But Now I'm Found

A Quinn Campbell Novel

J.W. Vincent

36th Parallel Press

BUT NOW I'M FOUND Copyright © 2025 by J.W. Vincent, 36th Parallel Press

https://www.jwvincent.com

Cover designed by Dawn McCracken

Edited by Amy Buz (https://buzwordink.com)

Printed in the United States of America.

ISBN 979-8-9930423-0-5

The Library of Congress Cataloging-in-Publication Data is available upon request,

10 9 8 7 6 5 4 3 2 1

CONTENTS

ACKNOWLEDGEMENTS

This novel would never have been completed without the love, support, and encouragement of my beautiful wife and partner-in-crime. She and I talked through the beat sheet for this crazy idea for a novel on a road trip coming back from vacation, and I wrote the entire outline before we got home. She is my muse, my permanent alpha reader, and easily my most favorite person in the world. She even designed the cover for this novel. *Plus ultra, best-o friend-o!*

I want to show my extreme gratitude to all of my beta readers. Quinn Campbell and I both thank you from the bottoms of our hearts.

I also appreciate my amazing editor and longtime friend, Amy Buz. Thank you for adding your expertise to this project.

My Wake Forest University freshman English composition professor, the late Dr. Bashir el-Beshti, holds a special place in my writing journey. He told me at one point during my first collegiate semester, "Son, you're not a writer; you're a *re-writer*." He was commenting on the fact that I have never finished anything, because I either lose faith in the story or in myself, and end up deleting everything and starting over. That advice has stuck with me to this day. I finished this story, with the help of my wife and my friends, to prove to myself that I *can* actually finish a story. Now I can officially call myself a writer.

I hope you enjoy this story, and I want you to know this is the first of many Quinn Campbell adventures!

Yours in writing,
J.W. Vincent

Hymn XLI

Amazing grace! (how sweet the sound)
That sav'd a wretch like me!
I once was lost, **BUT NOW AM FOUND**,
Was blind, but now I see.

 'Twas grace that taught my heart to fear,
And grace my fears reliev'd;
How precious did that grace appear,
The hour I first believ'd!

 Thro' many dangers, toils and snares,
I have already come;
'Tis grace has brought me safe thus far,
And grace will lead me home.

—Excerpt from the original words and verses by John Newton, from the 1st edition of the Olney Hymns, 1779, Book 1, Hymn 41

PROLOGUE

She couldn't see anything in the total darkness, but knew she didn't want to be here.

Dazed and confused, she rubbed her bloodshot hazel eyes, trying to bring the world back into focus. Besides the absolute silence, the first thing she noticed was that she was surrounded by gray metal bars. Bars? Why had someone locked her away in something resembling a large metal dog crate?

She recalled leaving an office party thrown by her legal firm. She was walking along an Atlanta side street, trying to get back to her car, which was parked near an alleyway. It was dark, she'd had a couple of drinks, and she was walking at a faster-than-normal clip. As the picture continued to develop, she remembered looking over her shoulder in paranoid fashion, making sure no one was actually following her. Then, the memory of a mask-wearing guy jumping out at her from behind a pickup truck and grabbing her suddenly rushed in, followed by a recollection of trying to fight back.

But he was way too strong.

Chills covered her coppery brown skin at that thought and the taste of bile swiftly entered her mouth.

Fighting for consciousness, she realized her head was still killing her. She touched a tactile sensitive spot on the nape of her neck and winced. Her scalp, sticky and swollen beneath matted curls, throbbed with pain.

Increased awareness also led to rising anxiety levels, a sudden wave of nausea, and an incredible need to use the bathroom. She also realized she was no longer wearing socks or shoes, which she thought was kind of weird. Everything about this felt wrong. Why her? Why now?

As best she could, she continued examining her surroundings through the soupy darkness. The floor of the cage appeared to be simple concrete, as if the cage had been plopped onto a pre-poured concrete slab, then bolted down tightly onto the hard surface. It was cold, rough, and quite uncomfortable. Her whole body ached as she continuously kept adjusting herself in a futile effort to sit comfortably. She crawled over to the door of the cage, and started rattling its locked metal bars back and forth. She screamed, slamming the bars, praying someone—anyone—would hear her pleas for assistance. She stopped rattling the bars when she realized the locked door remained securely in place.

An older man's voice with a deep southern drawl echoed from the dark. "Well, well, well. She ain't dead after all."

She swung her head around in various directions, trying to echo-locate the source. Since it was pitch black, she couldn't see very far in front of her at all. She detected a faint sound in the distance, hearing metal on metal, like the clink, clink, clink of something being dragged along the metal bars.

"What do you want with me? Where am I? Why am I here?" the woman nervously stuttered through question after question. "I'd really like to know why I'm here. *Please*."

"You ain't really in a position to ask anything of me, wouldn't you agree?" the bodiless voice continued.

"Look, my husband and family will be looking for me. If you just let me go, I haven't seen anything. I won't say anything, I *promise*."

"That's what they all say," boomed a younger-sounding male voice from somewhere else in the darkness.

There were at least two of them. Her breathing quickened—shallow, panicked. She turned her head back and forth, trying desperately to figure out where the voices were coming from. The foreboding sense of fear quickly crept in; combined with not knowing when and where she was, it left an indelible mark on her fragile psyche.

"I swear, I haven't seen *anything*, so I can't tell the cops what you look like." The woman's voice was weak and trembling. "Come on, now—I'm no threat to you."

From out of nowhere, wave after wave of electricity flooded into her body. Her muscles contracted involuntarily, and for just a moment, her lungs refused to work. Her eyes rolled back into her head, her face twisted in pain, and her movements seemed frozen in time. Her mouth opened as if to scream, but no sound emanated from her vocal cords. After a few seconds, the electrical charge stopped, and she collapsed weakly onto her side. Both men laughed in the darkness.

"I agree, you haven't seen anything. But as far as you not being a threat, on that, we disagree." One of the men whistled, and a weak, yellow light above her enclosure came to life, illuminating her and the older man squatting in front of her in a porous flicker. The tell-tale fluorescent buzz hummed monotonously as the fixture swung overhead. A younger man stood behind the woman's cage, carrying what appeared to be a modified cattle prod, which must have been what bathed her body in high voltage horror. A small trickle of smoke rose from the woman's upper back where the prod singed her clothing.

Her eyes watered continuously even after the surge of electricity ebbed, but she slowly pushed herself up, wiping the tears off of her skin with the sleeve of her blouse. Through those tears, she saw an older white man in front of her with gray hair pulled back into a ponytail; sporting a long, scruffy, gray and white beard; wearing a red flannel shirt, light-blue denim overalls, and a construction-orange beanie; and displaying a creepy smirk on his severely wrinkled face. His skin had a yellowish tint to it, and the fluorescent lighting made him look as if he had a horrible case of jaundice.

"Wha...what do you mean? I'm really...no threat to you," she said weakly, still recovering from the shock.

"Look, I am bound by the word of God to return this country back to a pure status, of which is currently made unclean by the likes of someone like...well...*you*."

"I don't understand."

"See, you made a few mistakes," the old man continued. "Mistake One? You stumbled onto us in the wrong place at the wrong time. Mistake Two? You were alone at night in a sketchy part of town. I mean, who does that? There are some seriously crazy people out there. And Mistake Three? You were simply born the wrong color. That mistake requires a *different* sort of solution." The man's accent dripped syrupy sweet with a deeper, more sinister edge to it.

"What does that have to do with anything?"

"I'm so glad you asked." The old man readjusted his crouching position in front of her cage. "Jesus' teachings tell us we, the children of Israel, are the chosen ones. All others, especially those of a darker skin color than us, are foreigners in the world of the Lord. It is our responsibility—since we are covered in the blood of Christ—to purify those who are unclean, and prepare them for the Kingdom of Heaven."

"Purify? Prepare? What in the *hell* are you saying?" The woman was still confused as to the old man's intentions, but she was beginning to realize her situation was becoming more and more dire by the second.

The old man whistled two long trills, and the lock on her cage door unlocked. He held the door closed, as two men walked up beside him—one on each side.

"Now, when I open this door, don't do anything stupid, alright? We can do this the easy way, the hard way, or the fun way."

He opened the cage door, and the woman instinctively tried to rush quickly through the old man's grasp, almost as if her body reacted of its own volition. The younger man on his right side backhanded the woman so hard she flew back into the cage, up against the rear wall. She just sat there, stunned. In her weakened state, she was easy to control through physicality.

"Fun way it is," the old man laughed.

The man who slapped her crawled inside the cage and grabbed one of her bare feet. He was dressed similarly to the old man, wearing flannel and denim, but instead of a beanie, he was wearing a black balaclava-style mask. All she could see was his yellowish-white skin and soulless eyes staring at her as he dragged her towards the open door. The woman did not fight back, because she was having serious trouble putting any thoughts together at all after the hard blow. She was rattled, probably concussed, and completely terrified.

The younger man dragged her across the cage and out of the door, easily throwing her over his shoulder like a large bag of rice in a fireman's carry. He brought the dazed and submissive woman to a different part of the darkened building, with another buzzing overhead fluorescent light barely illuminating the area. There was a tarp on the floor, and three flannel-and-denim-wearing, pale-skinned, masked men were waiting there, along with the old man. The younger man threw the woman's limp body onto the plastic tarp, her right side landing with a sickening thud. She groaned loudly after colliding with the hard floor, then tried unsuccessfully to get up on her knees. Two of the men grabbed her left arm, and the other two grabbed her right arm. The old man faced her as the four men held her down—arms out wide and on her knees in the middle of the plastic tarp.

"In order to cleanse an impure soul, we are charged with the responsibility of spilling its blood and blessing the body as its soul transcends. To honor the life of the Lord and that of my late wife—both of whom were sacrificed—another unclean one shall be reciprocally taken."

The woman was already wracked with fear, but now she was completely frozen with panic. Her mouth dropped open. One tear slid down her cheek.

In between quoting scripture, the old man hummed and sang a tune the woman recognized, but hadn't heard in a long time.

"*Amazing Grace, how sweet the sound—*"

The old man walked up to her, and placed a plastic bag slowly over head. She swung her head wildly back and forth but the old man pulled it all the way down onto her head. The bag reeked of bleach and candle wax. Once the old man fastened the bag's collar tightly around her neck, the air flow into the bag ceased, and to the woman, it felt like all time stopped.

She gulped for air that wasn't coming, but the sound of the hymn could still be heard inside the plastic, even though it was acoustically muffled. She still had no clue where she was, who these people were, or what exactly was happening. Her fear froze her, with nothing left to scream.

She gasped—no air, no time—and through the bag's haze, she saw the baseball bat rising in the old man's hands. Then, nothing.

Chapter 1

The story *always* comes first, even before family and friends, and *especially* before me.

The tires of our news vehicle scream as we jerk to a stop, just shy of a red light we never planned to obey. My photojournalist, Jason Armstrong, slams the truck into park. "We gotta be live in less than ten," he says.

"Got it," I reply, already halfway out the door, grabbing my stick microphone and earpiece like we've done this a hundred times before. Because we have. I excitedly run out of our vehicle and into the fray.

A crowd quickly gathers behind the yellow caution tape surrounding the accident scene, murmuring in a low, uneasy hum that says *something bad has happened*. I do not have all the details yet, but that doesn't matter. The story is here—and so am I. I quickly find the police spokesperson and ask him a few quick clarifying questions about what had happened here while Jason dials in the live shot. I scribble notes onto a blank page of my reporter notebook and run back over to my photojournalist.

Thirty seconds to air. I pull my long red hair into a hasty ponytail and ignore the drizzle of rain peppering the collar of my station jacket. My breath plumes in the evening air, and the lights from police and emergency vehicles repeatedly blink. Jason frames the shot with his usual precision. My heart races—not from nerves, but from the anticipation. *I live for this.*

The anchor tosses to me, and I step into reporter mode. *Who. What. Where. When. Why. How.* No other station is here yet, even though this accident has snarled rush hour traffic on Atlanta's downtown connector. The adrenaline drains almost as quickly as it arrives, because just like that, we are done.

"And we're out. Good job, Campbell." My producer's voice crackles in my ear. "Network doesn't need you tonight, so shoot some video of the accident scene and head back to the station."

I exhale, step away from the tape, and turn toward Jason, who is already tearing down the shot like the sidewalk itself owes him money.

I like efficiency—but damn. "Somebody's in a hurry."

Jason grunts, half amused, half over it. Backwards Braves hat. Hawks t-shirt. Jeans. And a photog vest with enough zippers to house a bomb squad. I know he has spare batteries, SD cards, and probably a fossilized granola bar tucked in there somewhere.

I grab the tripod and the stick mic—still rocking its WQX mic flag—and walk them over to him at the rear of the truck. I don't tolerate reporters who leave photogs to break down alone. Many hands, light work, all that. Teamwork makes the dream work, right?

That's when my phone rings.

I check the screen. WQX assignment desk. I grin, knowing this call probably means breaking news and a long night.

I answer with my usual snarky charm. "Overtime–R–Us, Quinn Campbell speaking. How can I earn my paycheck tonight?"

Laughter bubbles through the receiver like he's just heard the best joke of the week.

Tommy Jackson, whom I normally call T-Jack for short, is on the other end of the line. He has managed the WQX assignment desk since he left Georgia Tech with more degrees than I have pairs of shoes. Son of a Georgia legislative lion. Keeper of newsroom chaos. A legend in his own right. He's the only man who can talk faster than I think. His gorgeous coppery, deep reddish-brown skin and runner's physique make him pretty easy on the eyes, too, but I'll never give him the satisfaction of hearing that from me. Well, *maybe* never.

"Quinn, are you listening?" Tommy continues. "Torn down yet?"

I snap back from my mental biography of Tommy and watch Jason coiling cable with silent, passive-aggressive fury. I know he's getting ready to speak my love language.

"Almost. What's up?"

"We got a tip—a dead body was found in the Chattahoochee National Forest. Up near Springer Mountain."

That stops me, and excites me at the same time.

"U.S. Forest Service and Fannin County both confirm something's going on, but they won't say what. I figure you would want first crack."

My pulse quickens, and he is right. I *do* want first right of refusal. I want *all* the smoke when it comes to breaking news. This isn't just news. It has *potential*. And I always chase story potential like a bloodhound hyped up on adrenaline.

"Tell me everything you've got," I say, pulling out my notebook.

I yell out to Jason, "Story breaking up north in the Chattahoochee near the Appalachian Trail. Let's hurry up and hit the road."

Most photojournalists who go out on stories with me either love the fact I get handed all the big stories or hate me because they rarely see their families awake while with me. Jason is a part of the latter group. I would tell him to suck it up, buttercup, but this is why I'm still single. I'm married to the job, and I tell myself I'm just fine with that.

I turn my attention back to Tommy on the phone. "Just text me the specific address and numbers, and we'll head that way. I've dealt with the Fannin County Sheriff PIO before, so I'll call him on the way." I hang up the phone, and help Jason finish packing up.

Within seconds, my phone pings. Gosh, I love working with Tommy. He makes my life so easy, and I return the favor by always giving him the best breaking news coverage in the market. It's a win-win for us both. He sends me the address and the Fannin County dispatch number, as requested. Now I don't have to fumble around myself trying to locate this stuff on the road.

It's been a minute since I've been up on or near the Appalachian Trail. Some say the Trail begins (or ends, depending on your point of view) at Springer Mountain. In 1958, according to my research on the Interwebs, officials moved the Southern Terminus of the Trail to Springer from Mount Oglethorpe due to overdevelopment in the area. It's about an hour and a half from Atlanta, as the crow flies, so we pull into evening rush hour traffic, hop on Georgia 400, and start moving north.

It is the quietest ride ever, with Jason not even turning on the radio. Passive-aggressive much? Oh well, I'm my own best company anyway. I fire off a quick text to T-Jack.

Hey, could you send another photog/truck to replace Grumpy Mc-GrumperPants here, and is AB avail?

My favorite photog in the world—Alahna Bernard—is indeed available, and she's already on her way up the mountain. She might even beat us there. Man, my assignment desk sure knows how to keep a reporter happy. I've known Alahna ever since I moved to Georgia, and we have grown as close as blood sisters. She's my best friend and truly my family, and we are pretty much inseparable.

I call her to find out where she wants to meet and do the trade-off, and we work out the details for the handoff.

I tell Jason we are meeting up with Alahna in Dawsonville, right off US-19 N, so we can trade out equipment and vehicles before we head up the mountain. Once we arrive in Dawsonville, I quickly see Alahna's Ford Explorer with a bright WQX-TV shrink wrap on the side parked in a restaurant's lot right off the highway, and Jason pulls in beside her. After we get out of the truck, I give Jason—who is now extremely happy because he finally gets to go home—a high-five.

"Thanks for the taxi service, Jace. Go enjoy your family."

Jason laughingly gives me the one-finger salute, trades vehicles with Alahna, and then drives her Ford Explorer back to the station.

Alahna Bernard is twenty–five–going–on–forty, and is one of the strongest, most opinionated, and intensely passionate women I know. I adore her dark, thick, curly hair, which pairs perfectly with the warm bronze color of her skin. I'm just jealous her hair is naturally curly, while mine only holds a curl for about 0.0084 nanoseconds. She doesn't put up with anyone's crap—especially mine—and to top it all off, she's one of the best photojournalists in town. I also love that she is not afraid to put her camera in anyone's face, and her passion for capturing the perfect shot matches my aggression to tell the best story possible and to be the first on the air. Forever partners in crime.

***

Driving up the mountain, I notice a rather empty Amicalola Falls parking area near the hotel, where some hikers start the Appalachian Approach Trail up to Springer Mountain. You'd be stupid to start the Trail after sunset anyway, especially with all the bear activity in the area. There's a cool arch you can go through and hike up the Appalachian Approach Trail along the Falls, but those one hundred and seventy-five steps to the top are a *bitch*. Like, for real. I did it once on a dare, and did not like it *at all*, but the view of the Falls was worth it. From there it's *only* about a seven-mile hike up to the Springer Mountain parking area. I'm not *that* crazy of a person. Instead, we drive up to the parking area along Forest Service Road 42.

As soon as we arrive at the upper parking area, we see Fannin County Sheriff deputies, local fire trucks, and US Forest Service vehicles lining the narrow forest service road up to Springer Mountain, which makes it a little treacherous for our live truck to get through.

It's dark, well after eight, and we have until the eleven o'clock lede to find out *something* and throw at least a live voiceover (VO) and sound-on-tape (SOT) together. There won't be a whole lot of visuals right now besides all the police and fire vehicles, caution tape, and various trail signage because it's so dark already, but we'll put together the best package or VO/SOT we can.

"One of my contacts told me on the way up here it was a female body that was found along the Benton Mackaye Trail, just up from Springer," Alahna says.

"Looks like we're gonna be here for the long haul then. Someone taking care of your puppy?"

"Yeah, Ian is looking after Bobo."

Ian Bernard, Alahna's oldest brother and a successful defense attorney, is looking after Bobo, who is the most adorable little pit bull puppy in the history of dogs. Little meaning one hundred pounds of pure muscle and tongue-licking power. Alahna loves him more than anyone should be able to love anything else. It's cute and sickening at the same time.

"How about you? Oh, that's *right*—still no human *or* animal attachments. Got it," Alahna smirks.

"You know it. I'm too young to settle down yet."

"*Settle down*? That's hilarious, Q. You're thirty years old, and you don't even have a plant in your apartment."

"Just the way I like it. No one depends on me, but me."

"Spoken like a true narcissist."

I punch her playfully in the shoulder, and smile.

"Let's focus. You can dissect my personal life—or lack thereof—once we get back to civilization."

About that time, I spot Mike Rutherford, the Fannin County Sheriff public information officer, walking across the staging area. I know it is him because his windbreaker has the letters "PIO" emblazoned on the back. We're still the only station here. *Bonus.*

"I'll be right back." I start running over to him. "Hey, Deputy Rutherford? Got a second?" I worked a story with him about boat racing and water safety on Blue Ridge Lake a few months back when two boats collided on Valentine's Day weekend, resulting in a couple of fatalities.

When he sees me, the roll of his eyes is extremely loud and visible—even at this time of night.

"Look what the cat dragged in. How come we keep running into each other like this, Ms. Campbell?"

"Stop finding dead bodies and chasing criminals across your county's beautiful forests and waterways, and I'll stop hounding you."

"Deal. But all I can tell you right now is we will have a press conference at 9:30pm, and we'll fill you in on the situation then."

"Come on, Mike, give me at least a little crumb. I have to tell the station *something* so it looks like I'm doing my job." I'm trying my best to seem vulnerable, which is hard for me to do.

Deputy Rutherford looks around, sees no other reporters, and then sighs audibly.

"Alright, ask your questions."

I whistle for Alahna to bring her camera.

Rutherford lets us know a partially clothed Black female—with hands and feet bound by thick rope—was found by other hikers just off an ATV path near the Benton Mackaye Trail, also known as the BMT, about five o'clock this evening in some underbrush and foliage. She was not dressed for hiking the AT in the spring, and had no form of ID on her body. The hikers found her wearing a button-up blouse, an undershirt, and khaki slacks, but no socks or shoes, so at this time officials do not believe this was hiking related. He also said the body had weird bruising and burns which were inconsistent with anything found naturally on the Trail. Off the record, he told me there was an issue with facial recognition, but they are waiting on the autopsy results before they speculate. Rutherford didn't give me anything relating to the age of the victim, and told me I'd just have to wait for the press conference for anything else since the Georgia Bureau of Investigation has been called in to lead the investigation. I am beginning to have a bad feeling about this whole situation.

"An issue with facial rec, Mike? What exactly does that mean?" He refused to say. *Sigh.*

I thank him, briefly shake his hand, and then call the desk to give them an update.

"I'd like to offer you a dead body for the eleven o'clock. You interested?" I quip.

"Is it worth the delivery fee or service charges? I don't have to tip you, do I?"

Tommy is probably referring to the alleged diva rider in my contract. No such thing exists, but I do like to keep up appearances.

"All I know is the Black female victim was not a hiker, and she was not dressed for the AT. I don't think she was killed on the Trail, because she had wounds inconsistent with hiking. My gut tells me since she was bound by thick rope, someone probably killed her elsewhere and just wanted to dump her here." I can't go on the air with any of this conjecture, rogue allegations, or gut feelings—even though I really trust my gut—until I can get someone to corroborate the information. That's Journalism 101, or at least it is for me.

I also tell Tommy about the 9:30pm presser, and the fact the GBI has been called in.

"10-4. Keep us posted. I'll tell the eleven o'clock producer and you can fill her in later."

See, this is also why I don't hike. Get turned around, don't bring the right food or access to water, weather turns nasty, and you're toast. Get me too far away from amenities and creature comforts, and I break out in hives.

"Thanks, T-Jack. We'll start trying to dial in the live shot, and I'll send you what I have when I actually have something. I gotta get ready for the presser, at which I assume the GBI agents will tell me exactly what Deputy Rutherford told us. I'll keep you posted."

***

After our eleven o'clock live shot, I didn't want to miss any updates by driving all the way back to Atlanta, so I talk my assistant news director into letting us spend the night at the hotel at the base of the AT. I always have my go-bag packed and ready, so I have everything I need—change of clothes, hairbrush, toothbrush, makeup, boots, 100 SPF sunscreen for my usually pale skin, you know, the essentials. I'm used to living on the cheap, ready to move at a moment's notice when breaking news happens. Saving minutes matters when you're in a rush to be live before anyone else in town.

Once we get to our room, I fully acknowledge to Alahna there are very few things that feel better than a hot shower after an eighteen-hour day. I set the alarm on my iPhone for 3:15am since our first live hit is at five in the morning. Give me a strong cup of coffee and the adrenaline of a breaking news story instead of sleep any day. One of the GBI case agents told me if anything breaks overnight, he'd let me know. I hope he is a man of his word, because Lord knows I will chase him down every five minutes tomorrow if he doesn't keep me in the loop. My reputation of being aggressively tenacious and of never giving up on a story or on a lead definitely precedes me.

3:15am comes quickly, but we are up and out in plenty of time for our live hit. Alahna fed back a bunch of video and our interview soundbytes last night before we broke down our live shot, so editors back at the station already have my stuff ready to go. I just have to look good for the camera, because everything else is laid out perfectly. Two other stations have limped their way up the mountain, and they have nothing as far as video or sound. I really hate being in that position, because my news director, William "Wild Bill" Tucker, would be all over me. "Get *something*. I don't care *where, how*, or from *whom*. Your live shot better not be naked. *Do your job*." My mental impersonation of his voice didn't do it justice, but I cringe just the same.

I've seen Wild Bill eviscerate reporters like that before, and I vow never to let that be me or the photog with me. We're a unified front in a situation like this, and I always stick with and support my photo-journalists.

The GBI and the Fannin County Sheriff's Office plan a morning press conference at 9:15am, conveniently after our morning newscasts are over, just to inform the media vultures about any new developments in the story. They deflected all of my questions last night, so I'm hoping they have more answers for me now, especially in relation to the facial recognition issue. That tidbit of information is still eating at me. It is like a hangnail or a loose thread on a comfy blanket. I see it, and I just cannot help but tug on it. I run through several scenarios in my head about why a forensic field agent for the GBI cannot use facial recognition on a dead body—and none of them are good. I resist the urge to pull my long red hair into a ponytail and put on a WQX hat, because I only do that in natural disasters or rainstorms. Instead, I stick with just the ponytail, and I leave the hat in the go bag.

We do our morning live shots, and notice we had way more than any other station in town. *Score*. After our last hit, Alahna begins breaking everything down while I go over to bug the GBI folks one more time prior to the 9:15am presser. It's kind of my thing—in order to prep myself for the actual presser. Information is power, right? But I got nothing new before they started the press conference. Can't blame a girl for trying, right?

What news do we have? Any new updates? Any identification on the victim? Can you tell us any more about the body itself? Why are you having so much trouble identifying the victim?

That last question stops everyone in their tracks. I could visibly see a shift in posture from the people leading the presser, and they all clam up and give me nothing actionable. I could feel a sense of foreboding—a real feeling of dread and horror coming off of them, like the body was in a condition they've never seen before. *Noted.*

The GBI presser continues, and they only end up mentioning the few confirmed details to the story we already have: Black female, no identification or age as of yet, waiting for autopsy to help with identification and to determine an official cause of death.

The sun is up by this time, and the heavily wooded area is in full view thanks to the bright sunshine above the horizon. Thankfully, it has not been too rainy of a spring so far, so the roads and trails aren't too mucked up. I'm wearing jeans, my hiking boots, a WQX polo, and my hooded station jacket. Alahna is similarly dressed, wearing a t-shirt over a long-sleeved undershirt, jeans, and hiking boots that look like sneakers. Even though it is early April, temperatures usually fluctuate up on the mountain, not to mention all the fog and intermittent rain. It could go from soup to sun and then back to soup with just a flick of Mother Nature's fingers. I also make sure to cover my pale exposed skin with insect repellent before we traipse along the overgrown AT.

The Chattahoochee National Forest has a lot of twisting, turning roads and trails, and several hidden away spots—with open-face trail shelters and such—but the Appalachian Trail cuts a nice swath through the Forest, which is usually packed with day hikers and the more courageous Georgia–to–Maine hardcore Trail geeks. I totally stand out like a redheaded sore thumb on the mountain, because I'm not the most outdoorsy kind of person. I mean, I always *wanted* to try hiking the AT, not because I enjoy being outside—you know, a girl needs her amenities like indoor plumbing and room service—but just once, I want to say, "Hi, my name is Quinn Campbell and I hiked the Appalachian Trail." If you laughed at the possibility of me *ever* actually saying that, then you already know me too well.

I talk to some of the less media-savvy law enforcement folks, as well as the firefighters and EMTs who actually found the body, trying my best to glean more info from them. Reporters from the other stations follow me around like seagulls looking for crumbs I leave behind, which I'm used to and find rather humorous.

I can't talk to the hikers that originally spotted the dead body because they gave their statements and then bolted long before I got up on the mountain—just my luck. I got their names, though, and I'll track them down later if need be.

I see this young EMT putting away gear, so I saunter over to him to try and covertly extract some details from him.

"Hey, it's been a crazy last few hours, amirite?" My chuckle usually disarms unsuspecting interviewees.

"First all–nighter I've pulled in quite a while. Since college, actually."

Which could have been yesterday, if my mental age calculator is anywhere near right. He continues to put equipment away in a mindless, methodical fashion, not even looking at me.

"All I need is a little adrenaline in my veins—maybe a cappuccino—and then I'm good to go for hours. Just call me the Energizer Bunny." I chuckle again as I play an invisible bass drum. The EMT finally looks in my direction, laughing at my feeble attempt at humor. *Score.*

"What was it like last night? Did you see the body?" I ask, just going for it.

"I helped load her into the coroner's vehicle. She was a mess, though."

"Define *mess*?"

"All I can say about it is there's a reason we couldn't identify her. And it isn't because she didn't have any ID on her."

That particular response really piques my interest. "What...you couldn't see her face?"

"What face?"

Damn. One of the largest red flags ever immediately pops up in my brain. Did he misspeak?

"What about fingerprints? Did you see anyone try printing her?"

Suddenly, another more veteran EMT comes around the corner and sees me chatting up the other first responder.

"Cooper, what in the hell do you think you're doing? Don't you know who she is?"

Busted. I pirouette in front of him and mouth a quick "thank you" before the senior EMT whisks Cooper away and out of my reach.

What face? That can only mean a few things, and my vivid imagination is working in overdrive. What could have possibly happened to this poor woman? Something just feels off about this whole deal.

I ask other Sheriff's deputies, a couple of grumpy Forest Service rangers, and local GBI forensic techs if they've finished clearing the scene and if we can go up there. The agents mumble something about "yeah, it's cleared" and "knock yourself out" hiking up to it. I kind of hoped someone would volunteer to take us up there on their Bureau-issued four-wheeler, but that didn't happen. They give me the basic location and tell me there isn't a lot to see up there since they have basically scrubbed the area for any possible remaining evidence.

"Just look for the red flags, pun intended," one of the agents tells me.

I call the assignment desk and tell them everything I have learned about the story. The dayside producer wants us to stay on the mountain and try to find new information for a noon live shot. I have the desk do a little internet sleuthing about the area for me, which hopefully will give me some better bearings since the WiFi and cell signal on this part of the mountain are absolutely horrific.

There are a few personal cabins and shelters sprinkled throughout the area, some luxurious AirBnBs in neighboring towns like Dahlonega and Ellijay, and a few local churches scattered in the region—and those are just the ones we know about. These woods are ancient, and the Appalachian Mountains themselves are the oldest mountain range on the planet, according to some geologists. Before Alahna and I head up the Benton Mackaye though, I need to call my buddy in the GBI. He owes me a favor anyway—several actually—and this might be a good time to call in a chit. And I know he's involved with this, since this scene is in his assigned region.

The phone rings a couple of times, then GBI Special Agent Daniel Brown answers the phone.

"Damn it, Campbell, you *know* I can't talk to you about this."

Caller ID outs me before I can even ask a question. I love it when people are immediately on the defensive when they talk to me. It really does my heart good, and makes my job a little more fun.

"Aww, come on Brownie, how do you even know what I'm going to ask? I could be asking you to take me to dinner."

"I'd rather give you sensitive information that could get me fired and/or permanently imprisoned than be wholly responsible for you having a good time at my expense or in my company."

Ouch. I'm not sure how to take that.

"Awww, I feel so special. Look, I only have two questions. Feel free to answer them specifically, generally, indirectly, or even tangentially."

"That's assuming I'm going to answer you at all."

"After the gift I secured for your mom and dad's 50th wedding anniversary, that rare bottle of wine from that winery near Lake Lanier? You *owe* me, Brownie."

I can hear the rolling of his eyes, and then he sighs loudly.

"Just *ask*."

"OK, first question—can you give me any information about the victim's age?"

"Not exactly. Her fingerprints aren't in our system, but we're thinking she was somewhere in her twenties or thirties." I *knew* someone with the GBI would have tried printing her.

"Based on what? Gut? Intuition? Tea leaves? A Magic 8-Ball?"

"Forensic science isn't based on gut feelings or magic, Campbell. We use radiocarbon analysis to get a ballpark year of birth, but also use a basic racemization analysis to better determine the chronological age range of the victim, among other things."

I love it when he starts talking in scientific ten-penny words. He really knows how to woo a girl.

"OK, fine. Second question. Why were we told there is an issue with facial recognition?"

Maybe if I keep pressing, somebody will *actually* address this absolutely fascinating nugget of information Rutherford and the young EMT gave me.

Brown sighs hard, probably knowing I am like a dog with a bone on a detail like this. His reaction tells me he actually realizes resistance is futile, and he knows I usually get what I want. At least I hope that is what it means.

"I can't believe I'm telling you this, but knowing you, you are going to find out sooner or later anyway." Brown stops briefly, and I'm assuming he's trying to either gather his thoughts or figure out what he can or can't officially tell me.

"I was told there was something wrong with her face."

"Please tell me one of my agents didn't tell you that." He sounds truly agitated.

"You're off the hook for now. A rookie first responder gave me that piece of information."

"Ok, I'm glad I won't have to bench someone now. Look, I can tell you the woman was found with a plastic bag over her...well, locked

securely around her neck...and it looked as if it was...she was...umm..."
He stutters and pauses after each new detail, which dramatically
heightens my anticipation. The sound of unease in his voice is troubling, but I push on anyway.

"Come on, Brownie. You can't simply lead me to a discovery like
this and then hold out on me. Spill it."

"It wasn't pretty, Campbell. At all. The pictures my agents sent me,
I...I've never seen injuries like this before."

Now I *have* to keep digging. "Well?"

"Her head was completely bashed in. Absolutely crushed, and there
really wasn't much of it left. It is almost as if it exploded *inside* the
plastic bag."

CHAPTER 2

Plastic bag. No face. Head was just...gone.

My mind is racing and my thoughts are so scattered. Come on, Quinn, *think*. Put it together and figure out what it all means. Sitting in our news vehicle parked at the staging area, Alahna and I try to talk through our game plan, to see if we can come up with anything that makes sense. I give my producers the information GBI Special Agent Brown gave me, and I get the assignment desk to do some deep background from the newsroom. I keep mentally going over the horrific injuries this poor woman suffered, and I'm trying to visualize what kind of person could do such a thing. I have to figure out how to report the brutal details of this incident while also humanizing the victim at the same time. She was someone's daughter, wife, best friend, and/or colleague. I have to treat her with some kind of respect. It's the right thing to do, and once again, I find myself walking a moral tightrope between honor and honesty.

"So, I think we should first hike up the Benton Mackaye Trail to where the body was found and then figure out a plan from there," I suggest to Alahna.

According to our assignment desk, the BMT is an almost three hundred-mile trail that ends in Davenport, TN, so who knows what is *actually* up there buried in the brush, or how long it's been there. Man, I wish I had some kind of WiFi so I could do my own research.

"Personally, I wish we had some sort of police escort or backup." Alahna sounds unusually apprehensive. "This woman died horribly, and I'm uneasy about poking around the forest looking for someone to do the same thing to me."

"It's broad daylight in the middle of a beautiful spring day. Nothing's gonna happen to us, alright? Besides, if we run into zombies, I just need to outrun you."

"Ha ha ha. I am not worried at all about you and your stupid zombie apocalypse conspiracy theories, but bears? They're what I'm concerned about. Not to mention the alleged killers in the woods."

I instinctively let out a baby roar, and she responds by playfully cowering away.

I put my hand on Alahna's knee. "We'll just poke around a bit, shoot some video, and we'll be back here at the staging area before you know it. Besides, when have I ever let you down or ever let anything bad happen to you?"

Alahna's side eye makes me a little uneasy.

***

I find it odd no other station is following us onto the dense forest Trail. Oh well, they can continue to play catch-up if they want. Not me, not ever. It's in my nature to always push forward. I refuse to pass up the opportunity to fully flesh this story out, leaving no stone unturned and no trail unwalked.

We walk along a short stretch of the BMT until we see the evidence marker flags still stuck in the ground, just like the GBI agents told us there'd be. So much for the idea of *leave no trace*. I make a mental note to come back and remove these flags in the interest of trail conservation, but not today. I admit it looks like the GBI folks removed every single bit of non-natural evidence that may or may not have been connected to our Jane Doe. I cannot even tell anything had even gone down there.

The Trail is dense with spring green foliage, sporadic river/stream crossings, moss-covered rock outcroppings, and is marked by 5x7 white diamond blazes. I overheard one of the Forest Service guys saying officials named this Trail after the guy who planned the original Appalachian Trail idea. I should file that tidbit away for the next time we do AT trivia at our local sports bar.

Most of the AT is a footpath, meaning motorized vehicles—even horses—are frowned upon over much of the two thousand, two hundred-mile thruway. However, some locals over the years have been rumored to take dirt bikes and four-wheelers on some wider sections of trails, leading into the woods to God knows where. I keep hoping to find one so I could hitch a ride with them instead of hoofing it all day.

"Alright, my number one photog, what do you see?" I always like to stroke Alahna's ego, making her understand how much I appreciate her eye.

"Nothing. Absolutely *nothing*. Especially since we left the main Trail a while ago."

The only video we have so far is of the red evidence flags, and I haven't seen anything else to shoot since we headed off into the deep woods. It's better than nothing, right? Speaking of nothing, I don't see a single white diamond in sight. We are indeed way off the Trail.

"Alright, how about this? Let's hoof it a little way up in this direction, and see if we can maybe see something the feds missed?" I point in the direction I want to go, and Alahna scrunches her face at me. "We see things through a different lens than they do. If we see nothing, then we will just turn around and head home, OK? Easy peasy."

"You're absolutely right, Q. Your masters' degree in journalism and mine in digital media communications will help us see the unseen before any trained special agent with degrees in criminology, forensic anthropology, and who knows what else can. Yep, we're definitely gonna see the smoking gun first."

I cannot tell if she was just being sarcastic or if she actually just took a dig at me. I will let it slide this time, so I stick my tongue out at her in a childlike response.

I look at my watch. Tuesday, April 12, 10:17am. It is a beautiful sunny day, but we are deep under the Chattahoochee canopy with absolutely no new information. Plus, I have zero cell signal. Not even the ability to send an SOS. I'm beginning to truly regret this decision.

After a few more minutes of scrabbling through the heavy underbrush, we enter a small clearing. The views are gorgeous, and I stop just for a second to soak everything in.

"Hey, do you hear that?" Alahna asks, stopping dead in her tracks.

I stop my visual scenic tour and start listening for whatever it is Alahna hears. There it is. In the distance, I hear a motorized vehicle of some sort, maybe multiple ones, somewhere in the forest. It is hard to triangulate the sound because of how it bounces all around us. It starts to get louder, and then stops. Maybe it was just my imagination.

"It's probably just a GBI scrub crew. Maybe they'll take us back down to the Springer parking area," I say, looking around our current location. At least I *hope* it's the authorities.

"I hope so. Hiking through the undiscovered country with a camera is a lot harder than it looks."

Just a few more minutes, and then we will definitely turn back, I promise her. My gut rarely lets me down, but my active imagination is worried this might be one of those times I regret being me.

***

One of three four-wheelers stopped just before coming out into a clearing near something that caught his attention. The man raised his right fist in the air, signaling the two other men with him to hard stop, shutting off their engines. The first man saw two women who appeared to be walking by themselves, discussing something about a "few more minutes off trail" and then they were "gonna turn back." *Too late.*

"They ain't supposed to be here, especially *that* one with the camera," the first man said.

"So, what should we do? You know Pa's madder than fire at us right now for dropping that cleansed body out here," said a second man.

"At *us*? It ain't *our* fault, and I'm so sick and tired of cleaning up my dumbass brother's messes. He's gonna end up destroying everything Pa has worked so hard to build," said the third man, with anger and resentment dripping off his words.

The three men got off their ATVs and stood together for a moment. It was obvious they were very familiar with the area by how they navigated the deep brush. They were all dressed in flannels, jeans, and work boots, sporting beards of varying lengths. The men did not appear to be day hikers, but seemed to be something else entirely.

"We're gonna have to grab 'em both 'cause the redhead happens to be with the dark one."

"Ain't got much of a choice, do we? Pa will know what to do with 'em."

The men pulled balaclava-style masks up over their faces, started grabbing things out of their packs, and quietly walked through the brush on foot towards the two women.

***

The woods are completely and eerily silent. All hopes of catching a ride back down the trail vanish.

"Come on, Q. Let's turn back, OK? There's nothing else for us out here. At least let's get back to the BMT. God only knows where we are right now." Alahna is even less of an outdoorsy type than I am—which is nearly impossible, if you think about it.

"OK, fine. Let's backtrack our steps and get out of this creepy ass forest. I'll do what I can to cover the noon show with what we have," I tell her, much to my chagrin.

Alahna pumps her fist in a *yes* fashion, and immediately turns around. When she does, she comes face to face with a man that appeared out of nowhere. She shrieks in surprise, then falls backward. The man is wearing a balaclava-style mask, completely obscuring his face, except for his unusual eyes.

"Damn it, man. You can't just walk up on someone like that." I can tell Alahna is pissed he knocked her over, but she keeps the camera from hitting the ground. A true pro. The man's skin is sandy beige under the mask, and his eyes are cold and heartless. I can also see evidence of a shaggy beard underneath. He wears a blue flannel shirt, light blue denim jeans, and a camouflage jacket. My reporter's eye tries to memorize everything about him out of habit.

"You ain't 'sposed to be out here." His voice is accented with a slow, melodious, yet creepy southern drawl.

"Look, we're just a little off the public trail, trying to track down some information about what happened up here last night." I have what I think is a bright idea, so I run with it. "Hey, you look like you're familiar with this area. Did you see anything out of the ordinary last night?"

I feel someone or something walk up behind me, so I instinctively spin around and see two more masked men appear. Alahna and I are now standing back-to-back, keeping the strangers, who are slowly walking around us, where we can see them. They are all wearing varying degrees of flannel and denim, seeming almost like that and their masks are the uniform of choice out here. The men have us surrounded, keeping their distance at first, but it feels like they are slowly creeping closer. Is it just my imagination? I'm not sure, but now I can feel my heartbeat pounding through the veins in my neck. This is *so* not good.

"OK, you guys keep multiplying. You know it is kind of rude to stalk up behind someone like that." I wonder how they could move so quietly along the forest floor. If I wasn't so creeped out right now, I might actually be impressed.

"Why are y'all out this way?" one of the mountain men asks us, almost staring right through me. All of them have unkempt beards underneath their masks, and their yellowish skin looks as if they all have some level of liver disease.

"Hey guys, we're just journalists with WQX-TV in Atlanta, trying to put some missing pieces together on a story about the woman's body that was found up here last night. If you can help us get back to the BMT, we'll be so out of your way." I point to the station logo on my polo.

Out of the corner of my eye, I notice the illuminated red light on Alahna's camera. Smart cookie. If anything happens to us, it'll be recorded for posterity—reminiscent of those horror movies with found footage from long-dead main characters.

"So, you're not from around these parts then?"

It is all I can do to follow along with the mountain vernacular. "We both live and work in Atlanta, but I'm from North Carolina. My photog is at least from Georgia, though."

Alahna elbows me in the ribs and glares at me for giving that nugget of information away. I ramble a little when I'm nervous or on edge.

I said it. I'm nervous. Doesn't happen often, but I'm there now. I may even have a little fear mixed in for good measure. The forest is completely silent except for my heartbeat pounding in my ears.

"Then we can disappear ya, and no one will mind."

I freeze as one of the men swings a collapsible shovel and hits Alahna in the back of the head, crumpling her to the ground in a heap. The hit was so hard the solid thud echoes deeply throughout the eerily quiet underbrush around us. Her camera tumbles away from her body after she hits the ground.

"Dude, what the—"

At that very moment, I feel the dull crash of something very hard hitting me, too. The world quickly goes dark.

***

"It's not like Quinn to miss her live shot window, much less not answer her phone." Tommy Jackson looked at the clock—12:32pm—as he continued pacing up and down behind the WQX assignment desk. "Maybe she just lost track of time? I don't know...I just have a bad feeling about this."

News director William Tucker came out into the newsroom, weaving his way through the cubicles full of writers, reporters, and producers. A man in his sixties, Tucker's wrinkled brow and pursed lips adorned his stark white face. He walked briskly up to the desk, which caused Jackson to stand completely still. "Did you try her photog?" he asked. The top knot in his blue tie was loosened ever so slightly, the sleeves of his white dress shirt rolled up to the elbow, his hands on his hips.

"Yes, sir. She's not answering either."

Wild Bill ran his hands through his head full of salt-and-pepper hair, and stared off into space for a moment. "Send another crew up there pronto. Not being live on the air at noon screwed us, and the other stations all reported information from the morning presser we did not have. And that *really* pisses me off." He pounded his fist onto the assignment desk so hard a box of half-eaten doughnuts flew into the air and onto the floor. The whole newsroom froze.

"Yes, sir. I'll send Thomas and Washington up to the scene and they'll lead the 5 and 6. I've also got calls in to the Forest Service, GBI, Fannin County Sheriff, and the hotel up at Amicalola Falls. Maybe somebody will know something—" Jackson's words trail off.

"—about Campbell and Bernard, I know," Tucker finished his assignment editor's sentence. "Let's hope so. Keep me posted."

As the gruff news director walked back to his office, newsroom workers finally unfroze and started back to work again. The clicking sounds of fingers on keyboards filled the air.

"Hey, maybe the GBI can ping Quinn's phone?" a veteran reporter asked Jackson. "They did it for me for a story I worked on last month, and they helped track down a stubborn source I couldn't find." The reporter handed him a business card. "Here's the contact information for the agent that helped me out."

Jackson took the business card for ASAC Daniel Brown, GBI Assistant Special Agent in Charge for Region 8, and thumped it with his finger. "I know Campbell has used Brown in the past, and knowing Quinn, she would have run some of this information up his flagpole. I bet dollars to doughnuts he's heard from her."

***

Fuck me.

As I slowly come to, I shake my head trying to clear the cobwebs and stop the ringing in my ears. I soon realize I am lying on a concrete floor in some kind of cage. I don't even remember hitting the ground. I try to look around, but my head and neck are killing me from that dude crowning me with something hard. I rub the back of my neck, not sure how long I have even been laying there. My eyes are still very blurry, so I blink and rub them repeatedly, hoping they clear up.

I'm in some kind of a cage in a big barn or holding area or warehouse of sorts, a wide-open floor plan with several other cages, rows of shelving, and other machinery. In the absence of any discernible light, I can only see but so far in front of me. I try to listen for any identifying sounds, but all I hear is the ringing in my ears. And where the *hell* are my shoes and socks?

"Quinn! Thank God you're alive." I hear Alahna's voice, but I can't pinpoint her. *Damn this tinnitus.* "Over here. Look left."

As I turn my head, a severe pain shoots from my neck, down my spine, into my left hip. I instinctively recoil. I finally get a bead on her, in a cage catty-corner to mine. I feel like her dog Bobo in his crate.

"AB! Dude, what the hell happened? Are you OK?"

"Aside from a splitting headache, my internal diagnostics say I'll live. You?"

"This really isn't my idea of fun. You know when the last time I slept on the floor was? Yeah, me neither." Humor, my defense mechanism, falls kind of flat at this moment, pun intended. "How long have I been out?"

"I have no clue, Q. They took my phone and watch, so I literally have no clue when or where we are. I've been in and out of consciousness myself, and I've been waiting to see if you were OK."

I, on instinct, check all of my pockets. No phone. I look at my left wrist. No watch either. Damn. "There are no windows I can see, so I have no clue if it's breakfast, lunch, or dinner."

"It feels like we were brought here an eternity ago. I haven't been able to tell if you were breathing or not, so I've spent the last few moments praying you weren't dead."

As bad as my head feels, I kind of wish I was. "You know me. It'll take more than some mountain man to get the best of me." False bravado for the win. I'm actually quite nervous, really anxious, and totally afraid at the moment. I hate not being in control of my life. "However, something tells me we've been relocated, and we might not even be up on the mountain anymore."

Suddenly, a door creaks open and heavy footsteps walk slowly toward us. A fluorescent light fixture flickers on above us with that annoying repetitive buzz, which does absolute *wonders* for my headache. The man in front of me is much older and bigger than the ones we encountered in the woods, but looks just like them—balaclava covering his face, red flannel shirt, denim coveralls, and generic work boots. I see the hint of a gray beard underneath his mask. His eyes have a curious edge to them, almost as if he is studying me with them, and the skin I can see appears to be abnormally yellowish and pale. He looks like a stereotypical survivalist buried deep in the woods awaiting World War III or the coming apocalypse. I wouldn't be surprised if he has a surplus of military-grade mystery meat MREs stashed somewhere.

"So, Sleeping Beauty finally woke up. Glad my boys didn't kill ya."

His boys? Damn, we've fallen into some Deliverance-type shit.

"I'm glad for that, too. Now, sir, as you can see, we're of absolutely no threat to you, so why don't you let us out of these cages and let's just have a conversation, like adults." Come on, social psychology class, don't fail me now. I keep using rational thought to problem-solve, while my heart remains in my throat and my blood pressure skyrockets.

"You know, that's what everyone says. As far as I'm concerned, you definitely ain't a threat to me from behind bars, neither. I say you stay where y'all are at, for now."

I'm trying my best to memorize every square inch of him and this place, so that if, or when, we can make it out, I can describe them to anyone who will listen. There are no signs, no posters, no identification markers at all, anywhere near me I can see. All I see are cages, cinder block walls, random machinery, and metal shelves full of God knows what. Anxiety and dread continue to course through my veins.

"So, why did your boys knock us out up on the mountain? I mean, we were on our way out of the area."

The old man chuckles. "Not fast enough. See, you all was diggin' into that body they found, and we can't be having that."

Shit. I'm no longer chasing a story. I'm *in* the story, which breaks a longstanding and unwritten journalism rule. And I dragged Alahna into the story with me. Damn it.

"Look, we saw nothing. We won't say anything to anyone, I swear." I cross my fingers behind my back, knowing full well I'm going to tell anyone *and* everyone. He probably knows it, too.

"Again, that's what they all say. Oh, I know you won't say nothin' to nobody, darlin'. That's why y'all are here."

Alahna is absolutely silent, and I wish I was in the same cage with her, to let her know I won't let anything happen to her—like I promised.

"You know who we are, right? Every cop and fed in this area will be looking for us. It's only a matter of time before—"

"Before what?" the old man interrupts me and leans in close to my enclosure. "They don't even know where you are right now. And they're never gonna find you because they are probably lookin' for you in the wrong place."

Keep fishing, Quinn. Keep him talking. He'll give up something, guaranteed. "So, where should they be looking for us? Are we even still in Georgia right now?" My fear is beginning to take complete hold of me.

"Nice try, darlin'. I've watched enough cop shows on TV to know authorities can remotely turn on phones and watches and stuff," the old man says. "Too bad they won't be able to use these to find you."

The man walks over to a massive hydraulic press. He turns to me and smiles as he reaches into his overall pockets, and pulls out one of our phones. He puts it under the press, then a second phone, and then both of our watches. He turns on the machinery, and he brings the piston slowly down onto our devices, destroying them with a sickening crunch of plastic and glass. He raises up the piston, laughing at us as he scrapes the pieces of the pulverized devices into a box on the ground.

I sure as hell didn't peg these morons to be high-tech hillbillies. They knew our devices could be used to track us. *Damn it.*

One of the younger men brings Alahna's camera over to the hydraulic press. The old man takes it, and sits it lens up under the press. The piston comes down onto the lens, shoving it into the camera housing with several loud crunches. I instinctively look away from the technical carnage, knowing any video or sound AB shot on it is now lost. The old man scrapes more broken pieces of plastic, metal, and glass into the same floor box, which he hands back to the other man.

Then the elder whistles like he was calling a dog or something, and another one of his mask-wearing boys shows up with a long white rod or metal stick of some sort. He sticks it into Alahna's cage and she flings herself wildly into the opposite side of the cage from what appears to be some form of electrical shock. That must be one souped-up cattle prod.

"AB!" I shriek in her direction. "Tell me you're OK. Why'd you do that? She poses no threat to you."

Alahna starts sobbing, but still gives me a weak thumbs up, her thick curly hair falling in front of her face. "I'm...I'm OK," she squeezes out.

"You know why you pose no threat to me? Because you're in a cage with no hope of ever gettin' out. Unless you can pick an electric lock." He whistles again, in three short trills, and another man flips a lever on an older-looking wall switch directly out of Victor Frankenstein's old-school laboratory. A loud hum comes to life all around me, and I realize suddenly that son of a bitch just electrified our cages.

"Don't touch the cage, AB. Stay away from the bars."

"Too late. I found that out the hard way before you woke up." She holds up a hand to me, and I can see the blistering on her palm. The old man starts laughing.

"It was fun to see *that* one fly back from the cage door," one of the men says.

That one? Rude. She does have a name, you know. My temper continues mixing with my anxiety and fear, which can be a potent combination if left unchecked. Right now, however, my fear is winning.

From behind, I didn't see another of his boys shove one of those prods inside my cage. Electricity courses through my right shoulder blade, causing my body to involuntarily tense up, and all of my nerve endings to come to life all at once. I scream silently at the waves of intense pain pumping through my body. The man removes the death stick from my upper back, and I can smell burning flesh. *My* flesh. It was an acrid smell, similar to meat sizzling on a hot grill, but with faint coppery, metallic undertones. 0/10, would not recommend.

"Now you know what it feels like." The old man waves to the men surrounding our cages. "You are not in control here."

I am both enraged and petrified at the same time. I start to wonder if we're ever going to escape, and I immediately shake those thoughts out of my head. I made a promise to Alahna, and I'm going to try to keep it.

"Now, we're gonna leave you for a bit. It's supper time, and it's waitin' on the stove for us. So, bye for now." He mentions food, and my stomach lurches. I wonder if the smell from the smoldering blisters and burns on my skin reminds him of food. *Yeesh, I hope not.*

The old man stands up, smiles creepily, and nods in my direction. One of the men prods Alahna again, this time against her lower back, which causes her to scream wildly. Tiny wisps of smoke curl up from the combination of her burning skin and the smoldering hole in her shirt.

"Come on now, *stop that*," I scream, trying to get them to leave her alone. I absentmindedly grab the bars in front of me, forgetting they are electrified. The next thing I know, I'm lying on my back on the ground towards the rear of the cage as a result of the force of the electrical charge. My arms are outstretched above me, and I look up at the still sizzling flesh on my injured hands.

"Damn, that was fun. We got two for one that time," one of the men says.

All the men laugh and walk out of sight. I hear the heavy door close, and then the loud click of its locking mechanism.

I feel something wet near my jawline, and I notice blood is coming out of my ears. I also have an odd, rusty, metallic taste in my mouth, and I immediately curse Thomas Edison, Nikola Tesla, and even Ben Franklin. Electricity sucks. That last jolt from the bars really did a number on me.

I notice Alahna is lying motionless in her cell; the force of that last prod must have made her pass out. My thoughts are in overdrive. My anxiety and fear levels surge and my heart races, because I don't know *anything*. I don't know where we are. I don't know if we can make it out of here. The words *I don't know* aren't normally a part of my lexicon, and that frightens the hell out of me.

What if no one ever finds us?

I didn't even notice the tears running down my cheeks. The overwhelmingly pervasive realization of our current predicament weighs deeply on my conscience, and all I can feel at the moment is fear and regret, both feelings I need to find a way to get rid of.

It's *my* fault we're here. It's *my* fault Alahna is laying in that cage. *It's all my fault.*

Therefore, it's up to me to stay focused and get us the hell out of here.

***

The old man closed the inner warehouse door behind him. All the men removed their balaclavas in a relieved whoosh, and tossed them on a center table in what appeared to be an old control room with a huge pane of glass looking over the warehouse floor.

"Damn, it's so fun to watch 'em bounce and flail when the electricity goes through 'em," one of the older boys said.

"Now damn it, Beau. You're the reason we are in this predicament," the elder man groaned at his youngest son. "If you hadn't dropped the package out on the Trail, we wouldn't be in this mess."

"I already said sorry, Pa. It was Clyde's fault for not cinching it down to my 4-wheeler right. It was my first time actually carrying a delivery, and all I had to do was transport it." Beau tried to plead his case.

Clyde did a spit take with his lukewarm, knockoff-brand beer. "MY fault? Don't you even put that on me. I have never lost a package. *Ever.* Couldn't your dumb ass tell when it fell off?"

"Do you have any idea what kind of mess we're in now because of you?" The old man moved slowly over to Beau as the words trailed out of his mouth. "You have brought unwanted attention to my name and my works, and I can't have that."

"Nobody saw nothing, Pa. Except that white woman and her girlfriend we currently got out in the barn. The Custer name is safe now, right?"

The back of Custer's hand reactively found purchase across Beau's left cheek, with enough force to knock the young man to the ground. Clyde and the two other men stepped back quickly, out of Custer's range.

Elijah Custer was an extremely well-built man, quite muscular and ripped for his age, and over his sixty plus years on this Earth, he had obviously developed little to no patience for failure. Because of his unusually strong frame, the slap of his son hurt a lot worse. Beau still sat on the ground, stunned.

"We will deal with those two, and then we're gonna have to lay low for a spell. Clyde, you, Zeke, and Lee need to prepare everything for tomorrow. Beau, you better figure out a way to clean up this mess moving forward. Otherwise, I'm gonna have to deal with you myself."

"Sure thing, Pa. You can count on ole' Beau."

"Make sure to shut everything down before you come over to the house for supper. We will save a seat for ya."

"But we can't guarantee any food'll be left. Might have to eat some crumbs," Leland laughed.

Beau made a mental note to turn off any and every electrical switch that's on right now before heading back for supper. He knew Pa could count on him.

***

The silence in the darkness of our holding area is so eerie.

No noises outside. No trains. No airplanes. No street noise. I keep remembering the movies where the sound of the L-Train was recorded, letting authorities know exactly where the people were being held. No Hollywood sound effects are present to save us now. I absolutely have zero idea when and where we are, and that scares the bejeezus out of me.

Alahna is still out cold. I have been sitting in the middle of my cage for what feels like weeks, just toying with the electrical blisters on the palms of my hand. Suddenly, Alahna takes in a deep breath, and jerks to an upright seated position.

"Damn, you scared me, girl," I say, happy she's still alive.

Alahna struggles to sit completely up, rubbing her eyes as if to get rid of the cobwebs. "I...I guess now we're even."

"We have to try and keep our wits about us, AB. So, just hang on as long as you can, OK? You know people are out looking for us."

Alahna chuckles weakly. "Yeah, I know. Between Wild Bill and my brother, they probably have half the state out combing the woods."

Alahna's middle brother Aaron Bernard is a case agent with the Georgia Bureau of Investigation, and is *fiercely* protective of family. He's probably hell bent for leather by now, trying to find AB. And me.

The gentle hum of the electricity running through the cage bars is almost soothing in an *if you touch me again, I'll kill you* kind of way. I begin to go through everything on my body that could potentially shield me from the bars' electricity. Nothing. What I'd give for a pair of rubber or leather gloves right now.

Suddenly, all the rickety fluorescent lights overhead shut off, bathing the warehouse in total darkness again. Only the hum of the cage electricity remains.

Until it doesn't anymore.

Could it be? I think to myself.

There's only one way to find out. Thankfully I decided to wear a sports bra today, so I blindly take off my WQX polo, wrapping my hand in it as if cotton could actually prevent electrocution. It's the thought that counts though, right? Cautiously, I touch the bars of my cage quickly and remove my hands again. Nothing. On a hunch, I take my polo-wrapped hand and push against the inside of the cage door. With the electricity apparently off, the mechanized door lock pops right open.

Holy shit.

"AB, push open your door. Trust me."

I hear her door unlatch in the darkness, and we both scramble across the floor to find each other in the dark. No hug in the history of hugs ever felt as good as this one.

"I got you into this, and I'm gonna get you out of it. You trust me, right?" Both of my hands are firmly on Alahna's shoulders.

"With my life."

"Alright, let's blow this popsicle stand." I put my polo back on, and try my best to steel my nerves. "Stay *right* behind me."

CHAPTER 3

It takes a long time for my eyes to adjust to the pitch darkness. I can hear nothing but my heartbeat in my ears. I reach my hand behind me, searching for Alahna in the dark. "Grab my hand so I know you're behind me." I feel her hand touch mine, and I instantly feel a little better.

"Where else am I gonna be?"

"You know, with all these idiots around, I won't feel safe until we both get out of here."

I put my free hand out in front of me, feeling out into the darkness for anything I might bump into or trip over. The last thing I need to do is alert Jethro Bob and his backup singers. We have to be as quiet as a mouse as we move super slowly in the pitch black. I don't even know what time of day—or even what actual day—it is, because I didn't see any windows earlier to let natural light in. It could be either 12 noon or 12 midnight right now, and I'd never know the difference. If I can just make it to a flat wall, I can try to find an exterior door, and hopefully not one that leads me back into the arms of my redneck concierge.

The old man mentioned food before everybody left, so I'm assuming lunchtime or dinnertime. Speaking of dinner, I could use some of Alahna's mom's chicken salad right now. I can get pretty hangry, but maybe being hangry right now will actually help me keep my focus.

We shuffle our feet slowly and quietly in a straight line, hoping for the best. The only sound I hear is our stifled breathing, trying to stay quiet and hidden in the sea of dark. Step...reach...step...reach. Suddenly, my hand finds pay dirt—a wall, which is about 50 paces or so from my metal prison.

"Got something here. Come help me find a door."

We spend the next few minutes slowly combing the wall for some kind of exterior door. Hell, any door will work at this point. I can't believe how blind I am right now. This darkness is suffocating, or maybe it's just my paranoia closing its grasp around my windpipe. I'm subconsciously gasping for air.

I find a round door knob, and I gently test it back and forth. Locked. Alahna finds one. Also locked. This place isn't that big, if I'm remembering correctly, but it might as well be the entirety of space. The longer we're loose, and the longer we struggle to get out, the higher the probability Mr. Hayseed Plowboy and his goons will find us. I know this, and I'm sure Alahna knows this, but I feel responsible for her right now. I *will* get us out of here. How? I'll cross that bridge when I get there.

As I'm sliding my hands over the wall, the electrical blisters on my palms are incredibly sore to the touch, but I don't care. I keep sliding my hands along the cold wall, and I find what feels like a huge pane of glass. I can weakly make out a table and some chairs behind the massive window. I hear Alahna testing another doorknob, and then she gasps quietly. "This one's unlocked."

Don't get too excited, Quinn. Might just be a closet or something.

"It's about damn time we had a spot of good luck. Hey, but let me go first, OK?" Alahna taps me on the shoulder and slides around behind me. I really wish I had some kind of weapon on me besides my razor-sharp wit.

"Well, here goes nothing." I turn the knob and push the door slowly forward.

***

Custer and the boys were in the dining room of a double-wide trailer sitting adjacent to the meagerly sized warehouse structure. A meal for the men was bubbling on an electric stove surrounded by dirty dishes and varying degrees of other filth.

"Did you shut everything down like I asked?" Custer asked Beau, as he took a swig from a cheap store-brand bottle of beer.

"Yessir. They're sleeping in the dark right now just like you asked." Beau reached for another beer out of the disgustingly packed fridge. There was no way to know what was good or bad in there, because everything was piled on top of each other. Ezekiel and Leland were already sitting at the table, and Clyde was standing in the living room, all staying quiet and chugging cheap alcohol.

"Good, because you and I need to talk." Custer took a 9mm sub-compact pistol out of his waistband and sat it on the bar between the two men. Beau just looked at it, and then cautiously looked up at the old man. "You know how bad you screwed up, right?"

"Look, Pa, the package was tied all nice and tight like to the rear grill of my four-wheeler. Clyde even checked my knots himself." Beau's speech was speeding up—a clear sign of nervousness. "At least I think he did."

"If that be the case, then why'd you lose it? How'd it come loose then?"

Beau looked over at Clyde who threw up his hands in a *don't look at me* fashion, and then at Ezekiel and Leland, who looked away and continued trying to stay out of the conversation.

"Umm...Clyde showed me how to tie the knot, and I did it just like he—"

Clyde interrupted him, screaming. "Don't you bring my ass into this again, 'cause it ain't my fault! I told Pa you weren't ready to go on a run."

Clyde stormed over to the table, and when Beau stood up in response, Clyde crowned him with his beer bottle, showering Beau and the kitchen in shards of glass. Ezekiel and Leland jumped out of their chairs and put their backs to the wall of the trailer, trying desperately to get out of the way. Beau crumpled to one knee, blood running down his forehead. Clyde immediately grabbed Beau and put him into a headlock. Beau struggled against the much stronger and older man, while the others just egged on their other brother.

"Let the boy go, Clyde." Custer said, calmly.

"But he can't go 'round blaming me for his screw-ups," Clyde huffed. "I've been on dozens of pickups and drop-offs and I've *never* let you down. But he's going to blame me?"

"Look, he's gonna make this right. Tomorrow, when we take care of our new guests, all will be made right. God don't care how or when we do what we do, but we just need to continue our mission. Our purpose."

Custer walked over to Beau, whose head was still wrapped up in Clyde's chokehold.

"You do know what this means, right?" Custer asked, putting one hand on Beau's shoulder. "Your screw-up could jeopardize our whole way of life, our mission from God. We need to pick up packages and deliver them from this life in a way that honors God's word, my promise to your late Ma, and our larger mission. Don't let Him think your mama died in vain."

"I understand, Pa. I do." Beau coughed out, as Clyde released his headlock. "I ain't about to let you down again."

"Good, boy. Good. Because if you screw up again, you will need to be cleansed just like all the others. None of our lives are worth more than our ordained mission. Do you hear me? It all started after your mama died, and God placed us on this important path, and we find our own ways along this spiritual journey every single day." Custer's tone became deep and somber at that last part, as he aggressively patted Beau's face. "Tell me you understand, boy."

"I understand, Pa." Beau was deathly afraid of his father, but he followed him as if he was a true life prophet. Clyde, Leland, and Ezekiel all nodded at Custer in affirmation.

"Boys, let's eat. We need to praise Him for this food, pray to Him to forgive this stupid boy's screw-up, and then mentally prepare for tomorrow. We have two to deliver to Him tomorrow, and then we will return them to the ground with all the others."

The five men sat down at the table, held hands, and then praised the good Lord, from whom all blessings flow, for the food and for their livelihood. Custer looked around all his boys as they began to eat their food. It's hard to believe they have delivered eighteen souls so far, and two more will be added to their tally tomorrow. God be praised.

***

The door opens into what appears to be an office or conference room of sorts. The white cinder block walls match what I remember from the internal walls of our mountain prison. It is small, with a row of TVs and what appears to be a switch panel covered in red and green lights. This must be where they keep eyes on us and make sure the juice is flowing to our cages. I look a little closer at the panel, and all the lights are red. According to little labels underneath each light, green means on and red means off. Good thing for us, someone hit the wrong switch.

What if this was meant to be? What if they meant for us to get out so they could hunt us and kill us as we tried to escape? This seems too easy, doesn't it?

Damn it, Campbell. *You can't think like that.* That only happens in the movies, TV, or in some poorly written novel. Do you actually think these guys are *that* insidious?

I shake my head to get the creeping doubts out of it, and I push on. I notice you can't see shit on the TV screens since the main floor is so dark. I'm surprised—and appreciative—that these guys don't have better technology like infrared or lowlight cameras. I'll have to send them a thank you card if I make it back to civilization.

The ambient lights from the screens and light panels give the room an eerie subterranean glow, just bright enough for me to see another door on the far side of the room. I walk over to it and turn the knob, realizing it too is unlocked. I slowly pull the door inwards, and I notice it thankfully leads outside. It is dark, but not artificially so like inside the warehouse, with the moon casting a smooth glow over the entire area. At least now I know what time of day it is. I just wish I knew *where* we are.

I take a quick look around, and reach behind me to grab Alahna. I see some four-wheelers and a couple of trucks to my left, and nothing but wide-open fields in front of me and to the right. I also see a trailer ahead of me, which is where I assume the men are. I notice zero light pollution, which means we are probably deep in the woods, far from any city limits. I start trying to put together some kind of a plan, but nothing good comes to mind.

"Hey, do you remember that story we did a few months back, about the chop shop ring in Alpharetta?" I ask Alahna.

"Yeah, the guy we interviewed spent so much time flirting with me and showing me how to hot-wire cars." Alahna has a perfect memory for those kinds of things. I sometimes forget what I had for breakfast that morning.

"If we get over to one of those trucks, do you think you can recall enough from him to get it started?"

"It's worth a shot. Let's try the older Ford. The guy said they were the easiest models to boost." People remember all sorts of things when placed under duress. Maybe once we get there, they'll have left the keys in the ignition. That will be the lucky break we'd need.

This is our chance. This is our plan.

We slide alongside the wall to our left, slowly moving towards the white pickup truck.

"We have to be stealthy right now. As soon as we crank that truck, they're gonna hear it, and we have to be ready to floor it and hope there's a road to somewhere."

We slither up to the truck, an older model Ford F-150, white in color with a blue stripe down the side. My dad had a similar truck when I was a kid. You could have driven that truck through a wall, and it would have done more damage to the wall.

I look in the driver's side window, and notice the door lock is popped up. I guess there's no need to lock a truck in the middle of nowhere. I've lived in Atlanta too long, I guess, because I lock everything—my car doors, windows, and triple lock my front and back doors. I even lock my bathroom door when I'm alone in my apartment. Just because you are paranoid doesn't mean they're not actually out to get you.

I press the button on the door handle quietly, and slowly, slowly, slowly open the driver's side door. These old doors are prone to squeaking, and I don't want to give us away before we even have the chance to start the truck.

Alahna slides behind the steering wheel, and checks the ignition. No key. She looks around the cab, checking the ashtray, glove compartment, and other places someone might stash a key. Then she leans up and pulls down the sun visor. A ring of keys falls into her hands, and I did everything I could to hold in the *woohoo* whoop that welled up deep within me.

The door to the trailer swings open, and Alahna instinctively lowers herself onto the truck's bench seat. I notice Mr. Green Jeans walk out onto the porch, searching the pockets of his coveralls for something. His mask is off, and I clearly see his face for the first time. I stare at it, hoping to memorize any little details. Gray hair in a ponytail. Long gray beard. Wrinkled face. Height. Weight. Everything.

I couldn't get around to the passenger's side now without him noticing, so I try to climb into the cab behind Alahna. I climb about halfway in, squeezing Alahna up against the steering wheel. Then, the worst possible thing that could happen...actually happens.

Shit.

***

Custer opened the trailer door and walked outside to grab a quick smoke. Dealing with these boys makes life so difficult for him, in ways he was not familiar with. He pulled out a pack of cigarettes and popped one out of the pack. Then he pulled out a silver-plated lighter that had a huge cross engraved on one side, and the words *By the Grace of God* on the other. He flipped open the top, pulled his fingers down on the wheel, and watched the flint spark enough to create a solid flame.

Finally, a moment's peace. Grace be to God. That's when he heard it: the horn blaring from his pickup truck.

***

"*Shit*," I curse to myself.

"Get in!" Alahna slams the door and then puts the keys in the ignition. The old Ford whines a little and then fires up. I see her put her seat belt on, and I feel like that was a good decision, too.

"Gun it. *Now*."

I hear the old man scream something toward the trailer before flicking his cigarette in our direction. He reaches into his waistband for something as Alahna puts the truck in drive. I instinctively yell for her to get down, as we hear the gunshot. The passenger side window erupts, covering me in a shower of glass as the bullet destroys the window.

"Go, go, *go*!" Alahna guns the old truck, and it fishtails slightly before lurching forward. I look through the shattered window and see all the men barreling out of the trailer for the other vehicles. Our escape window is closing rapidly.

Minus the shattered glass, the cab of the truck is unusually clean. About four or five cross pendants hang from the rear-view mirror, swinging left and right as Alahna barrels down the dirt road in front of us. The high beams show there is nothing around us but darkness and the unknown. No lights, no people, no nothing.

I instinctively look at the fuel gauge. This is where the victims in a horror movie would notice the truck was empty and some serial killing whack job would catch up to them and chainsaw them up into little pieces, but I am relieved to see three-quarters of a tank. Sometimes I hate my brain for betraying my confidence—or lack thereof. Stupid monster movie marathons.

Despite the glorified horse path we are on, the speedometer keeps going faster and faster on. The bumps and ruts toss us around in the cab, but I *so* don't care. The truck flies down the path like a missile in the darkness, not knowing where we are, what we are doing out here, or who will be there to save us. *IF they save us.*

Suddenly, the back window of the truck shatters when a bullet comes through from behind. My hands instinctively fly up to cover my head while shards of glass shower the inside of the cab. They have caught up to us. Alahna just stares out in front of us, making sure to keep the truck on the road.

One of the other trucks comes barreling up behind us, with three four-wheelers flanking it on either side. A masked man hangs out of the passenger side window, squeezing off rounds in our direction.

"You played video games as a kid, right?" I ask. "Like Mario Kart?"

"Q, now's not the time for you to fly your nerd flag, unless it'll help me drive this truck any faster."

Blam! Blam! Blam!

"Seriously, listen. All I'm saying is, if those four-wheelers come up alongside us, turn the steering wheel in their direction and run them off the road. Every car chase scene in history employs that technique." I ramble when I'm scared, so I'm not surprised I'm blabbering on about Nintendo games at a time like this. *Focus, damn it.*

I turn to look behind us again, and notice the truck right on our bumper. I can't see the other ATVs; the bright high beams of the oncoming truck obscure them from my view.

Blam! Blam! Blam!

Three more rounds come into the cab, shattering the windshield—blinding us for a split second. Alahna cranes her neck to better see the path through one of the shattered holes in the web of splintered glass.

The truck behind us falls back a little, and I allow myself to feel a little hope, like this crazy ass plan might actually work. It is short-lived, however.

The truck following us comes flying back up behind our truck, on the right side of the truck bed, and Alahna does what she can to try and block them.

Blam! Blam! Blam!

More bullets come into the cab, but the adrenaline rushing through my veins isn't enough to block the searing pain as one of them pierces my left shoulder. I immediately feel a wetness on my left side, as blood pours out of the wound. I slump forward in the cab, unable to make even the slightest of sounds.

"Quinn!"

Alahna's screams break through the tinnitus in my ears, trying to check on me and keep the truck on the road. The burning sensation in my shoulder is so intense that I can't breathe, I can't think, I just...can't. I am essentially paralyzed with pain and fear as I grab for my shoulder. The throbbing of the wound matches my racing heartbeat.

"I'll...live," I weakly say out loud. "Just...keep...going..."

Right at that moment, the truck behind us speeds up again and strikes our right rear at an angle, causing the backend of the truck to slide around about ninety degrees. Alahna attempts to course correct from the PIT maneuver, but our truck then flips over and over and over for what seems like an eternity. The last roll of the truck ends with us right side up, the cab crushed all around us. I look over at Alahna through the blood pouring down my face, and I instinctively grab out for her, forgetting about all of my pain. "Alahna? Can you hear me, AB? Say something."

My peripheral vision catches something out of the corner of my eye just in time to see the stock of a rifle connect with my face. Hard.

***

The bright sun brings me out of my concussive slumber, and my head is killing me even worse than before. I try to look around but the pain in my head, neck, and shoulder prevents me from doing a whole lot of that. I try to move, but my seat belt holds me firmly down on the seat. I gasp when I remember Alahna was with me, and I look over to the driver's side of the cab—and she's not there anymore.

"Alahna! Where are you?" I forget all about my pain for a minute as I try desperately to scan the scene and scream out for my friend. "Say *something*."

"It's about time you came to. I was hoping you weren't all the way dead yet."

I recognize the old man's voice, but can't see him. "Show yourself, you coward." Here's hoping my false bravado doesn't actually get me all the way dead.

I try to unhook my seat belt, but it's jammed. I angrily fight with it for a couple of seconds, frantically jerking it back and forth, then give up. I'm pinned in the cab, with metal and glass crushed all around me, making movement a little precarious. "Where's my friend? You better not hurt her."

"Oh, you did a good job of that yourself, trying to escape. I figured you both were smarter than that." A masked man walks up in front of the wrecked truck I am still in.

"You mean smarter than one of your moron children that screwed up and turned off all the electricity last night? How else do you think we got out?" My fear is mixing with my rage, which makes me say things I probably shouldn't. This is not the time to kick the hornet's nest, but I'd rather him be angry at me, and not Alahna. "Look, there's still time to forget all about this and let us go."

Silence out of the old man. Either he just found out a hard truth about his "boys," or maybe something else.

"I'll deal with him later. Right now, you need to see what mess you've gotten yourselves into."

I hear a vehicle of some sort heading our way, with the engine sounds growing louder as they approach. I notice the truck pull past us, then back up right in front of the wreckage that remains of our getaway plan.

I observe a curious detail of the truck in front of me, and I wonder to myself. *Why is the truck bed covered with a plastic tarp?* Then I feel my eyes grow wide.

I hear some commotion coming up from behind me, then coming right outside the destroyed passenger side window. Two of the bala-clava-wearing men drag an unconscious Alahna from behind us and then throw her into the truck bed in front of me in a lump.

"Come on now! Don't hurt her, OK? Take me instead, and let her go," I scream. "Escaping was my idea. She had nothing to do with it."

One of the masked men balls up his fists and does the "Boo hoo" gesture near his eyes while the old man says, "Oh don't worry, little lady. You'll be here soon enough."

The old man comes into view on my left, and climbs up into the bed of the truck behind Alahna. Two of the boys pull her up to her knees, and hold her arms outstretched. The old man slides up behind her, and smacks her twice across her right cheek. "Wakey wakey, eggs and bakey."

Alahna slowly comes to, and instinctively tries to pull away from them, but she is too weak and disoriented to do so effectively. The elder puts his hands on her shoulders.

"Ladies and gentlemen, we are gathered here today as a part of our ordained mission. A mission given to us by the Father, the Son, and the Holy Ghost himself. A mission that began when I lost the love of my life, and when I made a sacred promise to her in front of God Himself as her soul transcended to Heaven from this mortal plane."

The fear coursing through my veins makes it hard to pay attention to the old man, but I try to focus on helping Alahna. I start looking around the cab of my truck, looking for something, *anything*, that can free me from my current situation. Unfortunately, an intense feeling of dread begins creeping into my subconscious. My breath shakes rapidly, and my heart pounds out of my chest. *This can't be happening.*

He grabs a handful of Alahna's hair and jerks her head back hard, causing her to cry out.

"Just remember, red...whatever happens next is because of you. It's because of your curiosity. It's because you failed this one. Remember, *you* brought her to us."

I survey the area around me, deep woods to my right, with what appears to be a huge drop off. Wide open field to my left. I start trying to unjam my seat belt again. *This isn't happening. It can't be.*

"Ok, look. I get it. Somebody screwed up and you think we saw something. If you let her go, I'll sign whatever form you have to prove my silence. I promise you we saw nothing, so please, please, please let her go. She has a family who will miss her, and I've got nobody. Please take me instead. *Please.*"

The old man starts laughing. "You think a scribble on a piece a paper will protect you? You think I care about your *word*?" He pulls out a long hunting knife and traces it along the nape of Alahna's neck. "You brought this unclean soul to us, so purification *must* happen. *Has* to happen. We're bound by the word of God and my promise to my beloved to return this country back to a pure status that ain't kept unclean by the likes of this...this *mistake*. But like I said, we'll be taking you soon enough, though."

Pure status? Unclean? This is some racist bullshit, and it doesn't seem like I can talk my way out of this one. Queue the dueling banjos instead.

The old man continues. "Let's go back to the time between the Old and New Testaments. No prophets. No miracles. No nothing."

The men on either side of Alahna pull her arms straight out beside her even farther, causing her to grimace in pain. It makes her look like she was on a cross herself.

"In Matthew, Chapter 15, Verses 21 through 28, a Canaanite woman chased after Jesus of Nazareth with a daughter demonized by what she thought were dark forces, which made her skin far darker than anyone else's. She asked Jesus to save her baby, to show her the might of His grace, and He denied her request, saying it wasn't right to take the food meant for the children of Israel and toss it to dogs like her."

One of the boys holding Alahna laughs, and says to her, "You hear that? You're a *dog*."

The elder lifts his hand up to the masked man, telling him to be quiet. The irony is not lost on me that Jesus probably looked more like Alahna than anyone else here, but I don't expect these men to believe that.

"Continuing on, Jesus' teachings tell us that we, the children of Israel, are the chosen ones. All others, especially those of a darker color than us, are foreigners in the world of the Lord. It is our responsibility—since we're covered in the blood of the Lord—to purify those not of our skin color, and prepare them for the Kingdom of Heaven. I'm a man of my word and I keep my promises, especially to my God and to the love of my life."

As soon as he finishes the sentence, he takes his knife and slices Alahna's face from nose to ear on her right side. A bloodcurdling scream escapes her lips, and as the blood pours out, it combines with her free-flowing tears.

I feel even more trapped now—physically in this truck, and emotionally watching my best friend in the world, my sister, suffer. I've never felt this level of fear and helplessness before. I start to shake and I feel my skin get cold. I pull even more desperately at the seatbelt holding me securely against the truck's bucket seat.

"Please, sir. *Please.* She was born in Alabama. She lives here with her family. She's not a foreigner. She is one of us. A true American in the eyes of God." I don't know what else to say, so I think appealing to his twisted sense of Christianity is the right move.

Alahna isn't saying anything, her body language shows total defeat. *Come on, AB...be strong*. I wish my telepathy broadcasted out to someone other than my own subconscious.

"In order to cleanse an impure soul, we are charged with the responsibility of spilling their blood and blessing the body as its soul transcends. To honor the life of the Lord and that of my long-lost love—both of which were sacrificed—another impure one shall be reciprocally taken."

The old man's knife slashes Alahna's left cheek from nose to ear, matching the first slice. More screams come out, but weaker this time around. She's quietly sobbing at this point.

"*Leave her alone, you racist bastard*," I whisper to myself. I feel the heat from a level of anger and rage welling up inside me that I've never felt before. A carnal, primitive, ancient anger starts taking over my faculties. I start yanking on my seatbelt in an unconscious adrenaline-filled rage. I kick my legs against the dash and door of the wrecked truck like a woman possessed, and I notice the passenger side door crack open.

I will kill you, old man. I will end your life. You better leave my best friend alone. My mind is racing with all sorts of irrational thoughts.

"We are the children of the Chosen One. We are the children of the one true God. And by the Grace of God, we will continue to live in His promised land. We will protect our land and avenge my wife's death by cleansing all unworthy people in her place. I will forever keep the promise I made to my beloved, and I will avenge her in all things. Thy and her will be done."

The older man snaps his fingers twice, and looks off to the side of the truck. "Bring me the bag."

No. No. NO.

Two more masked men walk up to the back of the truck, one of them carrying a small box. "Here ya go, Custer." The elder suddenly becomes enraged and clasps his massive hand around the masked man's throat, lifting him several feet in the air. The young man drops the box he was carrying in the back of the truck in the process.

"Damn it, you dumbass son of a bitch. No names. Not now, not *ever*." The old man throws the younger man several feet through the air with just a flick of his arm, the younger landing in a heap in the open field. The elder stands in the truck bed, shaking his head slowly from side to side, in a truly disapproving manner of the now-flattened man.

Custer. Custer. Little Big Horn. If I make it out of this, remember that name. Remember, Quinn. For Alahna's sake. I close my eyes, trying desperately to remember what his face looked like.

The old man, whom I now know as Custer, opens the box, and removes a clear plastic bag with what looks like a dog collar on the bottom. I suddenly remember what Special Agent Brown told me about the bag on the Springer Mountain dead woman, and bile immediately fills my mouth. The connection between the Springer body and Alahna in my brain has been made. These men are definitely the killers, and I'm not sure I'll survive long enough to identify them.

I can't talk. I can't move. I know exactly what is getting ready to happen, and I can't do a damn thing to stop it. And then I hear it. Custer starts whistling something. A familiar tune that shakes me to my very core. *Amazing Grace.*

He continues to whistle as he places the bag over Alahna's head. She struggles as much as she can, but Custer and the other men are just too much.

"Quinn, find these motherfu—" She mouths the last part as Custer clasps the collar tightly around her neck, cutting off any air flow. She starts gasping for air, gulping for something that isn't coming. She swings her head back and forth, fighting with everything she has left, which isn't much.

Custer starts singing the familiar tune he was whistling. "Amazing Grace, how sweet the sound…"

I can see that Alahna's eyes are wide, scared shitless, and I feel as if she is staring right at me. *Why did you do this to me, Quinn?* I hear her voice in my head, and I immediately regret everything.

"That saved a wretch like you…."

Custer cups his hands over her ears, as if he doesn't want her to hear his song. Her gasping starts to slow down, but her eyes are as wide as ever.

"You once were lost, but now you're found…"

She is trying hard to free her arms from the boys, but it isn't hard for them to overpower her in this state. Her legs start twitching as if she is trying to run away. As he continues to twist the lyrics, Custer pulls out what appears to be a baseball bat with a cross burned into the handle. It is light brown from barrel to knob.

"Impure, but now you're clean."

At that moment, he brings the bat down hard on the top of Alahna's head with a muffled crunch, the bag catching most of the carnage. The bile and vomit come rushing out of my body in heave after heave.

"'Twas grace that taught my heart to fear…And that grace helped to lead…"

I hear a second crunch of the bat as he continues to pummel Alahna's now lifeless body. More heaves. More tears. More regret.

"How precious did that grace appear, the minute your soul was cleansed."

A third, a fourth, and a fifth gratuitous swing of the implement of religiously racist destruction continues to rain down upon her. Custer laughs maniacally between blows.

I know she is no longer there, but I can't help but scream her name out loud.

"I love you, AB!"

Suddenly, in a stroke of good luck, I'm able to free myself from the jammed seatbelt. I dive out of the barely open passenger side truck door as Custer continues his ritual. My injuries from the truck crash are severe, but I don't feel them. Adrenaline, fear, sadness, guilt, regret, and rage all course through my veins at the same time as I jump into the deep, cavernous woods to the right of the truck. The crazed man continues to sing and swing, and I can't tell if anyone is following me. I just run as hard as I can, which is difficult with bare feet.

Suddenly the ground falls sharply off underneath me, and I tumble ass over tea kettle down the ravine. As my body rolls, I can see nothing through the tears in my eyes. I am honestly praying that I fall to my death.

Quinn, find these motherfuckers. Alahna's voice rattles in my head. She is already haunting me.

My body crashes into a tree and stops tumbling right at the edge of the ravine clearing, and it takes what seems to be an eternity for my marbles to stop scrambling in my brain. When I regain some semblance of focus, I look out ahead, realizing I am on the banks of what appears to be a huge river. I look back over my shoulder, fully expecting Custer and the boys to be chasing me with dogs or four-wheelers or something. All I hear is the sound of the river and Alahna's voice in my head.

Part of me keeps saying, "*You just gotta survive, Campbell. You just gotta make it out of this God damned forest.*"

"I'm sorry, AB. I'm truly sorry."

I close my eyes tightly, take a deep breath, and jump feet first into the water several feet below.

CHAPTER 4

"Help! Help! We need some help over here, because there's a woman in the water."

Dimly, I hear some kayakers calling out for help, and I can only assume it is because they spotted me. The sun shines brightly, and the weather is perfect to be out on the water. Just not the way I came to be here. I have been in this river for what seems like days, and I have been dragged over rocks, rapids, and body-scraping shallows. The only thing I know for certain—or I think is certain—is that I have absolutely no idea how long I've been in the water. I am freezing, waterlogged, and disoriented. I have no clue when or where I am, but one thing keeps bringing me back.

Alahna is gone. It should have been me. It's all my fault.

I'm the one with no real-world connections, no one to miss me. She had her family and her whole life ahead of her. *Why was I the one to survive?*

Several kayakers and someone who acts like a first responder rush out in the shallows to where I am hanging onto a rock, and attempt to get me to shore.

Questions fly in my direction. Are you OK? Can you swim? Who are you? Where are you from?

Standard operating procedure questions when confronting strange women lying in ponds. Only thing missing is my sword and a desire to be political. My mind works in mysterious ways sometimes, but I don't open my mouth to immediately answer any of their questions. For once in my life, I don't have anything to say.

I don't even realize I am crying again.

Many hands grab me out of the water and lay me down on the banks of the river. I hear and see everything going on around me, but in my injured mental and physical state, I can't comprehend the full magnitude of this situation. The heaviness of the guilt I feel—almost like a huge black stain on a perfectly white piece of fabric—surprises me, and I wonder why it didn't weigh me down enough to drown me in the river. I don't deserve to be the one still breathing, but deep down inside of me, something won't let me give up. I survived for a reason.

A few minutes later, first responders load me into the back of an ambulance with a police escort in tow.

"Excuse me, ma'am, can you tell me your name?" the officer asks.

"Quinn Campbell," I reply, weakly.

"Miss Campbell, how did you end up in the river?"

"I jumped in."

"By choice?" He didn't seem convinced.

"It was better than the alternative."

During their preliminary questioning, EMTs continue searching my body for potential injuries.

"We've got a gunshot wound here. Upper left shoulder." The EMT relays this information, and immediately begins to clean out and dress the wound.

"Ms. Campbell, how did you get shot?"

The room starts spinning rapidly, and the ringing in my ears gets excruciatingly loud. The officer's words slur, and I feel like I'm about ready to pass out.

"I...it was—" I feel my eyes begin to roll back in my head.

"Ms. Campbell, are you alright? Stay with us, OK?"

"Custer," I whisper. "It was Custer." Then the world goes dark.

***

I come to inside the ambulance, and I see first responders still working me over. When they notice my eyes are open, the questions start again. They again ask for my name, my birthday, my address, where I work, if I have any allergies. I'm not entirely sure the answers I give them are lucid. My hair is wet and matted, and the gunshot wound in my shoulder throbs uncontrollably. I have deep cuts from the truck crash all over my body; electrical burns on the back of my neck, shoulder, upper torso, and hands because of Custer's hillbilly hospitality; and bruises on top of bruises. It wouldn't surprise me if I had a few broken bones as well from the river bed and all of the shallow rapids. I am malnourished, dehydrated, and exhausted...just a hot mess express.

Why wasn't it me? She should be here with me right now. I can't get those thoughts out of my brain.

Then I hear the latest update come across the scanner in the ambulance, and it snaps me back to reality.

"Attention EMT4, your patient, Quinn Tallulah Campbell, age 30, from Atlanta, was reported missing from Springer Mountain on April 12."

That didn't take long. And someone reported me missing? I bet it was Wild Bill Tucker.

The EMT responds in the affirmative and tells dispatch they are headed to the closest Level 1 trauma center in downtown Atlanta.

"Ms. Campbell, can you hear me? Can you tell me how you got shot," the paramedic asks, trying to coerce me into conversation as he continues working on my injuries. Apparently, police and first responders care about why and how people acquire gunshot wounds.

"Custer," I mumble weakly.

"Is that a name? A location? Can you give me any other information?"

I can barely hear them because I'm fading in and out of consciousness again.

"Can you tell me anything about where you've been? What else hurts? I mean, your body's pretty beaten up."

Everything hurts, I think to myself. And he does not know what beaten up looks like, so I just turn my head to the side.

"What...what day is it?" I ask, in a despondent tone. "How long was...was I gone?"

"It's April 15. You have been missing for three days."

Sonofabitch.

***

After several hours, multiple surgeries, hundreds of X-rays, and tons of IV bags later, I wake up in a hospital bed. The beeps of the machinery keep me company as I stare out the window. Everything looks gray. For some reason, nothing has color in it anymore. One doctor tries to scare me by saying that if I don't eat, they are going to put in a G-tube, but I know my rights. As long as I have control over my faculties, they can't force treatment on me. My luck, they'd deem me a danger to myself, and as soon as I fall asleep, they would slip a sedative into my IV drip, wheel me back to the OR, and install it anyway.

Flowers fill my room, gifts from acquaintances, colleagues, college friends, and goodness knows who else. Plushie stuffed animals, candy, and cards are among the loot, and the nurses do a good job of hanging them all around my room. I vow to eventually read every single one of them, and then find a way to say thank you to each of them for caring.

A knock on my hospital room door draws my attention. Turning my head towards the sound, I see a face I recognize—a face I saw when I was pulled out of the river. He was one of the first police officers on scene, and a second officer is now with him.

"Ms. Campbell, are you feeling up to answering a few more questions?"

I stare at them for a few minutes, cutting my eyes back and forth to each of them, and then I lean my head deeply back into my pillows. "You were there at the river."

"Yes ma'am, I was. My name is Grayson Miller, and I'm a detective with the Dahlonega Police Department. This is Deputy Victoria Dillon with the Lumpkin County Sheriff's Office." Deputy Dillon nods her head, and then extends a hand in my direction. I look at it for a few seconds, and then I look up at her, showing her my heavily bandaged hands. She smiles knowingly, retracts her hand, and pulls out a little notebook instead.

"Ms. Campbell, can you tell us what happened to you?" Deputy Dillon asks, putting pen to paper.

"You need to be a little more specific." I chuckle weakly and turn my head away from them. *They do NOT want to know what happened to me.*

"Ms. Campbell, I know you've been through a lot, but we're just trying to piece together what happened to you between you being reported missing from Springer Mountain and turning up in the river in my town a long way away from Amicalola Falls," Detective Miller says. "I do have to ask, though. What happened to your shoulder?" He is obviously inquiring about my gunshot wound and I turn back to face them.

"Shaving accident?" Neither officer laughs. "Or maybe I fell down the stairs?" Stone faces. They really are a tough crowd. *I'm here all week. Tip your servers and try the veal.* "Alright, fine. I got shot, OK?"

"Do you know who shot you?" Deputy Dillon asks.

"It was either Custer or one of his boys. The shot came from behind me."

"And why did this Custer person shoot you?"

I close my eyes, and every sordid detail replays in my subconscious. "Because I was a threat to him. I guess I still am."

"A threat? How so?" Miller asks, his head sort of cocked to one side.

I stare at both cops, and just turn my head away from them. Every nerve ending I have is on fire, and I really don't want to relive things right now, but I start talking away. "Look, it's pretty simple. I poked my head into somewhere it didn't belong, and he was pretty confident I would ruin him and/or his way of life. End me, end the threat."

"Ms. Campbell, we're just trying to piece together how, from the Benton-Mackaye Trail, you ended up in my town over fifty miles away as the crow flies," Detective Miller says plainly, probably realizing I'm silent for a reason.

"Ms. Campbell, can you give us anything else to go on? Where exactly did this happen?" Deputy Dillon adds.

"Way deep in the Chattahoochee-Oconee near a big river. Not sure exactly where, because I was unconscious during my original transport. That's really all I got."

Deputy Dillon continues. "You also have some strange injuries that most hikers along the AT never suffer from, and frankly, they're quite puzzling to us."

I know they're just doing their jobs, and I really do want to tell them everything, but my body is telling me otherwise. Maybe if I tell them one more thing, they'll let me rest.

"They had some kind of turbo charged cattle prod implement of destruction they kept shoving into our bodies. Totally wasn't a walk in the park."

"And your bandaged hands?" Deputy Dillon quickly scribbles down everything I'm saying.

"They kept us in cages, and they occasionally electrified the bars." I look down at my hands. "I found that out the hard way."

"I know you're exhausted, but know we're just trying to find out more about who did this to you, so thank you for filling in some of the gaps." Detective Miller truly looks appreciative, and I smile in acknowledgment. "Since you've been missing for three days, time is of the essence."

There's no rush because the other missing person in this scenario is not really missing.

"Look, trust me. Time is really not of the essence. I really want to help, and I will definitely tell you everything I know, but now's not really a good time." My mind is ready and willing to cooperate but my body and my heart are not quite there yet.

Deputy Dillon then asks me a question that completely wrecks me.

"OK, one more question, Ms. Campbell. If time is not of a major concern, as you say, then can you tell us what happened to Ms. Alahna Bernard? Are you saying that she won't be found alive?"

My heart starts pounding out of my chest. My blood pressure spikes. I start rage bawling and hyperventilating at the same time. I gasp for air and scream at the same time. The nurses hear my screams, and notice all of my machines beeping like a frantic astromech droid; several of them rush into my room.

Quinn, find these motherfuckers replays on a loop in my head, and I can't hear anything over the sounds of Alahna's voice and the ringing in my ears. I can't catch my breath, and I suddenly feel like I'm falling through my hospital bed.

Detective Miller and Deputy Dillon quickly back away, with shocked looks on their faces. Miller slides his card onto my bedside table. "If you think of anything else, please give us a call," he says, in between and over top of my grieving shrieks. Nurses whisk both officers quickly out of the room, close the door, and pull the blinds, allowing me to finish my nervous breakdown in peace. A nurse injects something into my IV that starts taking effect almost immediately, calming every muscle in my body with a warmth that travels all over. My breathing is still ragged, but the air is finally flowing into my lungs. As I begin to calm down, all the nightmares and visions finally seem to fall away. *Thank you, ma'am, may I have another?*

***

Standing outside in the hallway, Detective Miller stared at the now-closed door, shaking his head as the nurses locked everything down. Locked the door. Pulled the shades. Cut everyone off. "Did you see her reaction to your last question? She completely melted down."

Deputy Dillon slid the small notebook back into her uniform shirt pocket. "Her reaction to my question about Ms. Bernard was both troubling and heartbreaking. I think her non-answer is actually an answer...one we really didn't want to get."

"I understand her reaction, alright?" Detective Miller responded. "She's obviously gone through hell and back, and doesn't want us poking around in a sensitive memory. But yes, I feel like her reaction means Ms. Bernard probably met an untimely end. We'll just have to come back tomorrow and try again."

"But we still don't know how she got from Springer to Dahlonega, especially since she obviously floated down the river for several hours, if not days? The entire Chattahoochee/Oconee vicinity could be our crime scene, Grayson. That question needs to be the first one answered and/or accounted for."

"Let's loop the GBI in, and see if the headless body they found a few days ago connects to Campbell or Bernard in any way," Detective Miller said. "We'll let their forensics team run ballistics on the bullet fragment pulled out of Campbell's shoulder, and see if we get lucky. Since both Campbell and Bernard disappeared looking into that case, maybe the evidence will give us the connection we need."

Miller and Dillon left the hospital and climbed into an unmarked Crown Victoria in the emergency room parking lot. Miller sighed audibly and grabbed the radio. "8419 to dispatch, I'm Code-4 at the trauma center, heading back to HQ."

Deputy Dillon began flipping through the notes that the hospital staff gave her, detailing all of the reporter's injuries, complete with pictures before and after her surgeries. The gunshot wound was the least troubling of her injuries. "Electrical burns from a superhuman cattle prod and cruelly electrified cages. She also had injuries indicative of and consistent with a serious motor vehicle accident. Where does one get shot, crushed, and electrocuted in Lumpkin or Fannin Counties, all at the same time?" Dillon rubbed her temple, and continued flipping through the notes.

"I'm truly at a loss, Vic. The biggest question mark, like you said, is how does a reporter and a photographer—who were both on foot near Springer Mountain—end up way over in Dahlonega?"

"I honestly have no idea. We have very few real clues to go on, and we have a witness currently having a nervous breakdown. She did give us something though. The name 'Custer,' the same name she gave you at the river." Dillon flipped back through her notes. "Now she's saying he or one of his sons shot her? Does that name ring any bells for you?"

Detective Miller pulled onto the highway heading back home. "Not a clue, so yeah, we're gonna need our techs on this, and maybe some federal help as well. And maybe Ms. Campbell will have calmed down enough tomorrow to help fill in more of the gaps. She wants to help us, I truly believe that."

***

Orderlies and attendants constantly go in and out of my room, and doctors refuse to let any visitors into my room after the police incident, which required a high dosage of ketamine to calm me down. Nurses were told to say I am in an area of the hospital that doesn't allow visitors because of the severe nature of my injuries. I appreciate the seclusion, because I'm having trouble facing the stark reality of my situation. No visitors means I can just wallow away in my sorrow and compartmentalize my mental, emotional, and physical damage all alone, which is probably not a good thing, but here we are. Mostly gone is the false bravado, the plucky sardonic wit, the charm that makes me...well, me. I'm a shell of the woman I once was, and that sort of pisses me off. I can't face reality in this mental shape, no matter how mad I get. The doctors even unplug my hospital room phone from the wall to keep me from pulling it out of the wall myself. I can promise you I'll never be the same, but I will adapt to my new mental surroundings. *Pull your shit together, Campbell.* I need to get back on my feet and put Custer in the ground or in a metal cage of his own. Wouldn't *that* be poetic irony? I've never felt such a potent combination of rage, determination, and guilt like this before. Who knows what I'm capable of now?

I slowly pull back the covers and look down at my pale, damaged body. There are bandages everywhere. Someone expertly wrapped both of my feet and ankles. A soft cast covers my right knee. My left arm and shoulder are in an isolation sling thanks to the gunshot wound, and both of my hands have burn wraps on them. I reach my right hand up to touch my face. I feel a bandage on my forehead, and there is a wrap around my head to keep it from sliding down. Deep purple bruises and deep jagged cuts cover a majority of my body, most of them from the wreck, even more from the river rapids I negotiated without a kayak. My five-foot four-inch athletic frame literally looks like a dime store mummy.

"Hey hey hey!" A nurse peeks her head in, and has a plate of food with her. "Here ya go, Ms. Campbell. You gotta keep your energy up, so I brought you a good plate of food and a surprise." She uncovers an orange popsicle. "Don't tell anyone I gave this to you."

The first thought that pops into my brain is, "*Whoopty freakin' woo. Like a damn ice cream popsicle made for kids is gonna bring my friend back and actually cheer me up, hmmm?"* Instead, I just weakly say, "Thank you."

"Oh, a man named William Tucker came to the nurses' station today, demanding to see you, but we were still trying to bring you down from your panic attack, and we wouldn't let him in. He left his personal number with the nurses' station and told her to keep him updated with any and all developments. Since he's not an emergency contact or an immediate family member, we couldn't give him any of that information, and he was none too pleased."

Wild Bill *hates* hospitals, so the fact he was here of his own free will means something. "I give you permission to release any updates to him, should he ask again."

The nurse scribbles something down on a notepad. "And some people who said they were family came up to see you around the same time. Two men with an older woman. When they couldn't come in to see you, the taller of the two men got really agitated and bullied the head nurse. They really tried hard to get in, too."

The Bernard family, it has to be. I'm not surprised Alahna's mom Beatrice and her two brothers, Ian and Aaron, came to see me. I know they're searching for clues as to Alahna's whereabouts, but right now I'm just not strong enough yet to tell them she won't ever be found alive, or admit to them it should be her lying here in this bed and me rotting away in some mass grave. Lying to them also would feel wrong. Therefore, I'm somewhat relieved they didn't get in to see me yet. As a trained GBI agent, Aaron would see right through any lie anyway, and he's known me long enough to know my tells. So, when I see them, they get nothing but the truth. I owe it to them. "I'm really sorry Aaron showed his ass to you guys. You're just doing your jobs."

"Yeah, the dude literally flashed a badge and said that since he was a federal agent, he should be able to get in to see you," the nurse chuckles. "I was like, 'Honey, you're gonna have to do better than that.'" She throws her head back and belly laughs, then starts checking my vitals.

"Thanks for taking care of me, truly. But if they come back, they are technically my family, so you can let them in. Just not today. Tomorrow, maybe."

She nods, and then walks out of the room.

I look up at the board that tells me who my attendants, nurses, and doctors are. April 17. Wow. My life forever changed five days ago out in the middle of freakin' nowhere. I know Alahna's family must be so conflicted, happy one of us was found and heartbroken that it wasn't AB. *It really should have been me.*

I lift the lid on my plate of hospital "food." I see what appears to be salisbury steak in a mystery brown gravy, mashed potatoes, a roll, a liquid that I assume is unsweetened iced tea, and my contraband orange popsicle. I cover the food back up and push it aside. I am just not hungry. I do eat the popsicle, though.

***

Beatrice, Ian, and Aaron Bernard waited impatiently in the empty lobby on Quinn's hospital floor. "Why can't we see her?" Aaron asked, bluntly. He continued to pace back and forth while Ms. Bernard, known affectionately as Mama B, and Ian both sat motionless in their waiting room chairs. Aaron wore a GBI windbreaker, polo, and cargo pants, while Ian sported a suit and tie. Alahna's mom dressed a little more casually.

"She's just trying to recover, honey. You've seen all the official law enforcement type people crowding this floor." Mama B shrugged her shoulders. "I assume they're all up here for her. Besides, the charge nurse said we can get in to see her tomorrow."

Ian continued, "You know how this goes, Aaron. They're probably trying to make sure she's stable before anyone can get info from her about what happened...and about Alahna."

The mention of his sister's name stopped Aaron in his tracks.

"I'm also trying to get that same information! My GBI sources have turned up nothing on her—zero, zilch, nada—so I hope she gives us something to work on." Aaron began pacing again. "Guess we're lucky Quinn survived."

"Of *course* we are, son. No guessing about it," Mama B quickly added. "She's a member of this family, and she looks at both of you like her big brothers."

"I'm more worried about my real sister." Aaron blurted out, blankly staring out the hospital window into the night. "Sorry, Mama. And speaking of, I know you're ready for her to come and take her damn dog back off your hands, bro." Ian shrugged, knowing how much Alahna's dog actually missed his mother.

"I know, son. We all are worried about her," she said in a pensive tone. "I just know she's out there somewhere. I have to keep telling myself that, and I'm not sure my heart can take it otherwise. But we can't take it out on Quinn. It's not her fault."

"We don't really know that yet, Mama. We don't know *anything*. But I tell you this—I will find Alahna and bring her home if it's the last thing I do, Mama." Aaron turned to look right at his mother. "That's an absolute *promise*. And I know Quinn will help me do that. I just know it."

***

Every single television station, news radio station, newspaper, and citizen journalist with a blog or social media account was talking about the reporter pulled out of a river in north Georgia, but also about the still-missing photojournalist. Both of their pictures were plastered everywhere. Everyone was going live from outside the hospital or from the river where the reporter was found.

The other part of the story was still the dead woman found up on Springer Mountain, and how she was possibly connected to the reporter and missing photog. The dead woman had now been identified as 24-year-old Jada Sinclair, a paralegal from Alpharetta, and there were confirmed similarities between the wounds found on the dead woman, and those suffered by the reporter.

Custer sat in the living room of his trailer, watching all of the media updates with a frustrated scowl on his haggard face. The door to the trailer opened, and four men dressed in construction coveralls walked into the tiny trailer's living room. A couple of them were covered in dried concrete dust.

"The press is callin' me the 'Mountain Mangler.'" Custer growled, polishing off a lukewarm beer, then slamming the glass bottle against the trailer's living room wall, crashing it into a million pieces. "She just got lucky is all. I was convinced she was pinned in the wreckage of what *was* my truck, so I wasn't in a rush to deal with or secure her. I am surprised the river didn't finish the job for us, though."

Clyde got some beers out of the fridge, and gave one to everyone. "We ain't done with her yet, though...right?"

"You cain't let her go, Pa," Ezekiel said, before swigging a mouthful of beer. "Because of Beau, she heard your name."

Beau stopped mid-swallow, and put his beer down. "But I worked all day today to finish securing our last package," he said in a nervous, frightened tone. "I worked the auger all by myself, and then helped

Lee and Zeke pour the concrete pad over her, along with the bits and pieces of her phone and camera. Why ya gotta pick on me more?"

"Not pickin', just bein' honest. Give me a seven-to-ten-day cure, and then we'll start light framing on that fresh pad," Clyde added, since he's the foreman for the family's construction business, Calvary Rock General Contractors. "Ain't nobody gonna find the body of that camerawoman like they did the one before her. *Nobody*." The contempt in his voice was palpable as he stared directly at his incompetent younger brother.

"But you're the reason we're in this mess, bro." Leland said, looking at Beau. "We've been doin' our thing up here for years, and nobody even knew we was out here."

"Shut your damn mouth, asshole." Beau chucked his empty beer bottle at Leland's head, crashing it against the wall of the trailer. Leland stood up, rage exploding in his eyes.

"*Stop* your shit, both of ya," Custer bellowed, freezing both men. Custer was both physically and mentally stronger than all the other men, so when he said stop, they stopped. "We have bigger fish to fry than Beau's obvious screw-up. We're on their radar now, so we gotta be careful. Better than careful."

Custer took another long swig from his fresh beer.

"Do y'all know anybody at that hospital? Anyone that could help us with our...problem? Anyone sympathetic to our cause? Anyone that owes us a favor?" Custer added. "We need a win right now."

"I got a buddy in maintenance near there. We built a house for his mama. Maybe he's got a contact that can get me inside?" Ezekiel said.

"Good, get ahold of him, Zeke. We need to find a way inside and deal with her before she tells everybody about us. Tell him only what he needs to know, and remind him what we do to people who fall out of our good graces."

"I got it handled, Pa." Ezekiel downed the rest of his beer and tossed the empty in the trash can. "I'll go call him right now."

"How many more open lots do we have, Clyde?" Custer asked.

"We currently have nine spots left in the lower subdivision." Clyde said. "We break ground on another subdivision in Dahlonega this summer—and that one will have thirty available lots."

"Good. Go ahead and start prepping one for the 'girl who ain't livin' much longer.'" Everyone laughed except Custer and Beau. "Actually, prep two of them in case Beau fails me again."

Beau nervously swallowed his mouthful of beer. He really hoped Ezekiel was as good as he thought he was. He really needed to get off Custer's shit list.

***

"*Get away from me, you bastard!*" I scream, as a nurse tries to wake me up in the middle of the night, with a scared look in her eyes.

"You're having a bad dream, honey. It's OK now," the nurse says, rubbing my good shoulder in comfort.

OK? I'm very far from OK. Every time I close my eyes, or try to sleep without a horse tranquilizer, I see Alahna with Custer and his inbred malcontents at the end of her life. The look of horror on her face. The swing of the baseball bat. His speech about "cleansing the impure" amongst us. Those racist bastards. Religious freaking bigots. Anger and rage flood my entire body, battling with the guilt and regret I still feel, and I feel like an EV car battery that just got plugged into a Level Eight supercharger.

I can't shake it. I can't change it. I can't deal with it. Every little thing pisses me off, and where my first thoughts used to be sarcastic and funny, they are now evil, vengeful, and volatile. I'm enraged, helpless, irritated, broken-hearted, and afraid—all at the same time. It's exhausting, yet I can't sleep at all. I'm powerless to fix *anything*, including me. It's like every nerve ending is on fire yet I feel nothing. Yeah, no...there's no rest for the traumatized. My mind is racing, my thoughts are coming fast and furious. I need to quiet the noise. I need to get out of this bed and find the son of a bitch that put me here and took my sister away from me.

I turn on the TV, and a stupid infomercial about a salad spinner is on. I check the clock—3:17am. My brain is so screwed up.

I need to find a way to keep people from asking me questions like "are you OK?" or telling me "Everything's going to be fine." Nothing will ever be fine again. At least not my previous definition of fine. I'm still trying to figure out what my new normal is.

I look back up at the TV, and lose myself in some As Seen On TV infomercial, just mindlessly staring at their paid block of time, trying to think of everything *but* her.

***

"Good morning, sunshine," my attending nurse, Bianca, says in a cheerful voice. I'm *so* not a morning person, not even before the incident. I look at the clock—6:36 am. Damn, I must have dozed off for at least a little bit.

"Good God, you're way too damn chipper this morning." I close my eyes, rub them, and try to stretch my neck. Jiminy Christmas, it's still way too sore.

"Now, you and I are gonna have to have a talk, Miss Quinn. You are barely eating your food, and that ain't gonna work for me. Either you eat it without me here, or I'm gonna force-feed you. Ain't losing nobody on my watch."

A week ago, I would have said something like, "I'd like to see you try," or "You and what army?" Now, I only say, "Whatever, boss."

"Don't you 'whatever' me. I got six kids at home, and I ain't got no trouble forcing a spoon in somebody's mouth." Ugh, what a pain in the ass.

"Hand me the damn spoon."

She takes the lid off the food, and the smell actually makes my stomach rumble. Soft scrambled eggs, toast with jam, and an orange juice. I disavow the coffee on the tray, because it and my body just will not get along. I grumble and take a bite of toast.

"Happy?" I say, with my mouth full of dry bread.

"You damn right I am. I put $20 on the fact I'd get you to eat without me holding the spoon. *Cha-ching*! I'm gonna buy a Lotto on my way home tonight." I groan and smile a tiny smile before I catch myself. Too late, Bianca saw it.

"You smiled. That means today's gonna be an extra great day."

"What, did you make a smile bet, too? I'm gonna have to take a cut of the winnings if this keeps up." Bianca laughs.

"Naw, no smile bet, but you sure made me feel good, Ms. Quinn. You went through hell and back, and yet you still managed a smile. Oh, and there have been tons of people here to see you this morning, but we turn."

They just want to see the girl who lived. Story at 11.

Every network is still airing the story of me being found floating down the river. It has been mainly an anchor story, using video from my BMT live shot the day those yokels kidnapped me. Some have used soundbytes from the GBI, some from local law enforcement, and some have even asked random people—called "man on the street" interviews—what their thoughts are on the whole situation. Some are trying to connect the dead woman on Springer Mountain to me and Alahna. They don't know how close to right they are. I bet Wild Bill shared my video with everyone in town, and probably racked up a ton of favors. Even the cable news channels run a story about me. I do not deserve the attention. I sure as hell don't want it. But I'd be doing the same thing if I wasn't stuck in a hospital bed.

"OK, let's go ahead and open up visitors today. I think I'm somewhat ready to interact with human beings again. But if I get too overwhelmed, I need you and the other nurses to step in and save me, alright?"

"I promise we'll be here for you. But now you have to do something for me. Clean your plate with me watching. Otherwise, no deal." Bianca puts one hand on her hip and points at my breakfast plate with the other.

Damn quid pro quo. I glare at her as I shove blackmail eggs in my mouth, and she just grins in my direction.

***

Ezekiel rolled his '70 Ford F-150 into the hospital lot, paint chipped, muffler growling. He cut the engine and sat for a beat, coveralls itching against his skin. The disguise was good—a maintenance hire, just another ghost with a mop. Rooms to clean, halls to scrub down. A janitor could slip anywhere, even into the reporter's room, and people wouldn't bat an eye.

Hank met him inside. No greeting, no small talk. Just a syringe pressed into his hand. The liquid inside shimmered an unnatural blue, like poison pretending to be medicine. "Finish her off," Hank said, voice low, eyes darting. A nurse he'd charmed had mixed the dose, but it wasn't her that Hank was afraid of. He owed a debt to Custer, and the old man doesn't bluff. If Ezekiel failed, Hank's family would be dead before sunrise.

"Look, she's on the seventh floor on the south side," Hank said, giving Ezekiel his fake ID badge. "If I help you here, I'm good with the family, right?"

Ezekiel smiled. "Ask me that once I've finished cleaning up my brother's mess, and let's hope this all works out. Thanks for helping me find her."

Hank smiled, weakly. He wasn't too sure if he could believe Ezekiel. "Good luck." Hank handed him a printout of custodial responsibilities, as well as nurse and doctor schedules in that wing, and the locations of empty rooms. "You're gonna have to get your hands dirty before just walking in her room. If you seem busy doing the things on that sheet, you'll be invisible."

Ezekiel slapped Hank on the shoulder. "She once was lost, but now she's found, brother."

***

Surgically repaired through-and-through gunshot wound in my left shoulder. Upwards of twenty fractures (hands, ribs, clavicle, right patella, shin). Grade Two whiplash. Second- and third-degree electrical burns on my neck, right shoulder, upper torso, and both hands. Bruises and deep cuts over two-thirds of my body (a combination of the wreck and the river rapids). Ruptured blood vessels in my right eye. The doctor came in to give me the rundown of "why I should feel lucky to be alive" speech. *Sorry, Doc, that is not what I'm feeling.*

As the doctor talks to me, I channel my inner *Peanuts* character, because all I hear is the *Wah, wah, wah, wah* teacher voice. Need to start PT, blah blah blah, you should talk with someone, yadda yadda yadda, seek help, badda bing badda boom. I guess the doctor notices that I have checked out.

"Ms. Campbell? I need you to take this seriously. It's imperative for your physical and mental well-being that you let us in and let trained professionals help you with whatever you're going through." Let you in? What are you, a vampire with an MD?

"Sure. Fine. Whatever you say, Doc." Sarcasm is, was, and will forever be my superpower.

"Look, since you've been here, our staff has done an exceptional job treating your physical wounds, but I fear your mental and emotional wounds run much, much deeper."

"What gave you that idea, Doc? Am I *that* obvious?"

"I get that humor and deflection appear to have both served you well up to this point, but since you won't truly talk to us, I reached out to one of your colleagues that has been here every single day trying to see you and help you." The doctor flipped through his notes to find the name. "A Mr. Thomas Jackson? He has been very helpful to us, forwarding information from your station's HR department, since you don't have anyone listed as emergency contact or family contact on any of your paperwork."

Good ole' T-Jack. I can't even be mad at him for telling my business. He's just trying to help, just like the doctor is. I told you he cares too much about me sometimes.

"Mr. Jackson told us how you will deflect and redirect conversation away from yourself as a coping mechanism. He said you are one of the smartest and most fiercely loyal people he's ever met, which will help us with some of your cognitive tests. He also said if you don't want us to know something, then we will never get that information."

Damn, he was three-for-three. I guess my reputation *does* precede me.

"Look, Doc. I know you're just trying to do your job, and thank you for trying to fix me up, but some wounds can't be fixed with a Band-Aid and some green Jell-O." I look away from him and back out the window. I start memorizing the sway of each individual tree that I can see. "And there's a reason I don't have any emergency contacts." He's not getting that sob story right now.

"Ms. Campbell, I have recommended that one of our clinical psychiatrists come by and see you today. It will also be good when you let some of your friends in to see you, a change that makes me happy." He looks over at all the get well soon cards lining two out of the four walls of my ICU room. "It might help you deal with some of these emotions you're shouldering on your own."

"Thanks, Doc. I'll take all your recommendations under advisement. My people will get back to you soon."

The doctor gives me a shake of his head, pats my bed, fires off a weak smile of defeat, turns and walks out of the room. Maybe friendly faces can actually help me deal with the crush of these tremendously heavy emotions. I need to find a way to compartmentalize things, though...to bury...these thoughts. The word "bury" triggers a chill throughout my body. I bet dollars to doughnuts that those rednecks denied Alahna a proper burial, and I hope she haunts those bastards for the rest of their lives. I know she's already doing it to me. And if she's not already terrorizing those country bumpkins, then I'll do it for her.

***

Ezekiel was tired of cleaning bedpans, removing soiled linens, and emptying some of the nastiest trash he's ever seen. *"I'm gonna literally rip Beau's head off when I get out of here,"* he mumbled to himself. But Hank was right. He was walking in and out of rooms and no one even acknowledged him.

He found the room where the reporter was recovering. There were so many people going in and out of her room. This might not be as easy as he once thought.

He would have to time it just right. Maybe after visiting hours are over? He looked at the information Hank gave him. Damn, he'd have to wait until 8pm for that. He looked at his watch—2:32pm. Looks like he's gonna have to play janitor a little while longer.

He just has to keep one eye on that room. As soon as she's left alone, she's all his.

***

Soon, my dance card is going to be full. I told the nurses they could go ahead and open my door to the public. Still, there is a limit to how many people can be in my room at a time. Some WQX colleagues came by first, followed by a few college friends and former roommates, you know, people who would not go too gaga over me. I told the nurses not to let any competing vulture reporters in to see me, because I knew they were just trying to use my story to further their careers. It's what I would have been doing if it wasn't me lying broken in a hospital bed, so I can't fault them for trying.

For the most part, the people coming by to see me create a nice feeling, a feeling of necessary distractions. They don't ask me details and I don't give them details. They genuinely care about my well-being, and spend their allotted time trying to either make me laugh, make me smile, or let me know they care about me. More people came than I expected. It really did make me feel better.

Then it happened. I heard a knock at the door, and I saw Aaron Bernard standing in the doorway, with Mama B and Ian close behind. I'm not going to lie, seeing them immediately made me feel better and awful at the same time, especially since I have bad news to tell them.

"Man, you look like shit," Aaron says with a smile.

"Takes one to know one, asshole," I respond almost instinctively.

Mama B shoves an elbow into Aaron's midsection, and literally runs to my bedside. Even though my body is bruised and broken, her hug makes all of that pain go away for a split second. She's crying, I'm crying, and Ian puts a hand on my shoulder. Aaron looks so relieved that I am OK, and I nod in his direction.

"Oh, Quinn honey. I'm so happy you're OK." Mama B releases her hug and starts looking me up one side and down the other. "Your poor body. I had no idea you were this injured."

The worst injuries I'm suffering from, they can't see.

"I'm tougher than an old piece of shoe leather, Mama B. I'll be out of here in no time."

"You know you don't have to act tough around us, baby. Be honest with me. How are you, really?" I look at both Ian and Aaron's faces, and they really look worried.

I close my eyes, and exhale slowly. This is going to suck, but they deserve to hear it.

"Pull up a couple of chairs, boys. You're gonna want to sit down for this."

I open up the floodgates, and let them know everything. The electrified cages, the car chase, the cleansing. I'm rage crying while I take them through the last few minutes of Alahna's life. I can't even look at them as I'm telling them what Custer and his boys did to my best friend and their younger sister.

"I knew I had to try and survive, so that I could come back and avenge what happened to AB. Even with all my injuries, I fell out of the truck, scrambled down a deep ravine, and jumped into the water. I had no idea where it would take me or if I would even survive, but I couldn't let them catch me."

I stop briefly to look at the three of them, through my teary eyes. Their faces are ashen white, and Mama B quietly sobs. Ian's head hangs low, while Aaron is standing with his back to me. I notice his fists are clenched, and I know him well enough to know he is already plotting his revenge. No one, and I mean no one, was to ever pick on, criticize, or bully his baby sister. And now I know he's going to add the word "cleanse" to his list of do nots.

"I was so helpless, Mama B. I was stuck and couldn't do anything but watch. And I don't even know anything about who they were, where they are, or what they're planning to do next. I was useless to save her then, and I'm useless to avenge her now."

Mama B rests a finger on my lips, and shushes me. She grabs me tightly, and she manages to squeak out a few words through her sobs. "At least one of my girls made it home. Thank God for that."

Aaron turns around and stares right at me, his eyes bloodshot from crying. "Q, you have to promise me something. Right *fucking* now."

"Anything, Aaron. Name it."

"When you get out of this bed, we—you and me—are going to go find those murderous motherfuckers and put them in the ground."

"You think I'm not already mentally planning something similar? We need every bit of your GBI pull, and you best believe I'll give you everything I have." Admitting this openly is helping me deal with the guilt and regret I feel. Joining my emotions with Aaron's, my rage and desire for vengeance now take center stage.

"I'm going to hold you to that. I'm going to make a call, and I'm gonna get the senior case agent who's assigned to this case down here ASAP. Those rednecks don't have any idea what's coming for them."

Our broken hearts are solidified by our white-hot rage. Mama B kisses my cheek, and pats my knee. "We're going to let you rest now, sweet one. I need to be alone right now, but we'll be back, OK? Please please please don't let your guilt or regret over what happened prevent you from getting better. I forgive you, my child. This is not on you."

Hearing forgiveness coming out of Mama B's mouth bathes me in warmth I didn't expect to feel. Maybe it *wasn't* my fault. Maybe I *can* get better—physically, mentally, *and* emotionally. I have to—for Alahna's sake.

Once the Bernards leave, I ask the nurses to give me an hour or so to myself. I need to recover from breaking their hearts. Even though it was cathartic to spill my guts and tell them everything, it never feels good to crush any and all hope in the hearts of those you love. I need some recovery time, and a couple of those damn orange popsicles.

***

Tommy Jackson has been in touch with the hospital every single day since they brought me in. He has sent trade journals, entertainment magazines, and all sorts of things for me to read, since he knows how much of a pop culture elitist I am. I didn't read them at first, but I have started using them as another distraction. Do you know how hard it is to flip through a magazine with wrapped hands and only one good arm?

"Knock, knock. Is the diva ready for her spotlight?" Jackson says with an apprehensive smile as he stands in the doorway to my room.

"Only if you brought me some of those little fun-sized candy bars. Otherwise, get the hell out of my room." It actually feels good to see his face, and I know I'm smiling a huge smile despite my attempt at subterfuge.

Tommy enters my room slowly, and the look on his face immediately makes me self-conscious, wanting to bury myself under the covers. He walks over, and tries to hold my right hand, which is still heavily bandaged, and I remind myself of Randy in his big winter coat in *A Christmas Story*. *I can't put my arms down...*

"Q, I can't tell you how happy I am to hear your voice, or to see your face." My tears once again start pouring down my face, and Tommy is immediately unsure of what to say or do. Sometimes his social awkwardness is cute, but now, I am the awkward one. It surprises me that I have any tears left, to be honest.

He pats my good shoulder as tears continuously stream down my face. I can't even look at him. "I'm so sorry, T-Jack. I'm so sorry I...that I...please don't look at me." My voice trails off as powerful body-rocking sobs take full control of me. "I'm just so broken right now."

Maybe I care more about Tommy than I originally realized. I don't know why I don't want him to look at me like this. Am I really ashamed of how I look? I feel like an idiotic schoolgirl with a bad haircut. *So stupid...*

Let people in, the doc said. *It'll help you*, he said. Screw him and his lack of bedside manner. He's not the one bawling over here, acting like a middle schooler just hitting puberty.

Tommy gets the point, stops talking, and just holds his hand on my good shoulder. Just knowing he is there allows me to let down my guard a little bit, and just hard cry. Again. This was my second cathartic cry in as many hours, but the first one felt completely different. I unburdened myself by coming clean to the Bernards, and I was worried about breaking their hearts, but Mama B forgave me. The rage I felt along with Aaron somehow made the guilt and regret seem like less of an issue. But this one? I can't speak, I can't breathe, I'm just sobbing, like one of those emojis with waterfalls coming from each eye. I feel like I'm letting down one of the most important men in my life.

"Hey," I say weakly, between sobs. "Will you stay with me for a while? No talking, just—sit with me?"

"I'd be honored, Q. There will be plenty of time for you to tell me whatever you need to tell me. Until then, no words."

He pulls up one of those weird hospital chairs, and just sits beside me, my bandaged hand in his. His presence feels really good, if I'm being honest. And completely different from the Bernards. I feel connected to Tommy, comforted and soothed by his presence. *Maybe I care about him too much sometimes, too.*

I didn't let anyone else in for the rest of the night, and I also talked the nurses into letting him stay past visiting hours. The charge nurse took pity on me, after seeing how much of a blubbering mess I am. It was just me, T-Jack, and all of my feels. The doctor would say today is a good first step to dealing with whatever it is I'm dealing with, because Tommy stays right beside me, never once leaving my side. I cry myself to sleep, hoping no one—including Alahna's memory—would bother me again tonight.

***

A tone went over the PA system, letting everyone know hospital visiting hours were over. Ezekiel had found a spot in a custodial closet to hide, so he wouldn't have to actually work. He was relieved to hear the announcement.

He grabbed a janitor's cart, made sure the syringe was still in his left pocket, and started walking towards the room where the reporter was.

He went to enter the room, but saw a man sitting in a chair beside her bed.

"'Scuse me, but you cain't be here. Visitin' hours are over." Ezekiel tried to act formal and intimidating.

"No, it's OK. I'm here at her request. The nurses' station knows who I am." The man turned away from him, refocusing his attention on the sleeping reporter.

"I have to clean up in here, so it'd be best if you left. Just so you won't get in my way."

The look on the man's face showed he didn't quite understand why a janitor needed the room empty in order to do his job. "Like I said, I'm not leaving. You can do your job with me sitting here. Just work around me."

Ezekiel felt the man giving him the once over, a closer inspection than he would like, so he tried not to seem too nervous or fidgety. Something seemed off all of a sudden about the entire situation. This was not going how Ezekiel had planned this event in his head.

He was having trouble thinking on the fly, so he just nodded his head and started acting as if he was cleaning the room. He didn't like this dude staring at him, and the tension building up between the two of them was palpable. The man by the reporter's bedside waited for Ezekiel to turn his back to them, and then he stealthily pressed the nurse call button.

A night nurse walked into the room, expecting it to be just Quinn and her friend but instead saw *two* men in the room, with her finally asleep. "What can I do for you, Mr. Jackson? Is everything OK?" she quietly asked.

Tommy glanced at the janitor, noticing that the man was acting even more nervous than before. He mouthed the words *I don't trust this guy* covertly to the nurse, and then cut his eyes towards the janitor in a "hey, look at him over there" fashion.

"Yes, ma'am, I was wondering if you could ask this gentleman to come back later?" Tommy whispered. "See, Quinn is finally sleeping, and I really would like her not to be disturbed."

"Hey, there, umm...do you mind coming back later?" she whispered, walking over to Ezekiel. "Besides, I don't think I've seen you on this hall before. We normally handle the ICU cleanup with the same crew every night. And you are?" She looked down at his ID badge for the unknown man's name. She looked a lot more closely at him than Ezekiel anticipated or had prepared for, because the face on the badge was definitely not the same as the man in front of her. The hat he was wearing didn't help matters any. She gave him a curious look, confused as to the facial discrepancy. "Ummm...I'll, um, be right back."

She spun around quickly to walk out of the room, but Ezekiel couldn't let that happen. He took a broom off of the janitor's cart and swung the handle as hard as he could, hitting the nurse just above her right ear. She crumpled into a pile on the floor, and Ezekiel swung at her two more times on the ground for good measure, with two gruesome thumps.

***

I shoot up in bed at the commotion, wondering what in the hell is happening. Through blurry eyes, I see the nurse lying bloodied on the floor, and a janitor standing over her. I look over at Tommy, who is holding tightly onto my arm, and then back at the man.

I know those eyes. I will forever remember them. He's one of Custer's boys! The last time I saw those colorless gray eyes and his yellowed skin, he was holding Alahna's arm as Custer sacrificed her. Creepily, the crazed janitor winks at me and then utters words that chill me to the bone.

"You once was lost, but now you're found."

He makes a move towards my bed, but Tommy instinctively stands between me and the man. The man takes his index finger, and points it straight at Tommy's head. He cocks his thumb back and fires off a shot from his intimidating finger cannon.

About that time, two orderlies come into my hospital room, and the fake janitor acts as if he needs a quick getaway. The much larger man barrels right through them—knocking them both out of the way. He reaches out his hand, grabbing the doorjamb, which helps him turn left on a dime.

They found me. I'm a sitting duck here. And now, so are my friends.

***

The commotion Ezekiel left in his wake followed him out of the room, and down the hallway—with hospital security chasing him towards the stairwell. The reporter's visitor stood in the doorway, making sure no one came back in.

Ezekiel ran down the stairwell, tumbling down several flights of stairs while also tossing off his cover clothes piece by piece—first his hat, then the coveralls—as he tried to hide in plain sight. He barreled through visitors, doctors, orderlies, all in an attempt to reach an exit. Hospital security gave a valiant chase, but lost him in the main lobby of the emergency room. A large accident with several casualties had just been brought into the ER, and Ezekiel blended expertly into the chaos. He slipped out of the entrance before police could lock down all the exits.

He ran as hard as he could across the parking lot to his Ford F-150. He saw a 9mm handgun in the bag sitting in the passenger's seat. He grabbed it, cocked it, and put it in his lap. The furious look on his face showed that if he had carried the gun with him, there would have been many, many dead bodies left in his wake...maybe even his own.

He cranked the truck, waited a split second, and then faded into the evening traffic on the Downtown Connector, headed towards Georgia 400.

Custer was going to be *very* pissed.

***

Tommy looks back at me, in total protective mode after all the commotion. I'm sure he sees my look of absolute horror, and I feel every bit of color fading from my abnormally pale cheeks. No sound is coming from my mouth, even though my jaw is completely agape. My eyes are wide open, as if I'd just seen a ghost. My breaths are short and shallow, my pulse and heartbeat both off the charts.

I look down at my nurse, who is being attended to by medical staff for the massive blows she suffered from the imposter's attack. She is the one that slid me the contraband orange popsicles. She didn't deserve to be brained by a sadistic, racist zealot.

One of those damn hillbillies *actually* came after me—hoping to finish the job they started. He must have been ordered to tie up loose ends. I now know people sympathetic to their cause work in this very hospital. I know at this moment I am not safe at all. Maybe no one I know is safe.

"T-Jack, he was one of them. He was...one of the men who kidnapped me and AB."

"Seriously? How did you recognize him?"

"Well, they all wore balaclava-style masks, but I will forever recognize that yellowish skin and those dead gray eyes. He was...he was...holding AB when...when they killed her."

Tommy completely freezes at my last statement. He stares at me blankly, trying to process what I just told him. Now I have to give him the rest of the story.

I once again unburden myself of the entire sordid story, and he sat there staring at me the whole time. When I get to the river jump and then present day, all Tommy can do is repeat "I'm so sorry" over and over again. Like he could have done anything to prevent what happened from actually happening. I notice my tears have stopped, and that I'm focusing on the single solitary tear sliding down Tommy's incredibly handsome cheek.

"There's nothing you could have done, T-Jack. We were just in the wrong place at the wrong time. AB's older brother, you know, the GBI agent? He's coming back tomorrow and I'm gonna give them everything—descriptions, names, the works. I did see the leader's face briefly, and we both just saw one of his sons, so it's only a matter of time before we find them.

Or they find me first.

CHAPTER 5

After the attempt on my life in the hospital, there's no way folks will leave me by myself again. I am not the woman I once was, which is somewhat difficult for me to accept because this guilt-fueled rage is changing the very way I see myself. Maybe this is how people have always seen me, and I was just too cocky to notice it. But like the fabled phoenix, I will rise from these ashes a changed, much stronger woman. At least I hope I will.

As the days go by, I keep replaying the screw-up of an assassin's words over and over in my head. "*You once was lost, but now you're found.*" The feral, heartless look in his coal gray eyes is burned into my retinas. He was apparently willing to do just about anything to get to me—such a frightening realization to have while his sickening southern drawl rattles around in my brainpan. Not the kind of earworm I'd prefer to have.

I look around my room, and it still looks like an Atlanta arboretum had a love child with a dollar store. Plants and flowers of every color. Get Well balloons in various stages of deflation. A myriad of stuffed animals scattered around the room. Cards taped to the walls, doors, and cabinets. I bet there isn't a Hallmark card left in the ATL. They should just label my room as the 7th Floor Gift Shop, and give me a cut of the earnings. It seems like I'm always thinking of a side hustle.

A nurse walks up to my room, knocking three times on the door. Two security officers that, according to Tommy, are bought and paid for by WQX-TV flank the door. I truly appreciate Wild Bill Tucker's gesture, even though I'll never give him the satisfaction of telling him so. One of the security guards checks the nurse's badge and allows her in. No doubt the powers that be enacted a new protocol after the failed attempt to end my life. The GBI has also locked down my floor, and stationed local law enforcement at the stairwells and at the elevators. I guess I shouldn't be surprised by that. Just one more layer of helping keep me safe while I try and get well enough to get the hell out of here.

Big picture moments are easy for me to recall, but little things like dates, addresses, and license plates intermittently blink in and out of my frontal lobe—which irritates the hell out of my reporter brain. I'm trained to be aware of anything and everything around me, knowing that small details can really add serious weight and heft to a story. Now, I can only consistently remember the intense emotions—fear, guilt, anxiety, horror, rage, regret—and their physical counterparts—my gunshot wound, full body pains, the nervous sweats, my accelerated heartbeat and ragged breathing—along with Alahna's face as it slides into the bag. *And that damn song*. Thanks for ruining *Amazing Grace* for me forever, you pricks.

The nurse double checks my bandages, looks over my gunshot wound, and gives me the general once-over. She picks up the lid to my lunch tray, giving me a disapproving side eye as she recovers my untouched leftovers. "Miss Quinn, you've been here for ten days, and you've barely eaten anything but your pudding, some fruit, and an occasional vegetable," she says, disapprovingly. "This form of weight loss is not covered under your insurance, and you're gonna be paying for it later." Insurance humor. 200 points for the nurses' station.

"As far as food is concerned, I'm doing alright. The night orderly sneaks me candy, chips, and sodas out of the vending machine." I pat my belly. "Dinner of champions."

The nurse gives me a blank stare reminiscent of all those animated GIFs. By the way, it's pronounced with a hard G, not like the peanut butter. Don't @ me.

"The doctor will be with you soon to talk about your discharge papers, your home care routine, and suggested physical therapy regimen." She pats me on the good shoulder. "Your wounds are healing nicely and you've passed our PT and OT guidelines for release. Pretty soon, you'll be back to life as normal." I give her my best fake smile.

I'm pretty sure the "normal life" ship sailed a LONG time ago.

A few moments later, I hear a knock at my door. I look up, and I see GBI Assistant Special Agent in Charge (ASAC) Daniel Brown, accompanied by Aaron Bernard, standing in the doorway.

"Penny for your thoughts?" Brown quips.

"You know I'm more expensive than that, Brownie. At least bring me chocolates or a warm Krispy Kreme doughnut before asking me to spill my guts."

"Ms. Campbell, I'm just happy to see you still above ground. Agent Bernard basically filled me in after what you told him yesterday, and I'm sure you know I need to ask you several follow-up questions. Especially now, after what happened yesterday with the disguised custodian and your injured nurse, who is in ICU right now. That will undoubtedly lead into more questions about your Appalachian Trail adventure." Brown pulls out a mini digital recorder. "Do you mind if I record our conversation?"

"Go for it. I'm sure it's a hell of a lot easier than scribbling notes down in shorthand."

Brown smiles at me, clicks record on the device, and sits it on the bed between us.

"First off, how was the attack on your life yesterday connected to your disappearance near Springer Mountain?"

I tell him about how the custodian was probably either a son or a close relative of a man named Custer, whom I saw kill Alahna Bernard and who also orchestrated our whole disappearance.

"So, let me get this straight. The man who tried to attack you last night was directly involved in your disappearance *and* in the death of Alahna Bernard?"

"Absolutely."

"Tell me about the others. What do you remember?"

I explain to both Brown and Aaron they all wore balaclavas for most of the time they were around us, but I describe Custer's face in as much detail as I can remember. An older man, probably in his mid to late sixties, unkempt gray beard, yellowish skin, about six feet tall or so, built like a brick shithouse. I also tell him there were five total men involved—including Custer—as best as I can remember.

"I also believe they killed the Springer Mountain woman, too."

"What makes you say that?" Brown asks.

"Remember the bag you told me that was on the dead woman's head? Well, they put one over Alahna's head, too. It had what looked like a dog collar that he pulled tightly around her neck before...you know...he killed my best friend."

"We didn't release anything about a collar to the press. How exactly did this man Custer kill Ms. Bernard?"

I sigh loudly. Remembering these details is causing a welling up of emotions I'd love to tamp down. "He had this baseball bat. It was light brown in color with a cross burned onto the handle." I tell them about the tarp covering the truck bed, the other men holding her arms, about Custer's racist "sermons," and then the repeated bashings of Alahna's skull.

"I see. What about your injuries—specifically your unusual burns. They perfectly match those found on Jada Sinclair's body. How did you come by these injuries?"

"Yeah, those bastards love their electrical shock toys. They had a couple of these souped-up cattle prods of death, and they loved sticking the prod inside the cage and watching us flop around like electrocuted fish. Oh, and they also electrified the bars of our cages."

"You were kept in cages?" Brown looks naturally concerned. "What else can you tell me about where you were held captive?"

I told him there were about 10-15 cages on the floor of the warehouse, but it was so incredibly pitch black that I couldn't make out much of anything else.

Aaron was just standing behind Brown, scribbling down notes of his own as I spoke. No doubt he's willing and/or planning to go rogue if the GBI doesn't do enough to avenge his baby sister.

After about thirty minutes of questioning, Brown picks up his recorder and hits stop.

"Ms. Campbell, thank you for your cooperation, and I'm truly glad you made it through this ordeal alive and are in a position to help us make some sense out of what happened to you, Ms. Bernard, and Ms. Sinclair. Maybe we can find the people responsible for this before they create any more problems."

"Brownie, you know when I get out of this bed, I'm gonna want in on the investigation. I want to be there when you find them."

"Just answer your phone when I call."

"Yeah, about that. My phone was crushed to dust under a hydraulic press, so I kinda need a new one."

Brown hands me his business card. "When you get your new phone, just let me know."

"Thank you, Q." Aaron finally speaks, and gives my heavily bandaged hand a solid fist bump. "Thank you for not leaving my baby sister alone."

"There is no way I was leaving her. Not then, not now—not ever. We *will* find who did this."

Soon after Brown and Aaron leave my room, the amazing hospital staff decides to discharge me from their care after eleven days, gives me a pair of crutches, and then releases me with a bag full of painkillers, antibiotics, steroids, stretching routines, psychiatric referrals, etc. The amount of paperwork also in the bag reminds me of one of those long-ass CVS Pharmacy receipts you get after buying only a bag of chocolates and an overpriced bottle of water.

The two security goons come along with me, one in front, and the other behind. You know the stereotype—the ones that take their jobs *way* too seriously and say absolutely nothing? Yep, those are my shadows now. The funny thing is that my trail shadow is carrying all the leftover cards, flowers, stuffed animals, and anything else the nurses were able to pack up for me. He looks like he just robbed the hospital gift shop. It is low key hilarious.

Nurses and my bodyguards take me out of the hospital via the service elevator, and we get into a black Escalade parked on the opposite end of the hospital, far from the front door. They don't want to risk a high visibility exit in case the hillbillies try to kill me again.

The security guard behind the wheel is huge, 6'5", 6'6" maybe, and built like a stone statue—which explains his expressionless face. The other one has a softer edge to him, and he looks a little younger than the driver. Both men have sleeve tattoos, and from the backseat, I can see a military insignia on the right arm of the driver. Eagles, skulls, lightning bolts, and the phrase "De Oppresso Liber" inscribed around the tattoo on a semicircle banner. I mentally file that away for later, because I want to look that phrase up.

After several minutes of silent driving—which was extremely hard for me—we pull up to a location I don't recognize. The younger man opens the rear door, helping me get out and get set up on my crutches.

"Where are we?" I ask. "My apartment is in Midtown."

"Look ma'am, someone tried to kill you in the hospital. We can only assume they have your home address, too." The older man actually makes some sense. "This is a safe house we have access to. One of us will go by your apartment later for a supply run, so be thinking about what you'll need to be comfortable here."

"How long are we talking?"

"Until further notice. You can't go home right now." Damn. I love my apartment. I mean, I am never there, and the rent costs me an arm and a leg, but I like the location more than the apartment itself. At least I have somewhere to truly call home. Well, I *had* somewhere...

I remember my purse was last seen in the racist rednecks' possession, so it makes sense they could track down my home. Hell, if I don't know where I'm at, hopefully they won't know either. We walk inside the door, and a set of stairs confronts me. "Want me to carry you?" my trail shadow asks. I shoot a *screw you* look at the younger guard, and he lifts both hands up in an *I'm sorry* gesture.

"Me and my crutches can manage just fine, thank you."

Of *course* it was on the fourth floor, and now I'm seriously winded. I should have worked more on my cardio, pre-hillbilly hoedown. The older guard unlocks the door to the safe house, and lifts up his hand in a full stop motion. He quickly slides inside and closes the door. We stand there for what feels like hours in awkward silence while he clears the safe house. The door opens, and I cautiously hobble inside. The furnishings are spartan, and the dust layers show this hasn't been a safe house for anyone in a *long* while.

"I guess you guys don't keep a cleaning service on retainer?" I decide to sit down on a couch easily made in the 1960s, but it matches the blue shag carpet. "Who all uses this place?"

"It's an interagency location. GBI, FBI, my company. This is just one of many in the metro Atlanta area."

The older guard grunts some kind of communication to the younger one, and hands him a small slip of paper. The younger man walks over to the front door, gives me a half smile, looks at the other guard, and then walks into the hallway, closing the door quickly behind him. My older shadow walks to the door and locks all four door locks swiftly with an easy back and forth flick of his wrist. *Impressive.*

"So, this relative silent treatment may work for the both of you, but it's creeping me out." The older bodyguard looks directly at me, and I notice a bit of softening around his eyes.

"Look, Ms. Campbell. We are here for your protection only, not for your entertainment or amusement."

Rude.

"At least give me your names, so I'm not calling you Tweedle Dumb and Tweedle Dumber."

The older guard sighs. "Call me Anderson. The other one's Barton. We'll be your protection detail for at least the next two weeks. Bought and paid for, so don't worry about a thing."

Lovely. I'm stuck with them, whether I like it or not.

"Are you gonna wash my back, too? Oh, and I prefer the soft 2-ply toilet paper."

Anderson rolls his eyes loudly, and walks over to the kitchen table. "You can't afford me for those services, so act like we're not even here. I sent Barton to the closest drug store to fill your prescriptions and get you some basic things to change your dressings with—gauze bandages, med tape, you know, like a first aid kit. This safe house doesn't have a lot of creature comforts, but at least you can have some sense of security while we're here. Our job is to make sure you are safe and taken care of, within reason."

"Speaking of comforts, I'm in desperate need of a long, hot shower."

Anderson picks up a folded newspaper and starts flipping through it. "I thought I smelled something." *Ass.*

I flick the newspaper as I crutch walk past him, and he grunts in disapproval. I've heard that sound a lot today.

I close the bathroom door behind me and just stare at myself in the mirror. I don't even recognize myself. Scars. Bruises. Gunshot wounds. Where is the wisecracking southern belle without a care in the world but paying her bills on time and making it to her car at night without getting wolf whistled at or hit on by some man or woman? *I'm sorry, but she's not here at the moment. Please leave a message at the tone.*

I lean toward the mirror and wipe my hands down my face. My ice blue eyes stare coldly at the reflection in the glass. Turning my head slowly from side to side allows me to really survey the damage. *At least I still have my head.* I slam my hands down on the sink and shake that thought out of my head quickly. Don't go there, don't go there, *don't...go...there.*

I glance down at the neckline of the "I Heart Atlanta" t-shirt that my favorite nurse bought me from the gift shop, pulling it down slightly to see the discolored flesh underneath. I slowly lift the shirt over my head and off with my good arm, and just stand there, frozen.

Negative thoughts, images, sounds, and scenarios begin flooding my subconscious. I stare at my mostly-healed bullet wound, noticing the scar tissue already forming on my pale skin. I lift my opposite hand up and trace my fingers across it, and I immediately feel a wave of helplessness engulf me. I don't even notice the tears pouring down my face until I sink down onto the cool bathroom tile into a mopey ball of despair. I cradle my knees to my chest and move slowly back and forth, my sobs matching the movements in perfect time.

Suddenly, Anderson knocks on the door. "You OK in there?"

No, you dense bastard, I'm not one bit OK pops into my subconscious but I merely squeak out an "I'm good" response.

I hear that familiar grunt of disapproval, and then his footsteps lead away from the door. I feverishly wipe the tears from my eyes, and slowly stand back up. I methodically remove my remaining clothes, turn on the shower, and step inside.

I stand under the warm stream of water for what seems like hours, letting the ribbons of warmth wash over my head and down my body. I can't close my eyes, because when I do, I keep seeing things I never want to see again. All of a sudden, my throat tightens, and I feel as if I am back in the river. *I can't breathe.* It is as if I am being pulled underwater by some unseen force. I brace my hands against the walls of the shower to steady myself, but I keep falling and falling into the deep unknown. I begin to hyperventilate, gasping for air that isn't coming. Even though the water is scalding hot, I feel the cold of the darkness below, grabbing me, pulling at me, trying to drag me back into the horrific moment. From out of nowhere, I hear Alahna's voice cry out to me from the darkness.

You failed me. You let this happen to me. I'm dead because you didn't save me. You get to live even though you couldn't save me. This is all your fault.

I try to scream. I try to respond. Nothing. I collapse into the tub, pulling the shower curtain loudly down onto me in a heap.

Quinn, find these motherfuckers.

The bathroom door explodes, and Anderson comes barreling in. He finds me in the fetal position, my head buried in my hands and my eyes frozen in a mixture of terror and soul-crushing guilt. Even though I thought I wasn't making a sound, the searing pain in my throat now proves otherwise. That's what must have caught Anderson's attention.

Anderson turns off the water, and wraps a large white towel around me while removing the soaked shower curtain. I am freezing, my body trembles under his hands. He stands me up on the carpeted bedroom floor, and notices I am frozen stiff. "Umm, I hope you don't mind, but I have to do this for you." I cannot muster a response.

Taking my silence as approval, he deftly removes my towel and gently pats me dry. Even though he has a seriously gruff exterior, he is gentle, caring, concerned. While other men might have taken advantage of the situation, knowing that I am in absolutely no condition to resist or fight back, Anderson does not. He dries me off in a very platonic way, even turning his head away from me when he could. He wraps me in a dry towel, and sits me on the edge of the bed.

"I can't guarantee you there are any clothes that you'll like here, or if they'll even fit, but let's see what's been left lying around."

He opens every drawer and closet door, acting as if he is on some great and all-important mission. He grabs an oversized t-shirt, a pair of sweatpants, and a pair of fuzzy socks.

He lays the chosen outfit beside me on the bed and pats his hand on them. "Now, come on, Miss Campbell. I'm gonna need you to put these clothes on for me." I look down at the hot pink paisley shirt, the big multicolored polka dot sweatpants, and orange creamsicle fuzzy socks. A giggle wells up from somewhere deep inside, and it pulls me slowly out of my catatonic state. I manage a weak response.

"Thanks...but I...would never wear...that combination."

"There she is. Look, I'm gonna turn around and let you get dressed, but I am not leaving this room until you do."

***

GBI Assistant Special Agent in Charge Daniel Brown sat behind his desk at the regional headquarters in north Georgia, tapping a pencil on his desk blotter. He stared at an open folder on the desk, looking at pictures of Quinn Campbell, Alahna Bernard, and Jada Sinclair, the dead woman found up on Springer Mountain that started this whole mess. Flipping through the pictures and case notes, he looked clearly deep in thought. He also added the transcript of his interview with Ms. Campbell to the file.

A knock on his door broke the silence. He looked up, and noticed a well-dressed man wearing a holstered firearm on his hip and a detective's shield around his neck.

"Special Agent Daniel Brown? I'm Detective Grayson Miller with the Dahlonega Police Department. Got a second?"

"You were there the day they pulled Ms. Campbell out of the water, correct? I remember seeing your name on the police report. What can I do for you, Detective?" Miller pulled up a seat on the other side of Brown's desk, and noticed the file folder open in front of him.

Brown instinctively closed the folder, preventing prying eyes from being tempted to look at the classified information inside.

"Yes, I was there that day, and I also visited Ms. Campbell in the hospital with a colleague from the Lumpkin County Sheriff's Office. It didn't end well. I was hoping maybe you could help me connect some of the dots?"

Brown looked at Detective Miller for a second before answering. "You know, knowing that Campbell is a veteran reporter who consistently and aggressively likes to bust my chops, I can tell you she was very forthcoming to us when I interviewed her again yesterday. I mean the woman is trained to be observant and mentally record details that the uninitiated never see."

Brown studied the detective silently for a moment, and then sat back in his chair. "Are you looking to pool resources? Work together? You do know we're running point on this, right?"

"Campbell was pulled from a river in my town, and with her injuries, you and I both know something criminal happened to her. I want in on the investigation, and I already have approval from my police chief."

Brown had just coincidentally secured approval from his boss, the regional Special Agent in Charge, to work this investigation with three very specific parameters: 1. Find the people who killed Jada Sinclair; 2. Investigate any and all connections between Sinclair's death and what happened to Quinn Campbell and Alahna Bernard; and 3. Find Alahna Bernard's body.

"After talking with Ms. Campbell, I am convinced the people responsible for the death of Jada Sinclair are the same people wanted for the alleged murder of Alahna Bernard and the attempted murder and kidnapping of Ms. Campbell." He'd never worked with Miller before, and needed to gauge his reactions. "The injuries suffered by

Ms. Sinclair and Ms. Campbell were eerily similar, so we feel circumstantially that these cases are connected. Unfortunately, we only have Ms. Campbell's testimony right now, so we need corroborating evidence."

"I can help you get that information, sir." Detective Miller added. "I really need to close this case."

"Have you ever worked with the GBI before?"

Detective Miller sat a little bit forward in his chair. "I have not had the pleasure yet, sir. However, I do play well with others, and I know my place. I just want to finish the puzzle in front of me, and find out once and for all what in the hell really happened."

"In that case, welcome to the team. We have an organizational briefing here tomorrow morning at 0800. Bring whatever you've collected with you, and we'll fold you into the group."

Miller felt energized at his addition to the team, and he was excited to hopefully get this puzzle of a case off his current caseload.

"How do you take your coffee?" Miller asked. "I was trained to never show up empty-handed, because our station house coffee is old and disgusting."

Brown didn't tell the young detective they have a fancy espresso machine in the kitchen lounge. "Surprise me." At that, he reached his hand across the desk, and Miller grabbed it.

"You'll find I'm a pretty good detective."

"We'll see...if you get my coffee wrong, that's strike one." Brown's lips curled up into a mischievous smile.

"Challenge accepted. I won't take up any more of your time, so I'll see you first thing in the morning." Miller stood up, and walked towards Brown's office door. "Thanks for including me."

"Don't thank me yet. Thank me when we close this case."

CHAPTER 6

I guess fifteen days of Jell-O, mystery meat in random sauces, and contraband orange popsicles might make a person crave *real* food. I weakly convince Anderson to have Barton go by my favorite Midtown restaurant—Juliette's—on his way back from running by my apartment for supplies and filling my prescriptions, and order me a veggie lasagna, some garlic knots, and her "world famous" homemade cannoli. I swear they are the most luscious, most scrumptious, most decadent pieces of food I've ever eaten.

I've been going to Juliette's at least once a week ever since I moved to Midtown from Athens, after graduating from the University of Georgia. Juliette Cotton, owner and a fellow Dawg alum, and I hit it off immediately. I even housesat for her when she and her wife went out of town. She has the cutest and most neurotic Jack Russell terrier I've even seen. Strider is just adorable, but I can only handle him in small doses. Probably like how people deal with me, and I'm just fine with that.

It's amazing how scents, smells, and sounds can trigger memories. I inhale deeply, and Juliette's culinary aromas put me in one of my happier mental places; I begin to not feel so completely crushed under the weight of my guilt and rage. I notice Anderson got the chicken parm, and Barton got a salad. A damn *salad*? From the best Italian restaurant this side of Sicily? All beauty and no brains, he is.

"So, how was my apartment? Was it disturbed in any way?" I ask, shoving a bite of the lasagna into my mouth like a person who hasn't had real food in, like, forever.

Barton shrugs. "Not that I could tell, unless someone broke in and put all those dirty clothes on the floor."

"Hey now, in my defense, I haven't had a lot of time for cleaning up lately." It's not like I'm seeing anyone right now either, so what does it matter if I throw my own panties on the floor anyway?

"Relax, I'm kidding," Barton laughs, getting a huge amount of salad onto his fork. "Kinda—"

"Any sign of surveillance? See any tails?" Anderson inquires.

"I know how to shake a tail, boss. I learned from the best." Barton points in Anderson's direction. "But to the best of my knowledge, there was nothing for me to shake. There was one vehicle that caught my attention, though—a lingering yellow cab—but I don't think it was actually a threat. Besides, I sat on the place for an hour to see what I could see. No sign of trouble, plus I didn't stick around for very long after that."

I put down my near-empty container of lasagna and walk over to the kitchen. "I wonder if there's anything to drink around here." I open several cabinet doors, and then find an unopened bottle of a cheap grocery store pinot noir in the fridge.

"Anyone else want a glass?"

"You shouldn't drink and take your pain pills together," Anderson grumbles. *Thanks, Mom.*

"Come on, Mother Teresa. Let me have at least one glass to calm my nerves. Besides, I haven't even taken a pill yet." I put my hands together in a praying gesture and give him my best *pleeeeeeeaase* sheepish look.

"Alright, alright, alright," he says, dismissively. "Just one glass, but that's it. The doctor told me the pills he's prescribed for you don't play well with alco—"

I interrupted his verbal finger wag. "Yadda yadda blah blah narcotics + wine = no bueno. Got it."

Anderson grumbles in my direction. "And to think I'm missing out on being with my family for this."

I stick my tongue out at him, pour the pinot, and then walk back over to the couch. Anderson moves a dining room chair, putting his back to the wall, keeping the fourth-floor window and front door in front of him. You can tell this isn't his first security rodeo. Both he and Barton wear holstered weapons, and I immediately pray I would never ever need to see them used. Guns freak me out, more so now after actually taking a bullet. I down the pinot in one gulp, feeling the wonderfully tannic liquid slide down my throat. I sit the glass down on the kitchen counter with a clink.

"So, my station hired you to be my guardian angels, but also to wait on me hand and foot, and satisfy my every whim, right?" I kid, but neither man flinches.

Barton chimes in. "We're here to keep you safe and make sure you do the things you need to do to get better. Your safety is our top priority." So much for the personal warm and fuzzies.

I shake my head at that emotionless response and start flipping channels on the television. Game show? Nope. Sitcom? Nope. Doctor/hospital serial? Ugh. I stop on a commercial for a local cell phone company advertising their latest and greatest tech. It reminds me that I have no cellphone, and that severely hampers my ability to communicate with the outside world.

"Hey fellas, can I use one of your phones?"

"No need." Barton puts down his salad fork and walks over to a bag sitting on the bar. He pulls out what appears to be a phone. "Here's a burner for you, and I've saved our contacts in it already. This is a short-term solution for you until you can get a new device."

"If something happens and you don't see one of us," Anderson grumbles, "you call us first, even *before* 911. I promise you we're not far away. Ever. And we've spoofed the number, so if you call anyone, it will show up as a different number every time, in an effort to keep you safe."

"Well, thanks for this. However, I think I'm gonna turn in for the night." I look around the open concept floor plan of the safe house. "But where are you guys gonna sleep?"

"We'll sleep in shifts. Tonight is Barton's turn. I'll be stationed right outside the bedroom door."

I grab the bag of feel-good meds off the bar, and notice the big duffel bag on the floor. When he went by my apartment, he must have filled it with handfuls of clothes from my closet, and more delicate things from my drawers—socks, panties, etc. At least he tried.

"G'night, Tweedle Dee and Tweedle Dumbass for ordering a salad." Barton smiles and points a finger gun in my direction as if to say *Good one*. Anderson just shakes his head in my direction. I swear he disapproves of everything I do, have done, and will ever do.

I close the bedroom door behind me, and I lean up against it. This is my life now. Nothing will ever be the same. I will never be the same. But maybe that's not a bad thing, you know? Like a river when you throw a pebble in. It causes ripples on the surface as it sinks down to the bottom. The ripples peter out until eventually the river looks the same. But really, it's not, and it never will be. The pebble is part of it now. I will figure this shit out. *Yay for the new normal.*

I unpack the clothes from the duffel and hang up all the blouses and slacks Barton grabbed from my apartment. I smile slightly realizing he actually brought some of my better clothes. I put my underwear away and leave out some pajama bottoms to wear to bed. I need to find some kind of routine to make me feel grounded.

I grab the burner phone and immediately punch in T-Jack's cell number. He picks up on the third ring, and he answers like a distrusting soul getting a spam call from a number they don't recognize.

"Umm...hello?"

"Those Yellow Jackets suck, but them Dawgs is hell, ain't they?" Typical UGA vs. Georgia Tech hate.

"Hey Q! It's good to hear your voice. But where are you calling from? The area code says Phoenix, AZ?"

"Look, the goons Wild Bill hired as my security shadows picked up this burner phone for me. It spoofs a different number every time I call, so there's that. I'm at some safe house in town—but I have no clue specifically where."

Everyone knows Tommy has a soft spot for me, but he has always had my back. That's more than I can say for some people. Hell, *most* people, because of the unscalable walls of protection I've built around my heart that keep everyone truly at arm's length. Maybe Tommy will eventually find the key I've left for him outside of my portcullis—under the metaphorical fake rock.

"How are you feeling? Obviously, you've been discharged from the hospital, so that means you're at least physically able to get around?"

"With Tweedles Dumb and Dumber surrounding me, I do actually feel pretty safe at the moment. However, I do miss my Midtown place, and being able to do what I want when I want. But yeah, physically I'm getting around. Mentally, that's a different story for a different day."

"Would it hurt for you to be a little vulnerable right now, and accept some help from people that are just trying to make sure you're OK?"

I don't know how to take that, but it felt a little like he was patronizing me, or criticizing my independent streak.

"I don't have much of a choice, ya know? I'm stuck between the doctors' orders and my bodyguards' orders. I don't have a say."

"The doctors said that you might be suffering from PTSD or maybe you have deeply buried trauma you haven't dealt with yet. I promise I won't push, and I know you're going to do what you're going to do, but maybe you should still find someone to talk to. Someone with a background that can help you unpack...well, everything?"

"Are you volunteering?"

"You know I would absolutely be that guy for you, but I'm talking about someone with a medical or psychiatry degree."

"Well, as a matter of fact, I do have an appointment with a doctor-ordered shrink tomorrow, so we'll see how it goes." I'd probably rather lie on Tommy's couch right now.

"That's actually really good to hear, Q. Please just keep me in the loop, OK? I want to be supportive, and be there for you."

Like I said, sometimes he cares TOO much. But I won't tell him I like it when he does.

"I know, T-Jack, and I will. I promise. Just remember you're still a ramblin', gamblin', hell of a friend to me."

"I guess that would make you the ramblin' wreck then?" He cracks himself up.

"When I get a new phone, I'll make sure to give you the number, OK? But I'm exhausted, and need to go. Good night, Tommy. I'm fine, I *promise*."

I hang up the phone before he can fully respond. I try to think about how lucky I am to have friends who just want to help. By my thoughts quickly shift over to Alahna, who used to be the one I *always* turned to for support. Now, the only thing she does is haunt my subconscious. I squeeze my eyes shut, whisper *I'm sorry*, and then open my eyes again. The intruding thoughts are gone—for now.

I climb off the bed, walk over to the door leading into the living room, and open it.

"Hey, Anderson? What time is my quack appointment tomorrow?"

"0800. I'll get you up at 0600 and we'll be wheels up by 0730."

Shit. I'm so not a morning person.

"We're gonna have to hit a coffee shop on the way."

Anderson slowly looks over at me, again with disapproving eyes. Barton is transfixed on some rerun of a bad sci-fi show on TV, and didn't even look my way. "Fine, we'll talk about the details tomorrow. Try and get some sleep, and we're right outside the bedroom if you need anything. See you at oh-dark-thirty."

I give him a quick *sir, yes sir* two-finger salute, and close the bedroom door. I can't remember the last time I got any kind of restful sleep, but hopefully tonight will be different. Red flags haven't popped up yet with these dudes, so I guess I can trust them. I mean, they've given me no reason not to, and besides, if I die on their watch, they'd probably either get fired or permanently demoted to the Motor Pool.

I look in the bag Barton brought back from the pharmacy, and I locate the bottle of oxycodone. I guess I do have a reliable option to help make the mental and physical pain subside.

Reading the oxy label, it says take one 5mg tablet every six hours for thirty days as needed for intense pain. And I probably shouldn't take too many of these at one time, because I do actually want to wake up in the morning.

Living on the edge, which is my usual MO, I crack open the bottle and pop one full pill into my hand. All of a sudden, I feel like the bottle of pharmaceutical painkillers whispers to me, which is a discomforting thought. Shaking my head swiftly back and forth to clear my thoughts, I cap the bottle forcefully and toss it onto the bathroom vanity with my other meds. I put the pill into my mouth and wash it down with a swig of tap water.

I turn down the bedcovers, and sit down on the bed, wringing my hands together and praying the drugs kick in soon. Tomorrow is gonna be Hell 2.0, and I need to be ready.

Readier than I've ever been.

CHAPTER 7

I wake up in a sudden fright, covered in a cold sweat, just like I have done every day over the past two weeks. My breath is shallow and ragged as I survey my unfamiliar surroundings. I rub both hands across my face and through my damp hair, finishing by rubbing my sore neck. I squeeze both sides of my head as I rotate it side to side, back and forth. Pain radiates from my neck, across my shoulders, and down my back, well down everywhere. I look over at the clock—5:42am. *Shit.* I also notice my bedroom door is standing open, and Anderson has his back to the door, constantly surveying the landscape of the safe house. Nothing was gonna get into the flat without him knowing. I hear Barton snoring from somewhere in the darkness, and I am immediately jealous.

I throw back the covers with my good arm and slowly slide my legs over the edge of the bed. I put my hands on my knees and lean my weight over the side, trying desperately to regain my composure. I haven't really found anything yet to help stabilize my psyche and prevent all these negative images and thoughts from flooding through my mind. I am bone tired, and I see Alahna's face every time I close my eyes. *I'm the girl who lived*. Yay, me.

"That was your fourth nightmare tonight." Anderson chimed in, never once looking back in my direction.

"Only four? Wow...I'm doing pretty good." Early morning + oxy hangover + sarcastic me = no fun zone.

"Did you ever catch up to him? To Custer?" he asks, pointedly.

"Wait...huh?"

"You kept screaming it over and over. You'd scream his name, and then you'd wake up, roll over, lay back down, wash, rinse, repeat."

Shit. What else have I said in my sleep? A wave of self-consciousness flows all over me.

"Umm, I guess I should fill you in, so you know exactly what you're protecting me from."

Anderson flashes a manila folder at me with a GBI emblem on it. "No need. We already know most of what we need to know."

OK, color me impressed. "Do I want to know how you came by that information?"

"I'm good at listening to your night terrors and taking notes." He thinks he's got jokes. "In all seriousness, my company is good at what we do. But if you want to give up any more information you might be holding on to, feel free to do so."

"Just keep an eye out for flannels, old trucks, and bad beards."

Anderson nods his head, and tosses the folder on the living room table.

I stand up on my wobbly legs, and walk over to close the bedroom door before heading to the bathroom. "By the way, I'm closing the door again. I don't want you listening to me pee."

Anderson puts two fingers in his ears, and he shakes his head.

As I close the door, I immediately feel grateful the men are with me, but simultaneously feel a pang of lost independence, thinking I don't really need them to take care of me. I've never depended on anyone in my entire life, and I really don't want to now. I refuse to be anyone's burden, because I raised myself to be vigilant and self-sufficient. Living in my house growing up, I had to be.

My attitude has been cantankerous lately. Almost three weeks of no restful sleep has made me a little less than Miss Manners-worthy. I'm irritable. I'm paranoid. I'm hypersensitive and reactionary. I'm pissed off, full of rage and regret, and bound and determined to somehow avenge Alahna. I'm just a total ball of fun to be around. Plus, the fact these nightmares absolutely scare the hell out of me every single night—even through the somnambulant effects of the glorious pain meds I've been on.

Quinn, find these motherfuckers.

Alahna's voice pops into my subconscious every second I close my eyes. I also hear Custer's backwoods ass blame me for him having to *cleanse* her soul just because she was with me. They tell me every night that what happened and what continues to happen is 100% my fault and something I need to correct.

One quick shower later, I rummage through the clothes Barton brought back. I choose a cream blouse, a pair of navy slacks, and an old pair of navy flats. Thankfully, he grabbed at least one of my bras. Can't be freeing the nipples on my first visit to the shrink. Doc might get the wrong idea.

I pull my tousled auburn hair into a ponytail and look at myself in the bathroom mirror.

"*Damn, girl...you look halfway normal,*" I whisper, trying to convince myself it was true. It isn't working. Normal's overrated anyway, because I'm just me.

I try desperately to rub some wrinkles out of my slacks to no avail. Oh well, shrinks don't care about style points. I walk out into the living room, and I notice Anderson is making breakfast for three.

***

Leland's phone rang, pulling him from a state of slumber in the front seat of his stolen yellow taxi, which was sitting outside the reporter's Midtown apartment.

"Um...hello?" Leland wasn't a morning person.

"Well, boy, have you seen anything?" Custer never sounded happy. This was no exception.

"Not since yesterday. I saw a Black man wearing what appeared to be military grade clothing come out of her apartment. I tried to follow him but I lost him on the Connector."

Custer growled. "You *lost* him? He was our best lead on where she's being kept, that is if you can trust a man of his...*persuasion*. This ain't good, Lee. Seems like my whole family's turned into nothin' but screw-ups."

Leland countered, "But I got his plates, Pa. It was a black Escalade, government issue. Somebody's tryin' real hard to keep the reporter hidden."

"OK, so maybe you ain't a *total* screw-up. Text me the plates, Lee. I got a weak-minded government suit who I can squeeze for an ID. Might be time to call him."

"Will do, Pa. Want me to hang out here?"

"Yeah, for now, until I tell you otherwise. The longer she lives, the more dangerous she becomes to our way of life. She knows too damn much." Custer growled, then the line went dead.

Leland tossed the phone into the front passenger seat of the yellow taxi, and finished off what was left of his hours-old cup of coffee. If the man in black comes back, or if the reporter shows her face again, he'll be ready. He looked down at his shirt, and tried to wipe off what appeared to be blood. He turned his head to the backseat, and scoffed.

"Why'd you have to bleed your blood on me, you unclean bastard?"

The East Indian man, whose face and name were both on the taxi medallion, laid motionless on the vehicle's rear floorboard, covered in several packing blankets. Blood, bone, and brain matter remained where his head was just a day before. He would not be able to answer Leland's rhetorical question. But Leland would have to deal with the literal backseat driver soon, and get this taxi off the grid.

***

We pull up to the doctor's office in Midtown Atlanta around 7:45am, with a grande espresso in my hand. The sign out front says Westlake Psychiatric Associates, Dr. Evelyn James, MD. I so do not want to be here.

I've never ever been a fan of shrinks. They're full of psychobabble and psychotropics, wanting folks to lie on couches and recount their life stories, all while absentmindedly doodling stick figures on a steno pad. I've read too many stories about whether psychiatric treatment was effective or not, or if psychotherapy was as much of a quack science as chiropractic medicine. I've also heard about too many shrinks who have fleeced their clients. *This is probably just my paranoia talking*.

Anderson gets out of the car and immediately starts surveying the parking lot for any potential threats while Barton opens the back door for me. They are both adept at multitasking—keeping one eye on me and the other on everyone else at the same time.

"No, not yet," Barton says, when he notices me starting to unbuckle my seatbelt. "Not until he gives the OK."

Anderson is still doing his threat assessment, and holds his fist in the air—I'm assuming telling Barton to stop.

"Code 4," he yells over to Barton. "Let's move her out of the open and into the building, pronto."

A wave of independent anger wells up in me when Barton reaches over and tries to unbuckle me.

"Dude, I'm not three. I can unbuckle my own damn seatbelt."

"Sorry, ma'am. Force of habit."

"Ma'am? I'm not eighty either."

I climb out of the Escalade, and Barton quickly shepherds me into the lobby while Anderson covers things from behind, looking like large male bookends.

Once inside, Barton sits with me in the waiting area while Anderson talks with the intake nurse. She hands him a clipboard, and he brings it over to me.

"Fill these out, and give them back to me," he barks.

"Aye, aye, Captain," I mock, and give him an exaggerated salute.

"It's Colonel, actually. If you're gonna make fun of me, at least get my rank right," Anderson grumbles. "And please don't disrespect my service with a fake salute."

A wave of a different kind of guilt comes over me, and I nod my head in his direction as a sign of submission and understanding. They really brought out the big guns for me.

"I'm not a captain either," Barton adds. "I actually just got promoted to Sergeant."

Anderson shoots a *that's enough* look towards Barton, and he goes back to reading a random magazine.

"We aren't supposed to give details about ourselves like this to our clients. So please stop being a reporter right now," Anderson interjects.

"So, you know everything about me and I know nothing about you. Got it." I start formulating a weak ass rebuttal. "How do I know I can truly trust you?"

Anderson responds without even looking at me. "You're still alive, right? I guess you can trust us then."

Touché. Can't really argue that point, Colonel.

I continue filling out the intake paperwork. Typical background questions, trying to get a picture of who I am—physically, mentally, and emotionally. Do you have a history of depression in your family? Do you have a history of alcohol or drug use? Have you experienced a recent traumatic event? I shiver as I read that question, but soldier on.

I flip the front page over and see the other two pages. Ugh. This is why they tell you to get here at least fifteen minutes before your appointment.

I finish filling out the Quinn Campbell emotional War and Peace, and hand the clipboard back to Col. Anderson. He huffs as he tosses his Field & Stream magazine onto a nearby table and walks my information back up to the triage nurse. I swear he hates me.

A few minutes later, a nurse's voice breaks the silence. "Ms. Campbell?"

I stand up, and Anderson and Barton do as well. "Don't even think about coming in with me, unless you want to hear all about my fetish involving a cartoon mouse and undercooked spaghetti."

"First of all, gross," Sgt. Barton adds, "but we have to clear the area before you go in alone. Standard operating procedure."

"It's OK, Ms. Campbell," the nurse says. "Gentlemen, you have to stay here in the waiting room. I promise Ms. Campbell is in good hands."

"I know you mean well, miss, but we have our orders. Can we at least walk through the rear offices and rooms in order to quickly assess security risks?" Anderson can turn on the charm when he needs to.

"You have five minutes," the visibly annoyed nurse says. "Please do not enter any occupied room or violate any patient's right to privacy."

Anderson nods, and raises his hand to Barton, telling him to stay with me. These guys are becoming kinda predictable. They don't even like me using the bathroom by myself, so it makes sense their panties would be in a bunch if they couldn't have their eyes on me 24/7. I guess that makes them good at their jobs?

A short time later, Anderson returns, and nods his thanks to the nurse. She smiles, and then holds her hand out in my direction.

"Well, let's get this over with." I punch Sgt. Barton in the arm, and try to steel my fluttering nerves as best I can. This is gonna suck twelve ways from Sunday.

***

"I think I've found the vehicle you were looking for, Mr. Custer," the very nervous rookie GBI agent said into the phone.

"You think? Or are you 100% sure?" Custer wasn't a very trusting man, especially not lately.

"Uh...yes...yes sir, I'm positive," the agent stuttered. "I...I got a hit on the plate you gave me."

"If you're wrong, then I'm gonna pay a visit to that lovely wife of yours. I don't like being lied to *or* let down." Custer always had something for leverage.

The agent's breathing picked up pace. "Now come on, Mr. Custer. I have no reason to lie, especially not to you. Please don't hurt my family."

"You got nothing to worry about as long as your information is good."

"The 2012 black Escalade is registered to Peachtree Technology Corporation, one of the biggest military contractors in the state. We work with their operatives all the time to protect high-value assets. They are freelance security professionals, usually with active or reserve military training."

"Does it have onboard GPS that you can tap into? Don't tell me no."

"Uh...yes it does, but I'd have to get approval from another department before I can—"

Custer cut him off. "Like I said, don't tell me no. Can *you* do it?"

The agent sighed loudly. "Yea...ahem...yes, sir. It'll take a bit of time, though."

He looked at his watch. 8:36am. "You have until noon. If I haven't heard from you by then, I wouldn't go home if I was you." Custer disconnected the phone and tossed it onto the table. What's the use of having a network of people who owe him favors if none of them can get this simple job done? He looked over at Beau sleeping on his couch, and the contours of Custer's face began to wrinkle in obvious anger. They wouldn't be in this mess if that screw-up of a kid hadn't dropped a body up on Springer. A sloppy tie job on the back of the ATV led to this whole fucking mess.

Custer pulled a Glock G42 9MM out of his waistband, quietly checked the magazine for live rounds, and slowly slid it back into the magwell. He silently racked the slide back, putting a bullet in the chamber. He brought the barrel up to his mouth, closed his eyes, and kissed it. He stared over at Beau, and leveled the Glock towards his wayward son. How easy it would be to just end this nonsense for good. This family had been cleaning up after this kid for way too long. Custer made sure the safety was still on, unchambered the round, and then lowered the weapon. It's not Beau's fault he was his late wife's favorite son. He looked over at a picture of his wife on the end table beside the couch. He stood up and walked over to it, picking up the frame. He rubbed an index finger over his wife's face, and the softening of his face meant he just allowed himself to think back to a happier time, but the softness was short-lived. He sat the photo down, and walked over to a desktop computer in the living room area of the trailer.

Above the old school computer was a pegboard covered in old newspaper clippings and construction blueprints. One clipping had his late wife's picture on it, with the headline "Drunk Driver Kills Woman in Fiery Crash." The drunk driver's name and mugshot were circled in red ink, and a pushpin with a red string tied to it was just above it. The string connected to another pushpin on a construction blueprint labeled Custer Property #1. The following words were written underneath the second pushpin: Original Cleanse. The drunk driver was a Black man who had just gotten out of jail that morning, and was returned to the earth the day after his wife's funeral—buried underneath the concrete slab foundation of the first house his crew built in that particular neighborhood. That started Custer and his boys on this "ordained" mission to rid the world of people of color who terrorize God-fearing White folk. It's a dirty job, but one that honored his beautiful bride who senselessly died on a Georgia highway just 10 miles from home. Several cleansed souls are buried under the concrete slabs of new home construction across four different subdivisions. The most recently cleansed soul, the photographer, is stashed underneath a freshly poured slab deep within an active construction zone. The augured hole was pre-prepared for the soul Beau screwed up and dropped on the Trail, so why not put it to good use?

Custer felt like it would be impossible to find their transitioned victims if they were hidden underneath cured concrete slabs—a fringe benefit of owning a construction company.

"My darling Emma, I will clean up this mess, and will continue to honor your memory by doing so. God be praised, and may all the unworthy be cleansed by my hand."

***

Case agent Aaron Bernard sat at a table in a conference room in the regional GBI office. From where he sat, he could see ASAC Daniel Brown meeting with a group of agents he knew were a part of the investigation looking into the Quinn Campbell case, among other things. He was white knuckled, holding onto the edge of his desk so hard it might crumble under the pressure.

Aaron rocked back and forth slightly, as if he was trying to talk himself into or out of something.

He shot up as if somebody kicked him, and walked over to the open door of the conference room. The agents continued talking about procedures, duties, protocols, and focal points of the investigation.

Detective Grayson Miller walked past Aaron into the conference room, carrying a coffee in his hand. "You know, we could use an extra set of hands."

Brown looked up from the team to see Miller walk in, with Bernard in tow.

"No, no, no. Bernard, you can't be here." Brown walked over to him, in an effort to escort him out. "I let you come with me to talk with Campbell in the hospital, but you are stuck behind a serious conflict of interest here."

"Wait, are you kidding me? Conflict of interest? Come on, man. *No one* in this city knows my sister better than me," Aaron pleaded. "I bring operational *and* historical knowledge to the team, and you *need* me. This is *my family* we're talking about here, Brown."

"You are way too close to this one, Bernard. Your temperament could compromise this whole investigation." Brown wasn't budging in the slightest. "I told you yesterday, you can't be here. Don't make me bench you."

"Wait, this is Alahna Bernard's brother?" Detective Miller asked Brown, inquisitively.

"Case agent Aaron Bernard. And you are?" Aaron stuck his hand out to Miller, who shook it firmly. "Detective Grayson Miller with Dahlonega PD."

Bernard looked at Miller, and then back to Brown. "Wait, he can work on *my* sister's investigation, but you shut *me* out? That's not right on so many levels, Brown, and you know it."

The other agents at the table avoided all eye contact with Brown and Bernard. The temperature in the conference room was rising rapidly. Bernard stepped chest-to-chest with Brown, while Miller slid his arms between them, trying to break them up.

"I *need* this, Brown. I need to help find my sister's killer. Do *not* bench me," Bernard insisted.

"If you step *one* hair out of line, if your temper gets in the way of this investigation, if you go rogue, even in the slightest, you will be suspended indefinitely," Brown said emphatically, pointing a finger at Bernard's chest. "Besides, you're lucky to still be on active duty after what you pulled last year."

"OK, *that's* a story I need to hear," Miller added, acting like he was eating a bag of popcorn.

"I just let a suspect get in my head on a kidnapping case we worked last year." Aaron admitted.

"And he put him in intensive care with a fractured skull, a cracked jaw, and three missing teeth," one of the junior case agents at the table said, causing Aaron to shoot a deadly glare at her. She quickly looked away.

"Bernard's temper compromised the entire investigation and the district attorney had to drop all the charges, in order to prevent a major lawsuit being brought against him, the GBI, and the entire state of Georgia." Brown continued. "Bernard was suspended for 90 days, and was ordered to go through Bureau anger management classes."

"Point taken. Remind me not to get on your bad side." Miller quipped in Aaron's direction.

"You are on a *very* short leash, Bernard. I call the shots, and if I say jump, you need to immediately ask how high and how many times." Brown reminded him and the whole team that this has to be done by the book. "I will not let the guilty walk away on this one. Not on my watch. Not this time."

"Sir, no one wants justice on this case more than I do. I will not let you down or compromise this investigation." Aaron said. "You have my word, on my sister's honor."

"You better not. Your definition of justice better fit the Webster's version to a tee, and not your own." Brown did not look happy, but he knew Bernard brought knowledge of his sister and of Campbell to this task force that no one else had. He believed rolling the proverbial dice by adding the brother to the investigation was an acceptable risk.

"Now, let's get back to work."

CHAPTER 8

Dr. Evelyn James reads my intake paperwork like it is a New York Times bestseller, taking notes every so often. I sit uncomfortably on a loveseat, wringing my hands together, waiting for her to say something to me. I don't do uncomfortable silences very well, so I do something to fill the void.

"So, what's the prognosis, Doc?"

"Ms. Campbell, this is a lot to take in, so I apologize for taking so long. I want to completely wrap my head around you and your scenario before we start our session today." Dr. James places my paperwork on her desk, and turns her chair around to fully face me.

"From what I can tell, you've been through the ringer the last few weeks or so." She reaches over to her desk and grabs a folder. "I called over to the hospital and had them send over your latest medical records." She whistles and shakes her head in my direction. "I take it you have a lot to tell me."

Quinn, find these motherfuckers.

I mentally shake Alahna's voice out of my head, and I continue trying to meet Dr. James' gaze.

"Doc, I'm not sure you want to hear everything I have to say."

"Ms. Campbell, you have doctor-patient privilege here. Whatever you tell me stays here, unless I believe you are a danger to yourself and/or others. You are clearly suffering from some form of PTSD, based on your medical records and doctor notes, so I don't think I need a medical degree to tell you that."

"Am I that obvious?"

"May I call you Quinn?" Most people don't ask, so I appreciate the respect. I nod.

"Look, Quinn, let's just get the basics out of the way, OK? According to your paperwork, you have trouble controlling your anxiety and nerves when thoughts of the recent trauma come to mind. I've seen that with my own eyes. Wouldn't you agree?"

Again, I nod.

"You get physically upset—heart racing, panic attacks, near hyperventilation—while you deal with some serious psychological trauma. You often use humor and/or sarcasm as a defense mechanism to either change the subject, ignore the trauma at hand, or distract folks like me. Am I right so far?"

I sigh heavily, and nod again. "It's a Bingo."

"Without giving me any details yet, do you feel as if you are responsible for the trauma you experienced?"

"Responsible? No. Helpless to have done anything to change it or keep it from happening again? Absolutely. Filled with white-hot rage and a deep-seated desire to avenge my best friend? You better believe it."

"Interesting. So you are experiencing both negative and unproductive emotional thoughts. I also see you have trouble sleeping, with multiple reports of you screaming yourself awake from some form of a nightmare. Tell me about your sleep habits of late."

"Doc, to be honest, I haven't been able to sleep without help lately."

Dr. James flips through my records again. "Oxycodone didn't touch you. Morphine didn't work on you. They had to use IV ketamine in the hospital to calm you down enough to rest. Your records show a prescription for 5mg oxy. You still have some at home, yes?"

"It's a thirty-day supply, I believe."

"Good, but be careful how you take it and how much of it you take, because it can become habit-forming. It can also help with major depressive episodes related to your trauma-induced PTSD, as well as other forms of depression."

"Other forms? Trust me, Doc...I wasn't really depressed at all before this."

"After reading your intake paperwork, looking over your medical records, and making my preliminary observation, I'm not so sure about that. I do think I can help you work through those feelings, though. May I please ask you a few more questions?"

Dr. James sets all of my paperwork aside once again, and leans over toward me. She makes and holds direct eye contact with me, and I feel like she's gonna hit me over the head with her next question.

"Of course you can, Doc."

"Does depression run in your family?"

"I was an English major in college. I'm pretty sure that decision depressed everyone around me. But I don't think anyone was officially diagnosed, no."

"Alright. Do you ever feel like your thoughts are racing a mile a minute? Like you just can't shut your brain off?"

"That's just a Tuesday for me. People tell me I only have one speed—and that's full speed ahead. It's helped me be successful and get to where I am today."

"There's that Quinn Campbell defense mechanism I've already heard and read so much about."

I shrug.

Dr. James continues her battery of questions. "During times of your 'full speed' feelings, do you ever start laughing out of nowhere? Do you shift between happiness, sadness, and irritability at will?"

I have to think a little about that. "People tell me I have a short fuse and a short memory, because I get pissed off at people at work, and then go out for drinks with them afterwards. I don't really hold grudges, I guess. Until now."

She has picked up a steno pad from her desk, and furiously scribbles notes onto it. She continues firing off questions left and right.

"Are you holding a grudge for anyone or anything right now?"

"Yes. Quite a big one, actually."

"Duly noted. OK, prior to your traumatic event, have you ever had a really good mood turn into a really bad or depressed mood and then quickly back up again?" I nod yes.

"Have you ever lost interest in activities you've previously enjoyed, for seemingly no reason and out of the blue?" I nod yes again.

"Do you normally need little sleep, like three to five hours? Do you have trouble concentrating?" I truly do my best work after midnight, and my ability to multitask is on point, usually. I nod again.

"Have you noticed little, subtle changes in your personality, rapid and intense mood swings, or feelings of guilt or worthlessness?" I feel like she's already in my head.

Dr. James continues documenting my life story, but it feels like she is heading somewhere with these questions.

"So, Doc, what does my screwed-up, awesome life prior to my current situation have to do with what I'm feeling now? I frankly don't see the connection, but I think you might see something I don't see."

"I'm getting there. May I ask you some rather personal questions?"

"More personal than you have already? Sure, go for it."

"Have you noticed any impulsive feelings or actions? Spending sprees you can't explain? Sex with multiple partners? Addictive personalities with regards to alcohol, drugs, or something similar.? Anything where impulse control was hard for you?"

She wasn't lying about the personal questions. "Retail therapy helps me deal with life sometimes, so yes. Also, my sex life has had its ups-and-downs—pun intended—but has lately been nonexistent. And wine is my best friend, but I don't get shit-faced at 11am, if that's what you're asking."

"And your impulse control?"

"Look, Doc...I'm a thirty-year-old female working eighty hours a week in a male-dominated field. I get questioned daily, and I have to work twice as hard as my male counterparts on every story every day. I don't depend on anyone but me and my best frie—"

My voice cracks when I remember at that very moment that my best friend isn't coming home. I don't even realize I'm crying until Dr. James hands me a tissue.

"Ssshhh, it's OK." Dr. James reassures me. "I have this effect on people."

Now *she's* got jokes.

"Are you currently or have you ever had suicidal thoughts or have you ever wanted to hurt yourself or others?"

"Besides my dad jokes creating pain in others, nope." I giggle awkwardly, but then tell Dr. James that I've never had suicidal thoughts of any kind.

"So, you do not currently have thoughts about hurting yourself, hurting others, or ending your life?"

"Hurting myself? Absolutely not, because I love me some me." Dr. James smiles briefly at my narcissistic admission. "But hurting others? To be honest, Doc...I really *really* want to inflict the same level of pain on the people responsible for my situation, for these feelings I've been made to carry, for the ones my best friend felt, and that her family is feeling now."

"OK, in my professional opinion, and based on your answers to my screening questions, I feel like we have some underlying mental and emotional issues we need to address if I'm going to help you fully process your current issues. And I promise you, I will help you through this—every step of the way."

"Underlying mental and emotional issues? Like what?" I squint my eyes at her, trying to figure out what she is talking about.

"Right now, you are feeling almost every emotion to some degree, some larger than others, some more real than others, while some might be used as an external or internal distraction. Have you ever heard of bipolar disorder?"

"You mean the mental illness that every crazy person on TV is blamed for having lately? Yeah, I'm aware."

"A lot of people misunderstand bipolar disorder, and most get it completely wrong. I'm going to ask you a couple of questions about your personality and behavior prior to your emotional trauma, OK?"

"Haven't I already answered enough? I feel like I am just a piece of frayed string, and if you keep pulling on it, I'm just gonna unravel."

"Quinn, listen to me, OK? Think about yourself as a home...four walls, a roof, a floor, lots of windows and doors, with a lot of memories inside, both good and bad."

I speak in analogies, so I wait patiently for the explanation.

"Say I paint the outside of the house because the siding was cracked and weather worn, so it looks good externally. However, termites have destroyed the foundation, the subfloor, the internal walls, everything. Do you want me to paint the outside of your house, or do you want me to help you manage the termite damage before it becomes irreversible and your house crumbles onto itself from the inside?"

OK, not the worst analogy. It actually makes sense in my warped brain. Now I see why they wanted me to see a doctor. Especially this one. I feel like she knows what she's talking about. How else could she make me blabber on about all of these intensely painful things without even breaking a sweat or batting one of her eyelashes?

"Does anyone ever choose the external paint job?"

"It is my job to discourage such things." She smiles a disarming smile, and my shoulders relax.

"I hope you know what you're doing, Doc." I close my eyes, sigh heavily, and turn on my emotional faucet.

I completely open up to Dr. James about *everything*...from growing up in a home with an abusive alcoholic father, and having a somewhat fractured relationship with my mother because of the abuse, all the way through my trauma in the dense woods of north Georgia, the death of my best friend right in front of me at the hands of Custer, and the subsequent attempts on my life. The tears flow fast and furious as I literally have a breakdown in her office. My body trembles, and I rock back and forth as I blast the psychiatrist with the firehose of my emotions, feelings, and memories.

I'm not used to feeling *all* these emotions at once. I'm not going to lie, though—it feels good once again to unload this guilt and further unburden myself from the weight of all this pain. It's one thing to witness Alahna's death and experience the anger and guilt that come with that, but couple it with the unresolved trauma from growing up in an abusive home and developing defense mechanisms to sweep those emotions under the proverbial carpet? To be honest, it's a lot.

No one, and I mean *no one*, knows about my fractured childhood. I've spent my whole life walling those memories away from the general public. Now I'm feeling both my fucked-up childhood *and* the intense emotions of my unplanned hillbilly vacation. What a whirlwind journey of human pain and suffering Dr. James is taking me on. I'm emotionally spent right now.

Dr. James puts her hand on my shoulder, and squeezes slightly.

"I can't even begin to imagine what you've gone through, but I honestly believe we just had a breakthrough. The first step to dealing with a problem is actually admitting you have one. Thank you for trusting me enough to share your harrowing journey—both recent and not-so-recent—with me."

Good thing I didn't wear any makeup today, because my face would have looked like a melting raccoon in a Salvador Dali painting.

"It's weird, Doc. I normally keep things so close to the vest, but as soon as I started sharing things with you, I couldn't stop. Sorry to unload on you, but, to be honest, I'm not sorry either. I don't feel quite as burdened or suffocated or held down now, under the weight of...of...all of it."

"Don't apologize, because that's why I'm here. I will help you deal with your current PTSD while also helping you deal with what I believe—in my medical opinion—might be Bipolar I disorder, which means you have more severe high or manic episodes with less frequent major depressive episodes—if at all. It also might just be emotional overload, since you are feeling so many emotions all at once, so together, we need to take this journey slowly, seeing where the rabbit hole leads. Do me a favor, though. I need you to understand that—either way—you are *not* broken. Regularly come and see me, stick with the treatment, and let me help you balance everything out."

I still feel jumbled up inside, but with a little help from Dr. James and my friends, just maybe I can reverse-Humpty Dumpty my current psyche.

"I'll have to take your word for it, Doc. However, I'll try to have an open mind about this, and I am willing to work with you."

I stand up and shake Dr. James' hand at the end of our introductory session. A lot happened today, and I'm still processing the bulk of it. My bulletproof confidence, my ability to quickly shift between happy, angry, and sad within seconds, and my ability to rationalize any of my impulsive or reckless actions are—according to Dr. James—all hallmark signs of emotional distress. I know she said not to focus on it, but I'm smart enough to understand Bipolar is still a mental disorder. I wish I didn't know now what I didn't know then.

"Don't forget to set up another appointment two to three weeks from now. I want to see how you're doing, balancing everything that's going on."

"Aye-aye, Doc. Thanks again for not making me feel like I'm crazy. You are going to keep what I said to yourself, right? What happens in Midtown stays in Midtown?" Vegas was a better analogy, but we are not exactly in Sin City. "I told you things today that no one in my life has ever known. I'm feeling a little vulnerable."

"Doctor's promise. Just between you and me, I don't really think you are any danger to yourself or others, so your secrets are safe with me. But God help the people you hold a grudge against. *Whew.*" The look on Dr. James' face is legitimate worry, I'm assuming because of my desire to inflict serious bodily harm on the Backwoods Boys.

I smile an appreciative smile, nod my head in her direction, and walk out of her office.

Back in the lobby, I check out with the triage nurse and book my return appointment. Anderson nods his head in the exit direction, and I assume he means for me to follow.

"You know you can use your words, right?" I say, trying to make him smile. Instead, he rolls his eyes at me *again*, and grumbles as he turns and leaves.

I'm always a disappointment to him.

***

Clyde arrived at Westlake Psychiatric Associates with Ezekiel in the back seat of his prized red and white F-150. It was a busy morning, so there were people and cars everywhere. There would be no chance of dealing with this quietly with so many eyes in the area. Clyde hit redial on his phone.

"We found the Escalade, Pa. It's right where that agent said it would be. Yes, Pa. Yes, sir. Can do, sir." Clyde hung up the phone, and motioned to Ezekiel.

Ezekiel popped out of the truck long enough to secure a tracking device underneath the Escalade's back bumper. He climbed back into the truck and opened up a device that looked like a laptop in a briefcase.

"Is it working?" Clyde asked.

Ezekiel didn't respond, he just continued fiddling with the device the GBI agent gave them. On the screen, a red dot started blinking on a map. "Got it. Workin' like a charm, man. Ain't gonna lose 'em now."

"Alright, I'm gonna park over there, where we can still see the clinic doors. When you see that damn reporter come out, let me know." Clyde moved and positioned the truck in the parking lot across from the Escalade.

"She's probably gonna have some dude dressed all in black helping her. Young Black guy, mid-thirties maybe. Lee saw him at the reporter's apartment." Ezekiel said. "He's gotta be current or ex-military."

"Fine by me. We got enough firepower in this truck to take on anybody *and* everybody." Clyde glanced at the bag sitting on the rear floorboard.

"Can't do nothing here, so let's trail them to where they're headed, and reassess our chances." Ezekiel said. "Pa's not gonna like it if we go back home and she's breathin' still. I done missed once, and we can't afford to miss again. Go ahead and text Lee to meet us in Midtown."

"And we all need to mask up. Can't let anyone see us again like they did you, Zeke."

Clyde was referring to the security camera footage of Ezekiel in his hospital custodial uniform plastered on every TV station and in every police station and post office in the metro Atlanta area. One of those "Have you seen this person?" flyers.

"To hell with you, man. I almost ganked the bitch before I had to brain that nurse and hightail it out of there."

"Almost only counts in horseshoes and hand grenades," Clyde joked.

"Speaking of, have you got any grenades? If so, we can end this right now." Both men laughed at the thought of maximum carnage.

A short time later, Clyde saw something he thought looked unusual. A woman came out of the office wearing a baseball cap, shades, and a hoodie, which was partially obscuring her face. She was flanked in front and behind by two men dressed all in black, the younger of the two in front. The older white-haired man had his head on a swivel, pushing her towards the Escalade. It was the reporter. Clyde took several pictures of the trio with his phone.

"Zeke, is that her?"

"Yup, that's her alright."

Ezekiel reached into the bag on the floorboard and started putting together what appeared to be an assault rifle, clicking together pieces of metal one at a time. "Tail 'em good like, bro. And don't get caught."

"Dude's probably good at avoiding a tail. Lee said they lost him yesterday."

"Good or not, they can't slip the tracker. You can keep your distance though, 'cause we got 'em tagged. She's ours now."

Clyde put the Ford F-150 in drive, and followed the Escalade out of the parking lot.

CHAPTER 9

———ele———

Col. Anderson was convinced my "undercover" look would prevent anyone from seeing me leaving the building. I feel like my outfit was less Clark Kent and more neon sign. I mean, who in their right mind actually wants to look like Amy Poehler chilling in the audience at the 2015 Emmys? I mean, seriously...

I remove the hat just as soon as Sgt. Barton puts me in the backseat of the Escalade and closes the rear passenger side door, and I shake out the kinks in my red hair, running my fingers through it to avoid a horrible case of hat hair. Barton opens the driver's side rear door and climbs inside. Anderson walks once around the vehicle again before getting in behind the wheel and starting it up.

"We'll take you back to the safe house before running a few other errands. We need to make sure you're safe first," Anderson says.

"No one knows where I am. Hell, I don't even know where the safe house is. Besides, you're the one who is convinced that my Unabomber outfit is a great disguise."

"I know that, and it is a great disguise, but it's standard—"

"Operating procedure, got it." Anderson hates it when I interrupt him.

"We've got rules to follow when guarding high-value targets like you," Sgt. Barton adds. "We need to get you back safe and in one piece."

"Plus, with the strange circumstances surrounding the attempt on your life in the hospital, and with Ms. Bernard officially still being listed as missing, law enforcement is not sure what role you play in this yet." Anderson's voice is cold and even. "I also know you have knowledge of things that are worth silencing. That will not be happening on my watch."

"I appreciate you, truly—but I am looking forward to the day where I can go to Publix by myself, shop for my own groceries, and come back to my home—alone. I've never been a big fan of dependency on other people. Plus, maybe I can go back to work soon?" Anderson shows no emotion or reaction at the mention of me returning to work.

"I'm looking forward to seeing my family again, too," Sgt. Barton explains. "We're stuck in this together for the time being. Nothing permanent."

We pull into the parking area at the safe house. I try to watch for street signs and landmarks, but the windows in the back are tinted way too dark to be street legal. I think that is probably on purpose. I did look at the time difference, though. It took about thirty minutes to arrive here, which might give me a perimeter of reference when I'm able to get online to check. The burner phone Barton got me is an old school dumb phone, and I don't see any web-surfing technology in the safe house. I guess they are on the protective side.

Col. Anderson did his walk 'round the vehicle thing, and then Sgt. Barton let me out of the backseat. I wonder silently if this is what being famous means, when you have your own personal security detail. Imagine that, I get shot and *then* I turn into Taylor Swift, and these two lug nuts are my Swifties. Guess it could be worse.

My mind immediately thinks about Alahna.

Quinn, find these motherfuckers.

I shake my head violently back and forth to get AB out of it as we walk up the several flights of stairs to the safe house. Anderson did the same thing he always does, clearing the house first before Barton and I are allowed inside. It only takes a few minutes, but the all clear signal is given. The 70s chic makes me laugh and cringe at the same time—shag carpet, bad wallpaper, hideous light fixtures. I wonder how long the powers-that-be have been using this residence.

I feel like I've been transported back in time to the Brady Bunch house.

***

Clyde positioned the truck in front of the apartment building, and scoffed at the fact there might be hundreds of units in this building.

"It's like trying to find a needle in a haystack full of other needles," Ezekiel said.

Leland climbed into the back seat of Clyde's truck with Ezekiel. All three men grabbed a handheld walkie out of a bag in the floorboard, and switched them to the same channel.

"I'll take Ol' Betty here and set up on the roof of this building across the street. Hit the radio if you find anything and I'll cover the front of the building," Clyde said, grabbing his Sako TRG 22A1 rifle and slinging a duffel bag over his head. "Catch y'all on the flipside." Clyde's years of military sniper training and experience comes in handy in situations like this.

"I'll stay here monitoring the front exit, because I know what she looks like." Zeke pointed to the building. "Go door to door if you have to, but find them, Lee."

Leland sighed. "Why am I always the one to do this? Alright, fine. Holler if you see anything through the windows." He holstered a Glock, grabbed an AR-15 from the bag in the backseat, and put a couple of magazines in his pockets.

Ezekiel stayed in the truck, using binoculars to scan the front and side walls of the building. It was a four-story brick tenement structure, with front- and side-facing windows. If anyone showed up that he recognized, it would not end well for them.

***

I go into the bedroom and change out of my shrink clothes into a more comfortable T-shirt and shorts combo. I grab the bottle of oxy out of my fanny bag in the bathroom, and pop a 5mg pill in my mouth. Even though I don't complain much outwardly, my body is still wracked with pain. One swig of tap water, and the pill slides easily down my throat. I continue to stare at myself in the bathroom mirror. The bags under my eyes are so big they resemble entire sets of hard-shell luggage, with my right eye still a little swollen and bloodshot. The burst blood vessels in my eye still look gnarly. I pull up my T-shirt and look at all the bruises dotted across my alabaster-colored rib cage, noticing they are turning many different shades of deep purple. If they didn't hurt so badly, I would probably think they are a beautiful shade of my favorite color.

I mentally do a diagnostic, standing in the small bathroom between the shower and the door. Gunshot wound still sore? Check. Still hurts to take a deep breath? Check. Still having a burning hot rage fest when thinking about a certain hillbilly? *Checkmate for him.*

I splash water on my face, trying to refocus my emotional center.

After changing clothes, I walk back into the living room where Col. Anderson sits in his chair on the outside wall, keeping the entire open space in front of him. Sgt. Barton unholsters his handgun, pops out the magazine to check the ammo count and then re-inserts it into the magwell. He racks the slide, then puts it back in his shoulder holster.

"I'm going to make a quick supply run for me and Anderson." Barton taps the phone on his hip. "If you need me to grab anything, let me know. I'll pick up Chinese on the way back."

Anderson hands a laundry list of items to Barton. "Thank you for stopping by HQ for me. We'll need these things if we're gonna continue to keep Ms. Campbell safe."

"10-4, Colonel. Be back in a jif."

Barton opens the door to leave, looks back at me, and jokes, "Don't let anything happen to him while I'm gone. He'd be one hell of a ghost."

Anderson actually smiles. Like, a real honest-to-goodness smile. I wasn't sure he could actually do that.

"And I'd haunt your ass forever."

"Ain't nobody got time for that," I laugh, then look back at Barton. "Ready for guard duty, *sir yes, sir.*" He closes the door behind him.

A few minutes later, a series of loud booms disturb the silence. They happen in groups of three, all in rapid succession. *Boom, boom, boom! Boom, boom, boom!*

"Shooters on the floor below us," Barton says, as he barrels back through the door. "I got sprayed as soon as I came around the corner,

but I got a few shots off. I have no clue how many more there are."
Barton pulls the emergency lock on the door. It is a thick metal bar
attached to the side of the doorjamb in case one of the four deadbolt
locks fail. He is as white as a ghost, trying hard to catch his breath.

Anderson is already on his feet, flying across the room to a tall
cabinet in the dining room. He pulls out what looks like bulletproof
vests. He shoves one of them at me.

"Shut up and put this on. *Now*."

In the face of sheer terror, I immediately go into survival mode. My
heart races so fast I can hear it in my ears, but I do exactly what I'm told
when I'm told. I've been in some serious situations before, but this one
feels *way* different. I slide the vest on, pulling the Velcro straps as tight
as I can. Barton and Anderson look like they are both preparing for a
serious gunfight at the ATL Corral.

Barton rapidly closes the set of window curtains on the side of
the apartment, pulling down what appears to be a blackout shade.
My heart is beating so rapidly in my chest as both men rush around
preparing the room. When Barton starts to pull the shade down on the
front window of the apartment, a sickening crack breaks through the
window that causes me to jump. The back of Barton's head explodes
backward, spraying blood and brain matter across the 70s upholstery.

"*Sniper*! *Get down now*!" Anderson yells.

It's as if time stands still, and Barton's body is still standing, slightly
swaying, until falling backward at my crouched feet. His lifeless body
is still twitching slightly, a bullet hole in his forehead, his eyes staring
off into nowhere. All I can think of is that he would have been with
his family if it wasn't for me. If he hadn't been charged with keeping
me safe. My life caused his death. I am frozen in a combination of fear
and guilt.

Not him. Not now. Not again. Me once again too helpless to do or change anything.

Anderson crawls across the living room floor to the front window, and quickly puts his back to the wall without being seen. In one motion, he grabs the blackout shade and pulls it quickly down while also falling to the ground. A puddle of blood forms underneath Barton's head, soaking into the blue shag carpet. The taste of bile in my mouth is strong and bitter, and I honestly feel every single emotion all at once. The overwhelming horror, the suffocating anxiety, the relentless pangs of guilt and regret, as well as soul-burning rage.

Something hits the shade, presumably more bullets, but they do not punch through the shade. Bulletproof curtains? Seriously?

Anderson's eyes linger on Barton's body for a breath too long before steeling himself and turning to me. He gets between me and the front door, gun drawn and facing the entrance. Bullets rip through the door, creating holes large enough for a hand to reach through and try to unlock the dead bolts. Without a second's hesitation, Anderson fires his Glock multiple times through the door, causing loud screams to echo in the hallway, followed by a thud. Then nothing but silence.

He whispers forcefully, "Move to the bedroom. *Quickly.*"

I am frozen solid, simply staring at the man on the ground who was literally just joking with me. Before this month, the only dead bodies I'd ever seen were already covered in sheets at crime scenes. I'd never had one look right through me before. I can't even begin to describe this ominous feeling.

"I said *go!*" Anderson shoves me toward the bedroom, while he stays gun drawn at the entrance. *Boom, boom, boom!* Bullets rip through the front of the safe house, like the walls were made out of paper.

"Go, go, *go!*" Another boom comes through the safe house wall, but this one sounds different, farther away, more distant. The hole it left in the wall is huge. Splinters of wood and other debris fly all around us as we crawl through the flat.

Anderson closes the bedroom door, and immediately grabs for his phone and quickly dials a number. "Mayday! Mayday! Foxtrot Two is down, I repeat, Foxtrot Two is down. Foxtrot One and package need exfil options now. Please advise."

I am motionless, with only my eyes skipping back and forth as if I were in a wakened REM sleep state. My ears ring, my heart pounds, my breath catches. I mentally transport myself back to the Custer escape, putting me not in a good way. Anderson's still on the phone.

"Affirmative. Foxtrot Two is DOA. Sniper stationed across from safe house, and main exit is more than likely compromised. Unknown number of shooters on site. I apparently hit one shooter in the main hallway, possibly DOA." He pauses, listening to the other end of the conversation. "Confirmed. Orders heard and accepted." He stands up, rakes all of my meds on the bathroom vanity into a small fanny pack, and locks it around his body.

Barton is dead because of me. Alahna is dead because she was with me. Death follows in my wake. I have *got* to end this vicious cycle somehow.

I start sobbing, my body shaking and trembling underneath me. *Boom, boom, boom!* More bullets enter the safe house, and like Pavlov's dog, I literally jump and flinch and tense up after each deafening shot. I don't even see Anderson grab me from behind and pick me up like a rag doll. He carries me over to the rear wall of the bedroom, sliding the chest of drawers to the side as if it was on wheels. A small access door is at the base of the wall.

"OK, we're going to open this escape hatch, slide down the chute, and it will carry us down to the rear of the building on the ground level. We have to do this right now, otherwise we're sitting ducks here."

Boom, boom, boom! These booms were much louder, as if the shooter was practically inside the safe house already.

"I'll go first, just to make sure no one is waiting for us down there, but you *have* to follow me. Can I trust you to do so? If not, I'll throw you down the chute first myself."

I say and do nothing, because all I can think of is that I'm cursed. People lose their lives around me. I might actually be a liability. I am respons—

Anderson huffs, picks me up by my shoulders, and tosses me down the steep metal chute which looks like it's right out of a poorly conceived death carnival. I collapse at the bottom of the chute in a heap, coming to rest in what appears to be soft sand in total darkness. Anderson rolls off to the side before landing on his feet like a cat. Superhero landing FTW. He pulls out a small flashlight, and quickly scans the area.

"This escape hatch was built in the 1970s, but hasn't ever been used—to my knowledge. You OK?" he checks.

"If I wasn't sore before, I am now. But I appear to be all in working order." I can hear my heartbeat in my ears. This is not the kind of first I wanted to be.

Anderson shines his flashlight around, looking for the exit door. It's a little exitway about the size of the chute entry door. He fumbles with the rudimentary lock, pushes it open, and rolls outside, gun drawn.

"Looks like the coast is clear," he whispers after scanning the area for a second. "*Move your ass.* They could figure out we're gone any second now."

I climb outside, and I am now in a small alleyway at the rear of the building. *Boom, boom, boom!* You can still hear gunshots tearing through the silence. Anderson grabs my hand and drags me down the alleyway. I can't get the sight of Barton's lifeless body out of my head, and considering I'm still covered by bits of him, it's not hard to understand why.

Anderson turns down one street, then another, weaving his way through the maze of buildings, alleyways, and side streets. I honestly feel like I am a kite and he is pulling my guide string. He locates an old car parked on a vacant, empty street, and busts out the passenger window with his flashlight. He opens the door and slides me inside. I reach over and unlock the driver's side door, so he wouldn't have to repeat the damage.

"Get out of sight as best you can. Do it quickly."

I climb into the passenger side floorboard as he pulls off a big chunk of plastic dashboard from underneath the steering wheel, trying to jumpstart this old car.

He touches the wires together a couple of times before the engine sputters, then comes to life. He shifts the car into gear and speeds us away. This is not me, this is not the life I want. *I don't want to do this anymore*.

Anderson pulls out his phone, and hits redial. "Exfil successful, and transpo acquired. I need a final destination." He cuts his eyes over to me, and then focuses quickly back on the road. "Confirmed. Orders heard and accepted. See you at Location Twenty-One Lambda Zulu."

He sits there in silence as the car flies down some random Atlanta street. He is cold, rigid, and devoid of any emotion, more so than normal. My usual instinct would be to add humor or levity to the situation, but this is possibly the worst time in recorded history for me to do that. He might shoot me himself, so I try a different tactic.

"Sorry," I squeak. "Sorry about Sgt. Barton."

"He knew the risks when he signed up. He was a decorated member of our regiment, and he was doing his duty. I trained him to be that way, and that is the way he was."

"But...we just...left him there."

"You are the top priority. Besides, my people will clear the scene, recover Barton, and scrub it clean of any involvement before police ever arrive. This is what we do." Anderson sighs, remaining somewhat stoic. "Don't worry, he would have done the same for me or you had the tables been reversed. Just know it's always about the mission."

I realize that I am the mission—protecting the girl who lived.

CHAPTER 10

A short time later, we arrive at a new location across town, south of downtown Atlanta, near the airport. It looks an awful lot like College Park or East Point, an area of little brownstones near U.S. Route 29 and Camp Creek Parkway. Lots of ways to hit a highway out of town if the need arises—if we are where I think we are. I am not paying complete attention in my less-than-lucid state. I just stared out of the broken passenger window most of the way here, letting the wind blow across my face and dry the tears as they slowly fell from my eyes.

Col. Anderson parks the old car on a side street, and we backtrack to a specific brownstone a couple of streets away. I assume he didn't want to take the chance that someone saw the junker we drove away in, which makes sense. He's been on a razor's edge ever since the safe house siege.

"Stay close behind me, no matter what you see. I have to clear the house, and I can't leave you unattended."

I want to protest, saying I'll be fine out here waiting for him, but think better of it, and just nod. He unholsters his pistol, and punches in an entry code to the lock box on the door. It opens and a little key pops out. He lifts a finger to his mouth as if to shush me, and he uses the key to unlock the door. He slowly opens the door, and goes in gun drawn. This is the first time I have actually seen him do this. He cautiously checks in every corner and crevice, behind every door and curtain, and systematically goes from room to room to make sure it is completely empty. I do not feel at ease until he re-holsters his weapon. Guns scare the hell out of me, especially when their bullets enter my body or when they whizz past my head. No bueno.

Anderson fishes his phone out of his pocket and hits redial again.

"Yes sir, this is Foxtrot One. Asset relocation complete. We arrived at Twenty-One Lambda Zulu moments ago and the safe house appears to be empty."

He listens intently to the other voice on the phone—and I assume it is his commanding officer.

"Not sure how they found us, sir. Either they found a way to track our vehicle or we have a leak somewhere they were able to leverage. Or both."

I still do not picture Custer and the boys being the technologically savvy type.

"Yes, sir. We left our previous vehicle in the garage at Eighteen Beta Gamma. Affirmative. We will acquire new transpo tomorrow and I'll relay that information at 0900." Anderson disconnects, and puts the phone back in his pocket.

"So, what now?" I ask.

"What do you mean, what now? My partner just took a sniper's bullet to the face, and I'm not in much of a chatting mood. Just go get comfortable while I figure out how to get out of this screwed-up mess." Anderson unhooks a fanny pack, tossing it my way.

"What's this?"

"All of your medicine from the bathroom. I didn't want whoever was burning down the door to get any more of your information. Your name and other identifiers were on the bottles."

Damn. Bullets whizzing all around us, and this guy thinks clearly enough to still protect me...or most of me. I unzip the bag and see my oxy, antibiotics, steroidals, and multivitamins. All the good stuff.

"Thank you, really."

Today has been emotionally grueling, from pouring my heart out to Dr. James about getting shot and running for my life and talking about seeing my best friend murdered, to watching Barton's life leave his body right in front of me. I am a bundle of emotions, and every nerve ending is on fire. My body is still suffering the effects from the gunshot wound and from the river. My heart breaks over and over again every second I'm awake, and every time I close my eyes. It seems like I can't escape any of these feelings without medicinal help. It's getting harder and harder to breathe. To be me. But I'm sure the fabled phoenix had a few symptoms after he resurrected from the ashes too, right? I'll find a way to deal with this. *I have to.*

"Hey, do all of your safe houses have a chutes and ladders escape plan?" Again with attempts at levity. I always have jokes, especially in the face of mortal danger. My timing couldn't be worse, but hey, a girl's gotta be true to herself, right?

Col. Anderson didn't give me much of an answer, just a shrug of his shoulders. He was too focused on his laptop to really engage with me. I guess I just remind him of his dead protégé.

I take that as a hint and give him some space.

***

Clyde and Ezekiel pulled their truck over at a back parking lot of a big box store just off of Georgia 400 near Coal Mountain. They called Custer and told him he needed to head down the mountain to meet them.

"He's gonna kill us. He's gonna kill us." Ezekiel's tear-streaked face twisted with anxious nerves as he just kept repeating the phrase.

"Naw, we got one, too. That's gotta count for something, ya know? How long ago did you call him? He's gotta be close now."

Ezekiel looked at his watch. "About half an hour ago, maybe?"

A few minutes later, Custer's F-series dent-side truck pulled to a screeching halt beside them.

"What in the hell happened?" Custer grumbled as he climbed out of the cab of his pickup truck, slamming the door behind him.

The two boys were standing beside their F-150, heads hung low. "They got him, Pa. They got Lee." Clyde motioned to the truck bed.

Custer went around to the back of the truck and let down the tailgate. He pulled back the camouflage tarp and saw Leland's dead body lying underneath. Custer's face showed an emotion somewhere between rage and grief. He slammed his fists down on the tailgate hard enough to make the entire truck bounce.

"I promised your late Ma that I'd look out for you boys, and I have failed in that promise." He spun around to face Clyde and Ezekiel. "You better tell me his death wasn't in vain."

The boys rattled off all the details, mouths going a mile a minute—following them to the safe house, Clyde killing one of her guards with the rifle, all hell breaking loose in the flat, finding Leland outside the door, locating the escape hatch, then losing them in the rear alleyway.

Custer grabbed Ezekiel by the collar and slammed him against the truck bed, his eyes filled with rage. He slapped his son hard across the face. "How is it that my whole family's full of screw-ups lately?" He slammed Ezekiel one more time for good measure, then let go of his collar in a huff.

"Sorry we lost 'em, Pa. We had to get out of there because the cops were everywhere." Clyde added.

"Don't apologize to me, idjit. Apologize to your dead brother that we now have to bury because *you* screwed up." Custer pointed at Leland in the truck bed. "Lee was the oldest and best of you. Lee never let us down. Never let *me* down. And now we have to put him six feet in the ground. Sorry just don't cut it, boy."

"But we can't avenge Lee's death from behind bars, Pa. It was all we could do to grab up his body and get it out of there," Clyde added.

"Alright, alright. Put him in my truck bed, and then head back home," Custer demanded, tossing Clyde his keys. "I have to get rid of these wheels now because you know some busybody saw enough of this truck to give a description to authorities. We'll figure out when and where to bury my boy tomorrow."

"But Pa, this truck's my baby. Can't we just paint it or something like they do on TV?" Custer slapped Clyde across the face, causing him to stagger backwards.

"No, because I'm gonna have to burn this bad boy. That's what happens when you screw up. You boys put our very way of life in jeopardy *again*. First, Beau's dumb ass and now you? Just...just get away from me. *Now*."

Custer grabbed a gas can out of the back of his truck and waved his boys away.

***

I awaken to the sound of some seriously mad banging on the bedroom door. Damn, dude...*calm the fuck down*.

"Up and at 'em, Campbell." Anderson bellows. "You have an appointment with Mr. Tucker in two hours."

I've been summoned back to WQX. I haven't been back there since before my disappearance. I'm looking forward to getting back to some semblance of normal. If that's even possible.

"Alright, alright. I'm up. Stop pounding on the door like a crazy person."

I can hear him roll his eyes on the other side of the door. He hates me, I know it.

I stumble into the bathroom, and stare at myself in the mirror. There's not enough makeup in the world that would cover my battle scars. It's such a double standard where scars on men are attractive and mysterious. Scars on women? Not attractive nor mysterious. Freakin' patriarchy.

I climb into the shower, letting the warm water pour over my body and soothe my sore muscles. The only shampoo in the bathroom is what appears to be an ancient bottle of Head and Shoulders. Note to self: we *have* to make a supply run on the way back from the station.

I turn the water off, pull a towel around my body, and wrap my wet red hair up in another one. I start looking through drawers and closets to see what clothing options I have. I only have the bra and panties I had on yesterday with me, but at least I have those because I am not about to wear someone else's undies. I find a few decent T-shirts that are my size, and I choose a graphic T-shirt with some random anime character on it. The jeans I pick out are stiff and unforgiving, but I am able to slide them on. There's no telling who wore these clothes last. A drug dealer? A mobster turned state's witness? A battered woman hiding from her abusive dick of a boyfriend?

I look like I am on vacation, but it's what I have to work with. I dry my hair, pull it into a ponytail, and slide the bottle of painkillers in my jeans pocket. Better to be safe than sorry.

I walk out into the living room, and Anderson is sitting at his laptop, drinking a cup of coffee. He seems haggard and exhausted, like he didn't sleep at all. *I know that feeling*.

"So, what's for breakfast?"

"Made a fresh pot of coffee. There's no food in this residence."

"And it looks like a fast food run is in our future." No response from Anderson.

He mentions he acquired transportation from a parking deck next to the safe house. A silver Honda Accord left by his company for use by the safe house inhabitants. The perfect car to blend in with—there are like a million of them on the road.

I quickly down a bitter cup of coffee as we head out to the car. Anderson's head is on a swivel as he holds me tight behind him. I feel like his shadow.

We make our way back downtown to the Atlanta newsroom. Since Wild Bill Tucker was paying Anderson to watch me, that kind of makes him the boss of both of us.

Anderson parks the car in the rear of the station, out of the view of the street and surrounding buildings—probably in an effort to avoid sniper or long gun firing opportunities. I am very appreciative to have him with me.

When we enter the building, I ask Anderson to stay back because I truly think I'm safe here...for now. Against his better judgment, he tells me to text him when I'm finished. He walks back outside, presumably to watch the parking lot entrance for psychotic hillbillies.

I walk into the newsroom just before 11am, and it is just as I feared. Even though people were scrambling to get the noon newscast on the air, word that I have arrived spreads like a north Georgia wildfire during a hundred-year drought.

People peek around cubicles, come out of offices, stand in the hallway, trying to get a glimpse of the girl who lived. People scatter when a familiar voice yells from behind me.

"Alright, folks. Show's over...nothing to see here. We have a noon show to produce, so get back to work."

Tommy Jackson. *Damn, I love him, but I doubt I'll ever tell him so. Maybe not.*

"Thanks, T-Jack." I hug him gently, like one of those side hugs that minimizes the pain from my still-battered body.

"No problem, Q. Wild Bill told me you'd be here this morning. Have you talked to him at all, since...you know..." His voice trails off.

"I know he came by the hospital, but I haven't had a deep conversation with him yet, no."

"I'm just glad to see you back in the newsroom. I'm looking forward to having you back."

I cannot wait to start doing my job again. Doing everything I can to uncover Custer's whereabouts, shining a fucking spotlight on him and his nefarious proclivities, making life a living hell. It's the *least* I can do.

I smile weakly at T-Jack. "You just need someone to carry the weight and uphold some standards around here."

Following the entrance spectacle, I walk over to Wild Bill Tucker's office. He is pouring over scripts and stressing over the upcoming newscast, as always. He looks up from his computer, sees me, and waves me inside. He stretches his hand out to me.

"Ms. Campbell, so good to see you still among the land of the living. Come on in."

I shake his hand and sit down at his desk. His office seems cluttered and scattered, but this man is one of the most organized men I know. Every pile is constructed that way on purpose, and he knows exactly what is in each one. This man knows more about journalism—or life, for that matter—than anyone I've ever known. The best leader I've ever worked for, he genuinely cares about his staff more than ratings. However, during sweeps, that feeling is tested in a big way.

"Thank you, sir. Good to see the station is still standing without me. I was legit worried about that for a hot minute." Even nervous, my false bravado screams loud and proud.

"Always with the jokes. Too bad you can't use your humor in your investigative pieces."

Oh, believe me I could. My sick sense of humor is sometimes dark...and all the time hilarious. At least to me.

"You don't win investigative Emmys with humor, sir. You taught me that."

Wild Bill lets out a brief chuckle. "At least somebody listens to me."

"There's a difference between listening and hearing. We all listen to you, sir...just some of us choose not to hear."

"And that's why *those* people cover school board meetings and pet of the week features down at the Atlanta animal shelter."

We both laugh awkwardly.

"Look, Campbell. I have to be honest with you. I need you back in the building. All this town has done over the past three weeks is talk about you. They need to know you're OK. They need to know you continue to be there for them."

I cock my head to the side, processing what he's really saying to me.

"Sir, you know there's nothing I'd rather do than get back to work. I can use WQX resources to do what I can to uncover the serial killers responsible for Alahna's death, and countless others around town." I begin to feel a familiar fire being stoked within me. "I *need* this, sir."

"I've missed that fire, Ms. Campbell." Will Bill takes off his glasses and tosses them on his desk. "You know, I thought about ending your contract and shipping you out of state—for your safety."

"Wait...you actually considered breaking up with me?" Always with the levity.

"I absolutely did, for at least a New York minute, especially after what Col. Anderson told me yesterday. There was another attempt on your life? You were involved in that apartment shooting in Virginia Highland?" Wild Bill leans forward in my direction. "The area was expertly scrubbed of any identifying evidence before law enforcement arrived. It was almost as if professionals didn't want anyone to know who and what was involved. I'm glad to see my trust and my money are both well spent."

"If you noticed the blood in the hallway, that was from one of the hillbillies that has been trying to kill me. I only saw a hand through the front door, but I was whisked away too quickly to see anything else. It *has* to be them."

"Then that's your first story. Use the information we gathered at the scene, and start digging into what happened. APD worked the situation, and I'm sure they'd love to talk to you. But we have to talk about a few things."

I am also overdue for a conversation with GBI Assistant Special Agent in Charge Daniel Brown.

"Truth is, Campbell, legal wants to distance itself from you after spending money to protect you and keep you safe," Tucker continues. "Most stations don't budget for mercenaries to keep star reporters above ground and in one piece. And since one of the safeguards was killed protecting you, they feel that you coming back under the WQX mantle might not be the best look."

Great. I've always hated legal staffers and consultants. They always treat newsroom staffs like a fantasy football roster and sometimes give news directors awful advice. However, this decision kinda makes sense.

Tucker cracks a sly grin. "But I told them to shove it. I told them the best look for WQX is to have my ace reporter back doing what she does best—investigating wrongdoers and being a voice for the voiceless. I told them I need you back, and soon. Therefore, I'm assigning you to our radio news division for the time being. You can use any phone to report for them, and not give away your specific location. That way, Col. Anderson can still work to keep you safe and you get back to doing what you do best. And Campbell, here's a newsflash for the uninitiated—you know I always get what I want."

Wild Bill Tucker definitely got what he wanted...me back in the fold. However, he relegated me to the news dungeon, working with elderly reporters, traffic mavens, and wayward board operators at WQX AM 880, one of the oldest and most prolific news stations in Atlanta history. I mean, it does make sense. He has access to my killer instinct, while the instinct of my killers can't lock onto my specific location.

"And here's something else I've asked for. Col. Anderson will continue to protect you for at least one more week."

"Mr. Tucker, are you sure that's a good idea? I mean, I think I'm good," I lie. If Custer attacks me again, I'd more than likely be helpless to stop it. I just hate having to depend on anyone, especially someone who literally hates me.

"No questions asked, Campbell. Already bought and paid for. I want you back in this building, I need your journalistic grit and intensity, but I also need you to remain safe while you attempt to burn your attackers and their sordid shenanigans to the ground."

"Yes, sir." A small price to pay to get back to work.

"Alright, go find Don Clark, the radio program director, and get set up with everything you need to work with them moving forward. Also, go to editing and have them rip you a copy of the Virginia Highland shooting video and interviews from yesterday. Go work your magic, Mighty Quinn."

Wild Bill Tucker only referenced my namesake Bob Dylan song when he was trying to pump me up. Not gonna lie, it feels kind of hollow without AB here with me, but this is the best way I have right now to honor her memory.

"You'll not see nothing like me, sir." He always likes it when I respond with this lyric from the song's chorus. Even Wild Bill Tucker has his corny moments.

"Welcome back to the fold, Campbell. I need you ready to go tomorrow."

I shake Tucker's hand, and nod my head.

On my way out, I stop to talk to several colleagues who all seem genuinely happy to see me. Lots of smiles, welcome backs, and good to see yas. Tommy eventually calls me over to the desk.

"I guess the radio program director gets to boss me around now instead of you. Sorry about that, but you missed out," I laugh.

"Campbell, you know as well as I do that I've never been able to *tell* you what to do. I just give you suggestions, and occasionally you choose one of them. You know it's true."

"Well, you'll have to live without me for one more day. My official first day back in the building is tomorrow. I'm just gonna go find the PD, get set up with station access information, and then also grab a copy of the Virginia Highland shooting sound from yesterday."

Tommy leans over and checks the big board of assignments. "Clark is still in the building, and should be in either his office or the studio. Go get set up for tomorrow, and I'll send the Virginia Highland video and soundbytes to your email, OK? They're on the server, so I'll just send you the links. Kill two birds with one stone, right?"

***

On the way back to the safe house, Anderson actually hits a drive thru for me. Such a big softie, knowing the best way to my heart is through my stomach. As I'm scarfing down lunch, he makes a quick phone call, and then tries to bring me up to speed.

"Look, there is no way in forty hells I am letting you set even one foot back in your apartment with those rabid rednecks on your tail, so I have some ideas about that." He acts like he has everything covered.

"In that case, we do need to make a few pit stops before we get back to the safe house, because I need some new clothes since I'm going back to work tomorrow," I say as I finish the last bite of my fast food fare—which is the very epitome of coronary heart disease wrapped up in gloriously greasy paper.

"Wait...you now have me for at least another week, and you think I'm just gonna hold your hand while you window shop at the mall?" There was a significant amount of incredulity in Anderson's voice. "Not gonna happen."

"I am the most efficient shopper you've ever seen. I know my exact size, and I don't wear anything flashy at all. A couple of pairs of slacks, a blouse or three, some intimates, and we're out of there—done and done." I wipe off my hands in the air, as if it isn't a big deal at all.

"Sounds like my own personal hell."

"Dude, look at what I'm wearing. I can't go to work looking like this, so let's put Tucker's money to good use. Since I can't get to my apartment, I'm gonna need some better options. Plus, I'm still wearing the same pair of panties I've had on for the last two days. *Gross*."

He gives me a wave of his hand and a grimace, much like when men hear women talking about their menstrual cycles or when we ask them to buy tampons for us at the pharmacy. They just don't want all the details about what it's like to be a woman...*ew, gross lady stuff*. Good thing they don't go through childbirth. Hell, even *I* don't wanna go through that.

"Look, Peachtree Technology is sending a group of folks to your apartment to make sure those rednecks A. Aren't watching and B. Don't try to intervene in any way. These guys are damn good at what they do, and are adept at hiding in plain sight. The relocation squad will expertly pack everything you own into a moving pod that will be moved to a safe location that I will be able to access with you. Since I am not letting you go back to your apartment at all for at least the very near future, our team will instead leave a secret present for anyone who might be following you, just in case they decide to snoop around your home."

A present? I don't even want to know what that entails.

"So, my apartment is off limits. Got it. Then how about Perimeter Mall? Mall of Georgia? Lenox Square? Hell, I'll even settle for online next-day delivery. But I need a change of clothes not purchased from the Six Flags over Georgia gift shop."

He begrudgingly agrees, and we hit a big box store on the way home. Since Wild Bill has paid for him for the next week, I might as well let him buy at least an outfit or three, along with some other necessities. Who knows when I will be able to get to my packed things, so I need a few clothing options. I smile watching him get quite uncomfortable at the clerk questioning with her eyes why an old guy is buying intimates for a woman half his age. Good times for which I'm sure I will have to pay for later.

He also stops off at a grocery store and buys bare minimum rations. He picks out some protein choices, a few vegetables, a loaf of bread, and the most important item to both of us—wine and beer. I already know Anderson's gonna impersonate my mother when it comes to alcohol and painkillers mixed together, but one of these days he's gonna realize I'm not going to do anything to jeopardize my health. Not intentionally, anyway.

I'm just ready to do what I have to do to get back to work. Routine does my body good.

Chapter 11

ele

Custer, Ezekiel, Clyde, and Beau all sat around a table outside their extremely secluded Georgia property deep in the Chattahoochee wilderness. You could scream for hours at the top of your lungs, and no one would ever hear you all the way out here in the boonies. That's why he and his late wife Emma built here, avoiding any and all unnecessary human contact at all costs. Clyde still looked grumpy because his baby of a truck was now a torched pile of rubble somewhere along the Georgia 400 corridor.

"Pa, none of my folk have seen hide nor hair of her," Ezekiel said, and then finished his beer. Clyde shook his head and Beau shrugged his shoulders. In frustration, Custer tossed his beer bottle as far as he could in the distance. A shatter of glass loudly broke the silence as the bottle hit up against something in the darkness.

"What good are _your folk_ if they can't help me when I _need_ them to help me?"

"Maybe we need to try somethin' else, Pa." Clyde said. "Why don't we try and grab one of them Peachtree Technology dudes and force 'em to tell us where they are?"

Custer scoffed. "You mean the paramilitary folk who are probably trained to withstand intense interrogation, and who could probably snap your ever-lovin' necks as soon as look at ya?" He rolled his eyes and opened another beer. "Waste of our time. Next idea."

"What about grabbin' one of their family members? Say we'll kill 'em if they don't give us their location?" Beau added, "We could each grab one, and say the first one who speaks saves their family." The boys all smiled and nodded together, apparently thinking it was a decent plan.

"It's a high-risk move. One where everybody dies because we can't risk 'em identifyin' us. Hard pass—for now." Custer took a swig of a newly opened beer and sat it back down on the arm of his chair. "I really don't wanna expose us like that, not right now. Any more than we already are, anyway."

"Pa, we gotta do *somethin'* different than what we are doin' now. It ain't workin' for us," Beau said flatly.

"If it weren't for *your* dumb ass, we wouldn't *have* to do anything different." Custer pointed a finger in his youngest's face. "The only reason you ain't dead, boy, is because you was your Ma's favorite."

Clyde and Ezekiel sat there quietly, drinking their beers and watching Custer fuss at their youngest brother.

"There's gotta be somethin' I can do to make up for that, Pa. Or are ya never gonna let me forget wha—"

Custer sliced through the air with a machete towards Beau's neck, stopping abruptly as the blade made slight contact with his son's carotid artery. A trickle of blood slowly slid down Beau's throat, his eyes wide with fear. The two other brothers just sat there, mouths agape.

"You don't wanna finish that sentence, boy," Custer snarled. "The only way your dumb ass can make up for your screw-up is to bring me that reporter's head in a box. That's the *only* way we can go back to our way of life. The longer she lives, the bigger chance she tells others about us, and then we'll have choppers flyin' overhead and cops all over, and then we spend the rest of our lives in some damn prison cell or die trying to stay outta one."

With the reporter also knowing his name, Custer's convinced it is only a matter of time now before people start digging into his background, trying to locate the Mountain Mangler himself. His safety and security are both on the clock now.

Custer lit a cigarette and took a long drag off of it. "Alright. Zeke, make sure *your folk* keep an eye on her apartment and see if she or anyone else shows up. I feel like she has to come up for air sometime. Clyde, work your contacts at the phone company and continue listenin' in to her dead friend's home phone." Clyde nodded in the affirmative.

"Will do, Pa. If she ever calls 'em, we'll know."

"Alright, stay on it. Maybe she'll turn up. When the time is right, we might be able to use them as leverage."

Ezekiel stepped away from the group while Custer was still talking to his brothers, and pulled out his phone. He quickly tried calling one of his buddies who was sitting on the reporter's apartment. *One ring. Two rings. Three rings. Voicemail.*

He tried the other buddy that should be there, too. *Three rings, and right to voicemail.* He tried three more times, and got the same result for each.

***

Two phones continued to ring in alternating chimes in the still cab of a pickup truck sitting on the side of a quiet Atlanta street. The two men slumped over in the cab of the truck would not be returning the phone call, now or ever, since they both have fatal bullet wounds—courtesy of the Peachtree Technology Corporation. Quietly, several people dressed completely in Kevlar hooked the vehicle up to a tow truck, while the phones of the dead men fell silent. One of the operatives slapped the back of the tow truck twice, and the driver removed the dead men from the scene, as if they were never there to begin with.

After the tow truck left, a flatbed trailer slid up to the reporter's building. The PTC relocation squadron began hurriedly packing up the reporter's residence. Dozens of people were packing, moving, and loading items with surgical precision. A moving pod sat on the bed of the trailer, and assembly lines trailed to and from the pod and the apartment building. The squad made very quick work of the relocation, and did as Anderson instructed, packing the reporter's clothes last so that they were easily accessible.

While the team finished the moving assignment, a technological "present" was installed by a couple of PTC technicians, preparing it for anyone who might gain unauthorized entry into the property.

***

"Damn it. I told those idiots to always answer the phone when I called. I guess if you want somethin' done right, ya gotta do it yourself." Ezekiel mumbled to himself, and then slid the phone back in his jeans pocket. He walked back over to the group, and he needed a new beer anyway.

Beau jumped into the conversation. "What do you want *me* to do, Pa?"

"Besides jump off a cliff?" Custer huffed. "Why don't you hang back here, and keep working on the plans for that new subdivision we're building. Make sure the crews stay on task. Hopefully, we'll have another "foundational" member to bury soon. And son, please don't screw anything else up."

Custer put the neck of his bottle out between the three boys, looking to clink them together.

"Bring it in, sons. I know we'll eventually make your Ma proud, God rest her soul, and we will avenge Lee's death. I know the reporter will be found, and she will soon be cleansed. How sweet the sound, that doomed a wretch like her."

Four bottles clinked together in agreement. "While y'all are working, I'll squeeze my GBI guy. He's gotta have some kind of access that can help us. Otherwise, we'll have to pay his family a little visit," Custer added, before downing his lukewarm beer.

Maybe soon the girl who lived will be the girl Custer had the chance to cleanse with his own two hands.

***

Anderson takes a swig of coffee, and turns to look me dead in the eyes.

"I know you're going back to work tomorrow, but I want to put some things into perspective." He sits his coffee cup down on the kitchen table, and turns to completely face me.

"Remember, be very careful who you contact, who you visit with, and who you call. I'll be here with you, keeping you safe, but I can't protect them, too."

"Well, part of my job is calling people in the know, and getting them to tell their truth on camera. Well, in my current situation, just out loud."

"Still, whoever you call, visit, or involve in your situation right now will potentially then have a target on their backs. If it were me, I would have someone monitoring phones every minute of every day, hoping you show or come up for air."

"You mean, if I call Alahna's mom, people might be bugging her landline, trying to find me? OK, yeah, that makes sense." He's right, of course. *He's always right.*

"And be careful calling any of your friends or loved ones, too. I would have tapped all of their phones too."

Paranoid much? I don't have many loved ones left in my life.

"Trust me—one way to stay safe is to think like they do. Ask yourself, 'How would you catch yourself if you were them?' I would know the Bernards are your only true familial connection, and that they really matter to you. If you're unpredictable, then they can't get a bead on your whereabouts. Be very careful calling your friends, seeing your friends, visiting old hangouts, giving an ex a booty call, or doing anything you have done before. If they anticipate your movements, based on your past proclivities, then they could get accidentally lucky and hit the Campbell jackpot."

"So you're saying I should zig instead of zag? Be anti...well...me?"

Anderson rubs his left temple. "In your simple terms, yes. Think about doing something and then know you need to take the left turn at Albuquerque."

I laugh at the reference before I can stop myself.

"So, act like I have ADHD? Be all focused like I'm gonna do this one thing, and then *bam*! I follow the shiny distractor and I'm onto something else, just like Dug the dog in *Up*. *Squirrel!*" I turn my head quickly to the side, and laugh.

Anderson rolls his eyes at me and quietly scoffs in his normal judgmental tone.

"Wait, so you can drop a Bugs Bunny/Looney Tunes reference and we're all good, but if I go all Disney/Pixar, you judge me? Such an animation double standard." His expression doesn't budge. *Typical.*

"Seriously though, I hope these cowards aren't inherently evil, because there's one other thing I could conceivably do to try and draw you out," Anderson adds.

"And what would that be?" I take a bite of a piece of toast as I see all expression slide from Anderson's face.

"Kidnap and torture your friend's mother, and then give you an ultimatum. Turn yourself over or she'll be killed in your stead. Or maybe your buddy at WQX. Squeeze them in a way that makes you come running."

A wave of nausea hits me as the thought of that possibility runs right through me. It is all I can do to swallow that piece of toast.

"Dear God, no. I couldn't let that happen." *Not Mama B...not T-Jack...*

"That's why I hope they aren't inherently diabolical and are just inbred and stupid."

There is also that Dahlonega detective that came by the hospital after they dragged me out of the river. I have his card somewhere—what is his name? Miller, I think? I should probably give him a call.

"Yeah, I agree. I need to widen the circle, especially since me being your problem is soon coming to an end."

Anderson grimaces and then finishes his coffee. He appears to have some kind of an idea, and he looks right at me.

"You know what? I got somewhere I need to take you." Anderson gets up, grabs his backpack, and throws it over his shoulder. "Let's go. Now."

A short time later, Anderson pulls up to the front door of a shooting range in Sandy Springs. He gets out, head on a swivel, and walks over to the passenger side. He opens my door, and quickly whisks me inside. He nods to the desk assistant, and he grabs two boxes of ammo and a couple of over-the-ear headphones.

"Your usual, Colonel?"

"We're gonna deviate a little, Pete. Give me a couple of boxes of 9mm, and keys to box A3." The assistant quickly complies with Anderson's request.

As we walk through the lobby and into the range itself, I realize I stick out like a sore thumb.

"OK, since you've brought me to a shooting gallery, I'm only assuming I'm getting a crash course in weapons training?"

"I can teach you everything you need to know in just one session, but I just need to make sure first you won't shoot yourself in the process."

Anderson underestimates my athletic ability. Or maybe he has me properly pegged. I guess we'll soon find out. I have never fired a handgun in my life. My dad took me hunting as a kid, and he let me fire a twelve-gauge shotgun that I'm convinced knocked the soul right out of my body with its recoil. My shoulder was bruised for a month.

So, maybe a handgun will be easier?

"So, are you gonna give me a Lady Derringer, or maybe a Noisy Cricket?" I doubt he got the Men in Black reference, but I laugh to myself anyway.

"Let's go get you set up. We're going to be using Sig Sauer M18s with a twenty-one-round magazine. I'll show you how to load the weapon, chamber a round, hold it, and squeeze instead of pull the trigger. When I'm done, you *should* be able to defend yourself."

Should? Thanks for the vote of confidence, dude. And he drops the full name of the weapon like I'm a lifetime subscriber to Guns-R-Us Magazine or something. All I hear are numbers and letters blah blah blah.

"Then let's go shoot some paper targets that may or may not want me dead." I laugh.

Anderson opens the door to Box A3, and pulls out two handguns. He grabs a couple of pairs of safety glasses from a box in the corner, giving one of them to me. He sets the guns on the counter at the end of the range, and attaches a paper target to the automated pulleys. He flips a switch, and the paper target slides away from him down range.

Anderson shows me how to load ammo into the magazine, then shows me how to put the magazine in the handgun. He shows me the slide, the safety, and the sights. He tells me to leave my finger off the trigger until I'm ready to squeeze it. He puts the gun in my hand, and tells me to look at the paper target.

Anderson tells me to aim and squeeze. I squeeze the trigger and the gun fires at the target, but misses wildly to the left. This is harder than it looks, but thankfully the recoil doesn't take my arm off.

He steps behind me and helps me point the gun at the target. He bends my elbow, and tells me to breathe slowly outward.

"Line up the black circle center mass, and try again."

I do as I'm told, lining up the sight of the gun on the X in the center circle, with nine, eight, and seven written on the circles, expanding outward. I squeeze the trigger, and I hit the nine circle just northeast of the center X.

"Well, that would have been in the heart, so I guess nice shot," Anderson says.

I immediately think of that 90s song, "Hey Man Nice Shot" by Filter, so I take it as a compliment. I'm such a nerd.

I empty the rest of the magazine, and most of my shots hit the paper person target. It looks more like a scatterplot, but hey, I'll take it. Not bad for a first-timer. I push a button and the paper person comes flying toward me. Anderson judges me quietly, puts another paper person on the rig, and sends it back down range.

Anderson slides his safety glasses on, puts on his headphones, and unholsters his Glock handgun. He pops out the magazine, checks it, and slides it back into the magwell. He racks the slide, loading a round in the chamber. I notice him look over at me, and a curl of a smirk slides across his lips.

"Watch and learn, kid."

Anderson rolls his neck, and holds the handgun at his side.

"Pick a number on the target." he asks, without moving his eyes from down range.

"What? Umm, OK. How about the number nine?" I suggest.

"Which one?" I look down range, and see four nines at the center of the target, and four more on the head of the paper target.

"OK, how about the nine just to the right of the center X?"

With lightning quickness, Anderson raises the gun and fires off a round—and it goes right through the chosen number. He smoothly holsters his weapon.

"Pick another one." He blows off his fingertips as he waits.

OK, now he's just showing off, but I play along anyway. I feel like I'm in an old spaghetti western, standing with the fastest draw in the West.

"Hmm, how about the center X on the target's hea—"

Before I even finish the selection, he draws his weapon, fires a round dead center mass through the upper X, and slides his weapon back in the holster. Damn, that was awesome.

"Remind me never to piss you off."

"Look, you're not going to be firing your weapon at a paper target. Moving targets are much harder to hit. I need you to get comfortable enough with holding, aiming, and firing your weapon, just in case you're ever in a situation where I'm not there."

"Wait, are you giving me a weapon?"

"Of course, I am."

"What about the fact I don't have a concealed carry permit?"

"Trust me, the people you'd use this on won't care if you do or not. Just keep it in your purse, and don't go through any metal detectors without me."

Guns still scare the hell out of me, and I don't want to be that person that shoots her own foot trying to get the weapon out of her purse. But I accept the fact he's not going to take no for an answer.

"Alright then. Let's get me more comfortable with this thing."

Chapter 12

Day One back on the job, and it feels incredible to once again have some sense of normalcy. A routine that makes me feel more like myself.

Stuck in the news dungeon ain't so bad. Anderson is still my shadow, but he's stationed out front, monitoring the only way in or out of the news complex. Knowing he's not far away is pretty comforting.

WQX AM 880 program director Don Clark happily greets me, and has already scheduled my first report on the Virginia Highland shooting for the eleven o'clock AM radio newscast. That gives me about two hours to craft a story that I actually lived through—easy peasy, lemon squeezy.

I sit down in front of a computer, and realize this is the first time since my unplanned hillbilly sequester that I've been able to access the internet. I smile deviously, crack my knuckles, and I get right to work.

My first internet search: *Custer*. Big surprise.

Millions of hits pop up, most of them related to Little Big Horn's George Armstrong Custer. A song by Slipknot. Custer County, South Dakota. Gotta refine the search.

My second search: *Custer Chattahoochee.*

Nothing of importance. A road along the Chattahoochee River. A school district. The name of a horse. Damn it. Of course, it wouldn't be that easy.

I decide to get back to work, and do something constructive. I download the soundbytes Tommy sent me via email, and I listen to the Atlanta PD public information officer, who basically doesn't know anything, and a couple of neighborhood interviews who also don't say a whole lot—heard shots, lots of them, don't know where they came from, worried about the safety of my family, crime in Atlanta sucks, etc. Barely useful out of context, since I was there and know the truth, but I have to use what I've been given. Suddenly, a wild thought crosses my mind.

"Hey Don, I have a crazy request," I call over to the program director, sitting in front of a mixer board.

"Day one, and she's already requesting things." Don Clark shakes his head. "Your reputation precedes you, Ms. Campbell, and I know all about your instincts. What's your request?"

I tell Mr. Clark the crazy story of what *actually* happened. He sits there, mouth dropped open, listening to me spin a story that's truly hard for him to imagine.

"So, do you have any way to corroborate this crazy story?"

"Don, I *am* your corroboration. I was *there* when it happened. I know details that law enforcement will never be able to uncover, because I saw it all happen. Do you want this exclusive bombshell report? If so, then let me tell the *real* story."

"Stick with the reporting from yesterday for right now, unless you can find someone to interview that will go on record on this story."

"Damn it, Don. I *am* the story. Isn't this what you want from me? What a way to welcome me back on air—telling a story that no one else has. The whole metro Atlanta area will be talking about my return on air, as well as the biggest exclusive this station has ever had. NewsRadio 880 will be on everyone's mind, and you can't buy publicity better than that."

Clark just sits there, stone faced.

"Come on, Don. Point me in a direction, and turn me loose. This is what I do."

"Alright, be very *very* careful. Don't mention anything you can't prove. Don't editorialize. Don't paint me into a legal minefield on day one, Campbell."

The story writes itself, and I make sure not to name PTC or Anderson or Barton, but I am extremely careful to draw a picture for our listeners so that they know exactly what went down in their neighborhood. I also connect this shooting to my disappearance a few weeks ago, saying that my captors were trying to finish the job. After the attack on my life in the hospital, I'm sure listeners are more apt to believe another attempt to get to me. I work the name Custer into the report, mentioning he is a person of interest in my kidnapping, among other things. I want him to know I know. I end up using a soundbyte from the PIO saying that the scene was basically gone by the time they arrived, but I'm careful not to make APD sound incompetent. It's not their fault that PTC works faster—and better—than they do.

Clark reads over my finished script, and just stares at me. "Did this *really* happen?"

"Absolutely." I tell him about our chutes and ladders escape, but I don't put that in the story. He just shakes his head in amazement.

"Alright, Campbell. Run with it. Let's go ahead and blow the market's doors off."

Happy about my first story coming up, I decide to log into my social media accounts for the first time in like forever. I quickly scroll through the hundreds of messages from my followers, saying things like *I hope you're OK* or *I'm glad you're alive,* to *You're a lucky hack* or *You did this only for the story.* After all the amazing things I've been able to say, do, and report in my career, the social media culture is super toxic nowadays. Trolls are gonna troll, so if you can't beat 'em, join 'em. I post the following:

To my loyal followers, thank you for your support and your words of healing, but I'm baaaack! Listen to my first report—a bombshell exclusive about yesterday's VA Highland shooting—today at 11am on NewsTalk 880 WQX-AM! Oh, if you see a man named Custer, tell him I said hello! #WelcomeBack #ThanksForYourSupport #NewsTalk880

Anderson is going to hate I'm doing this, but I am very careful not to paint a target on his back or on his company. I can't wait to see the comments after my report airs, because they should be...interesting.

***

Ezekiel has been trying for two days to get ahold of the men sitting on the reporter's apartment. He searched side streets, parking lots, and hotels in the area. Nothing has turned up.

His phone rang, so he pulled it out of his pocket

"Hello?"

"Found anything yet?" Custer asked, with normal tones of irritability in his voice.

"They just disappeared, Pa. I can't find my guys anywhere. Somethin' don't feel right."

Ezekiel heard a very obvious growl from the other end of the phone. "If they're not there, are you sure the reporter's stuff is still there?" Custer bitingly asked.

"Since I been here, I haven't seen her or her Peachtree goons coming or going from the building."

Ezekiel pulled the phone away from his ear as Custer screamed into the speaker. "*Then go make damn sure!*" The line went dead.

He hated getting on Custer's bad side. Some very bad things seem to happen to people who are on his bad side. He slid his phone back into his pocket.

Ezekiel looked at his watch, showing just after ten o'clock on Monday morning. The streets around him were busy but not abnormally so. He got out of his truck, and stood on the sidewalk facing the apartment building. He repeatedly looked up and down the street, noticing one traffic camera on the street. He made a mental note to get his Atlanta PD contact to give him the video. God knows how far back the video should go—and he knew he hadn't heard from his boys in days. Something happened, he just didn't know what.

He pulled a trucker hat out of his back pocket and put it on. He crossed the street to the apartment building, and realized the main door was locked and required a key fob to open it. He decided to wait for someone to either leave or arrive, and he'd try to slide in afterwards.

About half an hour later, a little old lady slowly opened the building's front door. Ezekiel grabbed it and held it open for her while also trying to hide his face.

"Well, aren't you a dear. Thank you," the lady said, smiling up at him.

He silently tipped his hat towards the lady. As she walked away, he slid inside the building as the door gently closed behind him. He pulled a piece of paper out of his wallet, with 21A scribbled on it—which was the reporter's apartment on the second floor. He decided to take the stairs.

The building was quite sterile and plain. Light beige walls with dark brown wooden doors. Paintings sporadically dotted the walls. No plants, no floor decor, nothing.

He walked up to 21A, and tried the doorknob. Locked, of course. He looked left, then right, and listened. No cameras in the hallway that he could see. No one on the hall milling around. All he heard was silence.

With a swift kick, the boot on his right foot ripped 21A's door almost off its hinges, and it opened with a crash.

The apartment was absolutely empty.

"Son of a *bitch*."

Ezekiel ran from room to room, opened every door, and pulled out every drawer. Not a single thing was left in the apartment. Frantic, he stood in the empty living room, trying to process what was happening. He knew Custer was *not* going to like this...not one bit. The fear in the pit of his stomach grew, knowing how Custer deals with dissatisfaction in his sons. He buried his fear deeply beneath rage, which helped focus him and allowed him to begin to figure out a way to get out of this situation.

Out of the corner of his eye, he noticed what appeared to be an index card pinned to the wall behind the door, which was now slowly swaying back and forth. He took a closer look at the piece of paper, with "Read Me" written on Peachtree Technology Corporation stationary.

He ripped the card off the wall and angrily turned it over.

"Under the cover of darkness, you lost your only leverage, and now you also have to say goodbye to two of your friends. Sucks to be you. By the way, we know you're here now."

Ezekiel balled up the card, and angrily tossed it across the empty room. "I *knew* something didn't feel right," he screamed. They knew *someone* would come. They were waiting for him. His anxiety level shot through the roof, and beads of sweat appeared on his forehead.

A man dressed in maintenance coveralls stuck his head into the now-open apartment, and locked eyes with Ezekiel. "Hey, what happened to this door?" He knew the man had seen his face and couldn't be left alive as a witness. With zero hesitation, Zeke pulled out his gun and shot the man in the head, causing him to fall backwards onto the tiled kitchen floor in a heap.

He then noticed a tiny blinking red light on the doorjamb above the door. He inspected it closer, and it was some kind of a radio transmitter. It looked a lot like a silent alarm of some sort.

"Those damn Peachtree jerks," Ezekiel mumbled, crushing the radio transmitter with the butt of his gun.

He knew he had to get out of there in a hurry, so he put the gun back in his waistband and hauled ass down the stairs and out of the building. Once outside, he saw several unmarked white Crown Victorias and black Escalades pulling into the parking lot.

Ezekiel pulled his gun back out and fired a few shots in the direction of the closest car. Windshield glass sprayed the air, and people dove out from inside.

A bullet whizzed by Ezekiel's head, then one struck him in the shoulder, knocking him back onto a brick wall. Wincing in pain, he started running in the opposite direction of the gunmen, spraying bullets at them, trying to cover his exit in retreat. He jumped over a pile of garbage, running in zig-zagged fashion. He ducked behind a dumpster to catch his breath and inspected his gunshot wound. He groaned quietly when he touched it, but he felt it was not in a vital location. He slowly leaned his head around the dumpster, and noticed the alley was empty.

Ezekiel wondered to himself why no one was following him.

He slid down another alley, and made it to a side street on the opposite end of the building, causing him to grin slightly as he crossed. He knew he needed to steal a vehicle quickly and then get the hell out of town.

Suddenly a bullet hit Ezekiel center mass from behind, dropping him to his knees. A surprised look came across his face as he looked down at the bullet wound. Then two more shots rang out, fatally dropping him on the sidewalk. A puddle of blood began to pool underneath him onto the alley surface street.

From out of the alleyway, a soldier dressed in all black walked up to the fallen man, kneeling down beside him. He was wearing a bulletproof vest with a PTC logo on it. He placed two fingers on the fallen man's neck, looking for some kind of pulse. He pulled a walkie off his hip, and pressed the talk button. "Falcon 1 to Osprey, target is neutralized. Everything's Code-4. Begin cleaning the scene."

The soldier quickly searched the man's body, pulling the 9mm handgun out of his dead hands. He slid the gun in a vest pocket and continued searching. He found keys, a wallet, a burner cell phone, and a folded-up piece of paper in the man's pocket. The soldier unfolded it, and it was a picture of Col. Anderson, Sgt. Barton, and Quinn Campbell coming out of the psychiatrist's office the other day. There was a red X on Barton's face, and Campbell's face was circled.

The soldier refolded the photo, putting it in his back pocket. He knew Col. Anderson would absolutely lose his shit when he saw that picture. He then opened the dead man's wallet, looking for some kind of ID, but it was not going to be that easy. It contained about $200, a fast food loyalty card, and a security card of some sort for a Georgia construction company—Calvary Rock General Contractors. No address. No identifiers other than the name and a cross logo. He closed the wallet and slid that into his vest pocket as well.

As the soldier stood up over the dead man, several more men dressed in military gear swooped in to grab the man's lifeless body off the street and completely scrub the scene like the professionals they are, including deleting CCTV camera footage from the area. PTC liked operating as ghosts, and this was no exception. The normal hustle and bustle of Atlanta life resumed, and it was almost like a fatal shootout hadn't just happened in broad daylight. Just another run-of-the-mill day in the ATL.

***

Assistant Special Agent in Charge Daniel Brown stood in front of a whiteboard. Pictures of Quinn Campbell and Alahna Bernard were taped to the board, with circles and words drawn around them. A picture of Jada Sinclair was also on the board, near the bottom. Two red arrows went out from her picture to Campbell and Bernard. Several GBI case agents also sat at a long table in the center of the conference room, all staring at the same board. Dahlonega Police Detective Grayson Miller was at the end of the table, randomly scribbling doodles in a notepad in front of him. Case agent Aaron Bernard was also in the room.

"Alright, folks. What do we know?" Brown asked, never taking his eyes off the board.

An agent bravely spoke up. "Only what Campbell told you, sir. We haven't found anything else to back it up."

Brown turned to glare at the agent. "Not good enough. Try again. Tell me what we *know*."

"We know that WQX hired a paramilitary mercenary group—Peachtree Technology Corporation—to protect Campbell and keep her off the grid," an agent piped in.

"We also know Quinn Campbell was involved in that shootout in Virginia Highland this week with. . ." Bernard checked the notes in front of him. ". . .two unidentified individuals. Fingerprints we pulled put Campbell at the scene, but the other sets of prints weren't in the system. They *have* to be from her PTC bodyguards."

"Whoever cleaned up the scene did so in a hurry, but effectively. A huge section of carpet was missing from the living room, which leads me to believe there was some kind of evidence there that someone didn't want us to find," a case agent added.

"We sent some of the hallway blood to the lab as well to see if we can get lucky and identify the person who left it there. With the amount that was there, the donor was definitely in a bad way," one of the younger case agents said.

Another case agent asked, "Why does Ms. Campbell always seem to be in the center of the action?"

"It's almost as if someone is trying to silence her," Detective Miller said, stopping his doodling long enough to enter the conversation.

Brown looked at Miller. "It does seem that way, doesn't it?" Brown turned back to the vision board. "Ms. Campbell said a man named Custer is responsible for her abduction, for the kidnapping and alleged murder of Alahna Bernard, and is also allegedly responsible for the death of Jada Sinclair. We need to double-time our investigation into that name. I feel like he's the lynchpin." He looked over at a few of the GBI techs in the room. "Run the name Custer and see if you can find anyone up in that area who may have sons or relatives working with or for him—*stat*."

The techs nodded in agreement, and started clicking away on their keyboards.

"Have we found any witnesses from last week's building shootout yet?" Brown asked. "Or have we been able to connect any dots between it and the reported shooting that just happened in Midtown outside of Campbell's apartment?"

"Nope. Both scenes were scrubbed in almost the exact same way." Aaron Bernard twirled a pencil in his hand. "I believe in my bones that PTC scrubbed them both. However, we were able to recover the slug from the dead building super found in Campbell's apartment, almost as if PTC left him just for us. It also looked like the door had been kicked in, but we're still combing through the scene."

"Maybe we'll be able to get a ballistics match between the super's slug and the one pulled from Campbell's shoulder we retrieved from the hospital?" Brown wondered aloud.

"Wouldn't that be a Christmas gift?" Det. Miller said.

"Did we ever get a hit on facial recognition from Ms. Campbell's would-be assassin in the hospital?" The janitor's photo is on the board, on the right-hand side. Question marks surround the photo.

"No, sir. No hits in CODIS or the DMV database," a junior case agent said. "Still working it, though."

"Bernard, help comb through all of the evidence we have. I need you to see if there are any connections to Campbell or your sister that we just can't see." Brown turned to the group. "Alright, people...let's get to work."

"Speaking of Campbell, maybe it's time to bring her in," Miller said, continuing his doodling. "I mean, she and her shadow protectors are the only three people we know of with firsthand experience against these ghosts."

"I'll reach out to WQX. I know William Tucker will have a way to contact Campbell or her bodyguards. Now, let's focus, people." Brown waved the team to leave the conference room and pound the pavement. Lots of yessirs emanated from the group, as case agents and forensic analysts split up and headed their separate ways.

Detective Miller wanted to connect himself with Aaron because right now, Agent Bernard gave him the best chance to find the missing clues to this fractured puzzle. No one wanted closure more than him, so that made him a very valuable asset. "Hey Bernard, need a partner to go back over the evidence?"

"Truth be told, I'll take whatever help I can get."

The two men shared a firm handshake, and Aaron gave him a *let's go* nod of the head toward the door.

CHAPTER 13

Leland's dead.

Ezekiel won't answer.

Custer is pissed.

The old man hung up his phone in disgust, after calling Ezekiel for the fifth time and failing to reach him. His son usually answered the phone immediately, so this was very out of the ordinary for him. The Mountain Mangler himself felt a little vulnerable as his family seemed to be unraveling right before his eyes. He, Clyde, and Beau sat around a table in the Calvary Rock construction trailer, drinking beer and working on a plan to recover some part of their way of life.

He tossed the phone onto the desk in the construction trailer, sighed dismissively, and then ran his hands through his long, shaggy gray hair, pulling his silvery beard downward.

"Somethin' just don't feel right." Custer muttered softly.

He stared at a family picture on the wall showing him, his late wife Emma, Clyde, Beau, Ezekiel, and his late son Leland, taken at the dedication/groundbreaking of their first new home build in north Georgia. The birth of Calvary Rock General Contractors.

He missed Emma. He missed Leland. The worry for Ezekiel was real. He missed the way things used to be. He realized he felt nothing but anger and disappointment for Beau, but remembered that his screw-up of a youngest son was Emma's favorite. Even through those big emotions, he still kinda loved the kid.

"It's not like Zeke to flat disappear like this," Clyde said. "When's the last time anyone saw him?"

"I told him to check the reporter's apartment in Midtown," Custer said, with zero emotion in his voice. "I think somebody musta grabbed him."

"That might be the only explanation," Beau added. "He lost touch with the guys he had watching the apartment, and then went to go find them."

"Think it was the cops?" Clyde asked.

"Not a chance. If the cops had him, we'd have heard from them by now. One phone call and all that." Custer pulled a cigarette out of the pack, fired up his lighter, and took a long drag. "I'll bet dollars to donuts it was those Peachtree assholes."

"I wonder if they're trying to get revenge on us for taking out that other guard the day they killed Lee," Clyde pondered. "I mean, we got one and they got one. I'd call that even."

Custer took another drag on his cigarette, and sat at the table, emotionless. "Bullshit. Lee was worth more than five of those rent-a-cop assholes. Lee was the best of us."

"Alright, let's say Zeke got grabbed. What's our next play?" Clyde looked to Custer and Beau for ideas.

"I got a feeling he ain't coming back," Custer said. "We just gotta move on without him, and keep our focus on the reporter. If we can silence her, then we can disappear and regroup. Until then, she's one helluva loose end."

"You saying we give up on Zeke?" Beau asked. The back of Custer's hand flew faster than it ever had before, catching his youngest son across his cheek with full force. The blow knocked Beau completely out of his seat. He sat on the floor, rubbing the pain out of his now-red face.

"We give up on no one. If he's alive, he'll be able to stay alive. If he's dead, he's dead. Either way, we have to stay the course." Custer took one last drag off his cigarette and crushed it out on the table. "Find. The. Reporter."

"How do we do that? The only ones who know where she is are those Peachtree goons." Clyde had a look of frustration and anger. "And you said grabbing one of them is off the table."

"She did post on one of her social media accounts, and she totally called you out, Pa." Beau said from the ground, still rubbing his face.

"Damn it, I knew it was only a matter of time." Custer stared out the window until his face showed an idea just popped into his head. "Didn't Zeke say there was a man in the reporter's room at the hospital when he tried to finish her off? One of her TV friends?"

"Yeah, one of her bosses, I think, or someone who worked with her," Beau remembered, climbing back into his chair.

"OK, we need to figure something out," Custer smiled, showing off an evil grin, beginning to formulate the crew's next steps. "It's time to ratchet up the pressure on the reporter, and I have some ideas on how to do just that. We've waited long enough. Ready to get your hands dirty, boys?"

***

Over the course of her career, Dr. Evelyn James had seen her fair share of patients with high levels of psychological trauma. That's why she was on the healthcare system's preferred referral list. High value assets with information locked away inside their minds came through the system periodically, and her locksmithing skills were locally renowned.

She sat in her Midtown office, flipping through her notes on her latest patient—the WQX reporter who had recently gone all the way through the wringer. Ms. Quinn Campbell had PTSD from major trauma and potentially latent bipolar disorder—probably genetic in nature—which is one of the best...or worst...one-two punches with which she could be diagnosed.

Dr. James was able to convince the reporter to trust in her diagnosis, and she opened up about some of the craziest stuff the doctor had ever heard in the history of her medical degree. Electric shock? Electrified cages? Crazy people with baseball bats? Watching her best friend die? Surviving two other attempts on her life? Dr. James was surprised the woman could even still muster a smile and/or crack a joke. She seemed like a very strong-willed woman who used humor and sarcasm to deflect her true feelings—which could actually be a side effect or a symptom of her Bipolar diagnosis. Feelings of being bulletproof? Rationalizing bad decisions? Rapidly shifting emotions? Classic.

She scribbled more notes in the margins of Ms. Campbell's paperwork and keyed in a screensaver password to unlock her computer. She started entering her evaluation of Ms. Campbell into the secure medical records database.

She wondered if she should tell anyone what Ms. Campbell actually told her? Confidentiality covered most—if not all—of her patient interactions, unless the patient was a danger to themselves. She honestly felt that Ms. Campbell wasn't a danger to herself, but believed she legitimately feared for her life every day. She did, however, believe

Ms. Campbell would unload every bit of pent-up horror, rage, and vengeance on her captors if she ever found them again. That bothered her slightly.

She typed into the online medical record the descriptions of the men who allegedly kidnapped and tortured Ms. Campbell and her friend. She described them as southern good ole' boys, wearing flannel and denim, all with long unkempt beards and wearing black balaclava ski masks and driving pickup trucks. They also appeared to be a close-knit group—maybe even a family. She only remembered one name, "Custer," which was the name of the apparent patriarch of the bunch. She said they looked like something straight out of a bad cable reality show.

She stopped typing long enough to stare out her office window. The woman she counseled in her office had no reason to still be the fighter she was. What she had seen could have—or should have—broken her mentally as much as it did physically. The fact she still exhibited such strength of character and will was a good sign, a sign she may very well turn the page.

The phone rang, snapping her out of her thoughts. She pushed the speakerphone button. "Yes, Diana?" Diana was her charge nurse.

"Dr. James, your daughter is on Line 1."

The psychiatrist looked over at a family picture on her desk, featuring her, her husband, and an adorable little girl in some picturesque mountain scene from a previous vacation. The little girl was her first and only daughter.

"Thank you, Diana. Can you please cancel the rest of my appointments for the day? It's Fiona's birthday tomorrow and I want to take her shopping."

"Yes, doctor. Can do."

"Thank you, Diana." Dr. James pressed the blinking button on her phone. "Fiona? Hey sweetie."

The young girl responded quickly. "Hi Mom. Did I call at an OK time?"

"Yes, baby. You have perfect timing." Dr. James looked at the wall clock in her office. "Are you still at school?"

"Yeah. We had an early release today, so I was hoping you could come pick me up. Most everybody else is gone. I tried Dad and he didn't answer." Her husband Derrick worked in marketing for the men's professional basketball team in town. Sometimes his schedule was worse than hers.

"Sure, I can do that. I'm just finishing up a couple of things here, and I have cleared the rest of my calendar this afternoon. How about I come and get you and take you shopping? You can pick out some nice things for your birthday tomorrow."

"That sounds great, Mom, thank you. When will you be here?"

Fiona's middle school is about twenty minutes as the crow flies from her Midtown office, which meant probably forty minutes with Atlanta traffic.

"Keep your phone handy. I'll call when I'm close, OK? *I love you, Munchkin.*"

"Ugh, Mom, that was so first grade. I love you, too." The call ended, and she placed the phone back in the cradle. She loved playfully embarrassing her daughter. She'd called her Munchkin ever since she played one in an elementary school play. She was so stinking cute in her Lollipop Guild outfit.

Fiona was her whole world, and she was going to spend as much time with her today as she could. She clicked save on Ms. Campbell's medical record, closed her folder, and walked over to her cabinet to file it away. She ran her finger along the top of Ms. Campbell's folder, sliding it into its place in alphabetical order.

"I'll figure out Ms. Campbell tomorrow." She closed the filing cabinet drawer, and locked the cabinet. She pulled off her white doctor coat and hung it on the coat tree by her office door. She grabbed her cardigan and her purse off the same rack, opened her office door, and left quietly to go pick up her amazing daughter. It's time to spoil her rotten.

***

After the six o'clock PM newscast ended, Tommy Jackson finished up his shift for the night. He gave updates on any working stories to his assignment desk replacement and the nightside producers, high-fived the daytime producers for a good day's work, and stopped by Wild Bill Tucker's office.

"Alright, Mr. Tucker, what did you think? Good day?"

Tucker turned around in his chair, smiling at the assignment editor. "Good job as always, Tommy. Are we all set for the eleven?"

"Yes, sir. All reporters have photogs, all live trucks are up and running, and the nightside editors have already started on the network pieces for the eleven o'clock. Need anything else before I head out?"

"Nah, I'm good." Tucker spun back around in his chair, and turned his attention to the network newscasts on the wall of monitors in his office.

"Alright, sir. Guess I'll see you in the morning."

Jackson's cell phone rang, and GBI Field Office came up on the caller ID. Jackson waved to Tucker and left his office before answering the phone.

"Tommy Jackson."

"Mr. Jackson? This is Detective Grayson Miller with Dahlonega PD. Got a second?"

Jackson knew Miller was the local Dahlonega detective working with the GBI on Quinn's investigation.

"Detective Miller, this is a perfect time. How can I help you?"

"I was hoping I could meet up with you tomorrow morning with my partner and Ms. Bernard's brother, Aaron. I was hoping we could go over some or most of what we know and see if you could help connect some of the dots."

"Sure, I can do that. Wanna say ten AM at the coffee shop across the street from WQX?" Jackson offered. "I can get the desk covered here for about an hour or so."

"Fantastic," Miller said. "Well, I won't take up any more of your time tonight. See you in the morning." Jackson disconnected the call, and put the phone back in his pocket.

Jackson badged out of the newsroom, asking the security guard about his family and how they were doing. The guard smiled and small-talked the assignment editor on his way out. Jackson thought to himself about how beautiful the night was, and also about what he was going to do for dinner.

He decided to hit a grocery store on the way home, buying a large supreme pizza and a bag of salad, making tonight an easy dinner night. Being a young, single man in Atlanta had some advantages—like easy dinner nights and no judgment zones.

Jackson parked his 2018 Jeep Wrangler in the driveway of his Grant Park home, grabbed the grocery bags from the back, and walked up to his front door. He opened it, tossed his keys onto the table in his foyer, and carried the grocery bags into the kitchen. He sat the bags on his kitchen counter and turned on his oven, pulling the pizza out of the bag and removing the plastic surrounding it. He reached into his refrigerator and grabbed a cold beer from the door. Beer + pizza + streaming TV service = a really good night.

A few minutes later, Jackson sat down on his couch, pizza and beer in hand. He picked up the remote control, and turned on the TV. He cycled through several screens, trying to find something to watch while he ate his dinner. Something non-newsy. He had his fill of that at work today.

Something caught his eye, and he turned his head to look out the window. He put the remote control and his beer down on the coffee table, and walked over to the front window. He looked outside, and scanned left and right. The night was peaceful, and the lights illuminated the quiet street in front of his home. He could have *sworn* he saw something. He spent a minute scanning the neighborhood, noticing his neighbor across the street taking out the trash. He shook his head and smiled. God, he's too paranoid for his own good lately. He laughed in partial judgment of himself. He pulled the curtains, and walked back into his living room.

Sitting back down on the couch, he resumed scanning through the channels. Eventually he settled on a sports channel talking about the latest events around the world of professional and collegiate athletics.

He was so focused on the TV screen that he didn't even hear the mask-wearing man slide up on him from behind.

***

Beatrice Bernard was in her kitchen, making dinner for her two boys. Aaron had been working so much overtime with the GBI task force lately, trying desperately to figure out what had happened to Quinn, that she hadn't seen a lot of him lately. Tonight was supposed to be a family dinner night. Ian told her he was going to finish up at the law firm in time to come and help with dinner prep, but Aaron said he was going to be a little late.

Ian's wife was out of town on business, so it was just going to be the three of them tonight—just what Mama B wanted. Quality family time.

She heard someone putting a key into the front door lock. "Mama B, sorry I'm late." It was Ian.

"No worries, baby. Come help me finish up these side dishes."

Ian strolled into the kitchen, and kissed his mother's cheek. He washed his hands, and began his responsibility as her sous chef. Chopped a few greens here, stirred the potatoes there, stuff he'd been doing most of his life. Mama B opened the oven door, checking on the ham she was slowly roasting.

They heard another car pull up outside, and Ian looked out the front window. His brother Aaron had arrived, carrying what appeared to be a store-bought pie or some other kind of dessert. He chuckled, because if it wasn't made from scratch, Mama B wouldn't touch it. More for both of them.

Ian laughed to himself when he heard Mama B chastise Aaron for bringing that "no good excuse for a dessert" to dinner, and again when he heard her tell Aaron that "she had raised him better than that." An *I told you so* response popped up in Ian's mind, but he kept it to himself. He was too busy enjoying Aaron catching hell for once instead of him.

After dinner, the boys helped clear the table and clean up after the meal. "Mama, do you mind if I crash here tonight? I have to be on this side of town early in the morning, and I don't feel like going all the way up to my house tonight," Aaron asked.

"Son, you know you don't have to ask me that. This is the house you were born in and in which you were raised. You can stay here any time you need to." It was just Mama B in this big house nowadays, since her husband, their father—who was a Decatur PD sergeant—was killed in the line of duty several years ago. "It'll be nice to have someone else in the house with me for a change."

Ian finished washing dishes and dried his hands off with a dish towel. "Yeah, Monique should be home tomorrow from her weeklong conference in Boston. I should probably head out and start getting the house ready. I can't wait to see her."

"I missed her tonight, son, so you guys can come over this time next week for dinner. I'll make her favorite pecan pie."

Ian walked over to Mama B and kissed her forehead. "Thank you, Mama." He walked over to Aaron and pulled him in for a hug. "Love ya, bro. Let me know if you need any legal help for the work you're doing. Our firm would be glad to help."

"Thanks, bro. I think the GBI has plenty of lawyers on the payroll, but you know you're my go-to if we need someone that always loses when playing spades." Aaron playfully punched Ian in the shoulder.

"Ouch, too soon, bro. You know I can't help but go nil. It's not my fault you can't cover my bags when I do it."

The two brothers laughed at each other, and Ian walked into the living room to give his mother a goodbye kiss and hug.

"Bye, Mama B. Call me if you need me. Love you."

Ian waved to them both, and walked out to his car. He pulled out his phone, put it in the center console, and cranked up the Audi. He loved his childhood home, and always loved spending time with his family—even though it has felt rather fractured without his youngest sibling around.

The night was crisp and calm, with very few people on the road. Ian had been driving these streets ever since he got his license at seventeen. There were lots of parking lots and strip malls in this neighborhood, and his father taught him to parallel park and three-point turn around here all those years ago.

He pulled up to a stoplight, and began fumbling with his car stereo. Didn't like that song, next...didn't want to hear that commercial, next...and then he finally settled on an old R&B song that made him smile. He instinctively began singing the song as if he was performing it live on stage. The light turned green, and the Audi slowly pulled out into the empty intersection.

All of a sudden, a huge truck slammed into Ian's car from behind, and the force of the truck shoved the Audi into a retaining wall on the opposite side of the intersection. The Audi was crushed between the wall and the truck, in an accordion fashion, showering glass, metal, and plastic all over the lot. Airbags deployed, horns were going off, and Ian slumped over the steering wheel.

A balaclava-wearing man walked up to the shattered driver's side window, and used a switchblade to cut through Ian's seatbelt. The man tried to pull open the driver's side door, but it was jammed shut. Instead, he pulled the semi-conscious Ian out through the window. About that time, Ian started to come to, trying to regain his bearings. He immediately realized something was wrong.

"W...wait, what's happen...happening? What are you doing?" Ian was still groggy from the collision. The man didn't even try to answer Ian's question before pistol-whipping him into unconsciousness.

Chapter 14

Detective Grayson Miller arrived at the coffeeshop a little before ten o'clock in the morning, and it was already packed. Aaron Bernard grabbed a table while Miller ordered drinks for the both of them. He picked up his order and walked over to Bernard.

"I'm not sure I can trust a fed who doesn't drink coffee," Miller joked.

"Well, you're stuck with me and my tea-drinking self."

The men sat in awkward silence drinking their beverages, watching the customers in the packed coffee shop move through with experienced precision, as if the employees and baristas there worked better with a packed house.

Miller watched the breakfast crowd, analyzing faces and mannerisms as they went about their day. People watching was kind of a calming mechanism for him. He analyzed patterns of behavior, signs of good or bad days, and tried to predict in his mind how they'd react in certain possible scenarios. It helped keep his mind sharp.

"He's late. Maybe you should call and remind him about our meeting?" Bernard asked, blowing on his chai tea to cool it before taking a mouthful of the caffeinated liquid.

Miller pulled out his phone, and punched in Jackson's number. Three rings and then straight to voicemail. He tried again. Same result. Then he called the WQX assignment desk and asked for Jackson. The woman who answered the phone said that Jackson didn't report for work this morning, and hadn't called in sick.

Miller felt a sudden wave of dread. He immediately called ASAC Daniel Brown.

"Brown."

"Hey, Aaron and I were supposed to meet Thomas Jackson this morning, and he missed our meeting time. Then I called the station, and they said he didn't come in this morning and didn't call in," Miller said. "Frankly, I'm worried."

"I'll text you his home address. Go do a welfare check and let me know. I'll also have APD meet you over there." Brown disconnected the line.

Miller finished his coffee in a gulp. "Alright, we're headed to Grant Park. Let's get out of here." He and Bernard fought upstream through the customers and headed out to the parking lot.

***

Dr. James arrived at her Midtown psychiatry office, carrying her purse and her jacket under her arm. She had just dropped her daughter Fiona off at school, and was still smiling after watching the love of her life run into the school building. Oh, how Fiona loved her teacher and all of her friends. She was such a little social butterfly.

"Good morning," she cheerfully said to her staff at the front desk, and several of them either waved hello or said it was good to see her, too. Most of the nurses and support staff in her office had been with her for years, and they worked really well together. It meant a lot to her to work in an environment that was inclusive and supportive.

She grabbed her mail out of a bin at the nurses' station, and proceeded to walk the hallways to her interior main office. Her routine in the morning was to open and read her mail, check any emails that her nurses had not responded to, and then look through any folders of patients she had coming in that day. She tried to do all of this in the hour or so before her first scheduled appointment time. She took great pride in the fact she meticulously stuck to a schedule, trying her best to hit every appointment time as close to spot on as she could. She was such a creature of habit.

Her patients were very important to her. All of them.

Her cellphone rang, breaking the silence of her morning routine. It was a blocked number. She did not answer it, but instead tossed her phone on the desk, and went back to what she was doing.

An incoming text message buzzed her phone. She opened the message, and saw it was a picture from her home this morning, showing Fiona eating the breakfast she made for her. A puzzled look crossed her face as she tried to figure out where it came from.

Another message chimed in. It was a picture of Fiona as she ran into school this morning. She was beginning to worry.

A third message arrived. It was a picture through the window of Fiona sitting in class. A text message accompanied the picture.

Answer this phone as soon as it rings again, or the next picture will be of your beautiful daughter in a less than favorable condition. No cops. No help. We will know.

Dr. James freaked completely out almost immediately. Fiona was her world, and she had no idea why this was happening. Her mind raced, and her breath was shallow and ragged. Tears began to well up in her eyes.

Not her daughter. She has nothing to do with whatever these people want.

The phone rang again, and she quickly answered with a worried voice. "Who are you and what do you want?"

An electronic vocal changer obscured the caller's voice. "Help us, and your daughter will live to see another day."

"Leave her alone! She has nothing to do with...whatever this is. I'll do whatever you want, just *leave her alone*." Her voice trembled as she tried to keep her composure. Hell hath no fury like a mother trying to protect her children.

"Meet in Piedmont Park in one hour," the electronic voice demanded. "There is a green bench overlooking the lake. Bring everything you have on Quinn Campbell. Her file, any notes you took, everything. Involve the cops, and your daughter won't show up for school tomorrow. Remember, we have eyes everywhere, and we'll know if you do anything stupid." The call disconnected.

She dropped the phone on her desk, and immediately broke down in tears, gasping for air. Then a thought crossed her mind—this *has* to be connected to the reporter's case. Ms. Campbell harbored some real entrenched fear about her attackers, and they must know she told her everything. Her heart was pounding out of her chest, and she continued to gulp for air. She considered calling the school to warn them, but thought better of it. Maybe if she cooperated with these people, and gave them what they wanted, maybe everything would be fine.

She was breaking doctor/patient confidentiality by even thinking of handing over Ms. Campbell's file, but what was more important? Protecting her oath to do no harm, or protecting the little girl who was her whole universe? Who depended on her for everything? Dr. James didn't care really what happened to her, but she had to protect Fiona at all costs. It's what any mother would do, right?

She walked over to her file cabinet and pulled out Ms. Campbell's folder. She then walked back over to her desk and put a flash drive into a USB port of her computer. She quickly copied Campbell's folder from her desktop and saved it onto the drive. She ejected it from her computer and put the flash drive into a manila envelope along with a note that said, "For your records. By the way, you were right to be afraid. EAJ." She quickly scribbled WQX and ATTN: Quinn Campbell on the envelope, and then sealed it shut. She put Campbell's file folder into her messenger bag, and walked out of her office and over to the nurses' station.

"Hey, Diana, can you do me a favor? Can you please put WQX's address on this envelope and courier it there ASAP? Do it quickly and quietly, please. I have to step out for a little bit this morning, so can you also please cancel my calendar appointments for the day?"

The charge nurse looked at the envelope and seemed a little confused, but nodded in acknowledgment.

"I'll let you know when I'm on my way back. Thanks, Diana."

She smiled weakly at the charge nurse, and turned to walk out of the office. She kept her head on a swivel, looking for anyone who might fit the description of the men Ms. Campbell described. Seeing no one, she quickly climbed into her car, and headed to Piedmont Park.

She'd do anything to protect Fiona, even if it meant exchanging her life for that of her daughter's.

***

Miller and Bernard arrived at Thomas Jackson's home in Grant Park, and Atlanta PD beat them there. The two agents flashed badges and credentials to the patrol officer enforcing the perimeter, and walked up the front door of the home. Miller noticed Mr. Jackson's Jeep still in the driveway.

Miller walked up to a plain-clothed APD detective. "Detective Grayson Miller, working with the GBI, and we're looking for Mr. Thomas Jackson. What do we have?"

"We have signs of a struggle in the living room, and some blood on the carpet behind the couch." Miller noticed CSI techs working all around the scene, collecting any evidence that might be found.

"Any signs of forced entry?" Bernard asked.

"Not that we can tell. There was an open window in one of the bedrooms. The perps could have climbed in through there. When we arrived, the front door was closed and deadbolted, so there must have been a secondary point of egress."

"Make sure to dust that window for prints," Miller said to one of the techs. "Detective, what about the back door in the kitchen?"

The plain clothes detective looked at his notes. "The back door was closed but not locked. When we got here, we found a half-eaten pizza left on the counter and an almost full bottle of beer on the living room coffee table. Someone must have interrupted his meal."

"Have you started canvassing the neighborhood yet?" Miller asked the detective.

"Not my first rodeo," he replied. "But yes, our officers have started going door to door, talking with neighbors and checking for doorbell camera footage. So far, they haven't found anything yet, to my knowledge."

Car in driveway. Back door not locked. Signs of a struggle. Miller's mind was on overload.

"Thanks. Aaron, walk with me." The two men walked outside through the police officers on scene, and over to their car.

"Grayson, this can't be a coincidence." Bernard said. "I'll bet my life Custer went after Jackson to get at Quinn."

"Abso-freakin-lutely," Miller agreed. "I bet they are either pumping him for information as we speak, or will try and use him to lure Campbell out into the open. To them, Jackson is either a means to an end, or just a loose end that needs tying up. Either way, I don't think this ends well for him."

"I'll phone it in. Maybe our techs can pull any additional CCTV cameras in the area, or work with APD to figure out what happened. The sooner we find Jackson, the better it is for him *and* for us." The two men climbed in the car, and headed back towards the main GBI office in Decatur.

While Bernard drove, Miller pulled out his phone and punched in a number. It rang twice before someone picked up.

"WQX newsroom." An assignment editor answered the newsroom phone, seemingly distracted and disinterested.

"Can I speak to Bill Tucker, please?"

"He's unavailable at the moment. May I ask who's calling?"

"I'm Detective Grayson Miller, working on a GBI task force looking into the Quinn Campbell case. I really need to speak with him ASAP. Please just tell him I'm on the phone."

"OK, give me a second." The assignment editor begrudgingly put Miller on hold, forcing him to listen to recorded WQX headlines. A meteorologist was in the middle of the 5-day forecast when a voice came back on the phone.

"Tucker."

"Mr. Tucker, Detective Grayson Miller with Dahlonega PD. I appreciate you taking my phone call. I was hoping we could meet with you today to go through a couple of new and disturbing developments the task force has uncovered."

"Let me guess, does this have anything to do with my assignment editor not showing up to work today?"

"That's one of the developments, yes. Can we meet later this afternoon?"

"It's not great timing for me, but if it can help get to the bottom of this story and help Ms. Campbell and Mr. Jackson, I'll do what I can. Email me the address, and I'll show up this afternoon." The line goes dead.

Miller looked at his phone, then sat it in the console between them.

"We have so many individual pieces, but nothing substantial to hold them all together. Tucker has to give us some glue to help connect the dots."

Bernard shook his head. "Tucker knows a lot about a lot. Alahna used to talk about him as someone who has forgotten more about journalism and about life than most people know in their lifetimes. He's sharp as hell."

Bernard continued. "We know he hired the bodyguards for Campbell, and we know he's got contacts inside that group. He's definitely involved, and may have pieces of hidden information. I need something to try and get back on Brown's good side."

"Look, Aaron. You will have a chance to make it right with him. And Quinn trusts you completely. If I've figured out anything about Ms. Campbell it's that she's tenaciously loyal to trusted people inside her circle, and I know she'll vouch for you. Help me work this case, do things the right way, and you'll get back to where you want to be. I'm sure of it."

Bernard grabbed onto the steering wheel even tighter. "I hope so. I just don't want to lose control again, especially if we actually find the men responsible for my sister's death. I need Quinn to help keep me balanced."

"This is one of the reasons you're working this case. Let's meet with Tucker and just go from there."

As their car pulled into the GBI parking lot, Bernard's phone rang. It was his mother. "Hey, Mama, I'm in the middle of a work thing, can I call you right back?"

He immediately heard his mother crying on her end of the phone. "Aaron, it's Ian. Police found his car after an accident last night, and it burned up in a fire."

Aaron couldn't believe what she just told him. "Wait...what? What are you talking about, Mama? Is he OK?"

"Thankfully, the police said they don't believe he was in the car when it went up in flames, but they also haven't found him yet." Mama B was squeezing her words out through loud sobs.

Aaron's mind began to race, unable to truly comprehend what was going on. As Mama B continued to talk into the phone, Aaron's mind whirled, going every which way all at once.

"Son, are you listening to me?" The heightened tone in her voice brought him back. He was still having trouble wrapping his head around the situation, so he needed to get a closer look.

"Don't move, Mama. I'm on my way." Bernard ended the call abruptly, and just sat in the car, motionless, with his mind still struggling to process things.

Rage, fear, and panic crossed Aaron's face all at once. He turned to Miller, angrily whispering the following command through clenched teeth. "Get...the hell...out of this car. *Now*. I've gotta go find my brother."

"Wait, what? Find your brother? What are you talking about?"

A mini mushroom cloud exploded in the center of Aaron's chest. "My brother's missing and my family's under siege, man," Aaron yelled. "I can't be responsible for my actions once I get there, and I don't want to drag you into my family business."

Miller continued to push. "No, let me go with you. You gotta have some backup. Partners stick togeth—"

Aaron cut him off. "Damn it, I said *no*. I cannot lose another sibling, and I will not stand by and let someone or something attack my family. Get the hell out of this car, Miller. If I need help, I will call for it. Promise. *Now let me go*."

Miller saw the emotion all over Aaron's face, and he knew he was not going to convince him otherwise. "Alright, text me the address once you get there. I'll have techs pull all the cameras in the area of the accident, and maybe we will catch a break. You gotta play this safe, man. Remember what you just told me."

Aaron had no intention of playing it safe. As Miller slammed the door shut, he shifted the car into drive and peeled all four tires as he flew out of the parking lot. So much for being under control, and doing things the right way. Sometimes a scene needs to be made.

***

Dr. James sat on the bench overlooking the lake in Piedmont Park, just as she was instructed to do. She had no clue who she was meeting, what they looked like, or what they would do once they arrived, but she brought everything they asked for.

She could—probably would—lose her license. She could lose everything she had spent her entire career building—her practice, her reputation, everything. But she'd rather lose all of that and her livelihood than have her daughter mixed up in all of this. Practices and reputations can be rebuilt, but Fiona was one of a kind.

She was there on time, but several minutes went by with no contact at all. Was she in the right place? Is her daughter still in jeopardy? All of these horrible thoughts began running through her mind. She could hear her heart pounding in her ears.

She jumped sky high when her phone rang, and it was from a blocked caller ID again. She quickly answered.

"Hello? Hello? Where are you? I'm here just like you asked, and I brought everything with me. Please don't hurt my daughter."

The voice on the phone was still electronically altered, as to hide their true identity. "Are you sure you did not call anyone or tell anyone where you were going?"

"Of course not. I did exactly as I was instructed. I promise I did." A lump formed in her throat, and she felt like every nerve ending she had was on fire. "Please, I'll do anything you ask. Just leave my daughter alone."

"Leave the folder on the bench. Do exactly as we ask, and your darling daughter will stay perfectly safe. If you tell anyone, if you involve the cops, or if you mislead us in any way, she will be anything but safe. You have my word."

The call disconnected. Her phone then chimed as a text message came in. She opened it, and a chill ran through her spine. It was a picture of Fiona in bed, just this morning, sleeping. She started crying almost immediately. This was all too much for her to handle.

The text message that accompanied the picture echoed what the man said on the phone call. "Give us everything and she stays safe. Involve anyone else, and we can't guarantee that she—or the people you love—will remain that way."

Her hands trembled as she pulled the folder out of her messenger bag. She left it on the bench as instructed, and she quickly walked out of the park and back to her car. The less she knew about these people, the better.

***

My first story was a major hit. Calls came into the studio from everyone under the sun, trying to get more information about my reporting. Police, neighbors, other stations—you name it, they wanted to talk to me. But I didn't return any of their calls. I let the story marinate in everyone's mind. The more people I have out looking for Custer, the better. Somebody's gonna get lucky, and it better be us.

There is no justice in my thoughts. No peace. No quarter. In my heart, only malice and vengeance exist when it comes to *him*.

My social media post also went viral, and I have several DMs from people in the market looking to connect with me. I even have one random comment from a troll asking if Custer was my new love interest. First of all, gross. Secondly, *not a chance in hell*.

Either way, I love the feeling I get from a blockbuster story, one that leaves the entire city buzzing. I also take back everything I have ever said or believed about the people working in the radio division. Now that I've been on the air with them, it's actually kind of fun, and I don't have to worry about makeup when all I have to do is press the live mic button. I could work in my PJs and no one would be the wiser.

I pull my WQX cell phone out of my pocket and punch in Tommy Jackson's number. Three rings, and then straight to voicemail.

"That's weird," I whisper to myself. "He's never let my call go to voicemail before."

I try again. Nothing. I look at the time, and it's 12:48pm. The noon newscast is over, and the evening editorial meeting starts at 1:30. He's always sitting at the desk right now with one ear on the scanners, one eye on the bank of TVs by the desk, and his phone always in his hand.

I fire off a quick text to his work phone.

LOSER. Answer your phone, dude. QTC

He's probably in the bathroom or something...or somehow indisposed, and can't answer my call. Oh well, his loss.

I tell myself I'll try him again later, and I start searching online again for Custer, hoping I'll get lucky.

***

Custer hung up the phone with the psychiatrist, and sat the voice changer on the ground beside him. He had Beau keeping an eye on the doctor, and he will hopefully bring everything she left back to the Calvary Rock compound.

He sat on a wooden crate in front of two of the metal holding cages on his north Georgia mountain property staring at something...or someone...very intently. There were two Black men lying curled up and unconscious on the floor of each cage, both facing away from him. Custer held two drivers' licenses in his hands, both with familiar faces and names—Thomas Jackson and Ian Bernard.

Custer picked up the supercharged cattle prod that was leaning up against the wall, and continued to stare down at the men. Clyde roughed Jackson up a little too much last night when he brought him up the mountain, and Bernard was pretty banged up after Beau crashed into his vehicle. With his injuries, Bernard must have been crushed in the car after Beau rammed him. To cover his tracks, Beau torched the man's car after he pulled him out.

Between having the psychiatrist's information and now holding onto two people the reporter cared about, maybe—just maybe—this will bring her out into the open. The reporter's been heard on the radio, mentioning his name and his connection to the death of the woman up on Springer Mountain. It's been really bad for business, and he needs it to stop. *Now*.

Even the reporter's social media posts about him have started people talking. Too many people know too many things. This is not good. Not good at all. Maybe holding two of her chess pieces hostage will get her to stop her on-air onslaught and return to them so that he can finish the job started so many days ago.

Custer pulled down his balaclava, reached the cattle prod through the holes of Jackson's cage, and zapped the man's lower back. The jolt of electricity forced him to wake up, and slam involuntarily against the back wall of the cage.

"Wh...what...what the hell, man?" Jackson was disoriented from being unconscious and from the electrical jolt, his face covered in blood from Clyde's blow to his head last night. His breaths were rapidly going in and out.

"There you are," Custer said. "Welcome back to the land of the living, at least for now."

Jackson looked around briefly, trying to quickly shake the cobwebs from his foggy mind. He saw cages all around him, and another man lying next to him in a neighboring cage. He was having trouble putting two and two together, and could barely even focus on the old man in front of him. His head was pounding, his ears were ringing, and he rubbed the back of his head with a wince.

"Where...where am I?"

"Wrong question, boy. 'Cause you know I ain't gonna tell you that."

A potential concussion wasn't making conversation very easy for him. "Oh, OK...how about who are you?"

"Again, wrong question, boy. But I think you're smart enough to figure it out."

"I have no idea what you're talking about. Wait—" Tommy's head turned to the side. Slowly, the look on Jackson's face showed he was beginning to put it all together.

Custer noticed it. "There it is, boy. Now you're starting to get it. You ready to answer your own question?"

"Wait a minute—you have got to be Custer, the Mountain Mangler." Bile immediately filled his mouth, and his heart rate skyrocketed. He tried to memorize his surroundings, and everything he could about the psychotic mountain man in front of him, all while horror flooded through him.

"Winner winner possum dinner. And now you're gonna tell me everything you know about your reporter friend."

"I don't know what you're talking about. I just—"

Custer shoved the cattle prod back into the cage and gave Jackson another dose of electricity, causing his skin to sizzle at the point of contact. He screamed, closed his eyes, and curled away from the implement of torture. The intensity of the pain forced every thought out of his brain except for one—protect Quinn at all costs.

The old man continued his interrogation.

"Again, boy...that's the wrong answer. I will tell you this, though. There are two of you here." Jackson turned to look at the other unconscious man, whom he did not recognize at first. "The first one to help me will not be the first one to die. That choice is up to you."

CHAPTER 15

Aaron Bernard arrived at the scene of his brother's vehicle crash, and noticed Atlanta PD and firefighters working all around the charred wreckage of Ian's car, which was crushed up against a retaining wall. Aaron threw the car in park, and jumped out of the vehicle. He flashed his GBI credentials, and walked over to the senior officer working the scene.

"Excuse me, I'm Case Agent Aaron Bernard with the GBI, and this is my brother's car. What can you tell me?"

"At first glance, it looked like a single car MVA, and then the car caught fire."

"At first glance?"

"Come here and take a look at this."

The officer walked around to the rear of the burned-out vehicle, and kneeled down at the rear bumper. "Did this car have any damage to the rear that you know of?"

"Not a chance. My brother babied this car. Besides, I just had dinner with him at our mom's house, and I would have noticed any damage then."

"Then how do you explain this?" Aaron noticed what appeared to be red paint transfer on the right rear bumper, which was caved in along with the rear quarter panel.

"Can you lend me an evidence bag?" Aaron popped out a ball point pen, and flaked some of the red paint into the small evidence bag that APD gave him. "I'll take this back and let our GBI techs run it through the system. Have you found any working cameras in the area? Any witnesses?"

"No working cameras that we've found, and no one was in this area at the time of the crash."

"Better question—is there any sign of what happened to my brother?"

"Not really. The car was doused, and then set on fire. Fire investigators found evidence of the accelerant towards the front of the vehicle, where they think the flashpoint originated. We did find blood on the ground by the driver-side door. If someone got out of this wreck, they would have had to be dragged out. Both doors were jammed shut after the crash, and aren't currently operational."

Aaron went over to one of the CSI techs, and started rummaging through one of their kits. He found a blood collection swab, a test tube, and an evidence bag. The tech just stared at him as he eventually found what he needed.

He rubbed the swab on what blood was left on the ground, slid the swab into the tube, and put the tube in the collection bag.

He stood up, and looked through the smoldering interior of the car, hoping to find something that the other folks missed. "Was anything else recovered from inside the car?"

"Not a lot, no. We did find the charred remnants of a phone in the floorboard on the passenger side."

"*Where the hell is he*?" Aaron muttered to himself. He slowly looked around the area, trying to figure out anything that could help him. Nothing immediately jumped out at him.

First Tommy Jackson, and now Ian. He texted the address of the accident to Detective Miller so that he could help put the entire weight of the GBI behind finding both Ian and Tommy. He had to still hold out hope they'd find his brother in time, and God help those who took him. The assholes behind this were getting sloppy, and they will eventually make a mistake. And when they do, he vowed to be there to put them away.

Not behind bars. Not in the throes of the justice system. No deals will be offered. Instead of putting them in jail, he thought more about putting them six feet in the ground.

***

"Hey guys, Agent Bernard just sent me this address, the one where his brother's car was wrecked and torched, with no sign of his whereabouts," Grayson Miller told the investigative team working out of the GBI field office. "We have to help him see what we can find out."

ASAC Daniel Brown stood up and walked toward a row of monitors on the wall. "Alright, people, eyes up. Bernard has just lost his second family member in 3 weeks, and we will not let that stand. Work the address, find me anything in that area that can help us figure out what in the hell happened at that crash scene. What model of the car was it again?"

"A 2024 Audi Q5, sir," an analyst replied.

"Did that model of car have any kind of cameras on board?" Detective Grayson Miller asked.

The analyst clicked several keys on her workstation. "Nothing standard, sir. They do make aftermarket front and rear universal traffic recorders, but there was no evidence that Bernard ever purchased them or installed them on his car."

"Of course he didn't. That would make our job too easy." Brown pointed to two senior members of the task force. "You two, load up and go out there to help Agent Bernard. Take whatever tech you need, and help police visit every single house, business, or establishment that just might have a doorbell camera, security camera, or eyeballs on that situation." The two agents packed up their equipment and headed out.

"Miller, you said that the WQX news director was on his way here?"

"Yes, sir. I could use you in that meeting since Bernard's otherwise occupied."

"Consider it done. I think he knows quite a bit, so I'm actually looking forward to talking with him."

***

Later that afternoon, William Tucker entered the GBI lobby, and talked to the desk attendant. "Um, hello. I'm here to see Detective Grayson Miller with the Campbell investigative team."

The attendant asked Tucker to sign in, gave him a visitor's badge, and then asked him to have a seat in the lobby while he called up to ASAC Brown's office. "They'll be right down to get you, sir."

A few minutes later, a young analyst came down to get Tucker, and escorted him up to the investigative division. They walked into the elevator as the analyst punched in the floor number. The elevator door opened, and the analyst walked Tucker over to an interview room to wait for Detective Miller.

The room door opened, with Miller and Brown both walking in. Miller extended his hand to Tucker, and Wild Bill shook it confidently. "Mr. Tucker, thank you so much for coming out on such short notice. I think you know ASAC Brown?" Brown also shook Tucker's hand, and smiled at him as they sat down at the table.

"Mr. Tucker, I'm not going to sugarcoat this," Brown said. "We need your help, and we need information I know you have."

"What is it that you think I know?"

"I know you used your family connections and station resources to hire the paramilitary group Peachtree Technology Corporation to protect Quinn Campbell and keep her safe, correct?"

"Campbell is currently under contract with WQX and PTC was merely protecting our investment. I asked my son-in-law to facilitate that protection."

"Investment? That seems kind of impersonal." Miller added.

"Think what you want about my vocabulary choice, but Campbell is a great journalist and an even better kid who has gone through hell and back. She is now once again able to use our unlimited resources and her killer instinct to work this story because I made that judgment call. I'm glad I did, and I'd do it again in a heartbeat."

Brown looked over at Miller and gave him a *take it easy* look.

Miller looked at Brown with a slight nod, before turning back to Tucker. "Sir, we have information leading us to believe that Tommy Jackson was abducted."

Tucker leaned forward in his chair, with a fearful look on his face. "Abducted? When? How?"

Brown told Tucker about the believed abductions of Tommy Jackson and Ian Bernard, and added that they believe the people who took them are trying to use them to find Campbell.

"Holy shit. Does that mean you believe that this Custer person, or people involved with him, are responsible for all of this?" Tucker had a horrified look on his face.

"Campbell is at the center of this investigation, and I just want to make sure the people involved don't get to her first." Miller added.

"Mr. Tucker, can you share Ms. Campbell's new number with us? We'd love to bring her in on the investigation...as well as her bodyguards." Brown asked.

"One of her security detail is dead. Died in the Virginia Highland shooting, according to Col. Anderson, her main bodyguard." Tucker noticed the surprised reaction from both men. "The colonel was able to obviously keep Campbell alive, but it was a mess of a situation. By the way, here are Col. Anderson and Ms. Campbell's numbers."

Tucker wrote the numbers down on a page in Miller's notebook that he brought into the interview room.

"Mr. Tucker, we appreciate your assistance." Brown handed Tucker his business card. "Please get ahold of me if you hear anything. One of our agents will see you out." Brown and Miller both shook Tucker's hand as all three men stood up.

Time was running out for Jackson and Bernard. Bringing Quinn and Anderson into the fold was a risk, but a necessary one. Anderson has tactical experience against Custer's men, so the GBI investigative team desperately needs their help. With Quinn, maybe they can harness her tenacity, and use it to their benefit.

***

Col. Brian Anderson sat in the WQX parking lot, facing the station's only entrance. Every vehicle that came onto the property was stopped by the gate guard, and Anderson was parked where he could see every interaction—coming and going.

There's a picnic table in a cute little courtyard where he sat, working at his laptop, knowing that Ms. Campbell was inside the building doing her thing. He was already pissed at her social media post, and he could not wait to really and truly call her on the carpet for putting herself in danger unnecessarily. On the flipside, he was slightly impressed by her attempt to shine a spotlight on Custer, but the mentor mentality in him didn't like seeing her put herself in a precarious position, one primed for retaliation.

His phone rang. Caller ID said it was Mr. Tucker.

"Anderson. What can I do for you, Mr. Tucker?"

"Colonel, I'm just leaving the GBI field office, and they are in desperate need for your services, and those of Ms. Campbell."

"You know we're light years ahead of them," Anderson quipped. "Why should I do their work for them."

"That's exactly what they need, Colonel." Tucker told him that two of Quinn's circle—Tommy and Ian—had been abducted, and the GBI thought that Custer was behind it. Anderson mentally cursed at this development, because he literally just told Quinn this was a possibility.

It turned out Custer and his men were just as diabolical as he had originally feared. Quinn poked the bear, and the bear just poked back.

"Alright, sir. Send me a contact number, and I'll set up a meet." Anderson closed his phone and slammed it on the picnic table.

"Son of a bitch, I told her this was gonna happen. I knew it," he mumbled to himself. He picked his phone back up, and dialed his PTC squad.

"Everything OK, boss?" the squad member asked.

"Look, the GBI is gonna reach out to me, and I'm gonna take Campbell in to help them with their investigation. I just found out two members of Campbell's inner circle were recently abducted—Thomas Jackson and Ian Bernard. This crew is starting to escalate, so we need to be vigilant and act quickly. Remember, Sgt. Barton was one of us. We need to find the people responsible for his death, and we still have to make them pay for it."

Anderson was still fuming about the picture that one of his employees found on the apartment crasher. The red X on Barton's face was callous, and made him want to put a red X on every single man involved with Custer—including the old man himself. He believed Barton died on his watch, making it his responsibility—one he does not take lightly.

"Sure thing, boss. I'll call my guy in the Bureau and get what I can. At the very least, I'll get the location of the two abductions."

"Good," Anderson said. "We also need to do a deep dive into that security card for Calvary Rock General Contractors found on the apartment dead guy. Grab the team and start digging into this construction business, and look for any connection between it and Custer. It could be either his first, middle, or last name. Cast a very wide net." Anderson had an irritated edge to his voice. "Rip the company to absolute shreds...get me tax information, land contracts, employment history, everything. When you get something, let me know, but send Sergeant Allen and Corporal Taylor to check out the construction business. Let me know if you find *anything* that connects back to this mess in any way."

He disconnected the call, then accessed a secure PTC website, pulling up everything they had uncovered to this point about Custer and his goons. He looked at the PTC vision board—a wall of pictures and notes from their investigation. Three pictures had red Xs on them, and a fourth unidentified man had an X, too.

One was the man their sniper killed leaving Quinn's apartment, and he matched the description of the janitor turned assassin that tried to kill her in the hospital, and who left a nurse with permanent nerve damage. His fingerprints were not in the system, and he had no identifying marks or information on him.

Then there was the gunman Sgt. Barton shot at and that Anderson dropped outside the first safe house. They didn't have a picture of him, but DNA from blood collected at the scene showed a familial relationship to the gunman killed at Ms. Campbell's apartment, and that he was more than likely a male.

Pictures of two other men—the ones killed in their truck while casing Quinn's apartment—had been identified because their fingerprints were in CODIS. Both men pulled a stint in the DeKalb County Jail, but were there at different times and had no apparent connection to each other. One of them was from Macon, and the other was from Augusta. The truck they were in at the time was stolen, so that was also a dead end.

The Company looked into both men, and found nothing of interest. No large financial deposits, no improper tax documents, nothing that led back to Custer.

All of this disconnection made Anderson uneasy. "They're hiding in plain sight, damn it. What are we not seeing?" he muttered underneath his breath.

Anderson felt so uneasy about not being able to see a pattern. Too many variables, and too wide a search area. He might have to start breaking some rules if he was going to figure any of this out.

But priority number one was keeping the reporter safe, from Custer *and* from herself.

***

"Thanks for the information. Keep making yourself useful, and we'll keep up our end of the bargain, meaning your family will stay safe."

Custer hung up the phone, sliding it back in his front pocket. He looked up at a screen on the wall, showing a camera feed of both men in their respective cages. The one from the car wreck's health was not great, suffering some serious injuries after Beau crunched his car.

He looked over at Beau and Clyde sitting at the table in the warehouse office.

"Our GBI guy just told me that some investigative team is trying to find information about us," Custer said. "He also said that the reporter fed them a ton of information—just like I feared she would. They are also working both crime scenes you boys left."

"Nothin' at those that can tie back to us, Pa. No one saw me leave that house in Grant Park." Clyde said, confidently.

"And I torched the hell out of that lawyer's car," Beau said. "I picked that intersection special to wreck him 'cause there were no houses or cameras that I could see. It was a blind spot."

Custer realized now was a great time for someone to start listening to him and to remain in the shadows. On the table was the file the psychiatrist left for Beau, with apparently everything she knew about the reporter. Custer flipped through it casually.

"This doctor's gonna be a problem, because she knows way too much." Custer slammed the folder shut. "We need to deal with her like we would any other loose end."

"Pa, I ain't gonna kill a kid." Beau shook his head no.

"Who said anything about killin' the kid?" Custer asked. "I'm talking about dealing with her. If others get in the way at the same time, then they're just collateral damage." Custer looked back over at the monitor. Both captive men were either sleeping or unconscious due to the damage from the cattle prod or the electrified cage bars. Custer had a little too much fun earlier.

"We need to go ahead and put her down." Custer looked at both of them. "One of you will have to do it."

What he'd give to have Leland or Ezekiel back. Lee was the most trustworthy of the bunch, and Zeke was the best enforcer he had. They were both pretty damn good sons. He had become convinced those Peachtree assholes either captured or killed Zeke. Either way, he's off the board.

"Tomorrow, I am gonna show both of our guests just how serious I am. One will talk, and the other will beg for us to put him out of his misery. Either way, it'll be a good day, thank the Lord."

Custer stood up, and walked over to a switch panel on the wall. He pulled the lever down, and the familiar hum of electricity buzzed to life. No one would be able to escape this time.

***

I pick up my phone and call Anderson, knowing he's sitting outside somewhere. "Hey, Tweedle Dumb, my shift is over. Wanna bring the car around?" I have levity in my voice, acting playfully like Anderson is actually just my chauffeur instead of my shield.

"Look, kid, I got some bad news to tell ya. Meet me in the parking lot ASAP."

"What? You can't just say that and then—" Anderson hangs up the phone mid-sentence. Damn, I hate it when he does that.

I shout over to Don, telling him my four o'clock story is recorded as-live, and is saved in the rundown. I literally run upstairs and into the newsroom, noticing Tommy isn't at the desk. He's *always* at the desk. Something feels wrong.

"Hey, where's T-Jack?" I ask the rando editor working the desk.

"He didn't come into work today, so I'm stuck covering for him."

Tommy *never* misses work, and now I'm legit worried. I break out into a dead run towards the back door, or as close to a run as my still-healing body lets me, knowing Anderson is waiting for me. My sense of dread is becoming tangible, and my heart is in my throat.

I blow through the back door, slamming it wide open and almost off its hinges, and I see Anderson and the car in the handicapped spot nearest to the door. I reach the car door, breathing way harder than I should be.

"What's happened? Where's Tommy?"

"Get in. I'll fill you in on the way." I climb into the passenger seat, and Anderson throws the car into drive.

"Spill it, Colonel. What do you know?"

"GBI Assistant Special Agent in Charge Daniel Brown just called me, and we're gonna go help him with the investigation."

"Where's Tommy? What has happened? I *know* you know something."

Anderson tells me that the GBI investigative team believes Custer or his men abducted Tommy and also Ian Bernard last night, and they believe Custer is trying to use them as bait to lure me back to him. Anxiety fills my soul, but it is quickly replaced by a toxic combination of fear and white-hot rage. I suddenly remember the gun in my purse, and I have visions of unloading the entire magazine into Custer. He cannot get away with this. *He simply cannot.*

And Tommy must survive. He *has* to survive. There is so much I need to tell him, stuff that is long overdue.

CHAPTER 16

Sergeant P.J. Allen and Corporal Jake Taylor arrived at the address that PTC techs uncovered from the security card found on the man killed outside of the reporter's apartment. The building appeared to be a normal construction company location, with trailers and equipment spread around areas of red clay and houses in various states of construction. With it being a Saturday, not a whole lot was going on. At first glance, nothing really looked out of place.

"Well, let's go check out the main construction office," Sgt. Allen said. "If you see anything weird, or that connects to Sgt. Barton or the reporter, take pictures of it and send it back to Col. Anderson."

"Roger that," Cpl. Taylor said. The two men climbed out of the SUV, and walked toward the construction office. Taylor and Allen were both dressed in all black, wearing Kevlar vests and PTC windbreakers. They scanned the landscape of the business, and nothing seemed out of the ordinary.

They walked up the stairs onto the porch outside the office trailer's front door. Three knocks, no answer. Allen leaned in to listen for any movement inside.

"Keep an eye out," Taylor said, as he pulled lockpicking tools out of his pocket. As Allen stayed on lookout, Taylor slid the tools into the door's lock. After a few seconds, the door unlocked.

"Like taking candy from a baby." Taylor packed up his tools, and stood in front of the door. He grabbed the doorknob and pulled the door open.

***

Custer's phone buzzed, telling him someone just opened the door of the Calvary Rock construction office. "What the hell?" Custer muttered. "No one's supposed to be at work today."

On his phone, he pulled up a live camera feed from inside the trailer. He saw two unfamiliar men walking around in the main office. A low growl emanated from his throat.

He closed the camera app, and punched in Clyde's phone number.

"Hey, Pa...what's up?"

"How close are you to the office?"

"Five, ten minutes, why?"

"Someone just broke in. I need you to get over there and handle them. *Now.*"

"On my way, Pa."

He disconnected the call and reopened the camera app, continuing to watch the trespassers snoop around the office.

***

Allen and Taylor continued looking through the office, trying to find any connection to Barton, Campbell, or the man they killed outside Campbell's apartment. They both wore gloves, and they were methodical, going through every drawer, every shelf, every piece of paper, and every nook and cranny they could find.

Taylor found a group picture on a shelf, from what appeared to be a groundbreaking of sorts. He pulled out his phone and scrolled through his image gallery. He pulled up the dead man's picture from the apartment shootout, and compared it to the people in the photo.

"Hey, Sarge, check this out." Taylor showed Allen the picture, as well as the dead man's photo. "Is that the guy we killed? The second one from the left?"

Allen looked at both pictures, and nodded his head. "Sure looks like it to me. Take a photo of it and send it to Col. Anderson."

Taylor snapped a quick shot of the group photo, and gently sat the original back on the shelf where he found it. He fired the picture off in a text to Anderson.

Allen looked through various documents on the desk, combing through unopened envelopes, blueprints, and other construction-related papers. One name kept popping up over and over.

"Found anything?" Taylor asked.

"Yeah, the name Elijah Custer is everywhere around here—envelopes, documents, everything." Allen threw some random papers down on the desk. "This must be the base of his business operation."

The sound of an approaching vehicle crunching gravel caught Taylor's ear, and he walked over to the front window of the construction trailer.

"Damn it, somebody just pulled up. Reset everything, and *hurry*." Both Allen and Taylor worked quickly to put the office back the way they found it before anyone came in.

***

Clyde climbed out of his truck, and stealthily walked over to the Escalade in the Calvary Rock parking lot. He'd seen one decked out like this before, when they were tracking the reporter.

"Damn it to hell, it's those Peachtree goons," Clyde muttered to himself.

He walked back to his truck and opened the rear door of the cab. A rifle case sat on the back seat. He opened it, and quickly began assembling the AR-15. He kept one eye on the front door of the trailer, making sure no one came out before he was ready, as he clicked the pieces of the rifle together. The last piece—the scope—locked into its channel position with a satisfying click.

He quietly closed the truck door, and climbed into the truck bed. That way he'd have an elevated position for when whoever was in the trailer came out.

***

Taylor went back to the window, looking out at the older Ford pickup in the lot. He watched for a few minutes, and saw no movement at all.

"Where in the hell did the driver go—"

At that moment, multiple gunshots erupted from the pickup truck, striking Cpl. Taylor in the chest, knocking him completely across the trailer. Sgt. Allen ducked away from the window and checked in on Taylor. "Hey, man...you good?"

Taylor groaned loudly and tried to catch his breath. "Damn it. It hurts like hell, but I'm OK. It hit my vest." Allen was still knelt down beside him.

A cacophony of bullets ripped through the trailer, from ceiling to floor, as the gunman tried to maximize the chance of hitting his target. However, all bullets whizzed past without finding purchase.

"We are pinned down here, Sarge, and there's only one way out." Taylor said, as he pulled one of the three bullets out of his vest. "What's our play?"

"I need you to lay down some cover fire so I can get out of this trailer and try and flank the shooter." Allen nodded his head towards the pickup truck. "On the count of three."

Allen grabbed the doorknob and looked at Taylor. *One*. Allen and Taylor both pulled out their PTC-issued Glock 9mm handguns. *Two*. They both chambered a round. *Three*.

Taylor leaned up in the window and sprayed the truck with gunfire, while Allen twisted the doorknob and opened the office door.

***

Clyde ducked down in the truck's bed as one of the men in the trailer returned fire. The spray of the bullets made Clyde think the shooter didn't know exactly where he was. Clyde knew he hit one of them, but he must have been wearing body armor. Next time, he would aim for the head.

He leaned back up over the truck bed, and noticed the door to the office was now open. *Shit*.

Clyde quickly slid out of the bed, and leaned down behind the truck, with the vehicle providing decent cover. He looked underneath the truck, trying to see if feet were running his way. There weren't many options for cover between the vehicles and the trailer, so maybe he would get lucky.

More spray gunfire from the trailer hit the truck, shattering the passenger side and rear windows. Clyde moved to below the tailgate near the back of the truck, and he saw someone kneeled down in a cover position just to the right of the office door. It appeared the man was still scanning the area, but did not know Clyde's exact location.

Clyde rested the AR-15 on the rear bumper of the truck to steady his shot. He quickly looked through the scope to line up his target, and squeezed off three shots in rapid succession. He smiled when he saw the man fall to the ground.

***

Cpl. Taylor still rubbed his chest through the Kevlar, grimacing at the pain but thankful the bullets didn't hit him about four inches higher. He continued spraying the truck with cover fire, ejecting an empty magazine and replacing it with a full one. He saw Allen exit the building, jump off the porch, and hide on the far end of the four side, which was to the right of the front entry door on the number one side. His military training labeled the side with the front entry door the one side, and then counted clockwise left to right around the structure—two side to the left, three side directly behind, and four side to the right of the front door. He laid down more cover fire, blowing out some of the truck's windows. He felt like the gunman was either in the truck bed or behind it on the ground.

Then he heard return gunfire, but the trailer wasn't the target. He heard a loud groan from outside the trailer.

"Sarge!" Taylor popped a third magazine into the magwell of his 9mm and angrily peppered the truck from grill to tailgate. He had to get out of this trailer, and check on Sgt. Allen, because he was a sitting duck in there.

He headed over to the door, which was standing wide open, and tried to get a look at the truck. He saw a glimpse of what appeared to be a rifle barrel peeking out from behind the tailgate. Taylor moved out onto the porch, focusing his gunfire at the right rear quarter panel of the truck. He jumped off the porch, grabbing at Sgt. Allen, and pulling him further out of sight. Taylor noticed the bullets missed Allen's Kevlar vest, and went into his neck and upper right shoulder. Blood was everywhere, and Taylor quickly tried to find a pulse through all the blood. Nothing. Allen was gone.

"*Damn it!*" Taylor growled.

Taylor pulled three magazines from Allen's waistband, and put them into his. He grabbed Allen's service weapon, put his back up against the siding of the trailer, and blew out a quick sigh. There was no way he was going to let them get away with this. He pulled out his phone, and attempted to send a message to Anderson.

Allen DOA. Pinned down by unknown gunman. Need help and/or exfil ASAP.

He loosely slid his phone into a side pocket on his pants, and focused on the problem at hand. Taylor raised both guns, closed his eyes, and knew he was about to jump out of the frying pan and into the fire. Taylor counted to three in his head, and then jumped out from beside the trailer. He got two shots off before a bullet hit him in the face, exploding out of the back of his head.

The force of the shot dropped him to his knees, and then he fell face first into the dirt beside the porch. His phone fell out of his pants pocket onto the ground, and a little red exclamation mark was beside the text to Anderson. A message accompanied the punctuation:

Send failed. Click to retry.

***

Clyde walked over to the two men on the ground, slinging his AR-15 across his back. He kneeled down beside them, smiling like a big game hunter that had just bagged two massive elk that were soon going to be mounted on his wall.

He saw one of their phones on the ground, and he picked it up. The screen was locked, so he pulled the glove off of the man's hand and placed his thumb on the screen. The phone chimed to life, showing the last text he tried to send.

"Must be their boss," Clyde muttered to himself. He put the phone into his pocket, and began cleaning up the scene, picking up shell casings and other signs that there'd been a shootout.

He took out his phone and called Beau.

"What's up, bro?" Beau answered.

"I need some help at the office. Get here double quick."

"On my way. I'll be there in ten." The call disconnected.

Clyde walked over to the Escalade, and opened the passenger side door. He started rummaging through the vehicle, trying to find anything of value. Two shotguns, an MK22 sniper rifle in a case in the backseat, along with various handguns and ammo in a canvas duffel bag. It's almost as good as Christmas. He also opened the glove compartment, hoping for registration or something, but it wasn't going to be that easy. Only thing in the glovebox was a silver .357 Magnum revolver. Must have been a backup weapon. He slid the revolver into the waistband of his jeans.

He moved all the weaponry into his truck, sweeping all the broken glass into the floorboard first. They needed to get rid of the two bodies and the Escalade, to move them very far away from the family business. They could probably drop the bodies down two holes at their latest construction site, but the vehicle needs to be left in a parking lot somewhere outside of Atlanta, far off the mountain.

He decided to call Custer, just to get his thoughts on the matter.

"I don't see anyone in the office anymore," Custer answered, referring to the video camera security app on his phone. "I assume since you're calling me that the situation's handled?"

"Yes, Pa. Both men have been dealt with. They were two of those Peachtree idiots, snooping around our stuff. I grabbed up one of their phones, and it looks like they only sent one picture to an unlisted number with no response.

Clyde told Custer it was the group picture from the groundbreaking ceremony of their first subdivision, with all family members present including his late wife Emma, a couple of local county commissioners, and the head of the local board of realtors.

"Damn it. Now they're one step closer to knowing who we are." Custer grumbled. "What are you gonna do with them?"

"I was gonna take 'em over to Lot Twenty-Four and drop 'em in a couple of pre-augured holes." Clyde responded. "What do you want me to do with their vehicle? I already grabbed everything of value out of it."

"Drive it down off the mountain and burn it somewhere very far away." Custer paused for a second. "Make damn sure you leave nothing behind to identify us. It's only gonna take those Peachtree jerks a short time before they pull the vehicle's GPS and try to connect the dots. We need to give ourselves as much time as possible to deal with this."

"Will do, Pa. Beau's on his way to help me out, but this will be done today."

Custer hung up, and Clyde slid the phone back in his pocket. He walked over to the two dead men, and started rummaging through their clothes. He found the other man's phone, and the keys to their vehicle. He opened the crawl space door under the trailer, grabbed two full gas cans, and put them in the back of the Escalade.

***

Sleeping on a concrete floor for several days had begun to take its toll on Tommy Jackson. His eyes started to adjust to the darkness in the area where he was being held, since the lights were only turned on when one of the men came in and demanded answers to questions about Quinn. When he didn't answer their questions the way they wanted him to, they shoved a cattle prod into the cage directly into his ribs. After their intense questioning, the men would leave him in the cage, and then electrify the bars. He learned the hard way that he'd rather get zapped with the prod than by the bars of the cage itself. The seeping blisters and painful burns on his hand reminded him of that every day

Jackson lifted up his shirt, and rubbed his fingers over the burns on his rib cage as a result of the cattle prod. He pulled his shirt back down, and rolled his neck a couple of times. The man who abducted him basically put a cover over his head and then beat the shit out of him before tossing him into a truck. Almost every part of his body hurt, but he kept trying to focus on his breathing in order to deal with the pain. And he had no clue where his shoes and socks were.

The hum of electricity let him know not to touch the cage, but he needed to check in on the other man being held with him. The man had been unconscious every time Jackson had been awake, but then he often passed out from interrogation before the other man came to.

"Yo, dude. You awake? Hey, can you hear me?"

The other man lay in the middle of the cage, curled up in a fetal position. He wasn't responding. Tommy patted himself down, seeing if he had anything to throw at the man to get his attention, but there was nothing left in his pockets.

Considering his present status and the fact no one knew where he was, Jackson was fairly positive he'd die in this cage regardless of who helped the Mountain Mangler first. Maybe he should just tell the old man what he wanted to know and just get it over with? What other choice did he have?

He just hoped that Quinn stayed safe, but he knew deep down that if she found out about what happened, she would immediately stick her nose right in the middle of things like she always did.

***

As Anderson speeds towards the GBI headquarters, his phone pings. He pulls it out, and then hands it to me.

"Check the message for me."

I take the phone and open the text message. It is a group picture, and then bile rises up in my throat when I see his face. Rage, guilt, vengeance, and regret bury me, and I can barely speak.

"It's a picture...and it's him. That's Custer."

Anderson snatches the phone out of my hand, and pulls the car off to the side of the road. He forwards the picture to someone, and then makes a call.

"Hey, check out the picture I just sent you. Hurry up and identify every single person." Anderson, on speaker phone, yells at the people working diligently in the office. "Custer is the older man in the center of the photo, and I'm assuming some of these other men are his sons and/or his relatives."

Anderson has heard nothing else from either Sgt. Allen or Cpl. Taylor since receiving the picture. "Also, find Sgt. Allen and Cpl. Taylor. They have gone radio silent. Track them down, because I have a bad feeling about this."

He sent off a group text to both of the missing soldiers.

Need a sitrep. Reconnect ASAP.

He pulls the picture up again, and just stares at it. I'm sitting there, numb and enraged at the same time, knowing we've just identified the man responsible for the death of my best friend and the one holding two people very important to me.

"You're the one pulling the strings on this puppet show, right?" Anderson speaks to the photo. "You're the reason Barton is dead, and that I had to make a promise to his family the people responsible for his death would never see the inside of a courtroom. I'm coming for you, asshole."

I'm feeling every single emotion at once. I am having trouble breathing, and I feel like I'm on the verge of a panic attack. I remember Dr. Evelyn James told me I could reach out to her at any time, especially if I'm having trouble dealing with the gamut of emotions. I pull her super secret business card out of my purse. She told me only her most needy patients got this particular card because it had her personal cell on it.

With my hands trembling, and while Anderson flies down the road at ungodly speeds, I punch in Dr. James' number. Three rings, then voicemail.

You've reached the private voicemail for Dr. Evelyn James. If you have this number, then you must be in distress, and you know how to keep a secret. Please leave only a number at the tone, and I will call you back.

Beep.

I did as I was told, and only left my number on her voicemail. When she calls back, maybe she will be able to help me compartmentalize the rage and the fear currently coursing through my veins.

***

The rings of a phone fell silent in the empty house. All lights off. No other sounds heard. Pictures of Dr. Evelyn James, her husband Derrick, and her daughter Fiona covered the walls of the dark living room. Shadows danced all around in the silence.

On the floor of the living room, behind the sectional couch, lay the psychiatrist's husband, with a kitchen knife sticking out of his chest. A huge puddle of blood covered the floor beside him, with what appeared to be drag marks heading out of the living room.

The trail of blood led into a room that looked like an office or a library, and all the way behind a big wooden desk.

There, on the floor, was Dr. Evelyn James, with multiple stab wounds to her back, and her throat slit from ear to ear. Doctor/patient confidentiality had been secured, because she was no longer able to tell anyone anything.

CHAPTER 17

GBI Assistant Special Agent in Charge Daniel Brown received a tip about bodies being found at the home of a Midtown psychiatrist, with notes on the office desk that had Quinn Campbell's name written on them. He had asked local PDs to keep an eye out for anything involving Ms. Campbell, and the desk sergeant relayed the information as soon as it came in.

Brown pulled up to the Decatur address with Detective Grayson Miller in the passenger seat, and Case Agent Aaron Bernard in the backseat. They climbed out of the sedan, flashed badges to the officer out front, and ducked underneath the crime scene tape. They walked up to the front door of the house, which stood ajar and had officers and forensic techs coming in and out.

Brown flashed his GBI credentials to the Decatur detective who caught the case. "Hello, detective. What do we have here?"

"Two adults, one male and one female, both found deceased on scene."

"Show me."

The detective led the team into the living room, where the adult male was lying underneath a yellow tarp.

"This is Derrick James, fifty-two years old, works in marketing for the local professional basketball team. His cause of the death is—"

Detective Miller interrupted him. "—the big knife in his chest?"

The Decatur detective rolled his eyes and continued. "The cause of death is multiple deep stab wounds in the upper torso. Coroner believes the knife was jammed into his chest postmortem."

Brown added, "Time of death?"

The detective checked his notes. "Coroner puts TOD around three in the morning, give or take."

"Show us the other body." Brown nodded his head to Miller and Bernard, silently asking them to follow the Decatur detective.

The men moved from the living room to the office, being careful not to step in the blood trail on the floor. The detective motioned everyone to go behind the massive oak desk in front of a large bay window. An adult female was lying on the floor face down, under a white sheet.

The detective pulled the sheet back, showing the woman's face.

"This is Dr. Evelyn James, age forty-eight, worked as a psychiatrist in Midtown. She had multiple deep stab wounds in her back, but the coroner believes the cause of death was the neck wound."

Detective Miller leaned down over the body, using a pen to pull back Dr. James' hair, so he could get a better look at her throat.

"It looks like she was stabbed in the living room, and then the killer or killers let her crawl all the way in here. Maybe then they straddled her from behind, pulled her head up, and gave her the *coup de grâce*."

"I'll bet the murder weapon was jammed into the husband's chest after they killed her," Brown said, scribbling in his notebook. "Make sure to run DNA on the knife, looking for multiple blood samples," he told the detective.

Aaron Bernard hadn't said a word. He was just absorbing and watching everything around him. He was going through the motions, hoping something somewhere would give him a clue as to where his brother was being held, or if he was actually still alive.

"How is this connected to Campbell?" Aaron finally asked.

Brown flipped back through his notes. "Looks like there were documents on the office desk and on the floor with her name on them. The doc must be her therapist."

"Was the husband just in the wrong place at the wrong time?" Miller asked.

"Or was the husband killed first? Did he happen upon the struggle and was killed trying to save his wife? The killers leaving the knife in the husband's chest suggests an air of finality, of a 'that's what you get for interrupting us or trying to stop us' vibe," Bernard said.

"Either way, it looks like this was probably not a random act of violence. It has to be connected to our work somehow. It can't be a coincidence that Ms. Campbell is once again involved," Brown added.

The Decatur detective came back into the office. "Oh, and a twelve-year-old girl is how we found out about this situation. She went to a neighbor's house and they called 911."

"Relative?" Brown asked.

"Yes, daughter of the deceased."

"Where is she now?"

"EMTs are checking on her outside."

"Was she injured in any way?" Miller asked.

"Apparently not, but she did have blood on her. EMTs wanted to make sure she was OK nonetheless."

"Maybe OK physically, but I bet there's no way she's fine mentally. Alright, thanks, Detective." Brown continued surveying the scene, and began assigning things to Miller and Bernard. "Miller, go see if the daughter knows or saw anything. Bernard, look through the stuff in Dr. James' office and see if you can find out what she knows about...well...anything connected to us. I'll work the crime scene."

Miller nodded his head and walked outside. Bernard sighed reluctantly, but walked over to the office anyway. Brown walked into the living room to talk with the forensic techs.

One of the techs called out from the office. "Hey, check this out."

Bernard walked around behind the desk, while Brown and the lead detective came back into the office.

"What do you have?" Bernard asked first.

"She's got something in her closed fist." The CSI tech pointed to what appeared to be paper sticking out of her balled-up hand.

With gloved hands, Bernard leaned down and pulled gently on the paper, trying not to tear it. Slowly, the doctor's dead hand released the paper. Once fully out of her hand, Bernard opened it to see what was on it.

One word was scribbled on the paper, which was torn off of a notepad on the psychiatrist's desk.

Custer.

***

Detective Miller walked up to the back of an ambulance where a young girl sat on the rear bumper.

"Ms. James?" The young girl nodded her head.

Miller gave the young daughter a quick glance, trying to determine what state she was in mentally. She had blood on her clothes, and her body was trembling under the blanket first responders wrapped her in. He had to be careful and tread very lightly with his questions, because he couldn't even imagine how traumatized she might be right now.

"I'm Detective Grayson Miller. Do you mind if I ask you a few questions?"

She shook her head no, and Miller sat down next to the young girl on the edge of the bumper.

"Thank you. What's your name, and how old are you?"

"I'm Fiona. I just turned twelve."

"Hi, Fiona. I also have a daughter about your age. She is obsessed with things like music and movies, but can't put her phone down for five minutes to tell me how she's feeling. Are you into things like that?"

"I love anime and manga. Does your daughter like those things?"

He had no idea what manga was, except that it sounded like the Italian word for 'eat.'

"She definitely loves her cartoons."

Fiona rolled her eyes at the cartoons comment.

"Anime is much better than simple cartoons, just like manga is better than comic books," Fiona said, judgingly. "The art is of a much higher quality than normal kiddie animation."

"I stand corrected." Miller smiled at the young girl, realizing she was still quite sharp despite the horrific events of the past few hours.

"Fiona, I need to ask some tougher questions now, alright? Is that OK with you?" She nodded. "What can you tell me about what happened this morning?"

Tears began to roll down her cheeks.

"It's OK. Take your time."

"Well, I was in bed when I thought I heard something from downstairs, like loud talking or yelling."

"Did you recognize any of the voices?"

"I heard Mom and Dad arguing with some other people, but I didn't recognize their voices."

"Were the voices male or female?"

"All male voices, I think. Except for Mom."

"Your bedroom is upstairs, right?" She nodded yes. "Did you come out of your room when you heard the voices?" She nodded again.

"I opened the door quietly, and I went to the top of the stairs, listening to see if I could hear anything."

"And what did you hear?"

"It sounded like they were fighting or something. I heard things being knocked over and breaking. I really couldn't tell exactly."

"Did you stay upstairs?" She nodded again, wiping more tears away from her cheeks.

"I was too scared to get any closer. I didn't know what was going on." Tears continued to stream down her face.

"Were you able to see anything?" She shook her head no.

"The house was really dark. I did see light from something like a flashlight, though." Miller scribbled notes on his pad as she retold her experiences.

"Could you tell who was holding the flashlight?"

"Not really. It was so dark I couldn't tell. I just saw the light bouncing around the room."

Miller continued to scribble information onto the pages of his notebook.

"OK, when did you come downstairs?"

"After I stopped seeing the light from the flashlight, and the yelling stopped, I counted backwards from five hundred, like my mom taught me, and then I went downstairs."

"Why did your mom teach you that?"

"She told me that if I ever saw something scary, that I should hide and count backwards from five hundred at least once, making sure whatever that was scaring me was over. She just wanted me to be safe at school or here at home, especially with all the school shootings we've had lately."

"Your mother was pretty smart. The world can be a pretty scary place, you know."

He noticed Fiona staring at her hands, covered in the dried blood of her parents. He immediately felt a pang of sadness for her.

"Fiona, you're doing great. I just have a couple more questions, OK? After you came downstairs, what did you see?"

"I walked downstairs, and then I—" She began to sob quietly.

"It's OK, Fiona. It's just me. You're being so strong, so thank you. You can tell me."

"I...I saw Daddy lying on the floor with blood everywhere. I put my hands on his chest, trying to wake him up, but he just laid there. I tried not to touch the big knife, because I didn't want to hurt him. That's when I realized I...that I had...I had blood all over my hands. I tried...I tried wiping them on my shirt, but I...I couldn't get it off. I just couldn't...it wouldn't come off." She cried a little harder, but wiped her eyes again with the towel.

"What else did you see?"

"I went...I went into Mom's office and found her...just...just lying there on her stomach behind her desk. She...she was..."

Detective Miller tried his best to comfort her in the face of the unbearable.

"It's OK, Fiona. I know this has been hard. You've been very brave, and we...well, I...appreciate your help." He smiled knowingly at the little girl, and he immediately thought about how his daughter would have handled the same situation. He knew this girl was stronger than her years, and he hoped she would be able to overcome this someday.

He stood up with his hand still on her shoulder. She did not look at him, but instead continued to stare at her hands, flexing her fingers and turning her palms inward and outward.

***

Custer sat beside the two cages that held Tommy Jackson and Ian Bernard, humming a song as if he was bored. There was no telltale hum or buzz, which meant the cages were not currently electrified. Someone had put a large bucket in each cage, in case they needed to use the bathroom.

Custer took a water hose and sprayed Bernard with it, right in the face. The force of the water jarred him back to consciousness. He began spitting the water out of his mouth, trying not to choke on it.

Jackson was sitting up in the center of the cage, watching Custer rouse the other man. He really needed to find out who he was, and why they captured him as well. It made sense for the Mountain Mangler and his crew to grab him, because of his relationship to Campbell, but he didn't recognize the other guy.

"Come on, now. He's awake already. You can stop with the water to the face." Jackson muttered.

Custer immediately turned the hose on Jackson instead, laughing as the force of the water knocked him over. "I spray who I want to spray, boy. No unclean soul like you can tell me what I should or should not do."

Jackson coughed up the water in his mouth and lungs, and shook his head. "Fine. Whatever, dude."

The other man appeared to be injured, like maybe he had a broken leg or other lower extremity damage. He was covered in dried blood, and he wore what was left of a shirt, tie, and slacks. He looked as if he'd been run over by something.

"So, have y'all gotten to know each other yet? Which one of y'all is gonna answer my questions? Remember, the first one to help me will not be the first one to die."

"So you're saying we're dead either way? If that's the case, why should we help you at all?" Bernard said as he tried to sit up inside the cage. The lawyer in him was beginning to come out. "And for the record, we've not been conscious enough together to talk. So, no, we haven't decided anything. You'll just have to wait."

Jackson agreed with what the man said. They really had no incentive to help Custer if they both were gonna die anyway. The two men made eye contact, and nodded to each other.

"Well, well, well...you're no good to me dead right now, so how's about we cut off a piece instead?"

Custer walked up to Ian's cage, opened the electronic lock, and swung the door open. Jackson almost wished he came into his cage like that, because he'd run like hell. Custer knew the other man had a busted leg and couldn't run.

Custer grabbed Ian's left arm and wrenched it forward. He pulled out a pair of pruning shears, and put Ian's pinky finger between the blades. Custer cut an evil glance at Tommy, curling up a wicked smile, before looking back at Ian. With a sickening crunch, the blades cut through flesh and bone, removing the pinkie finger from Ian's hand, just above the second knuckle. Tommy turned his head away, hearing the other man scream in pain, because he couldn't bear watching his cagemate suffer anymore. Ian recoiled back into the center area of the cage, as soon as Custer let him go. Blood continued to pour out of his injured finger, over all of his clothes, the cage, and the cage floor.

Jackson took off his outer shirt, and tossed it on top of Bernard's cage. "Here...take my shirt and wrap up your hand. Try and stop the bleeding."

Ian grabbed the shirt with his right hand, and appeared to wrap his left hand inside. "Thank you," Bernard said, weakly.

Custer laughed and laughed. "Proverbs Chapter 6, Verse 16 says, 'There are several things the Lord hates that are detestable to him, including haughty eyes and hands that shed innocent blood.' Neither one of you is innocent, so I'm still good with Him."

"I don't know what you think we've done, but we sure aren't the guilty ones here," Jackson said.

He growled, and then yelled his answer. "You both know *exactly* what you've done. You both know who she is. Deliver her to me, and I'll put you out of your misery and we will then cleanse your soul as a reward. Don't tell me, and we'll torture it out of one of you. One way or another, whether it's your intent or not, alive or cleansed, you will bring the reporter to me."

Neither man said anything after Custer yelled in their direction. Custer kicked Jackson's cage in frustration, and walked over to the inner door. He turned back to them, somewhat calmer now.

"You have until tomorrow. One of you will talk, and both of your souls will be cleansed and delivered to the Lord, our God...one much more painfully than the other. His will be praised." Custer turned off the lights, and walked out the door—still carrying Ian's pinkie finger.

A short time later, the buzz of electricity came on, which meant no touching of the cage walls.

"Hey man...you OK?" Jackson asked the other man, who was still cradling his left hand.

"I'll live. Do we even use our pinkie fingers anyway?" The man laughed awkwardly.

"I've been trying to figure out who you are, but they always seem to leave you unconscious when I'm awake. I'm Tommy Jackson, and I work for—" The man cut him off.

"Wait, you work for WQX, right? The assignment editor? My sister talked about you all the time. I'm Ian Bernard, Alahna's brother."

"The lawyer? Yes, I remember her talking about you. Your other brother Aaron is a GBI agent, right?"

"Yeah, that's him. These douche canoes want us to tell them about Quinn, so are we?"

"I've been trying to keep some information from them, in an attempt to keep her safe and prolong my usefulness to them. Something tells me once Quinn and Aaron find out we've been taken, they're gonna do everything they can to find us—no matter who's in the way. I have faith in her."

"Well, I'm glad you have faith in her. Mine is in Aaron. He didn't take the news about Alahna very well, and he's not gonna sit idly by and lose me, too. I will tell you this—the next time that redneck comes back in here, I'm probably gonna spill my guts. If I'm gonna die, I want to do it with a clean conscience."

"By putting her and Aaron back in harm's way? How exactly is that clearing your conscience?"

"Says the man with all ten fingers." Bernard turned away from Jackson, and curled back up on the floor of his cage.

"Just give her one more day, man. I know people are looking for us, I just know it. Hold out long enough for them to find us, alright? You can't give up hope, not yet at least. We just gotta hang on…"

No response. Jackson knew Wild Bill Tucker would pull out all the stops to find him, too. And now he assumed the GBI was involved as well, so they just had to survive until they were found, and hopefully found alive.

The Quinn he knew would never let it go, would never give up on them. He absolutely loved that about her…one of the many things he loved about her. Maybe once she found him, he would actually be able to admit that to her.

If she found them in time…

***

Anderson and I speed through downtown Atlanta, having not said a word to each other since leaving the side of the road. Anderson has been making several calls, trying to find out information about his two missing teammates. It is obvious he is distracted.

I can tell he also had a bad feeling about his men, since they apparently missed their mandatory roll call check in and they have failed to answer any subsequent call or text. The only communication he's heard from them was the group picture they texted him. Radio silence seems unusual for them, because if I've gathered anything about Anderson, if he calls you, you damn well better answer the phone. He makes another phone call.

"Hey, do me a favor. Ping Taylor and Allen's phones again." Anderson asks the PTC person on the other end of the line. "We have to figure out where they are."

Anderson gets an answer he doesn't like, and throws his phone on the dash with a huff.

"What is going on? What did they say?"

"Look, it's a PTC rule that phones must be turned on at all times. The fact their phones are currently off means the phones are either dead or they are no longer in their possession."

"Do you think…" my voice trails off.

"Unfortunately, yes. They've either been captured or killed."

Anderson's phone rings again. "Talk to me."

Anderson listens intently, and then hangs up the phone again. He looks confused. "Why in the hell would their vehicle be anywhere near the I-285/I-75 intersection in Cobb County, near the baseball stadium? That's a hundred miles away from their last known, which I believe is the address they found for Calvary Rock General Contractors."

He's never talked this much to me about PTC operations, so I keep him talking. Apparently, he trusts me now, and maybe that means he doesn't *actively* hate me anymore? Besides, I'm not sure I want to know how PTC found that supposed address for Custer.

"Maybe someone moved their vehicle to throw off the search?" I ask.

"Highly likely." Anderson rubs his face with his hands.

Joining forces with Assistant Special Agent in Charge Daniel Brown and the rest of the GBI investigative team might actually be the best play now, because time is running out for everyone involved. It's going to have to wait, because Anderson whips our vehicle around, heading north.

"Sorry, kid. I have to find out what happened to my men, and I can't leave you out of my sight. Therefore, you're coming with me."

Shit. Maybe I should have practiced shooting more paper targets before I run directly into danger.

At least I have Anderson with me to keep me safe, or at least I know he'd die trying to protect me.

***

Custer stared at the video screens, watching the two men talk to each other in the dark. *One way or another, they always turn on each other...they always do.*

His money is on the lawyer...as spineless as they are.

His phone buzzed, and it was Clyde.

"Hey...things under control?"

"Yeah, Pa. We torched those guys' vehicle way outside of Atlanta, and left their bodies out at the new construction site under the office trailer for the time being." Clyde cleared his throat, then continued. "We'll drop them in some holes soon at one of the new construction plots and stow them away like the others."

"What's Beau doing?" Custer asked.

"He stayed at the home office, clearing evidence of the shootout—boarding windows, picking up shell casings, etc. We wanted to reset the whole site."

"Well, hopefully Beau won't screw that up, too."

There was an uncomfortable silence before Custer continued.

"We need to strengthen our numbers. Send out an SOS to our work crews, and have anyone available meet us at the house."

"Why we doin' that, Pa?"

"Don't question me, boy. I just feel like people are beginning to stick their noses in places they don't belong. It's only a matter of time before someone stumbles into the right place at the wrong time."

"Alright, Pa. I'll recruit as many as I can to meet us at the house. When?"

"ASAP. We'll have a pig pickin' or somethin' then, and I need to make a beer run."

"Alright, Pa. Will do."

Custer shoved the phone back into his pocket, and turned his attention back to the video screen. The two men in their metallic suites appeared to be lying down now, no longer interacting with each other.

Tomorrow with the whole crew there, maybe they could have a cleansing party, where everyone could participate. He turned his attention away from the screen to a photograph of his late wife Emma on the wall.

"Everything I do is to honor His will as well as your memory, darlin'. Our work will be done."

Custer kissed his fingers and then placed them on the photograph.

"Something tells me there's a fair chance I'll be joining you soon, baby. And I'll be taking as many of them with me as possible on my way out. I vow to keep my promise to you."

CHAPTER 18

Col. Anderson and I just sit in his vehicle, parked at the Calvary Rock General Contractors construction address that his men were sent to check out. I am happy to have a smartphone again, so I am just scrolling through information about this business and anything else I can find. On the way here, I heard him send a recovery crew to check out his teammates' vehicle. A short time later, a follow-up phone call from the scene says the vehicle was torched and that there was no sign of Sgt. Allen or Cpl. Taylor.

I really feel for Anderson, because he is taking this new development to heart. I have never seen him so emotional. So angry. Not even after Sgt. Barton's death.

We both know something happened here, but exactly what, we don't know. With Custer being involved now, he's probably responsible for this, and for everything else.

"Kid, lock the doors and stay in the car," Anderson says to me, sternly. "I need to do my job for a bit."

I do as I'm told, and watch him work. His military training is evident, as he moves with such incredible expert precision. I keep my eyes open and my head on a swivel—just in case.

***

Anderson looked around the area slowly, scanning his surroundings. He popped the 9mm out of his shoulder holster, ejected the magazine to check for ammo, slid it back in the magwell, and then re-holstered it. He knew at least one of Custer's crew had a penchant for long guns, so he needed to be extra vigilant, which was probably why he wanted Quinn to stay hidden inside the car. He couldn't do his job and protect the reporter at the same time. He told himself he'd be quick.

He was a very detail-oriented soldier with extensive military urban tracking experience, so he slowly scanned the gravel parking lot up to the entryway porch. Nothing appeared out of place. When things look too clean, they usually are.

He looked back at the reporter in the vehicle, and he knew he couldn't dally. He needed to get in, get out, and get the reporter the hell out of here. Bringing her with him was a tactical risk he knew he had to make, because he didn't trust her with anyone else right now.

He stepped slowly onto the gravel driveway, stepping into each of the existing footprints. He suddenly noticed something in the gravel glinting in the sunlight. He crouched down, and grabbed at something between a couple of pieces of gravel. A spent 9mm shell casing. Standard PTC issue.

"Damn it. At least it looks like they got a few shots off," he muttered.

Whoever cleaned up the scene did an okay job, but it was clear a shootout happened here. There were huge pieces of plywood covering the windows which he assumed had been shot out. That wasn't suspicious at all.

He continued casing the area around the trailer, looking for clues of any kind. There wasn't a lot of anything that he could see, which might be a clue in and of itself. He walked onto the front deck, which was on the number one side, and walked to the right of the entry door toward the corner of the trailer where the number one and number four sides met. At the one/four corner, he found another shell casing, some broken blades of grass, and some blood. It looked like someone was crouched down here, maybe pinned by gunfire. There were a few holes in the trailer's siding. It was hard to tell if this was Allen or Taylor, or some other member of Custer's family. For some reason, Anderson didn't think the old man would actually get his hands dirty with scut work like this. He assumed Custer was more than likely the crew's shot caller.

He walked around to the rear number three side, which seemed largely untouched, as well as the left number two side of the trailer.

He peeked in one of the windows on the number two side, and most everything seemed in order. He did notice the glass in the boarded-up windows was shattered, and some was still on the floor inside.

It looked like someone got pinned down inside, and took heavy fire from the outside of the structure. That meant Custer probably had eyes on it somehow. He looked up at the light poles around the property, and didn't see any obvious cameras outside—at least where he would have put them.

Anderson wanted to cut the power to the trailer, just to make sure that if cameras were inside, they would no longer be operational. He walked over to where the power line fed into the trailer, took a multi-tool out of his vest, and cut the power cable. He made sure that was the only line coming into the structure.

He cautiously walked up to the front door and noticed more glass on the front porch. He looked around slowly, as paranoid as possible, and tried the doorknob. Unlocked.

He turned the knob slowly, and opened the front office door. He waited a second, surveying the open doorway, checking for potential traps or triggers. When he was satisfied it was clear, he slowly crept inside.

He needed to quickly recon the interior, and then vacate the premises. Protecting Ms. Campbell was still his priority, and he knew she was a sitting duck inside his vehicle. He couldn't afford to get pinned down by Custer's goons like he assumed Allen and Taylor did, so time was of the essence.

He took out his phone and snapped pictures of everything. He decided he'd look through them later. He took photos of bookcases, photos, and certificates on the walls and shelves, and stopped at one specific frame.

It was a building license issued to Elijah Matthew Custer.

Rage filled Anderson's soul as he thought about all the psychological and physical damage this asshole had inflicted—on Quinn, her friend, Barton, probably Taylor and Allen—and for what? Quinn had said he did some religious ritual on her friend before he killed her, but why? None of it made sense.

Anderson balled up his fist, and punched the license on the wall, shattering the glass frame and knocking it off the wall.

He took a few more pictures before moving to the desk in the corner. He rummaged through a few loose papers on the top of the desk, but then found a few pieces of mail in one of the drawers.

Most of them were addressed to Calvary Rock General Contractors at the current location, but there were a few different ones. Some were actually addressed to an E. Custer, and had a different address. Anderson folded one of the envelopes and shoved it in his vest pocket. Maybe he'd get lucky. Maybe this is the guy's home address.

In a petty move, Anderson took a red Sharpie out of a cup on the desk. He wrote a message for Custer on the calendar desk blotter in all capital letters:

I KNOW WHO YOU ARE, AND I'LL SEE YOU SOON.

Part of him hoped that Custer would see it, and suddenly realize his days were numbered. No quarter. No courts. No justice.

This moron had picked a fight with the wrong soldier.

***

Assistant Special Agent in Charge Daniel Brown, Dahlonega Detective Grayson Miller, and Case Agent Aaron Bernard were working diligently with the rest of the GBI investigative team when Brown's phone rang.

"Brown," he answered.

"Brownie," a familiar voice trilled. "Do you want anything from Starbucks?"

"Ms. Campbell, so good to hear your voice." Brown checked his watch, and realized the reporter and her bodyguard should have shown up at their field office a long time ago. "And no, you know our espresso machine is top tier."

"True, true," she replied. "Look, I know we should be there already, but Col. Anderson had to follow up on a lead. And since I'm his shadow, I'm here, too."

"Care to share your lead with us?"

"Calvary Rock General Contractors. Anderson somehow found a security key card for this location, and we believe that Custer is connected somehow to this company."

Brown ordered one of the GBI analysts to start digging into Calvary Rock.

"Also, Anderson has a picture of Custer that one of his men sent him. When we're on our way to you, I'll make sure to send it your way."

Brown scoffed at the fact Peachtree Technology Corporation was further ahead in their investigation than the GBI was.

"Look, Campbell, get us that picture ASAP."

"Absolutely, I'll do it first chance I get. FYI, we're also a long way away from you right now, so it might be a bit before we get there in person. But we *are* coming."

"Stay safe, Campbell. We need you in one piece."

"And I need me in one piece. I want to also find Tommy and Ian in one piece, too...and preferably alive. See you soon."

***

Before Elijah Custer opened the inner warehouse door, he flipped a handle that turned off the electricity to the bars on all the cages. He walked onto the floor of the warehouse, and the sound of his boots on the solid floor clicked and clopped as he methodically placed one foot down, and then the other. He twirled the cattle prod in his hands as he walked along several of the empty cages on the warehouse floor until he came to Jackson and Bernard.

The two men lay on the concrete floor of their respective cages with their backs to each other. Buckets full of urine and feces in the corner of the cages spread their foul stench throughout the warehouse. Custer got the feeling by the way they were positioned that they weren't exactly best friends. Maybe they were finally broken enough to help him find the reporter. Custer smiled as he slid the cattle prod between the bars of Tommy Jackson's cage, pressing the uncharged tines into his rib cage.

"Get up, boy. And damn, y'all stink." Custer recoiled at the smell of their excrement and shook his head judgingly.

Tommy jolted awake and rapidly blinked his eyes trying to focus his eyesight. "If you emptied this thing more often, then maybe you wouldn't have to smell it. Imagine having to sleep with it beside your head."

Custer looked annoyed at Tommy's retort.

"If you feel like your accommodations are unsatisfactory, then you can fill out the housekeeping survey before you leave," Custer laughed. "Your comfort and satisfaction with our services is not important to us. So, please, leave a message at the beep."

At the mention of a beep, Custer turned on the cattle prod and shoved it into the small of Ian Bernard's back. Ian was immediately roused from sleep by his own blood-curdling scream.

"You didn't have to do that," Tommy yelled, concerned about Ian.

Custer laughed hard at Jackson, almost like a predator who was merely playing with his food.

"Do you still feel like we are not providin' high quality services to you during your stay?" Custer asked, as he slid the cattle prod back into Ian's cage.

"Fine, fine, fine, I'll talk...I'll talk. Just stop hurting him." Ian whipped his head around, confused by what Tommy just said.

"W...wait, I thought you said..." Ian asked, but Tommy interrupted him.

"I know what I said, man, but I don't want him continuing to burn you when I can prevent it."

Custer smiled an evil smile, and his eyes crinkled up in anger. "Prevent it, you say?" Custer jabbed the cattle prod back into Ian's rib cage, sending mega doses of electricity into his midsection. Ian screamed loudly again, then crumpled in a pile in the center of the cage.

"Son of a bitch!" Tommy yelled, grabbing the bars of his cage, staring wide eyed at Ian while smelling his fellow captive's searing flesh.

"So, tell me again...still think you can prevent me from doin' what I want, when I want, to who I want?" Custer locked eyes with Jackson. "You can't prevent shit. Even if you talk, I'm gonna punish you in ways you've never seen. So, do not presume to think *anything* you do will prevent me from doin' *anything*. Understand me, boy?" Rage filled the old man's eyes as he stared right through Jackson.

"Look...look...I know you're just looking for information. We're both just looking to survive. Ask me anything, and I'll tell you what you want to know."

***

The ride to GBI headquarters is going to be a long one from Calvary Rock. Anderson gives me his phone when he gets back in the vehicle, and I start scrolling through the pictures he took. The first thing I do, though, is send the Custer family photo—with Anderson's permission, of course—to Special Agent Brown. I add the following message:

Told ya I'd send it to you. :)

Anderson uncovered a treasure trove of information. Addresses, pictures, the works. We found him. Now we just need to leverage this information to find Tommy and Ian before it's too late.

From my phone, I send a text message to Aaron.

We're close, A. Stay calm and stay focused. I need you with me when we take him down. Don't do anything stupid.

My relationship with Aaron hasn't always been this distant. When I first met him years ago, he tried every line he could think of to get me to go out with him. There was not a chance in hell I'd date him, because Alahna would not have approved at all of someone like me dating her brother. I didn't take it personally, because she was right. I was probably too much of a woman for him, anyway.

I know in my heart that AB would love us working together now to avenge her. Maybe we can fix the other stuff afterward. I mean, we actually grew sort of close back in the day. Ian was never around, so it was always me, AB, Aaron, and his flavor of the month. The three amigos.

For the record, Aaron left me on read. I know he received my text, but did not reply. I hope he's OK.

What seems like hours later, we arrive at the GBI field office, where Anderson has several members of the PTC team meet us. I shoot Brownie a message that we're here, and he tells me where to meet them. Anderson looks weary, but focused. We have a lot of work to do, and the hourglass is quickly running out of sand.

We make our way through security, the lobby, and to the central elevators. Anderson presses the floor button, and the doors quietly close. I instinctively press down the GBI visitor sticker on my shirt over and over, making sure it doesn't fall off. Anderson and the PTC team step out first, and he motions me to follow them. We walk into the GBI Joint Operations Command, and I see Brownie, Detective

Miller, and Aaron working away; I also notice my picture front and center on their investigation vision board. *Awkward.*

"Y'all want this party started...right?" No one reacts at all to my choice of 90s music lyric, so maybe my pop culture self is just too much.

Everyone turns around at the sound of my yelling, and a couple of the task force techs instinctively salute Col. Anderson. Brown immediately asks them to not do that.

"FYI, you only salute soldiers when they're in uniform," Brown says to the tech, as he fumbles awkwardly to save face. Anderson nods, and shakes Brown's hand firmly. "Thank you for coming, Colonel." The PTC techs put their stuff down in a couple of the empty cubicles.

"Assistant Special Agent in Charge Daniel Brown, I presume. Retired Marine corporal, last stationed at MCAS Camp LeJeune in North Carolina, working for the USMC Investigative Division before joining the Georgia Bureau of Investigation." Anderson easily spouts out Brown's military CV, and I think it is pretty much a shot across the bow, more of a *I know all about you, so don't screw with me* preemptive strike. Brown cracks a smile at Anderson, while everyone else is busy introducing themselves and shaking hands and nodding their heads.

"Do you know about my two failed marriages and the balance on my Vanguard IRA as well?" Both men laugh cautiously. "Good to know you can do your research, Colonel, because we're going to need that high-powered perception to help us work this case. Oh, and by the way, it's nice to have a retired Army Colonel last stationed at Fort Benning with extensive Special Forces training on the team." Brown totally gives him the *I can do research, too* counterstrike. I smile before I can catch myself.

Anderson walks over to the vision board, and takes a few minutes to absorb the work the GBI has done to this point. "Let's get down to brass tacks, shall we? We are miles ahead of you as far as specific details on this case, so we're going to have to calibrate our info. In case you don't already know, we are currently running an off-books unsanctioned op that began after Ms. Campbell's Virginia Highland safe house attack. While you do have the backing of the entire state of Georgia behind you, I can't wait to see what toys you have access to."

"Looks like we do need each other," Detective Miller adds, while the PTC and GBI techs begin opening laptops and setting up desk space.

"Then let's get to work." Anderson looks over at me, and motions his head toward the vision board. "Campbell, you're up. Tell the team what you see in the group photo you gave them."

Just looking at the five men on the screen again makes my skin crawl, my stomach turn, and my anger boil over. "Well, we now know the old man in the center is Elijah Custer. He is the man who killed Alahna Bernard, Jada Sinclair, and God knows how many others." I cut a look over to Aaron, who was standing motionless beside me. "And this one is the relative who tried to kill me in the hospital," she adds, pointing to Zeke.

"Our team neutralized the fake custodian outside of Campbell's apartment," Anderson said coldly. No one needs an explanation as to what 'neutralized' means.

"We also just came from Calvary Rock General Contractors. That's where my men—who I believe were either captured or killed by Custer or his goons shortly after sending me this picture—found the group photo, and it's also where I found some mail addressed to what might be Custer's home address. I haven't had a chance to run it down yet." Anderson pulls a crumpled envelope out of his vest, and hands it to Brown. "One of the guys in this picture is also allegedly responsible for the death of Sgt. Anthony Barton in the Virginia Highland shooting."

"Alright, team, get me everything you can on this Elijah Custer. Family records, financials, tax documents, property tax holdings, speeding tickets, Sunday school preferences, favorite foods, the works. And I need you to identify everyone in this picture. Like *yesterday*, people." Brown commands his team with a true sense of purpose. "Also, pull up satellite imagery from this address and the Calvary Rock address. I need to see what we're up against."

I'm watching all of the people in the room working feverishly together, even Anderson, Brown, and Miller—which surprises me, because they're all alpha males. But then I see Aaron, still standing in the same position, just staring at the photo. His face curls up in an uncomfortable position, and I see one solitary tear slowly sliding down his face. I can't take seeing him upset, so I slide over to him.

"Hey...you OK?" I ask, softly putting my hand on his arm.

"So, this is the bastard that killed her?" he asks in a monotone voice. I know he's exploding with anger inside.

"Yes, and I'm so sorry. We'll get him, I promise. We'll get closure for Alahna and anyone else he killed in the name of his screwed-up religious bullshit."

"I don't want closure, Q." He turns to look me dead in the eye, and the cold fire behind his eyes scares me a little. Actually, it scares me quite a lot. "I want to do to him exactly what he did to Alahna."

"Well, that makes two of us."

Analysts, techs, and case agents feverishly work around us, and I'm truly impressed with the quality and speed of their work. Anderson calls the rest of his team, and they work remotely with the JOC, combining investigative forces and manpower. Miller updates the vision board with the envelope Anderson brought back.

"Alright, people. The clock is ticking. What are we up against?" Brown asks.

One of the analysts puts a satellite image of the Calvary Rock business address up on their main screen. Nothing really looks out of the ordinary.

"Give me all you can about the address on that envelope," Anderson commands his techs on the speaker phone, while also addressing the GBI investigative team. "I'd like to see what they are working with."

"Give the man what he wants, people." Brown advises.

A short time later, new satellite imagery shows up on screen, and my heart drops.

The warehouse.

The homestead.

Bile comes into my mouth.

"Well, Ms. Campbell, you are the only one here that may recognize this place," Brown says. "What do you see?"

I walk up to the screen, running my eyes over the image. I feel the heat of everyone's gaze on me.

"Does this look familiar, Ms. Campbell?" Detective Miller asks me, and I look over the buildings in the image.

"That looks exactly like the warehouse structure where Alahna and I were held in those electrified cages. When we made it out of there, we grabbed one of their trucks and hauled ass out of there this way." I trace my finger along a dirt road until it goes into a treeline. "This is it. I'm sure of it."

My heart races and there's a ringing in my ears. I'm not used to dealing with all of these feelings at once—fear, regret, anger, anxiousness, and many more I can't even name. Yay for being mentally *and* emotionally unstable. Trauma can do that to you.

"Profile the man, Ms. Campbell. Do you think this is where Jackson and Bernard are being held now?"

My reporter brain kicks in. "I'd bet my life on it. There were too many cages on that warehouse floor and the tech was too sophisticated and widespread for me to think other locations exist. My gut says this is the right location. This has to be ground zero."

And since Custer wants me to come back to him, this feels like a full circle moment.

"Alright, people, it's almost 9pm. Col. Anderson, I'd like your help putting an assault plan together for tomorrow AM," Brown states. "Also, you have operational knowledge of the people we're dealing with, and frankly, I could use your help leading this team on the ground. Can I count on you, sir?"

Anderson knowingly looks over at me, and then turns to Brown. "I'm all in, sir."

Tomorrow, we breach this compound in the hopes of finding T-Jack and Ian, and of bringing Custer and his followers in before anyone else has to die. I'm so far out of my element here, but with Anderson and Aaron by my side, I have faith I'll make it out of harm's way.

I just hope Tommy and Ian do, too.

***

Custer left both men battered and bruised on the floors of their cages. He was somewhat satisfied that one of them told him some of what he needed to know. Tomorrow, they will both be cleansed for their troubles. They've earned that.

Before Custer left the warehouse, he made sure electricity flowed into the cages, and that the lights were turned out. He had enjoyed watching these two unclean souls lose their minds in complete darkness: they can't see, they can't escape, and they just sit there and stew. He has seen other "guests" have their brains turn to mush, and sometimes he has walked in to find blubbering idiots where grown adults used to be.

He even had one of the first he captured kill himself on the electrified cage bars. That's when he installed the cameras all throughout the warehouse. Suicide did the trick, but cleansing the impure souls himself was so much more satisfying.

When he opened the outer door to the warehouse, he smiled. Ten, maybe fifteen trucks were in the yard, which meant Clyde and Beau were able to round up some of the loyal construction crews. After what his guests just told him, he can only assume she will soon be returning to him, and assume she now knows of his two new captives. He was actually planning on it. It would make his job a lot easier if she came back to him, but that's why he needed reinforcements—in case she didn't come alone. He knew the Peachtree goons probably wouldn't be far behind.

"Hey, Pa. We did what you asked. Clyde and I grabbed a few loyal crews and day laborers we could count on," Beau said, still trying to impress his old man.

"What did you tell them?" Custer asked. "Do they know why they're here?"

"I just told them you needed help, and that was all they needed to hear," Clyde said, taking a swig from a beer bottle.

"Good. We need help, but we gotta tell them a little slower with what. Just tell them what they need to know to keep them around." Custer reached into the outdoor fridge and grabbed a cold bottle of beer. "Can't be too open with our truth just yet."

"I hear ya, Pa. Oh, we also brought food on our way back up the mountain. Fried chicken, collards, you know, the usual from your favorite grease spot." Clyde motioned over to a folding table with tons of food on it. The workers surrounding the table were obviously waiting for Custer before they got any food for themselves.

They stared at Custer, waiting for him to give the go ahead, so he addressed the group. "Hey folks, first of all, let me say thank you for coming up the mountain on short notice. See, me and my boys need your help, but we're still making plans as to what that help will look like. You all can sleep in this trailer, or the rooms above the warehouse." Custer took a swig from his beer bottle. "But I need you to stay off of the warehouse floor until we let you know what we're doing, OK? Can you all do that for me?"

The workers all raised their bottles, and murmured a chorus of "Yes, sir," "Yes, boss," and "Anything you say, Custer." Custer raised his beer bottle to the group in acknowledgement.

"Glad to see we're all willing to work together to finish this task. Hope you're ready to get your hands dirty. Now, let's thank the Lord for providing this amazing table of food. Thank you for your sustenance and for your love. Dig in, folks."

Custer looked at the group as they all grabbed forks, napkins, and plates of food, and wondered how many of the people in front of him wouldn't make it out of this alive.

CHAPTER 19

Five o'clock comes along way before I'm actually ready for it.

I've never been a morning person, so getting up before ten o'clock kinda sucks. Adulting is hard.

Anderson's typical wake up call, a frantic banging on the bedroom door, comes right at five, just like military clockwork, and I make a total fool of myself screaming at him in a half-asleep stupor to cut it out. Leave it to me to be super classy. He might as well have been playing reveille outside my door with a trumpet.

I take a really brief shower, wrap a towel around myself and one around my wet hair, and then brush my teeth quickly. I stare silently at myself in the mirror, noticing some of the bruising that still adorns my pale, freckled shoulders. Unfortunately, the wounds that hurt the worst are not, and have never been, visible.

I touch my healing gunshot wound, and a jolt of memory immediately floods my mind. I close my eyes and let the horrific event run its course. Maybe today will be the end of this sordid hillbilly story. I just wish I had Alahna back, because I miss her more than anything else I have ever missed.

My ice blue eyes are severely bloodshot due to the lack of sleep, so I rub them with the palms of my hands. I fumble for eye drops and put a couple into my super dry eyes, blinking rapidly to spread out the liquid. I unwrap the towel from my wet hair, and I use it to shake out a lot of the remaining water. I drape the towel over the shower door, turn back towards the vanity mirror, and pull my slightly damp red hair into a ponytail that falls down between my shoulder blades. I know today will not be a beauty contest.

Anderson had stopped by my pod on the way back to the safe house last night, and procured a lot of my more functional clothing, which I appreciate. I rummage through the boxes, and I pick a solid black polo and a pair of black cargo pants for today's mission. I feel like the extra pockets might come in handy. I toss the towel onto the bed, put on my underwear and sports bra, pull on the cargo pants and polo, and tug on a pair of compression socks. I'll put my hiking boots on last, because I hate wearing shoes of any kind. Alahna used to call them my shitkickers, so I'm wearing them for her today.

I pull the handgun Col. Anderson gave me out of my purse, knowing I'm probably gonna have to use it today. I think back to the old Ice Cube song, and I hope I don't have to use my Sig Sauer. *Today will be a good day.*

Anderson had made some of the strongest, most bitter coffee I've ever had, but I still squeak out a strained thank you. I should probably eat something, too, but my stomach is in knots at the thought of what is to come today. I don't want to hurl all over everyone. Instead, I grab a banana and call it even.

"You ready, kid?"

"As ready as I'll ever be."

With that, we load up the vehicle and head to the rally point.

***

All morning, the people who Clyde and Beau recruited to help outfit the compound worked diligently—boarding up external windows, gathering up weapons and ammunition, building makeshift barricades and fencing, and various other odd jobs Custer gave them to do.

Custer knew that after the two Peachtree goons were killed at the main construction trailer, time was not on his side. He knew it was only a matter of time before the full force of God-knows-what showed up on his doorstep, looking to make him atone for the atrocities performed in the name of the Mountain Mangler. They have no idea why he did what he did, and he knew he wasn't going to stop just because the uninitiated were coming to visit.

He knew this might very well be his last stand. His last chance to show Emma he was a man of his word, and that he would sacrifice everything and everyone to honor her memory.

And he also knew he had at least two more cleansings on the calendar. He had a deep-seated feeling that the reporter was coming to him, based on the information given to him by his guests, which would really save him a lot of trouble and effort. It's just the others that come with her that would be the issue. That's why he wanted pawns to stand between them and him. They would give him a fighting chance.

"Pa, what do you want to do with our cage dwellers?" Clyde asked, coming out of the main warehouse door. He walked over to where Custer was standing, surveying the work going on.

"They're gonna be the main event, son. Our last chance to honor my promise to the Lord our God and to your late mother." Custer took a final drag off his cigarette, and flicked the butt away. "They have to be cleansed."

"Do you think more of those Peachtree idiots are headed our way?" Clyde motioned over to Beau, who joined them.

"Son, how did you feel when they took Lee away from us? How did you feel when Zeke disappeared? You *know* they were behind it." Custer pulled a pack of cigarettes out of his shirt pocket, and popped one out. He put it between his lips, lit it, and blew out a puff of smoke. "Just imagine how you'd react if you were them. You know damn well they're probably coming up the mountain as we speak."

"To be honest, Pa...I want to kill 'em all. I want to punish them for breaking up our family." Clyde squeezed those words through pursed lips. A vein popped out on his right temple. "Those...those bastards...they just piss me off."

Beau just stood there silently, and Custer stared over at him with dead eyes. "Nothing to say, son? Nothing to add to the situation *you* caused?" Custer grabbed Beau's collar with both hands, and pulled him close—his cigarette mere millimeters from his son's face. "You still need to find a way to make this right."

"Pa, how can I make it up to you...to us? Tell me what to do and I'll do it." Beau's expression lost all emotion, as the color also drained from his face. Clyde just stood by and watched Custer threaten his only remaining brother.

"Son, Romans Chapter 12, Verse 19 says 'do not try to punish others when they wrong you, but wait for God to punish them with his anger.'" Custer released Beau's collar. "If you can't make this right, then your fate is in the hands of the Lord God Almighty."

The veiled threat made Beau look incredibly uneasy. Custer brushed off Beau's shoulders and took another long drag of his cigarette.

"Boys, just 'tween you, me, and God himself, no matter how you look at it, today is gonna be hell. If I was these guys, I'd be bringing every single weapon I could find with me." Custer took a second and looked across the yard, seeing all the workers preparing for war. "This might be the last day of our family. If we do somehow make it out alive, then that would be proof to me that the Lord our God has more work for us to do, and that means more people need cleansing."

"Pa, we'll stand with you 'till the end of us." Clyde said, and both he and Beau nodded to their father in an obvious show of loyalty. Beau reached out his hand between them, and Clyde put his hand on Beau's.

"Through many dangers, toils, and snares we have already come," Clyde quoted.

"'Twas grace that brought us safe thus far," Beau continued.

"And grace will lead us home," Custer finished, putting his hand on top of Clyde and Beau's. "We've no less days to sing God's praise than when we first began."

***

It had been hours since anyone had visited Tommy Jackson and Ian Bernard in their enclosures. They had been stuck in these cages for days, and had been given dirty, rusty tap water and crumbs of food to try and keep them alive. Their latrines—a couple of old five-gallon buckets—hadn't been emptied in forever. The stench was almost overwhelming.

"Hey, Ian," Tommy squeaked out. "You still with me?"

"Where else would I be?" Tommy could forgive the anger and frustration in Ian's voice.

"We just need to keep hanging on." Tommy encouraged. "I know people are looking for us."

Their clothes were stained with bodily fluids—blood, urine, etc.—and they were ripped and tattered. With no natural light or ways to tell time, it was impossible to know exactly when or where they were.

"If I know my brother, he's champing at the bit to get his hands on these yokels." Ian continued laying in the fetal position on the floor of his cage, facing away from Tommy. "He tends to hold a grudge."

"So does Quinn," Tommy added.

Tommy looked around the warehouse floor, continuing to search for ways to get out of this hellhole. The concrete floor of the cage was more rough than smooth, and comfortable it was not. Ian at least had his suit jacket as a pillow.

The electrical hum of the energized bars now qualified as white noise, but both men knew to stay very far away from them. Tommy looked down at his hands and he rubbed the calloused burned skin of his left palm. He silently stared at the wound, sitting cross legged in the center of the cage. All of a sudden, Tommy heard a noise coming from deep in the warehouse—the sound of a door opening, which meant his captors were coming in to see them. The hum of the bars stopped, which meant the bars were no longer booby trapped. Tommy leaned forward onto his cage door, trying in vain to see if the door would just magically open. Alas, it did not.

Out of frustration, Tommy wrapped both hands around the bars of the cage door and proceeded to frantically shake it back and forth, screaming loudly into the void. Sheer desperation and fear dripped from his scream, which was just as useless as checking the locked cage door.

"Oooh, we've got a screamer," he heard Custer say from somewhere in the distance. Shortly, he came into view as Tommy rapidly blinked his eyes to try and focus on the old man in the dark.

"If you let me out, you'd see you had a fighter, too." Tommy was not a fighter, but false bravado in a situation like this could be considered an instinctual response.

Custer laughed maniacally. "Don't worry, your time here is soon coming to a close, and not in a way you would prefer." Custer kneeled down in front of Ian's cage, where he did not even acknowledge his presence. "Boy, you still with us?"

"Sorry to disappoint you, but I'm still kicking," Ian responded, continuing to lay on the cage floor. Custer looked annoyed at this, and jabbed Ian with the cattle prod, but for some reason didn't press the shock button.

"Dude, will you stop screwing with me and just do whatever you're gonna do? I'm bored with you and with…wherever or whatever this is. I'm so done with you and all of this." The look on Tommy's face at Ian's response was sheer terror.

Custer whistled into the darkness, and Clyde walked in, carrying a large metal hook on a wooden pole. Custer took the pole in his hand, reached through the bars of Ian's cage, and jabbed the hook into his exposed calf. The squelch of the metal tearing flesh was drowned out by Ian's screams of pain.

"Fire up the cages," Custer commanded, and the white noise hum of electricity resumed. Custer handed the pole back to Clyde.

"Do it, boy." At Custer's insistence, Clyde pulled Ian's leg towards the electrified cage bars. Ian tried to fight against it but the pain was greater than his remaining strength. As soon as Ian's bare foot touched the cage, the sounds and smells of sizzling flesh caused Tommy to recoil. Ian was completely helpless and writhing in pain.

"You're killing him! Stop it!" Tommy tried in vain to sway the angry duo.

Custer waved his hand, and Clyde released the tension on the pole. Ian instinctively curled back into a ball, holding his injured calf and foot. The sounds of his sobs drowned out all other sounds.

"Oh, I will kill him, but not like this. Actually, I will deliver both of you—probably sooner rather than later." Custer jabbed the cattle prod into Ian's lower back and energized it, causing him to arch his back involuntarily. When Custer released the prod, Ian lost consciousness, with blood from his injured calf pooling underneath him.

Tommy was trembling with fear and fury, but tried desperately to hide it. He didn't want to give Custer any more ammunition than he already had.

"So, you want the easy way, the hard way or the—" Custer looked over at Ian. "—the fun way?" He and Clyde both laughed.

"What do you mean? What kind of choice is that?" Tommy looked confused and anxious.

"You'll have time to think about it, but I need you to go to sleep now. I can prod you with my boom stick until you pass out like him."

Custer twirled the prod in his hands.

"Or...we can hook you up and jam you into the cage."

Tommy shook his head at both of those choices, and slid backwards away from the prod and the hook, coming close to the bars at the rear of the cage.

"Or—" Custer whistled again, this time three short trills, and the hum of the bars stopped. Beau slipped up from behind Tommy's back, and jammed a needle into his neck, emptying the syringe before Tommy could react. "—he can do that. Nighty night, boy." Custer laughed again.

Almost immediately, Tommy started rapidly blinking, shaking his head as if to clear cobwebs. He then quickly collapsed face first onto the cage floor.

"Damn, boy. How much did you give him?" Custer asked, hoping his screw-up of a son didn't screw up again.

"The same dose we gave that last girl. It worked just as quick with her, too." Beau flicked the syringe needle and then threw it up on a neighboring table.

Custer waited a brief moment, shining a flashlight onto Tommy. When he was satisfied he was still breathing, he checked Ian, jamming him with the business end of the prod. Still out.

Clyde deftly removed the hook from Ian's leg with a squelch, but even the pain that it caused didn't help Ian to regain consciousness. Clyde wiped the blood from the hook onto his flannel shirt, and held the pole down by his side.

"We might need this again, Pa."

"If we get into close enough hand-to-hand fighting to use that hook, that might not be a good thing." Custer stared at the two men. "These two have outlived their usefulness. Prepare them for cleansing. I want the people heading our way to bear witness to our purpose. I want them to see exactly how committed I am to honor my dear Emma, and my wonderful Lord our God."

Custer had never really had an audience before, except for the reporter. It excited him slightly, as a smile curled onto his lips.

He was going to be ready for whatever happened—when and if it actually did. He wanted whoever coming after him to underestimate his resilience, for he had the Lord on his side.

He can do all things through Christ who strengthens him.

***

At the rally point, everyone is gearing up for a fight. Brown, Miller, and Aaron are there with the rest of the GBI investigative team, and a squad of Kevlar-wearing PTC members are there as well. Everyone is lacing up boots, checking straps, and doing quick inventory checks.

Today is *finally* the day.

"Alright, people. This is it." Brown looks at another investigative team member. "Call over to the Special Operations Unit and get some backup put on standby. SWAT is also on its way up here." Brown looks over at Col. Anderson. "Colonel, what's the play?"

"They like to spray and pray, but did use a long gun against us at the first safe house." Anderson looks over at me with knowing eyes. That's where we lost Sgt. Barton, and I know it still weighs heavy on his heart. "But they don't have the same toys we do."

"What are you thinking?"

"I called a drone pilot and former squad mate who owes me a favor, and he's on his way. If we can paint a target on ground level from high above, they'll never see it coming."

"We can and will throw everything we have at them," Aaron adds. "But the old man is mine."

Brown walked over to Aaron, looking slightly irritated.

"Bernard, am I going to have to worry about you out there? This is way bigger than just your sister and brother, you know that, right?" Bernard looks at Brown, emotionless. This is going to be a fight, I know it.

"Come on, Aaron," I say, calmly. "Let's color within the lines, OK?"

I turn my attention back to Anderson and Brown.

"I just know more people were captured before me. There were at least fifteen cages on the warehouse floor." I look around the rally point location, as people continue to prepare for battle. "Who knows what we might find in there. As organized as they were, with their little religious ritual they performed before killing Alahna, they may have all the cages electrified, and I know they've done this before, I guarantee it. And I know they'll be waiting for me to come and save T-Jack and Ian. They'll be counting on it, but they won't know when or where—or with who."

Brown shoots a look at me. "Do you have any evidence of previous abductions, Ms. Campbell? Or is this just journalistic intuition?"

"Look, people this organized, this radicalized, must have had practice before. They had the tarp prepared in the bed of the truck. They had the bag ready to put over Alahna's head. They had the scripture and creepy ass version of *Amazing Grace* prepared." My heart races, my breathing speeds up, my hands tremble, and words fly rapidly out of my mouth. "She wasn't their first, and if we don't stop them, she definitely won't be their last."

Everyone is looking at me with a mixture of interest and pity. I don't need their pity. I just need closure.

"Alright, people. Bag and tag everything after we confront the Custers. If Campbell is right and more people have been involved, then every shred of evidence might be important." Brown starts giving his William Wallace speech.

"On scene, we have no idea what we might encounter. Ms. Campbell has provided us with valuable information, so be on the lookout. Also, our suspects currently have at least two hostages—both connected to Campbell—and one is the brother of one of our own."

Everyone starts packing up, preparing for war.

"When we roll, we roll as one. Col. Anderson has operational control on scene. We stay aware, we stay alert, we stay alive."

Brown gives Anderson a fist bump, which surprises me. I've never known Brownie to play second fiddle to anyone.

Anderson pulls everyone together, and starts putting people in teams and giving them their orders.

"Campbell, you're with me at all times," Anderson says, looking right through me. "There's no way I'm letting these assholes get their hands on you."

I guess I'm still his mission.

"That's the most romantic thing anyone has ever said to me." Anderson loudly rolls his eyes again at me. *Damn, c'mon, man...that was funny.*

"The lead group—Eagle 1—will be with me, which includes Campbell, who is designated as Eaglet. Special Agent Brown will lead Eagle 2, Detective Miller will be on Eagle 3, and Agent Bernard will lead Eagle 4." Watching Anderson organize everything is damn impressive, like he's done this before. His Peachtree techs and the GBI analysts split themselves up amongst the teams.

Anderson points to a spot on the map a couple of miles away from Custer's property. "When we pull up to this staging area, we'll divide up and begin operations on my mark."

Brown pulls on his GBI jacket. "You heard him. Gear up, and let's roll out."

A rush of emotion floods through me. T-Jack and Ian, we're coming for you. Please hold on. *Please.*

CHAPTER 20

I'm nervous, nauseous, angry, and oddly excited—all at the same time.

Today is the day we get justice for Alahna and God-knows-how-many others, and today is the day we save T-Jack and Ian—or least I hope we do. If they were kidnapped to bring me back up the mountain, then it is working. I just don't think Custer and the boys are expecting the rest of the cavalry coming with me.

This is the quietest and most awkward car ride I've ever been in, and I am *not* gonna pull a typical Quinn and interrupt the silence with a dad joke or some other icebreaker. There is too much testosterone and Kevlar in here. Col. Anderson will not even turn on the radio. The only sounds are from the Google Maps voice, telling him to turn left or right as they wander through the Chattahoochee.

Anderson and five other Peachtree Technology folks are crammed into the Escalade, while I am in the passenger seat. They are all dressed to the nines in combat attire, like they are heading out on patrol in a war-torn country instead of driving up to north Georgia. The vehicle is full of black duffel bags packed with guns, ammo, additional weapons, and other mercenary paraphernalia. I scan the vehicle with my reporter's eye—cataloguing everything within my eyesight. When I tell this story—*if* I live to tell it—I want to make sure to get all the details right.

Anderson picks up the CB radio handset in the Escalade, and keys the microphone. "Eagle 1 to response team, this is a radio test. Sound off in order, over."

Brown responds as Eagle 2, Miller as Eagle 3, and Bernard as Eagle 4. The SWAT team assisting the Task Force responds as Eagle 5. All teams report in as requested.

"Radio check acknowledged. Stay in formation until we arrive on location. Keep your heads on a swivel, and expect everything." Anderson secures the handset back on the radio, and puts both hands on the steering wheel at ten-and-two.

"Campbell, I need you to listen to me." Anderson's voice has a very serious tone, one I've heard before. "Today is probably going to be like nothing you've ever experienced. You cover these things after the fact, but outside of the safe house incident, I doubt you've ever been in a firefight. Am I wrong?"

"As far as gunfire directed *at* me, you're right. The only times that's happened have been recently, and from these guys." Truth be told, I didn't like it, not one bit. Guns still scare the hell out of me.

"Fear keeps you honest, keeps you focused." Anderson is one of the coolest cucumbers under pressure that I've ever seen. He's the reason I'm still breathing. "When we get to the staging area, I need you to gear up. We brought extra vests with us."

The thought of getting hit by another bullet does not excite me. "Roger that."

"Also, today might get messy, and I need to know you can stay calm and do what I ask."

I will do anything to protect T-Jack and help save him and Ian. I'll do anything to avenge Alahna. I just hope I can do enough to keep myself safe. "I've got this. I'm good."

I forget Anderson has seen me at my weakest and at my most vulnerable. "Contrary to popular current belief, I still think of myself as quite the badass."

"Who are you trying to convince, me or you?" Anderson says with a smirk.

"Jerk." I say with a smile, and turn to look out the window. Honestly, I'm not completely sure I won't mentally freak out when I get caught up in the middle of a warzone, but I do know I've got plenty of people backing me up.

I can do this. I can do it for AB. I can do it for Tommy. I can't lose him; *I just can't*.

***

The caravan pulls off the long and winding road into a clearing large enough to establish our staging area. Techs and officers jump out of their vehicles and start setting up canopies and various other technology to assist in the upcoming siege.

Colonel Anderson's drone pilot buddy begins assembling the aircraft on the ground, with hopes of soon getting it up in the air for our eyes in the sky. I watch him intently, because I've always thought drones were crazy cool, and are the future of news reporting and video capture.

"Alright, let's get organized. Brown, Miller, Bernard, other group commanders, let's regroup over here." Anderson brings all group leaders over to his command canopy, and begins going over operational strategy. I see them all nodding and agreeing about something, and then it looks like they all synchronize their watches. Then I realize how much I miss my Apple watch. I bet pieces of it still litter the floor in that God forsaken warehouse.

One of the Peachtree techs hands me a Kevlar bulletproof vest. The tech helps me rearrange my gear, gives me a couple of extra magazines for my Sig Sauer, and slides them into my vest. If I empty the magazine in my gun *and* two more of them, then something tells me the plan must have gone to shit—if you know what I mean. I still have this incredible urge to stay back, observe, and report, almost as if I was a journalist embedded in a military regiment overseas. "Report *on* the story, but don't *be* the story." That's usually a phrase I live by, but I haven't been so good about that as of late.

"Get that bird in the air pronto, Sergeant," Anderson orders.

"Yes sir." The pilot puts on what appear to be VR goggles, and has cool looking controllers in each hand. He punches a couple of buttons on a keyboard in front of him, and the drone buzzes to life. This thing is massive, much bigger than the mini drones you can buy online.

The drone comes off the ground, and hovers at about my eye level. Then it takes off straight in the air and disappears out of view. The pilot expertly flies the craft toward the destination, hopefully giving us an idea about where we're going and what we're getting into.

Anderson, Brown, Miller, and Bernard all watch a monitor intently, on which I'm assuming is the drone's video feed. Anderson waves me over.

"Campbell, I want you to tell us again if you recognize anything." Anderson speaks very plainly to me, and his tone stops just short of giving me an order.

"I'll do what I can. Last time I was here it was dark, and I had been fighting for my life for a couple of days." I have tried hard to forget some of the emotions from that night, but now I'm glad my reporter brain prevented me from forgetting everything. Anything, for that matter. Some of those painful memories might actually come in handy now.

We watch the video feed from the drone flying high in the sky far above Custer's property. I had no clue how spread out his property is, so I watch and learn as the video feed comes into the staging area. A PTC tech records all of the drone's video, probably for use later.

Damn, this vest holds in every bit of body heat. I adjust it a little bit, feeling like I'm boiling underneath it. The price of safety, I guess. I stick my fingers under the neck of my vest, and pull it slightly outwards. Come on, breeze...work your magic.

I look around the staging area and see people quickly moving about, putting together weapons, organizing, planning, getting ready for a full-scale assault. The drone is supposed to give us an advantage, so I turn back to the monitor.

The drone pilot moves the craft around effortlessly, with some cool-as-hell tech that would make any gamer jealous.

"I think we're coming up on the main compound, Colonel," the drone pilot says.

"Make sure to hover at a safe distance, and try zooming in." Anderson leans in closer to the monitor. "Campbell, see anything you recognize?"

The area looks a little different, and there are a *lot* more people around. I see several makeshift fences and barriers in place on the road leading up into the compound's main area.

"The number of people there right now suggests they knew we were coming," Brown says. "That might be a problem."

"Not a problem at all," Anderson says. "The plan is still a go. Campbell, talk to me."

"This is definitely where we were held, and this is what I think was the main house." I point to both structures on the monitor. "The front office area of the warehouse was where they controlled the cage locks and the electrification of the cage bars." I look down at the scars on my hands from said electricity. "I think we came out of this door here."

Techs were looking at the feed on other monitors, figuring out the distances between structures, and trying to determine the best points of egress. There was only one main road in, but the plan was to find other ways to potentially flank them from multiple sides.

"Eagle 2, head around the left to the number four side, and Eagle 3, head to the opposite two side on the right. Park far enough out and come up by the warehouse on foot. Stay in place until I give the order." Anderson scribbles the play call on paper, like he was drawing up a backyard football play in the dirt with a stick. "Eagle 5, gear up and drive your vehicle right up Broadway. Eagle 1 will be right behind you along with—"

At that moment, a flash of light appears on the monitor and interrupts Anderson's order stream. Everyone recoils away from the apparent explosion.

"What the hell?" Anderson turns to the drone pilot. "Sergeant, what in God's name happened?"

"Something on the ground took out the drone, sir. I didn't even see it coming." Anderson bangs his fist on the table, and then spins the monitor almost off the table.

"Damn it, now we're going in blind. Things just got a *little* more complicated." Anderson runs his fingers through his hair and sighs loudly. "Eagles 2 and 3, your mission stays the same. Make sure to also keep an eye on the three side to see if anyone rabbits. Keep your radios hot, and we'll move in on my mark. Let's go ahead and re-synchronize our watches." Anderson, Miller, Brown, and Aaron all reach their hands out, and they beep their watches at the same time.

One of the GBI techs hands out printed copies of the Custer family photo. "Folks, remember the circled faces. You are likely to see these three men on site—Elijah Custer is the leader of the group, and Clyde and Beauregard Custer are his only remaining sons that we know of," Brown continues. "The other people on site must be workers from Custer's construction company or cult-like followers he has talked into helping defend the property. Clyde Custer also has extensive military training as a decorated Army sniper, so keep your heads on a swivel out there."

Techs also pass out pictures of Tommy Jackson and Ian Bernard.

"We believe these two men are being held hostage on site, probably in the warehouse, in an attempt to draw Ms. Campbell back to the property." My cheeks feel super hot when I realize everyone is staring at me. I wave my hand in a silly attempt to say hello. *Super* awkward.

"Our mission is to rescue the hostages and take at least one of these three men alive." Anderson pauses for a moment, and looks around at everyone within earshot. "Hear me loud and clear on this next part: lethal force is authorized, but be smart, people. We need at least one of the Custers alive to give us information about their operation. Are we clear?"

I look over at Aaron, and he's visibly frustrated. He hasn't been given his orders yet, and I can tell he's mentally pacing back and forth.

"Colonel, what about me and Eagle 4?" Aaron finally speaks up.

Anderson sighs loudly, and turns to look at Aaron. "Your brother's one of the two men in there, Agent. Can I trust you not to go all Rambo, jeopardize the entire mission, and get yourself and possibly your brother and everyone else killed?"

"Respectfully, sir...what would you do if it was your brother being held in there?" Aaron challenges. "Wouldn't you do everything you could to spring him? I've already lost my sister, and if I have a chance to save Ian, I'm going to take it."

"Nothing gets in the way of the mission, son. *Nothing*." Anderson takes a step toward Aaron. "However, if you see an opportunity to safely extract the hostages, then take it. Do not, I repeat, *do not* do so in a way that jeopardizes you, the hostages, or *any* of our people. Copy?"

I watch both men like I'm watching a tennis match, where players are volleying back and forth at a championship level. Aaron says yes sir to Anderson's demands, but I know him. He's going to do whatever it takes to save Ian, even if it puts him and the mission in harm's way.

"Colonel, what am I doing?" I ask, afraid of his answer.

"Eaglet is your designation, which means you stay on my six—no matter what. You stay behind me in lockstep." Anderson checks my vest and makes sure my weapon is holstered properly. "When I move, you move."

"Just like that?" I nervously laugh, as I quote the finished hip hop lyric.

Anderson's lips curl into a sly grin, and it is gone just as quickly. "Just focus on staying alive. They've been after you from the beginning of this ordeal, because of what you saw up on the mountain. Once we raid the compound, you probably won't be their sole concern anymore."

Oh yeah, how could I forget that I'm the one thing Custer wants most. I'll hopefully be able to draw him out into the open. "Yeah, something tells me he will still want my head in a bag just the same. It's the principle of the matter to him, I'm sure of it."

***

Clyde ejected the cartridge from his long gun with the bolt action lever after bringing down the rogue drone. He looked over at Custer near the entrance to the warehouse.

"I told you they'd try some military shit like that." Pieces of the drone fell down onto the ground near the main house. Clyde walked over to the debris, and held up a piece with U.S. Army identification on it. "See? Good thing I had Ol' Betty with me." He patted his long gun proudly.

Custer screamed out to the people manning the barriers and enclosures along the main road. "Get ready. They are here sooner than we thought. Eyes open, people."

He looked out at the twenty to thirty people Clyde and Beau managed to talk into being their human shields during this encounter. Custer made a mental note to ask his sons what they said to convince these people to potentially throw their lives away for the cause, if they actually made it out of this.

"Alright people, tick tock. The job is in motion." Custer stood in the middle of everything, standing tall and staring out into the distance. Workers began scurrying around the compound, finding places in the barricades to hide behind, preparing for the fight of their lives.

"Prepare our hostages," Custer ordered Beau, and he and several others ran into the warehouse. He wanted to hold onto the things he knew the cavalry wanted, putting the captives between the oncoming force and himself. He was going to force them to make a choice. An impossible choice. Or they could give him the reporter in 'exchange' for the two men—but he had no intention of letting any of them stay alive. All three of them would die today by his hand, if he has any say in the matter. A promise is a promise, and he was damn tired of loose ends screwing everything up.

***

I pull Aaron aside, and I look him straight in the eye.

"I need you to promise me that you won't get dead today." Neither one of us blinks. "*Promise me*, damn it."

"I promise I'll try. That's all I can give you, Q." Aaron puts his hands on my shoulders. "I've already lost Alahna. I can't lose Ian, too. I promised Mama B I'd bring him home, no matter what."

"And you can't do that if you're dead, you know that, right?"

"I know, I know." He sighs, and pulls me in for a hug. "And you need to not get dead either."

"They've tried four times, and haven't gotten me yet."

"Don't make it a fifth."

"Speaking of fifths, if we make it out of here in one piece, the first round of Glenfiddich is on me." I know how much Aaron likes his Scotch.

"Now I have to make it out of here." We both smile out of habit. "Deal."

Anderson sends Brown's and Miller's groups out into the surrounding fields, as SWAT finishes their preparations. Their SWAT vehicle is an armored tank of sorts, with armored gun positions on both sides and a bubble turret on top armed with one of the biggest guns I've ever seen. I'm also assuming it's bulletproof, since Anderson is basically using it as a battering ram through the makeshift barricades. And these SWAT guys haven't said word one to us today. They're like well-oiled machines, taking orders from Col. Anderson and performing their duties with pinpoint precision.

They'll be leading the way as the Escalades from Eagle 1 and Eagle 4 follow closely behind. Our vehicles are *not* bulletproof, so there's that.

"Eagles 2 and 3, when you are in position, and are ready on foot, let me know." Anderson squawks on the walkie. "We'll execute a pincer move on the sides as we drive right through the front gate and ring the doorbell."

Both Brown and Miller say, "Copy that," and the walkies go silent.

Anderson turns his attention to the SWAT driver. "Your goal is to drive through the first barricade, and use your roof and side gun positions to take out as many bogeys as you can. We'll be right behind you."

The SWAT driver nods his head, and climbs inside the LEO Speed-wagon. That's what Aaron told me law enforcement officers call the SWAT vehicle, and I give them mad props for their surprisingly creative wordplay. Even scared out of my mind, with adrenaline pumping through my veins so loud I can barely hear, I have to give credit where credit is due.

Anderson gives instructions to the crew monitoring the operation from the staging area. Earlier, I watched crews putting trackers on each of the vehicles, and now I know why. Before it was shot down, the drone provided a new layout of the area, which the techs are now using to pinpoint the locations of each of the vehicles.

I climb into the back row seat of our Escalade, surrounded by Peachtree techs. I watch Aaron slide into the passenger seat of his vehicle, with his GBI crew filling the rest of the seats. Anderson speaks to the SWAT vehicle driver, then walks over to our vehicle. He closes the door, and grabs the radio handset.

"Eagles 2 and 3, are you in position?"

"Eagle 2, in position and standing by," Special Agent Brown says.

"Eagle 3, in position." Detective Miller says they are also standing by.

"Eagle 4, remain behind Eagle 1 until Eagle 5 establishes a front line." Anderson runs through the rest of the plan. "Eagle 1 will go right, while you go left, both flanking Eagle 5. Copy?"

"Copy that." Aaron signs off.

"Alright, let's roll out. Eagle 5, we're on your six." Anderson maneuvers all of the teams deftly. "Eagles 2 and 3, hold your position until I give the order."

"Copy, Colonel. Eagle 5 rolling out."

The walkies fall silent. We are now passing the point of no return.

I listen to all of this while scribbling notes down on my reporter's notebook. This is going to be one hell of a story if and when we make it out of here. I can hear the potential teaser copy now: *The Mountain Mangler captured in north Georgia mountains. All hostages rescued alive. Story at 11.*

Time is running out for T-Jack and Ian, so I *really* hope the plan works.

***

Both Tommy Jackson and Ian Bernard lay crumpled on the floor of their respective cages. They have been tortured day and night since they were kidnapped, and for no good reason other than for the entertainment of their captors. Their clothes are in tatters and are stained with blood in varying stages of drying.

"Ian, are you still with me?" Tommy asked, weakly, still coming off whatever sedative they injected him with. "You still hanging in there?"

Tommy heard a groan from the other cage. "Yeah, man...but I don't know for how much longer. I'm so done with these freaks."

"We've lasted this long, what's a little longer?" Tommy asked. "I just know someone's coming for us. I know Quinn and Aaron won't forget about us."

"Then why'd they let Quinn go then? Was she just lucky?"

"Hell if I know. I just have this feeling that, with Quinn being the normal Quinn, she just made their lives difficult."

"And man, I'm not far behind. I don't have much left in the tank." Ian's head sunk low.

Tommy just couldn't let himself lose hope. He just knew Quinn was out there, shaking trees and knocking down doors trying to find him. Maybe he should have told her how he felt about her. Maybe she would have gotten here sooner had she known. Maybe she'll never know, but the thought of her saving them gave him just enough hope to stay strong.

"Hey, look, man. Tell me about Aaron. Is he as relentless as Alahna is?"

"Dude's like a dog with a bone when it comes to family. He is the epitome of loyal to a fault. And his temper...Jesus Christ, his temper..."

"Then you should lean into that. Stay with me a little longer, and let Aaron do his job. That's how I feel about Quinn. And if she and Aaron are coming here together, then God help these guys."

"I felt that way a couple of days ago, but my body is broken, man. My will is broken. I'm just not sure there will be enough left of me to save."

They heard a door open in the darkness, and several men came walking towards them.

"Alright, folks. Time to get ready for the big finale," one of the balaclava-wearing men said, as he turned to the others with him. "Knock 'em out, boys."

One of the men opened Ian's cage first, and Tommy watched him plunge a syringe into Ian's thigh. Once the man depressed the syringe, Tommy watched Ian slowly lose consciousness and fall over in a lump.

A second man opened Tommy's cage door, and from out of nowhere, Tommy gathered the courage to bum rush the unsuspecting man. Tommy pushed the man backwards out the door, and tried to make a break for it. However, in his weakened state, two of the other men easily overpowered him, and held him down on the ground.

One of the men walked up to him and kicked Tommy squarely in the ribs with a crunching sound. "You actually thought that was gonna work, boy?" He struck Tommy's face with a closed fist so hard that blood splattered out of his mouth onto the floor. He grabbed Tommy's hair, and craned his neck backward. "Pa's gonna make an example out of you, but not before I have a little fun."

The man stuck out his hand, and one of the others gave him the cattle prod. Tommy started shaking his head back and forth, begging for mercy. "Please, please...I didn't mean to—"

The man shoved the cattle prod into Tommy's ribcage, sending wave after wave of electricity through Tommy's weakened body. He was even too weak to scream, so he gritted his teeth and squinted his eyes in agony, trying to ride out the pain. After a few seconds, the man withdrew the prod, and Tommy collapsed on the warehouse floor—still being held by the other men. The man who Tommy knocked ass over tea kettle got up, and kicked Tommy square in the face. His head flew back from the force of the kick, then rolled back down in front. The embarrassed man started wailing on Tommy, punching and kicking him over and over again, before the youngest man stopped him.

"Easy, man. He is Custer's to cleanse, not yours to kill because of your stupid pride," the man said. "Knock him out proper like, and let's move them over to the office."

He continued wailing on Tommy, and then reared back for one last measured punch, which connected with Tommy's right temple. Tommy lost all consciousness and collapsed at the feet of the men who surrounded him.

***

LEO Speedwagon rolls down the entrance road with us and Eagle 4 in a single file line behind them.

"Eagles 2 and 3, still in position?" Anderson asks. Both Eagle 2 and 3 confirm they remain in position.

"Continue to hold until I give the signal to move in." Anderson re-hangs the radio on the dash.

The Peachtree tech in the passenger seat tells Anderson they are about one klick out. I had to quickly Google what a klick was, and it turns out it is a little less than a mile in military speak. And I thought journalists spoke with a lot of jargon.

"Alright, folks. Keep your head on a swivel, and be prepared for anything. Campbell, make sure your gun is loaded properly." Anderson barks from the driver's seat. I pull out the 9mm he gave me, and one of the techs beside me sticks out his hand.

"Let me help you with that," he says.

"Dude, I'm not helpless," I say. "How about this, watch and make sure I do it correctly before trying to mansplain it to me." The tech puts his hands up in an 'excuse me' gesture. I point the barrel of the gun toward the roof of the Escalade, and I rack the slide back a couple of times to make sure no rounds are in the chamber. I pull one of the magazines out of my belt, and slide it into the magwell until I hear it click. Then I rack the slide back again to put a round in the chamber. I make doubly sure the safety is on, and then I put it back in my shoulder holster.

"So, how'd I do?" I confidently ask the tech beside me who had tried to mansplain his way into loading my gun for me.

"Top notch," he says, and gives me a thumbs up. See, I'm not *completely* helpless. But I'm also not going to lie, guns still scare the hell out of me.

All of a sudden, LEO Speedwagon slows way down in front of us, which causes us to slow down as well. I assume we're just getting close to—

And that's when we see and hear the huge explosion.

CHAPTER 21

LEO Speedwagon lilts to the side up on two tires, and then crashes back down to the ground.

"IED! Get down!" Anderson screams in the cab, and grabs for the radio. "Eagle 5, is everyone Code 4?"

No response at first.

"Eagle 5, do you copy?" Anderson has more emotion in his voice now.

"We copy, Eagle 1. We're all Code 4, but our tires are toast after the explosion," the SWAT commander replies. "However, we're still good to press on, even if we're limping to do it."

"Copy that. Any idea what set it off?"

"Negative. I couldn't tell if it was a mine or something that was triggered remotely."

"10-4. Proceed forward with caution and watch out for more incendiaries from here on out." He puts the handset back on the radio and then turns his attention to us. "Everybody good?"

I do a quick self-diagnostic, and I give him a thumbs up. Our windshield is cracked but nothing else appears to have gotten through.

"I'm glad that it hit LEO Speedwagon instead of us," I say. "That thing's a straight-up tank."

"That's why it's in front of us." Anderson taps his temple as if to say he occasionally makes smart decisions.

The smell in the air is undeniable—gunpowder mixed with a sizable dose of fear. I've had friends embedded in war zones who have had plenty of experience with IEDs, but that was my first one. I think my heart briefly stopped before trying to pound itself right out of my chest.

I look out the front window, and the SWAT driver is no longer driving straight on the road. He is zig zagging left to right, trying to be a little less predictable. I bet that thing is even more of a beast to drive with four flat tires. Can't really call AAA at the moment.

I pull out my phone and text Aaron.

You OK? All good here. LEO Speedwagon took most of it.

Three little dots tell me he is replying to my text.

Yeah, all good. Glad u're OK.

I give his reply a thumbs up and slide my phone back in my pocket. I'm not even scribbling details into my notebook anymore. Hell, I'm not even sure where it is right now. I dropped it at some point during or after the explosion.

I rapidly scan the surrounding area, and everything seems still. *Too* still.

"Stay liquid, team," Anderson tells the rest of Eagle 1. "We will peel off at any moment, and you'll need to be ready to run and gun." I remember we're pulling alongside LEO Speedwagon's right side, while Aaron and Eagle 4 head to its left side. I'm in the middle of the rear seat, so I guess I'll go to the side of the faster Peachtree tech and away from any gunfire. Mama didn't raise no fool.

Suddenly, gunfire erupts from all around me. I hear bullets ricocheting off the SWAT vehicle in front of us. "Target barricade acquired. Engaging hostiles." Eagle 5 radios to the response team.

"Eagles 2 and 3, *engage engage engage*." Anderson orders into the radio, as he pulls the Escalade perpendicularly off to the right side of the SWAT vehicle. Eagle 4 does the same to the left.

Officers in Eagle 5 slide guns out of the sides of LEO Speedwagon, engaging shooters behind the first barricade. I see an officer climb up into the roof turret, and the big gun on top roars to life.

Boom! Crack! Pop Pop Pop!

The sounds of gunfire echo from every direction. The tech to my right gets out first, so I follow him out of Escalade and hide near the rear wheel well. Soon, I feel like I've been left behind, so options begin whizzing through my brain like bullets through butter.

I decide to attempt to get behind LEO Speedwagon. If it's bulletproof, then that is a good thing for me. I slide to the right rear quarter panel of the Escalade, and try to time the gunfire.

Pop Pop Pop! Bam!

I take a breath, then run behind the SWAT vehicle. I have zero clue where all the bullets are coming from. It seems like I'm surrounded, and I really don't have a clue about where to go.

Suddenly, a hand forcefully grabs my shoulder. It is Anderson.

"I thought I told you to stay behind me."

"Well, I did. Just too *far* behind you."

"That ends now. Get in my back pocket and stay there. And pull out your weapon for Christ's sake. I thought I taught you how to defend yourself, so get ready and stay ready. Just don't shoot a friendly. Or yourself."

A friendly. With all the chaos going on right now, how in the hell am I gonna figure out if it's a friendly until it's too late?

"When I say go, I want you to run towards that retaining wall to the left of Speedwagon. See it?" Anderson points, and doesn't even look back at me for confirmation.

"Yeah, I see it."

"Alright. 3, 2, 1, go." Anderson jumps out from behind Speedwagon and lays down some cover fire. I run behind him like my life depends on it, which it realistically does. I slide down behind the wall, and Anderson places his hand on my upper back. "Stay down."

Anderson pulls a walkie off his hip. "Eagle 5 is engaging hostiles at the first barricade. Eagle 1 and Eaglet are in position to the left of the first barricade."

I notice a SWAT officer get shot and I watch him fall to the ground. Then I see two or three of Custer's crew fall by the barricade. The big gun on Speedwagon cranks out multiple rounds and drops bogeys left and right until a shot drops the roof turret gunner with a sickening crunch. The sound makes me throw up a little in my mouth. *Keep it together, Campbell.*

Anderson motions to another spot of cover behind the first barricade over by the main house. "Go, go, go." He pushes me towards it as he lays down more cover fire. I once again kneel behind the barricade, and Anderson quickly joins me. I see him pop out his empty magazine and rack a fresh one into the magwell.

"Here." He shoves binoculars in my hand. "Find one of our three main hostiles or our hostages. I can't do that and engage at the same time."

I lean around to the left of the new cover spot, and put the binoculars up to my eyes. I see a ton of people I don't know either shooting at us, getting shot by us, or running in the opposite direction—right in the direction of Eagles 2 and 3. No Custer. No sons. No T-Jack or Ian.

A few rounds hit the fence way too close to my head, and I instinctively go further behind the cover, but drop the binoculars. *Damn it, Ms. Clumsy.*

Anderson leans out to get the binoculars and a round hits him, knocking him backwards.

"Colonel!" I grab out for him, and help him scramble back behind the cover.

"Relax. It hit my vest. It hurts like a bitch though, but I'm good. Not my first time getting shot." He hands the binoculars back to me. "Try not to drop them again."

My heart races so loud that I can hear every beat in my ears. Speaking of ears, mine hurt so badly from all the gunfire in front of me, behind me, and around me. So damn loud.

I see Aaron behind me to the right, and he gives me a thumbs up. He's hanging out behind Speedwagon, but then he peels out and runs toward the shooters behind the second barricade.

"Damn it, no!" Anderson must have seen him as well, because he takes two fingers and motions to the rest of Eagle 1 to back him up. "I knew he'd do something like that. We gotta move. Now."

I lean up to get a better vantage point with my binoculars. In the distance, in front of the warehouse, I see him, just standing there, smiling and waving at me.

Custer.

***

Standing in front of the warehouse, Custer surveyed the hellish landscape that was once his front yard. His plan was working. All of these
meat shields stood between the law and the Lord. No one appeared to
be worried about him at all because he's not shooting at anyone.

"She's gotta be here. I just know it," he mumbled to himself, looking for the reporter.

He saw Clyde take out the roof gunner from the lead vehicle with
a perfect shot. He was impressed at how much better Clyde's sniping
skills had become since he had given him Ol' Betty and the scope he
had picked out. It had been amazing to see. He knew Clyde wanted
every single one of these usurpers dead for what they did to Leland
and Ezekiel. Their family had been busted up because of these goons,
and Custer knew Clyde was gonna take as many of them down as he
could.

He also knew Beau had prepared both of their 'guests' in the warehouse. Once he saw the reporter, Custer would fall back into the office
and hopefully draw her to him. This whole war zone charade had been
for her, and he hoped she was enjoying the show.

He noticed something, or someone, in front of his house was drawing fire from the front line. Was that a red ponytail he saw? Could that
be her? He took a few steps sideways to get a better vantage point. He
saw someone get shot leaning around the retaining wall. He focused
more on that location, trying to figure out if his eyes were playing
tricks on him.

Then he saw it. A woman with a red ponytail leaned up over the
barricade with a pair of binoculars pointed directly at him. He knew
it. There she was. The reporter.

He waved in her direction, and then retreated into the warehouse
with Beau and their two 'guests.' He truly hoped she would soon
follow him.

If not, then Clyde was his back-up plan.

***

Clyde had taken up a position in one tree facing the side of the warehouse closest to the main house. He watched as one vehicle stopped on that side, and five agents got out on foot, walking stealthily toward the warehouse.

He put one agent in the rear of the group in his sights, and fired off an armor piercing round. The agent crumpled to the ground.

"Sniper!" Agent Brown yelled to the rest of Eagle 2, but there was no remaining cover on that side of the building.

Clyde fired off a second and a third shot, dropping two more of the agents.

Brown and another agent scrambled back in the direction of the Escalade. He went to grab his radio, and it wasn't on his hip. He had dropped it in the open field. He closed his eyes and banged the back of his head against the vehicle.

"I gotta get that radio." he said to the last remaining Eagle 2 agent.

"Don't worry, sir," the agent said. "Stay here, I'll grab it." She jumped out from behind the vehicle.

Clyde looked through the scope, needing just a small sliver of agent to show themselves. As soon as she came out from behind the vehicle, Clyde dropped her almost immediately.

"Damn it," Brown screamed, knowing he was pinned down with no way to radio for help. And he was a sitting duck, so he slid into the driver's seat of the Escalade and tried to start the vehicle. Clyde, seeing him trying to drive away, fired a couple of well-placed shots into the radiator and front axle well. However, Brown was able to limp the vehicle away into the open ground, heading back to the staging area. He was no good out there by himself.

Now that the 4-side was clear, Clyde scampered down from the tree and headed to the left side of the structure. He knew Custer had a surprise for whoever opened the front warehouse door first, but he had his marching orders.

Find the reporter and bring her to him...alive.

***

"There he is! There's Custer!" I scream to Anderson. "He just smiled at me, and fucking waved in my direction! The gall of that bastard! Then he retreated into the warehouse, and that's where Aaron and the rest of your squad are also heading."

"Maybe Bernard saw Custer too, and wanted to take his shot." Anderson ejects his spent magazine and loads another. "Let's move. Cover me, guys." He yells out to the SWAT officers and any other response team folks still fighting. They lay down suppressive fire so that Anderson and I can move closer to the warehouse door. There are lots of barbed-wire and wooden improvised fences between us and the door where Custer went in. I can't believe I'm actually trying to get back into a place from where I barely escaped.

T-Jack and Ian need me. I know they're still alive, and I know I can save them. Once we stop, I say something to Anderson that surprises even me.

"Custer wants me, so I'm going to trade myself for Tommy and Ian."

"The hell you are!" Anderson looks me dead in the eyes. "There is no way in hell I'm going to let you just turn yourself over to that murderer."

"Alright then. Got a better idea? He saw me and then he just waved at me." I close my eyes and take a deep breath before continuing. "He is luring me inside the building."

"You and every other gun we have available. There is absolutely no way you are going in alone."

"Then come with me. His boys killed Sgt. Barton. I know you want a piece of the man who ordered it."

"And I know they got Sgt. Allen and Cpl. Taylor, too. They have too much of our blood on their hands, but—"

Bullets continue whizzing above us and all around us.

"Look, the clock is ticking. He may be killing Tommy or Ian right now because he thinks I'm too chicken shit to face him." I steel my resolve for the next sentence. "I'm tired of him killing people in my name, or hurting people I care about. Either come with me, or handcuff me to this God damned fence."

Anderson takes out his radio. "Eagle 1 and Eaglet are heading to the warehouse door. Eagles 2 and 3, continue covering the sides of the building, and remove any bogeys from the playing field. Eagle 5, get that roof gun back operational, and cover the front door." He didn't wait for radio confirmation.

"Are you really sure you want to do this?" Anderson asks me, knowing exactly who he's dealing with.

"I'm done hiding from them. I am so sick and tired of being scared. I am done with him *and* his bullshit." I'm sure Anderson hates my answer.

"Screw it. Let's move." Anderson keys the walkie again. "Eagle 4, hold your position. Cover Eagle 1 as they enter the building. Me and Eaglet will enter right behind them."

"And I'll be right behind you." Aaron replies on the radio. "Eagle 4 will cover all of us."

I hear Aaron's voice on the radio, but then I scan the courtyard for where he actually is. I find him just to the right of the door, ready to join us as we enter the building.

"Eagle 1, *breach, breach, breach*." Anderson runs ahead, and I tag along closer than his shadow. The cover fire from LEO Speedwagon makes it possible for us to get to the wall beside the door. The rest of Eagle 1 and Aaron are to the right of the door, while Anderson and I have our backs to the wall on the left. As soon as the Eagle 1 tech opens the door, a huge concussive blast hits him and knocks him several feet backward through the air. Everyone immediately turns away from the blast and from their fallen squadmate.

As the debris settles, the rest of Eagle 1 enters the space where the door was, leaving me and Anderson waiting outside. Suddenly, I feel something whizz past me and Anderson groans, falling forward.

"No!" I scream, just as someone slides a fabric bag over my head, and bear hugs me. "Get off of me! Help!" I yell through the bag, but the person easily overpowers me. "Put me down, damn it!"

I realize the explosion was a distraction, something to cause people to close their eyes and look away while some idiot grabs me up. And I don't know if Anderson is OK or not. I hear a couple of shots hit the warehouse in our direction, but they are probably worried they'd hit me instead.

Looks like I'll be seeing Custer sooner rather than later after all.

***

Custer was glad the reporter wasn't the first one through the door, and he kind of counted on that. He had rigged and armed the explosive device as soon as he came inside, knowing they'd send a couple of grunts in first to clear the building. He wished it would have been that behemoth of a security blanket the reporter has had since Zeke screwed up at the hospital. No matter. His time will come.

As Custer stared at the opening where the door used to be, behind glass in the office vestibule, he wondered what would happen next. Would they come in, guns a-blazin', or would they retreat for fear of another explosion. He had only rigged one device, but they didn't know that.

Either way, the plan was in motion. Both of his guests were unconscious lying on tarps just inside the warehouse floor, and there was a third tarp just waiting for the reporter.

Suddenly, the interior door to the office opened, and Clyde came stumbling in with someone in his arms. Could it be?

"Pa, I got her. I got the reporter," Clyde said, triumphantly. "And I put a bullet in her security guard." He dumped her body on the floor in the middle of the room. She was cursing and fighting, trying to get the bag off of her head.

Custer leaned over and pulled the fabric bag off of her head. He was staring into the eyes of the person he most desperately wanted to see. He pulled her red ponytail to the side, and she immediately spat in his face.

"Excellent," Custer trilled, as he wiped the saliva from his cheek. "Prepare her with the others."

The reporter tried fighting back, but Custer pistol-whipped her in the head. She collapsed in a heap, falling completely silent.

He had finally found her, and this time, he wouldn't let her escape. *Praise be to God.*

***

"Son of a—" Anderson sat up by the exploded door, as the rest of Eagle 1 and Aaron Bernard fussed over him. "I'm alright, damn it. It's just my shoulder. Give me a sitrep."

"Most of Eagle 2 is down, but Agent Brown made it back to base camp. A sniper laid waste to them on the four side."

He began looking around, and fear covered his face. "Where's Campbell?"

"During the explosion, and right after they shot you, someone nabbed her and dragged her around the side of the building," Aaron said.

Anderson screamed loudly, and banged his fist against the warehouse. He grabbed his radio.

"Eagle 3, copy?"

Detective Grayson Miller responded, "Go for Eagle 3."

"Your mission now is to breach the warehouse somewhere other than a door. Be careful—IEDs are likely being used on most every entrance."

"Copy that." Miller disconnected the radio.

"Some of these assholes are using armor-piercing rounds, so be careful. That last bullet went right through my vest." Anderson groaned as he moved his injured right shoulder around slightly.

"Since they have Quinn, we need to move in *now*." Aaron had fear in his voice. "He's not gonna waste time killing her or my brother and the assignment editor as well since he doesn't need them anymore."

"Eagle 1 to base camp, call in air support. We need more eyes in the sky." Anderson barked into his radio, the pain from the bullet wound negatively affecting his personality. "Also call for backup and several RAs to this location. Have the RAs remain at base camp until this situation is Code 4."

"Base camp, copy that, Eagle 1. Air support, backup, and rescue ambulances will be called to the scene. Will update you with ETA when we know it."

"10-4." Anderson replied.

"I'm going to go find that side entrance, where that bastard dragged Quinn," Aaron said.

"Not without me, you aren't." Anderson stood up and quickly did a self-diagnostic. "She's my responsibility. What's left of Eagle 1 and Eagle 4, follow us to the four side."

Anderson and Bernard led the remaining group around the one/four corner, and that's when they saw the remnants of Eagle 2 lying dead on the ground. They moved quietly, scanning the area for snipers and other bogeys. They found a small side door with no window and a simple door handle.

"Careful opening the door, might be booby trapped again." Anderson reminded them.

One of Eagle 1's techs tied a rope around the door handle, and pulled the door open from a safe distance, while Anderson and Bernard flanked on either side of the entrance. When no explosion happened, they cautiously and quietly entered the building—remaining on high alert.

***

Det. Miller and the rest of Eagle 3 found a small entrance on the two side, with no window and a simple door handle. It was marked emergency exit.

"Hey, can you disconnect a possible alarm from this side of the door?" Miller asked one of his GBI agents.

"Let me look at it." The tech walked up to it and examined the door as best he could from that side of it. "I can't see any way to disable the alarm, sir. Or if there is even an alarm active on the door."

Miller shrugged his shoulders and said, "Well, they definitely know we're already here, so screw it." He grabbed the door handle and pulled it. It didn't budge. "Locked from the inside, maybe? Hey, got anything to open this door?"

One agent pulled out a circular disc and placed it on the door just below the door handle. "Fire in the hole." she said, and everyone turned away from the potential blast. The small device punched a hole in the door, which quietly obliterated the inside lock. The door opened slightly, and much to everyone's relief, no alarm went off.

"Guns at the ready. Be very careful and keep your heads up." Miller instructed. "Remember, they have friendlies, and we don't need to mix them up with our bogeys."

Miller and four other agents slid quietly inside the door of the warehouse.

***

As I come to, my head is seriously killing me. I stared right in that asshole's eyes when he hit me in the face. I swear they've given me at least two concussions now.

I notice I'm sitting in a chair, with my hands bound behind me and my feet zip-tied in front of me. I look around and realize I'm back in the warehouse. *Sonofabitch.*

But then I notice Tommy to my right, bound in the same way I am, but he's slumped over in his chair. My heart leaps through my chest as I scream his name. "T-Jack!"

That gets everyone's attention, and they all turn around to look at me, including Custer.

"You inbred hillbilly, I will kill you where you stand for what you've done to me and my friends!" Instinct kicks in and that response comes from a very dark place inside me. I probably should have not said that part out loud.

"Well, ain't we just a peach," Custer said. "You ain't in any position to be doing any killing right now." He and all of his crew laugh at me. I notice two of his sons are with him, along with several faces I do not recognize.

I turn to the left and see Ian in a similar state as Tommy. They both look like hell, and my blood begins to boil. "Look, you got me, you got what you wanted. Now let them go." I'm overwhelmed with anger and fear as the words slide forcefully out of my mouth.

"Now you know I can't do that, darlin'. Don't you remember anything from the first time we were in this position?" Custer tsk tsk tsked through his teeth, mocking me. I instinctively look down for my gun, but yeah, it's not there anymore. Custer pulls my gun out of his pocket.

"You looking for this little pop gun? What exactly were you gonna do with this thing?" Custer asks, smiling. He aims the gun at Ian and shoots him in the leg. The pain pulls Ian out of whatever unconscious state he was in, and he groans wildly as the bullet sears into his flesh.

"You coward," I scream, pulling at the zip ties binding my hands behind the chair.

"You think I'm a coward? A coward?" Custer asks sternly, as he points the gun at Tommy. "Say it again." In all the commotion, I notice Tommy is slowly regaining consciousness. I see him look around, confused.

Time stands still as I try to work out all the details around me. "Please, please don't..." I beg.

"You need to keep better control of that mouth." Custer laughs and shoots Tommy in the thigh as well.

Tommy screams bloody murder, and I hope and pray Custer missed both of their femoral arteries. Blood floods his pants as Tommy sobs loudly. Both of my friends are screaming and crying around me and I'm powerless to stop it. I've been here before.

All of a sudden, I hear Alahna's voice in my head.

I'm dead because you couldn't save me, and now my brother is going to suffer the same fate.

I shake my head vigorously, focusing on what I can control. "Look, OK...you've made your point. Just stop hurting my friends, alright? Just leave them out of it." I plead with everything I have left.

"No can do. It's only a matter of time before all three of your souls will be cleansed and you will be sent to meet the Lord, our God." Custer spouts this religious bullshit like it should scare me. Problem is, it does.

"Bring out the bags, boys," Custer says. "Let's prepare for the cleansings. They'll be here soon." Beau and Clyde put bags down in front of Ian and Tommy's chairs, and then smile at me when they sit one in front of me. Clyde smacks my face...hard.

"That is for breaking up our family, you little whore." Clyde laughs in a way that scares me to my core.

Shit. Our time is quickly running out. I pray Anderson heard the gunshots, and that he finds us in time.

***

"Gunshot, straight ahead," Anderson said, holding up his hands to stop Aaron and the remaining members of Eagle 1 and Eagle 4. He took two fingers and pointed them to the right along the wall, and the techs slinked away with guns drawn. "Aaron, you're with me."

Anderson and Aaron moved silently under the cover of darkness. The sound of a second gunshot echoed throughout the vast building, but it was hard to pinpoint exactly where. While the other techs were working the wall from the inside, the men closest to Quinn worked through the middle of the space. Rows and rows of packed shelves lined the walkway. They systematically cleared each row, and Aaron tapped Anderson's good left shoulder to confirm he was behind him.

Anderson turned and whispered quietly to him. "Let's hope Eagle 3 found a way in. Maybe we'll flank the bastards."

***

Detective Miller heard the gunshot and immediately froze in his tracks. The rest of Eagle 3 stopped as well.

"You heard that, right? A gunshot from somewhere forward from our position?" A GBI tech asked Miller.

"Yeah, I heard it." Miller said. "You guys clear the wall heading in that direction, and I'll take an agent with me. Stay together, and keep your eyes open. Do not advance on any bogeys until we're all together."

Then they heard the second gunshot. *Shit*.

"We need to hurry, just in case they're getting rid of loose ends," Miller said.

The agents immediately split up and started clearing their areas. As Miller and the other agent slowly processed through the warehouse floor, they saw several metal cages in rows, just like Quinn described. The smell of urine and feces was almost unbearable. He pulled out a flashlight, keeping the light close to the floor to not attract attention, and he saw evidence of blood on the concrete floor in several of the cages.

"I wonder how many people never made it out of these cages," Miller whispered quietly, almost to himself.

***

My heart races, and I keep looking around, hoping to see friendly faces.

Custer turns around with his back to me, and begins spouting the same religious crap I've heard before. My time is quickly running out.

"In order to cleanse impure souls, we are charged with the responsibility of spilling their blood and blessing the bodies as their souls transcend. To honor the life of the Lord and that of my late wife Emma—both of whom were sacrificed—other unclean lives shall be reciprocally taken."

Custer continues, "Jesus' teachings tell us that we, the children of Israel, are the chosen ones. All others, especially those of a darker color than us, are foreigners in the world of the Lord." He turns around and walks over to Ian. He unsheathes a huge knife and slashes Ian's right cheek with a flourish.

"It is our responsibility—since we're covered in the blood of the Lord—to purify those not of our skin color, and prepare them for the Kingdom of Heaven." He walks over to Tommy with the knife in his hand, and T-Jack spits in Custer's face. Custer pauses, wipes the saliva from his face, and jams the knife deep into Tommy's left shoulder. "I'm a man of my word and I keep my promises, especially to my God and to the love of my life."

Beau secures a bag on Ian's head, while Clyde slides one on Tommy's. It is now almost impossible to force air into my lungs, and words no longer come out. I am powerless to change any of our fates. I can only sit back and watch. *Again.*

"We are the children of the Chosen One. We are the children of the one true God. And by the Grace of God, we will continue to live in His promised land. We will protect our land and avenge my wife's death by cleansing all unworthy people in her place. I will forever keep the promise I made to my beloved, and I will avenge her in all things. Thy and her will be done."

One man I don't recognize hands Custer his baseball bat with the cross burned into the handle.

***

Anderson and Aaron met back up with the rest of Eagle 1, having cleared that part of the warehouse. They saw spotlights, and could hear a man's voice speaking loudly somewhere, up ahead.

As they made their way towards the sound, Anderson noticed a flashlight to his left. He pulled out his flashlight, and clicked it on and off three times in that direction. The other flashlight holder did the same. "That must be Eagle 3," Anderson whispered.

He pulled out his radio and keyed it softly. He whispered, "Is that you, Eagle 3?"

Miller responded quietly. "Affirmative."

"Move toward the sound of the man's voice. Remember, our mission is to save the hostages and Campbell. Take Custer and his boys alive if you can. Now going radio silent." Anderson beeped the radio twice and waited for Miller to get the message. Two beeps. Anderson then turned his radio off, and Miller did the same.

Anderson and Aaron slid up quietly toward the spotlight from the right, and noticed three people sitting in chairs in front of five men. One was Custer, two were his remaining sons, and two others were unidentified. He watched Custer slice into Ian Bernard's face.

"Bastard!" Aaron spoke instinctively, but Anderson quickly shushed him.

"Quiet, Agent. I know that's your brother, but if they know we're here, we might force their hands," Anderson whispered, while grabbing Aaron's shoulder. "Focus. We somewhat have the element of surprise, and I want to keep it that way."

Concurrently on the other end of the warehouse, Miller and Eagle 3 crept up from the left, just in time to see Custer shove a knife into Tommy Jackson's shoulder.

"Showtime," Miller whispered.

"Let's do this," Anderson whispered.

***

And then I hear it again. Custer starts whistling that same tune he corrupted for all eternity. *Amazing Grace*. It once again shakes me to my core.

I look at Tommy, and then at Ian. The bags aren't fastened around their necks, so they can still breathe for the most part. Good. *Come on, Quinn, think. Do something to buy some time.*

"Amazing Grace? Really? Why did you choose to weaponize that song?"

Custer holds the baseball bat in his hand, but now focuses all his attention on me.

"It's simple, really. It was my wife's favorite hymn," Custer says, plainly. "I didn't really think about it, actually. The first soul we cleansed, I whistled it while we worked. It just seemed to fit."

"But you changed the lyrics, though. Isn't that sacrilegious?" I'm just trying anything at this point.

Custer stops and stares right through me. "I'm saving a wretch like you. The words matter less than my actions—trust me. This is ordained work. This is a promise I gladly intend to keep."

"Pa, she's just stalling you. Get on with it," Clyde says, seeming a little anxious.

"What are you afraid of, huh?" I ask.

Clyde walks quickly up to me, and punches me hard in the stomach, forcing every bit of air out of my lungs. "It sure as hell ain't you, bitch."

Damn, that hurt. I'm not going to give him the satisfaction, though. I steel myself again, trying to slow my breaths, staring right at Clyde.

Custer cuts an evil look in Clyde's direction.

"Sorry, Pa. I just can't stand a woman who back-talks."

"Oh...you haven't...seen me...back-talk yet. This is just...pleasant conversation." I squeeze out through the pain. Breathing is still an issue after the gut punch.

Get in their heads, Quinn. Slow them down. Make them make a mistake. Anderson will get here in time.

"Have you ever even been with a woman you're not related to?"

From out of nowhere, Beau hits me in the cheek with a left hook, and I once again hear bells ringing in my ears. *C'mon, man...not in the face. It's my moneymaker.*

"Enough of this bullshit. It's time for the show, the one you missed out on last time, girlie." Custer grabs the bag in front of me, and starts whistling that damn hymn again. He slides up to me, and I'm still dazed from the sucker punch, so he easily slides the bag over my face. Physically fighting back just isn't an option for me at the moment. He fastens the collar around my neck, and I immediately realize no air is coming in.

"Amazing Grace..." Clyde sings, pointing a gun at Ian's head. The sound is muffled through the bag, but it is unmistakable.

"How sweet the sound..." Beau adds, pointing a gun at Tommy's head.

"That saved a wretch like you..." Custer finishes, then pulls the baseball bat above his head.

I close my eyes, knowing this is the end. Anderson didn't get here in time. *I'm sorry, AB...I'm sorry I couldn't avenge you.*

I hear several gunshots, and I just know I'm next.

After a second or so, nothing happens. I open my eyes slowly, trying not to gasp for air, saving what little I have left. I can't really see anything through the bag, but commotion happens all around me. Suddenly, someone fumbles with the bag over my head from behind, attempting to unlock the collar. I hear it click, and a rush of air slides in underneath the bag. I see Anderson pull it off of my head.

I look around for a moment, and see Clyde lying on the ground with a fatal headshot bullet wound. Agents have the two men I didn't recognize in custody, as well as Beau on his knees with his hands behind his head, being held at gunpoint. Custer is standing in front of me, hands up, still holding the baseball bat in his right hand.

"Drop the bat! Drop it!" I hear Detective Miller and others scream from behind me. "Do it now!"

Custer looks at them and then looks at me. He smiles and starts whistling the hymn again. His eyes widen, he puts the bat in both hands, and goes to swing the bat down at my head. I flinch when round after round enters his body, knocking him backwards through the office plate glass window, dead before he even hits the ground. Classic suicide by cop.

"T-Jack...Ian..." I say weakly, trying desperately to refill my lungs.

"They're OK, all things considered." Anderson puts both of his hands on my shoulders. "I told you I wouldn't let them hurt you."

"I'm just glad you found us in time."

"Me too, kid. Me too."

"You're hurt." I notice the blood covering his shoulder.

"Flesh wound, kid. I've had worse."

Aaron works hard to free his brother, cutting the zip ties around his hands and feet. They hug it out, and my heart swells. Anderson frees me from my restraints, and I stumble over to Tommy.

"Them Dawgs is hell, ain't they?" I say, trying to get him to smile.

"I guess I really am the ramblin' wreck now," he laughs weakly, and then winces in pain.

"Awww, shut up, you." I grab his face and kiss him, much more intimately than I expected, but we both lean into the affection. The fear of almost losing him, the regret of not having told him exactly how I feel, all of that rushes into one of the most passionate kisses I've ever been a part of. I break off the kiss, and lean my forehead onto his. "I'm just glad you're OK."

Tommy looks at me with wide eyes after the kiss, motionless. I begin to feel very self-conscious. "Wait...did you...did you not like it?" I ask.

"You know," he smiles, "relationships that start under intense circumstances never last."

"Did you just quote *Speed* to me, jerk?" I laugh. "You know I'm hotter than Sandra Bullock anyway, right?" I hug him tightly, trying to avoid causing him any more pain.

I guess I finally found something new today—someone I can truly love and can trust completely with my life. Someone I was so afraid to lose.

For once, I put myself and my needs *before* the story, and it feels kinda good, to be honest. And you know, I'm OK with that.

Epilogue

_____ele_____

It's over. _It's finally over._

Custer is dead, and will no longer be terrorizing me or my friends or anyone else because I was simply in the wrong place at the wrong time.

As I sit in the back of one of the rescue ambulances letting the EMTs triage me, I scan the landscape in front of me. The dead—of both friend and foe—litters the ground. GBI forensic techs flutter about, collecting evidence from the intense gunfight. I see an agent put Beau in the back of a police car, undoubtedly being taken somewhere to be interrogated as to the depth and breadth of Custer's depravity.

The fact he made it his mission to "cleanse" anyone of non-white skin because of his late wife's unfortunate death, and that he justified it by claiming religious motivation and loyalty, is beyond me. I became a target because his screw-up of a son grabbed me along with Alahna out on the Appalachian Trail, and I allegedly knew too much. They were afraid I'd bring down their whole house of cards.

In a way, they were right to be afraid of me, because I did bring about their downfall—just in a different way than any of us anticipated.

Col. Anderson walks over to me, his arm in a sling. I remember wearing a similar sling from my own bullet wound.

"Hey kid, how're ya holding up?" he asks.

"Better than you, it looks like." I smile, and nod toward his battle scar. "I know how bad that hurts."

"Like I told you before, it is seriously just a flesh wound." Anderson shrugs his shoulder slightly, and then grimaces. "It missed anything of importance, just tore through fatty tissue—of which I have plenty. Simple through-and-through."

I know there's nothing simple about a gunshot wound. They burn like a sonofabitch.

"How are T-Jack and Ian?" I ask, since the ambulances took off with them a short time ago.

"Both are extremely dehydrated, suffering from some of the same wounds you had when we first met." Anderson runs the fingers of his good arm through his hair. "Their gunshot wounds to the thighs were the most worrisome, but they're in good hands. EMTs stopped the bleeding on scene, so hopefully surgery will not be necessary. They also focused on Ian's missing finger and fileted calf."

"If you had been just one minute later—" My mind drifts into bad territory. Anderson puts the hand from his good arm on my shoulder.

"Stop thinking like that, kid. A lot of us made it out in relatively one piece. Our mission was a success, we saved the hostages and we have one of them in custody. He's singing like a songbird, by the way."

Special Agent Brown walks over to us, and sticks his hand out to Anderson. They shake and nod to each other.

"Colonel, we couldn't have done this without your help." Brown says, and turns to me. "And thank you as well, Ms. Campbell. Your ability to stall them gave us the window of opportunity we needed."

"Brownie, you know talking to people is what I do for a living, right?" I laugh awkwardly. "I'm just glad he decided to listen."

"Special Agent Brown, sorry to be a buzzkill, but I have to tell you Peachtree Technology's involvement ends here. However, can I ask that you please keep me informed as to the tea our suspect is currently spilling?" Anderson shrugs his good shoulder. I know he's still looking for closure for Barton, Allen, and Taylor. "Looks like you have a lot of paperwork in your future."

Did Anderson just say someone was spilling tea, and actually *use* the slang correctly? Wow, wonders never cease.

"Story of my life, Colonel." Brown rolls his eyes and gives a resigned shrug. "But yes, if we get information on your two missing teammates, you'll be the first to know."

The two men nod knowingly and respectfully to each other.

"Guess I should get back to work." Brown turns his attention to me, and smiles in my direction. "'Til the next dead body." He walks back into the fray, leaving me with Anderson.

"How many life debts do I owe you now?" I ask. "I've honestly lost count."

"More than you can ever repay, kid. Let's just say you will forever owe me."

"You wish." We both laugh. "Life debts have a shelf life."

"Then you need to take me to that Midtown restaurant again—the one you like so much—and get some more of that veggie lasagna. It wasn't that bad, you know."

"Juliette's, it is. You know I'll have to get a salad in honor of Sgt. Barton."

"He would have really liked that, and would have teased you mercilessly about it if he was still here." Anderson pats my shoulder again. "Time for me to ride off into the sunset, kid."

"Yeah, you better leave before I try and talk to you on camera."

"That, I can *promise* you, will never happen."

"Never say never to a reporter. It then becomes a challenge that I will happily accept."

"Get used to disappointment, kid." Anderson lightly punches my shoulder, nods, and turns to walk away. "You know if you ever need me—"

"Yeah, yeah, I know. Don't call." I laugh.

"Took you long enough, but I think you finally get it." The man who saved my life multiple times grabs his remaining PTC techs, climbs into a waiting Escalade, and pulls away from the property. Something tells me this isn't the last time I'll see Col. Anderson.

I smile almost without even realizing it. A GBI tech walking near me catches my eye.

"Excuse me, but can I borrow your phone really quickly?" The GBI tech hands their phone to me.

I instinctively dial the WQX newsroom, and an unfamiliar voice answers. "WQX, how may I direct your call?"

"Hey, it's Quinn Campbell. Please let me speak to Wild Bill Tucker ASAP."

The producer puts me briefly on hold, probably checking with Tucker as to where to send me. A short time later, a familiar voice comes on the line.

"Campbell, please tell me everything's OK?" Wild Bill says, with a pensive twinge to his voice.

"We found Tommy and Alahna's brother in time, and the Mountain Mangler has been killed by the GBI." I say, breathing a sigh of relief. "Want the story?"

"Does a bear shit in the woods? You damn right I want the story." Wild Bill's tone completely changes, knowing he's being given a true gift—a WQX exclusive.

"Send me a satellite truck and a photog, and it's yours." I smile, once again being in my element. "Get ready, because this story is gonna be a doozy."

Wild Bill Tucker transfers me to the six o'clock producer, and I feed her all the information I have. When I tell her no other station is up here, she decides to devote the majority of the A-block segment to this story. This is a bombshell report, one that everyone from Atlanta to Amicalola needs to hear. Hopefully Beau will continue to come clean with the locations of any and all cleansed bodies, especially Alahna's, so that we can find them and give them proper burials.

Some people find closure to be a powerful thing, and I'd settle for some of that, too. My life has been way too topsy-turvy, to say the least. I'm just happy I don't have to hide anymore.

Until then, it's back to work. I have to remind myself that in most cases, the story will *always* come first.

Appendix A

«ROLL INTRO VIDEO»

— TONY —

"Good evening, everyone, and welcome to WQX Action News at 6:00, I'm Tony Lipton. We begin the six o'clock newscast with breaking news.

«ROLL EXCLUSIVE GPX»

{VO}

In a WQX exclusive, there have been major new developments in the Mountain Mangler case up in the north Georgia mountains. This morning, GBI agents infiltrated a compound in the Chatta-hoochee-Oconee National Forest, looking for the person or persons responsible for the death of Jada Sinclair, and potentially many others.

— TONY —

Quinn Campbell joins us live on scene to give us the latest. Quinn, what can you tell us?"

— CUT TO QUINN, FULL —

*cg n2 QUINN CAMPBELL \ WQX Action News at 6

"Tony, today's scene was reminiscent of any western gunfight or Hollywood shoot-em-up movie. GBI agents, in cooperation with local law enforcement, located 62-yr-old Elijah Matthew Custer—whom we now know is the Mountain Mangler—and his crew here at this property buried deep in the Chattahoochee. The ordeal plaguing the city the past several weeks has come to a fiery close after an intense standoff in what some would call a classic battle between 'Good' and 'Evil.'"

— QUINN —

{PKG / SOT}

*cg n2 DANIEL BROWN \ Asst. Special Agent in Charge, GBI

*cg n2 GRAYSON MILLER \ Detective, Dahlonega PD

— QUINN —

"It will take several days for the GBI to comb through this area, in an effort to piece together the extent of the Mangler's operation. The main thing to note is that Elijah Custer's reign of terror is now officially over. And I, for one, am very happy to hear that. Reporting live from north Georgia, Quinn Campbell, WQX Action News."

— TONY —

"Crazy stuff. Thank you, Quinn."

[PAN - AB SHOULDER BOX (Photo of Bernard)]

"We also want to report that authorities are also investigating Elijah Custer for the alleged kidnapping and disappearance of longtime WQX photojournalist Alahna Bernard while she was investigating Ms. Sinclair's death on the Appalachian Trail. We'll have more information for you as it becomes available."

— TONY —

"Also, one of Custer's sons is currently in police custody, and authorities are working hard to bring more information about this operation to light, so stay tuned to WQX for the latest on this exclusive story throughout the evening. When we return, meteorologist Kara Connolly will give you Atlanta's 5-day forecast, and will tell you when you might need an umbrella this week. You're watching WQX Action News at 6..."

{SLOW FADE TO BLACK}

Author's Note

First of all, thank you so much for checking out *But Now I'm Found*.

Word-of-mouth is crucial for any author to succeed. If you enjoyed *But Now I'm Found*, please leave a review online—anywhere you are able. It would make all the difference to me and would be very much appreciated.

Thanks!

J.W. Vincent